THE
TRIAL

ALSO BY LARRY D. THOMPSON

So Help Me God

THE TRIAL

Larry D. Thompson

THOMAS DUNNE BOOKS

St. Martin's Press

New York

THOMAS DUNNE BOOKS.
An imprint of St. Martin's Press.

THE TRIAL. Copyright © 2011 by Larry D. Thompson. All rights reserved. Printed in the United States of America. For information, address St. Martin's Press, 175 Fifth Avenue, New York, N.Y. 10010.

www.thomasdunnebooks.com
www.stmartins.com

ISBN 978-0-312-60735-7

First Edition: April 2011

10 9 8 7 6 5 4 3 2 1

For my wife, Vicki,
who encouraged me to become a writer and
inspired me to succeed

Author's Note

The FDA is responsible for protecting the public health by assuring the safety, efficacy, and security of human and veterinary drugs.

—Mission Statement,
United States Food and Drug Administration

THE
TRIAL

Prologue

———◆———

Luke got the bad news on a Friday. On Monday he and Samantha drove to San Antonio to see Dr. Shepherd Stevens. They worked their way through the maze of buildings at the UT Health Science Center to the hepatology department and signed in. When they were escorted to the treatment area, they were met by a distinguished-looking physician with a calm, gentle demeanor. He invited them to take a seat.

"I'm pleased that you could come on such short notice. I've been following your case and advising Dr. Hartman as necessary. After looking at your last blood work, I thought it was time for a full workup."

"I don't understand, sir," Samantha replied, her voice cracking with alarm.

"Samantha, your liver is still failing, even with the interferon. We've been following the results of your blood work. Now it's time to do more testing."

"Doctor, I'm only nineteen. Am I going to die before I'm twenty?" Samantha asked.

It was dusk when the red sports car turned into the upscale suburban neighborhood. In the driveway, the driver killed the engine and rested his head on his hands, which were clenching the steering wheel. His mind drifted back through the disturbing events of the past few months.

When the young executive finally entered the house, he kissed his pregnant wife and talked briefly with her before he excused himself and headed to their bedroom. He sat at a small desk and extracted several computer discs from his briefcase, the same ones he had been studying all afternoon. Absentmindedly flipping through them, he continued to mull over seemingly random events from the recent past. Finally, he picked up the phone and placed a call. After a brief discussion he confirmed an appointment for the next morning and walked back to the kitchen to tell his wife that he would be out of town on business for a couple of days. Before she could ask where he was going, his cell phone rang. He glanced at the caller ID and excused himself. This time he shut the door to the bedroom. He listened to the caller, nodded his head several times, and clicked off the phone.

He replaced the discs in his briefcase and was about to close it when he suddenly changed his mind. Instead he turned to his computer and burned a duplicate of each of the discs. When he had a complete second set, he put both in his briefcase and grabbed his coat. Leaving the house, he called to his wife that he had forgotten a business appointment and would be back in about two hours.

He drove slowly from the neighborhood, then turned into a small shopping center, where he parked and took his briefcase into a store. Five minutes later he was back in his car, heading down the freeway toward Rock Creek Park, where he stopped in a lot that only a couple of hours earlier had been full of cars, trucks, and SUVs. Now there were only two vehicles, both empty. He had waited ten minutes before a dark, nondescript sedan parked beside him. Taking his cue, he got out and stood beside the car. A large man dressed in black jeans and a black T-shirt came around the back of the sedan. The young executive looked around nervously. This was not who he was supposed to meet. He'd never seen the guy in his life. He was about to run when he was met by a second man who stepped from the shadows and quietly stood behind him, his hand gripping a syringe. Before the startled executive could react, the second man drove a small 22 gauge needle into his neck, expertly piercing the left jugular. He slumped into unconsciousness when the man pushed the plunger with his thumb and Versed was forced into the vein.

The two men, both wearing latex gloves, glanced around the parking lot. Satisfied they were alone, they picked up the victim and carried him along the jogging path that ran beside the creek. When they arrived at a small clearing, one of the men pulled a .22 revolver from his back pocket. He placed it in the executive's right hand and put the gun to his temple. Using the victim's forefinger, he fired the weapon once. The victim jerked and then was quiet. The two men arranged the body beside the path, gun in hand, and retraced their steps. When they got to the victim's car, they opened the driver's door, grabbed the briefcase, and, after taking one last look around the parking lot, slowly drove the dark sedan back to the freeway.

1

The elevator doors opened at the penthouse level of Ceventa Pharmaceutical's headquarters just outside Washington, D.C., and a group of executives from the lower floors stepped into the executive suite. They talked among themselves as they waited for the CEO's assistant to end a phone call. When the blond assistant hung up, one young man grinned. "Hey, beautiful, what's going on? Why the command performance with only fifteen minutes notice?"

"You'll have to ask Dr. Kingsbury," she replied. "Please join the others in the boardroom. Coffee and sodas are on the credenza."

The penthouse housed Dr. Kingsbury's office along with a private health club, a gigantic boardroom, and the reception area. The reception area was thirty feet by twenty. At one end was the assistant's desk guarding the door to Kingsbury's inner sanctum. The remainder of the area was covered with antique chairs and sofas from the eighteenth century, part of Kingsbury's private collection. The burnt gold carpet was thick enough to absorb all but the loudest voice. At the end opposite the assistant's desk were two double doors with ornate brass handles.

The group walked to the double doors and opened them to find the boardroom full of other Ceventa executives. Some were seated in the twenty-four leather chairs around the long oval conference table.

Others stood behind the chairs, drinking coffee from porcelain cups, also burnt gold in color. The room was filled with an expectant buzz of conversation and questions. Several managers speculated on why they were summoned to the penthouse. A few merely drank their coffee and waited quietly as they gazed out the windows on the panoramic view of green Maryland hills and the Washington Monument in the distance. All conversation stopped when both doors flew open and the man himself entered, trailed by three assistants.

Dr. Alfred Kingsbury was an imposing figure. Six feet six inches tall, he had long gray hair that he parted in the middle and combed back above his ears. A Vandyke beard gave him a decidedly European look. In fact, he was originally from England, where he had graduated thirty-odd years before with two degrees, one in medicine along with a PhD in pharmacology. Shortly thereafter he joined Ceventa and rose through the ranks to become CEO of the North American subsidiary. His next step to the top of the ladder would be at Ceventa's global headquarters in Copenhagen, where he expected to be placed in charge of the one-hundred-billion-dollar pharmaceutical giant. With no apology for the delay, he stood at the front of the room, unbuttoned the jacket of his Armani three-piece suit, and spoke in a clipped British accent.

"Good morning. We have some exciting news. James, please lower the screen and start the PowerPoint."

The screen dropped silently from the ceiling at the opposite end of the boardroom. The projector came into focus with the company logo, a blue and green globe showing CEVENTA in burnt gold script looping around the earth.

The logo disappeared and was replaced by EXXACIA.

"Most of you are familiar with Exxacia. It's an antibiotic proven efficacious for pneumonia, bronchitis, sinusitis, tonsillitis, and several other infectious diseases. We developed Exxacia at our research and development facility in Copenhagen. It took ten years and nearly a billion dollars before we were ready to take it to market."

As Kingsbury spoke he walked around the table to stand beside the screen, motioning James to bring up slides designed to emphasize the points Kingsbury was making.

"We launched Exxacia in South America originally, and with some carefully crafted promotion, it soon was bringing in over a billion dollars a year on that continent alone. Next we took it to Europe, and combined sales approached five billion."

A self-satisfied grin crossed Kingsbury's face as he extended his arms, palms up. "Now, my dear colleagues, it's 2007 and we are ready to market in the United States. We will be—"

Kingsbury was interrupted by a young researcher who had been standing, arms crossed and leaning against the side wall. He dropped his arms as he spoke. "Dr. Kingsbury, haven't we had some significant problems with that drug in other countries? I've read some of our internal reports that describe liver failure, heart problems, and even death following use of Exxacia. Don't we need to be studying this drug, maybe halt sales in Europe and South America until we figure out what's causing these problems?"

"What's your name, young man?"

"Kinney, sir, Ralph Kinney. I'm a statistician on the third floor."

"Mr. Kinney, your concerns are misplaced," Kingsbury replied sternly. "We all know that any drug has side effects, complications. It's true that some of the people who have taken Exxacia are very sick. Many are elderly, and in flu season no matter what the treatment the elderly will die from the flu." Kingsbury's eyes darted around the room to look for any disagreement with his comments. Blank stares were all he saw, except from Kinney.

"Do you really think we should be selling a drug that may cause liver failure and death just to cure a sinus infection?"

"Mr. Kinney, no one has proved with certainty that Exxacia causes liver problems. Undoubtedly, those who took the drug and died from liver failure had a compromised liver that would have failed in spite of any drug. We can expect to save hundreds of thousands of lives in the United States alone. And I should add that our financial people expect United States sales of between five billion and ten billion dollars three years after FDA approval. That process will start within three months. Our timetable calls for the drug to be approved in eighteen months. No more questions. This meeting is adjourned."

Kingsbury left the boardroom. He stopped briefly at his assistant's desk and in a low voice said, "Get me the personnel file on an employee named Kinney who works on the third floor. I want it this afternoon."

As he turned to walk away his assistant said, "Oh, Dr. Kingsbury, don't forget that tomorrow is Teddy's sixth birthday."

Kingsbury looked back. His scowl had turned to a smile. "Don't worry. I never forget a grandchild's birthday. I'll stop at Toys 'R' Us on the way home this evening, and I'll be leaving early tomorrow for Teddy's party."

2

Lucas Vaughan parked in an open lot across the street from the old Harris County courthouse in downtown Houston. As he came to a stop, he looked in the rearview mirror and studied his face. *I don't like what I'm seeing,* he thought. It's only 2004. *I'll be forty next month. My hair is turning gray, and I've got dark circles under my eyes. The lines on my face make me look fifty. No wonder. I was up half the night with stomach cramps. Maybe it's time to be doing something else.* Luke sighed at the mirror, reached for a bottle of Maalox in the cup holder of his Toyota Sequoia, and took a giant swig. As the Maalox settled into his stomach, a determined look crossed his face. *Last day. It's the biggest case of my career. Time to win it.*

He grabbed his oversized briefcase from the back, tossed the Maalox in it, waved at the parking attendant, and waited at the corner for the light to change.

"Morning, Luke." Another lawyer approached. "You in trial?"

"Hi, Jock. Yeah, I'm in the third week of a products case against Ford. My client's husband was killed in a rollover."

"I thought the tire manufacturers were responsible for all those SUV deaths. Who's up today?"

"We settled the tire case for a large but confidential amount, enough to pay back six-figure expenses that I borrowed from the bank and put some money in my widow's purse. Hopefully, today is my payday. My experts say that Ford has at least equal responsibility, maybe greater. I'm crossing the Ford design engineer this morning."

Luke entered the courthouse, walked through a metal detector, and boarded the decrepit elevator that creaked and moaned its way to the sixth floor. When he stepped into the hall, he found it crowded with lawyers and clients. He smiled at two jurors and entered the courtroom.

Luke's client was seated on the back row, obviously deep in thought. "Morning, Nancy," he greeted her. "This should be the last witness. Good chance we can argue this afternoon." Pain shot over Luke's face, and he grabbed his stomach.

"Luke, you okay?"

"I'm fine. Just some indigestion. Happens a lot during trial. Let's get seated." Luke led the way to their counsel table.

"All rise."

Judge Ruby O'Reilly came through the back door as the jurors entered from the side.

"Good morning, ladies and gentlemen. Mr. Vaughan, you may recall Mr. Alberson for cross-examination."

A slender, graying gentleman who could have been a college professor rose in the first row of the audience and made his way to the witness stand. He had done an excellent job the day before, establishing that the plaintiff's car had some risk of rolling over, but no more than any other SUV. He blamed the crash on a tire that had lost its tread after only twenty thousand miles. As to the roof design, which was a major issue in the case, it met every federal standard. Fred Ayers, Ford's lead lawyer, knew that he had some problems in the case, but was satisfied that Alberson had managed to handle all of them quite nicely.

"Mr. Alberson, you would agree that Ford markets these cars as SUVs that are safe and passenger friendly?" Luke asked.

"Yes, sir. I certainly would."

"You understand that we're not here to talk about tires?"

"Sorry, Mr. Vaughan, but I disagree." Alberson shook his head. "The jury has already heard that the accident was caused when the tire tread on the right front came completely off."

Several jurors had puzzled expressions, wondering why the tire manufacturer was not in the case. Of course, they didn't know that the Texas rules of evidence barred them from learning that the tire company had settled.

Luke put his hands in his pockets and walked away from the witness to stand at the rail behind his client. Switching gears to get away from a discussion about tires, he continued, "You know, don't you, that my client's husband died from a fractured skull, following the crash?"

"Mr. Vaughan, I'm very sorry for your client's loss," the professional witness said sympathetically.

"And you automotive engineers have to anticipate that a crash may happen. You've got to meet certain federal standards with regard to crashworthiness of various parts of the vehicle, including the roof."

"If that's a question, Mr. Vaughan, the answer is yes."

"Yet you folks at Ford twice reduced the roof strength on this vehicle to save a few bucks on each one, right, Mr. Alberson?"

"Mr. Vaughan, the roof was changed in an overall design overhaul. Money was not the issue," Alberson said, exasperation in his voice.

"Still, Mr. Alberson, the design of the car driven by my client's husband just barely met federal standards most of the time, and, allowing for manufacturing variance, some of the cars came off the assembly line with roofs that were below federal guidelines, true, sir?"

Alberson folded his arms and looked to his lawyers for some help, but they had their faces buried in documents. "Probably so."

"And those design changes saved Ford tens of millions of dollars that went to bottom line profit, right, Mr. Alberson?"

"Yes," the witness answered, but before he could explain his answer, Luke's legs buckled as he broke out into a sweat. He managed to take a seat before he collapsed. Judge O'Reilly saw his condition and called for an early morning recess.

As the jury left the courtroom, the bailiff rushed over to Luke. "What can I do, man?"

"I'll be okay in a minute. Just get me some water and that bottle of Maalox from my briefcase."

After a half hour Luke assured the judge that he could proceed and then, to her surprise and that of the defense lawyers, said that he had no more questions. The defense team sized up where they were and elected to rest, satisfied that Luke's cross had barely scratched the surface.

Luke had worked hard on his closing argument, even rehearsing it before his mirror three different times. He had been prepared, but not for what had just happened. He had no fire, no enthusiasm, no thunder. It was a bland and ineffective closing statement, causing a number of jurors to switch their attention from Luke to the minute hand on the clock on the back wall. Three hours after retiring, the jury returned a verdict in favor of Ford. Luke could only apologize to his client. At least he had recovered on the tire case. That would give Nancy enough to raise her children, but after the gigantic expenses of a fight against Ford, Luke knew there would be little left for his three years of work. Certainly not the big payday he had anticipated. Then he collapsed on the courtroom floor.

3

———◆———

Luke was wheeled on a stretcher from the ambulance into the emergency department of Memorial Hermann Hospital, conscious but in severe pain. After a cursory examination, the emergency physician admitted him to a medical unit. Over the next twenty-four hours, Luke was put through a battery of tests. Finally, Dr. Vincent Lee, a general surgeon, entered Luke's room for the first time. After introducing himself, he said, "Mr. Vaughan, all of our tests are conclusive. You have a perforated ulcer. Surgery is the only solution."

"Then let's get it over with." Luke nodded in agreement. "The sooner the better."

Lucas Vaughan had been born and raised in San Marcos, Texas, a college town perched on the edge of the Texas Hill Country about halfway between Austin and San Antonio. His father was a real estate agent who sold rural land suitable for second homes. His mother worked as a nurse in the community hospital. By the time he graduated from high school, he was six feet tall and pushed two hundred pounds. His undergraduate grades at the University of Texas were barely good enough to get him into UT Law School, where he graduated in the lower half of his class three years later.

Unlike those at the top of his class, he didn't have offers of summer internships with big firms, and no job offers came as he completed his senior year. When he graduated, he figured that Houston was the biggest city in the state and there had to be room for one more lawyer. After pounding the pavement for weeks, he moved in with a plaintiff personal injury lawyer who had billboards on most of the freeways. All he got was an office and a promise of cases that the

billboard lawyer didn't want. Still, it was a start. He leased an effi-
ciency apartment close to the office and learned to move the small
cases with a minimum of expense. Within three years he was making
a decent living and opened his own law firm, putting up a few of his
own billboards. The cases produced enough fees to pay his landlord
and his secretary and to live comfortably but not lavishly. He taught
himself to try lawsuits. At first he was clumsy and ill prepared, but he
eventually developed a reputation as a fender-bender lawyer who
could try a very respectable case when the need arose.

He tried to find time for sports, even signing up for a flag football
league one fall, but his trial schedule interfered. By the time he was
in his early thirties, his weight had ballooned to well over two hundred pounds. One day he looked at himself in the mirror after a
shower and was disgusted. He postponed work while he took a slow
jog around the neighborhood. Thereafter, he squeezed forty-five minutes out of his hectic day for an early morning run, and the pounds
disappeared in a year.

Luke really had very little interest in getting married and chose to
have no serious girlfriends. There were a few one-night stands, but
that was it. Then he made what turned out to be a colossal mistake.
He had a few too many drinks on a Friday night at the Inns of Court
Club in downtown Houston and picked up an eighteen-year-old waitress at closing. They had a few more drinks and ended up in his bed,
where they had boozy sex. Three months later she called to tell him
that she was pregnant and he was the father. Luke wasn't sure that she
hadn't just chosen him from a number of lovers and anointed him as
the father of her child, but he had no proof to the contrary. So he did
what he considered the right thing and married Josie. Six months later
they had a daughter they named Samantha.

The marriage was rocky, to say the least. Luke continued to work
long hours and rarely had time for Josie and Samantha. He began to
suspect that Josie was running around on him, but he really didn't care.
When Samantha was three, he got home one night to find a note from

Josie: Samantha was next door, and she was leaving him to move to Nashville to become a country music star. He didn't go after her. In fact, he was happy to close that chapter of his life. Only now he had a daughter to raise.

Luke sold their condo and bought a small house in the Memorial area of West Houston. The most important feature was that it had servant quarters over the garage. He hired a Hispanic nanny and housekeeper named Teresa Delgado, paid her well, and moved her into the garage apartment so that she could always be available for Samantha. Satisfied that he had provided well for his daughter, he returned to his long hours, seeing Samantha only on an occasional night when he would get home before her bedtime and for a few hours on Sunday, after which he would usually retire to his home office.

4

The elevator doors opened on the fourth floor of the hospital, and Samantha, now thirteen and with yellow roses in hand, burst out, followed by Teresa. She paused only long enough to check a sign for the location of room 414 and then was off to her right.

"Samantha, knock on the door if it's closed."

Samantha got to room 414 and ignored Teresa's admonition. She pushed open the door to find her dad asleep.

"Dad, are you okay?"

Luke opened his eyes and smiled at his daughter. "I'm fine, Sam. Just a little tired, and I've got a sore belly."

"I brought you these," Samantha said proudly, as she put the flowers beside her dad.

"Thanks, Sam. They're beautiful."

Just then Teresa got to the room. "Here, let me have those. I'll bet there's a vase around here somewhere. I'll get them in some water and we can put them on the windowsill."

Luke reached for a remote control and pushed a button, and the head of the bed rose. When it got to a comfortable position, he adjusted himself. "How was school today?"

"It's okay, Dad. I'm still making all A's," Samantha answered as she sat in a bedside chair. "Why'd you need an operation?"

"I had an ulcer in my stomach. I've probably had it for a long time, and it finally ate through the wall of my stomach."

"Yuk! Are you going to be okay?"

"Doctor says I should be just fine. I'm thinking about some lifestyle changes, though."

"What does that mean?" Samantha asked, a look of concern crossing her face.

"Why don't we talk about it tomorrow? I just got out of surgery this morning, and I think I need to sleep."

"Sure, Dad. Here, let me have that control. I'll lower the bed for you."

Luke didn't hear the last words. Samantha lowered the bed, adjusted his covers, and tiptoed out of the room with Teresa following.

5

Samantha and Teresa were back the next afternoon. Teresa stopped in the waiting room by the elevators and told Samantha to visit with her dad alone. Samantha looked puzzled but walked down the hall and this time knocked on the door.

"Come in."

Samantha found Luke sitting up in bed, watching CNN. "Hi, Dad. How's your stomach?"

"Still tender, but feeling a lot better. I'll probably be able to go home tomorrow. Where's Terry?"

Samantha nodded her head in the direction of the hall. "She stopped to watch TV in the waiting room."

Luke raised the head of his bed higher so he could better see Samantha. "Sam, I told you yesterday that I've been thinking. I've got to make some changes in my life. I'm only forty, and trying lawsuits is going to kill me. If I keep this up, I won't see sixty. I'm going to start an office practice."

"Okay with me," Samantha said, nodding. "What's an office practice?"

"Doing wills, real estate documents, contracts, that kind of thing. We won't make as much money, but we'll do just fine."

Samantha looked at her dad, not sure what to say.

"There's one more major change, too, Sam. We're going to move from Houston. My secretary brought my laptop this morning, and I've been on the Internet. We're going to move to San Marcos. I've got my eye on three houses over there."

Astonishment filled Samantha's eyes, then turned to anger as she rose from her chair. "No, Dad. I'm not going to leave my friends!"

"Sam, calm down and lower your voice. This is a hospital. You'll like San Marcos. You used to like visiting there when Grandma and Grandpa were alive."

"You can go to San Marcos. I'll stay here with Terry. She's the one who's raised me anyway, not you." Tears filled Samantha's eyes as her voice choked. "Dad, you don't understand. You don't even know me. You don't even know that I still lie awake at night, wondering why my mother left me. I was abandoned by her and by you, too. Only you didn't just disappear. Instead, you turned me over to Terry and I've seen you for a few minutes at night and a couple hours on a weekend. I tried to please you. I even made good grades because I knew that if I made a B you'd be disappointed."

Luke had never realized that he might not have been a good father. He'd always thought that he was there for Samantha. Certainly he knew he had done his best, but as Samantha cried beside his bed, it hit him that he might have failed.

"Sam, I'm sorry. Look, when we move to San Marcos, I'll have more time for you. You'll see."

Samantha shut her eyes and clenched her fists. "I don't need you anymore. You've never been my dad, just my biological father."

She turned and ran from the room, almost knocking over an attendant bringing a dinner tray. As she ran crying down the hall, she vowed that she would never call Luke "Dad" again.

6

Roger Boatwright smiled as he replaced the receiver. He pushed himself out of his chair, thinking he really had to get serious about losing that forty pounds, and walked to a coat rack where he kept a coat and tie for just such occasions. He tried to wipe the wrinkles from the front of his white dress shirt before donning the tie and jacket, then gave up and figured it would have to do. If he had known this morning that he was having lunch with Alfred Kingsbury, he would have put on a nice suit and tie along with a freshly ironed shirt. Unfortunately, it was only now, ten thirty on Thursday morning, that Kingsbury's secretary called, asking if he could meet Dr. Kingsbury for lunch at his club at twelve thirty. Silly question. Of course he could. Still, he put the secretary on hold while he feigned checking with his assistant before confirming the lunch.

At a quarter to twelve Boatwright told his assistant that he had an unexpected meeting out of the office and would return by mid-afternoon. He retrieved his eight-year-old Toyota Corolla from the third floor of the garage and turned onto I-95 for the fifteen-minute drive to Kingsbury's club. As he drove he surveyed his life. He was forty-eight. After getting a PhD from the University of Pennsylvania, he had joined the Food and Drug Administration, expecting to stay a few years and then be lured away by a huge salary to a major pharmaceutical company. It hadn't happened. Not even a small pharmaceutical firm came calling. So he learned to play the game of politics in the FDA and eventually rose to be director of the Center for Drug Evaluation and Research, known as CDER in the industry. It was an important job with only moderate pay, certainly not what he expected as he entered middle age. Every new drug application had to cross his desk. If a drug wasn't safe or wasn't efficacious, a big word meaning the drug didn't work, he could kill it with one signature. He rarely exercised his veto. In his mind the pharmaceutical companies were his clients. New drugs rarely proved to be unsafe, and effectiveness was in the eye of the beholder. Besides, he hadn't given up the idea of moving into industry. Maybe that's what Dr. Kingsbury was calling about.

Boatwright turned off the freeway and took the first right, a tree-lined lane that led to the country club entrance, where he stopped at the security gate.

"Can I help you, sir?" the guard asked.

"I'm Dr. Boatwright here to have lunch with Dr. Kingsbury."

"Yes, sir." The guard checked his clipboard. "You're thirty minutes early. I'm sure that if you go to the bar, they'll serve you a drink while you wait for Dr. Kingsbury. Please drive up to the porte cochere. They'll valet your car."

Boatwright glanced at the porte cochere and realized his vehicle didn't fit with the other cars lining the driveway. Instead, he parked at the back of the parking lot and walked to the entrance, where he was greeted by two uniformed attendants.

"I'm here to meet Dr. Kingsbury."

"Good afternoon, sir," one said as they opened the double doors. "You must be Dr. Boatwright. You're welcome to wait for Dr. Kingsbury in the foyer or the bar."

Boatwright stepped into a living room right out of *Architectural Digest*. The arched ceiling towered thirty feet above him; a crystal chandelier dropped from its center. At the back of the room was a fireplace twelve feet tall, with a fire cracking and popping on a day when the outside temperature was seventy-five. Boatwright found a straight-backed chair against one wall, perched on the edge of the seat, and watched the front door.

The double doors opened, and a tall man in a three-piece suit was silhouetted in the doorway as he allowed his eyes to become accustomed to the change in light. When Roger Boatwright rose from his chair, Kingsbury spotted him.

"Roger, delighted that you could join me."

"Thanks for inviting me, Dr. Kingsbury," Boatwright replied as he took Kingsbury's outstretched hand.

"Look, Roger, my name is Alfred. We should be on a first-name basis unless I'm sitting in on one of your committee meetings or we're appearing before Congress. Agreed?"

"Sure, Alfred," said the smaller man, who was pleased to be on a first-name basis with Kingsbury.

"Now, this way to the dining room. I've reserved a table overlooking the eighteenth green, best table in the house."

The maître d' seated them at a giant window overlooking the green expanse of the golf course.

"You a golfer?" Kingsbury asked.

"Yes, sir, I mean Alfred," Boatwright replied, trying to hide his nervousness. "I play with a foursome most Saturdays. I'm usually happy to break ninety."

"Then I must get you out here some weekend, maybe when the club has a member-guest tournament. Now, take a look at the menu, and I'll order us a glass of my favorite wine. I recommend the lamb special. Best thing the chef cooks."

The men made small talk as they ordered and waited for their meal. They talked about Tiger Woods, the upcoming election year, major league baseball, and families. Kingsbury knew Roger's wife's name and that he had three daughters. Roger was impressed that Kingsbury had taken the time to research his background. Kingsbury took great delight in talking about his daughter and three grandchildren, particularly when he pulled photos from his wallet that showed them playing in the sand at the beach. Roger commented that the kids looked like their grandfather. Kingsbury beamed his agreement.

After they finished lunch, Kingsbury got to the reason for the meeting.

"Roger, my company has an annual seminar for our managers. We try to combine some business with pleasure. This year it's being held at the Ritz-Carlton in Montego Bay, Jamaica. We've invited three congressmen, key committee members, of course, to provide legislative updates. We'd like you to speak on the first day on a topic of your choosing, perhaps something about a current overview of the FDA, policies and procedures and maybe pitfalls to avoid in new drug applications."

Roger was disappointed that there wasn't a job offer on the table, but he figured one might come if he made a good impression at the seminar. "I'll have to check my calendar when you give me the date, but I'm flattered that you would ask."

"You'll need to check your calendar for six days. We have other speakers for about three hours every morning, and then we hit the golf course. You'll want to bring your clubs and your A game. And we want your better half to join us. She can go to the spa or go shopping with the other wives while we're on the course. We'll cover expenses for both of you."

"Maybe I ought to pay for my wife, Alfred."

"Nonsense, my boy. It's all completely on the up-and-up. You're our featured speaker and will be attending other lectures throughout the week, and spouses are expected. I promise there won't be an eyebrow raised. I'll e-mail you the details. Now, if you have five more minutes, let me tell you about a new antibiotic you'll be seeing a new drug application on shortly. It's called Exxacia, and it's going to revolutionize how we treat infections."

After Boatwright left, Kingsbury stepped outside to the edge of the golf course and called his home office in Copenhagen. With confidence in his voice he reported that he had just met with Boatwright and was certain that he could get the FDA on board with their new antibiotic. He was convinced that Exxacia was going to turn their company around in North America, probably tripling their earnings in two years. He also had a plan in the works that would more than triple his own net worth. That it involved insider trading was of no concern to Kingsbury. *My plan is foolproof,* he thought as he returned to the clubhouse with a spring in his step.

7

Kingsbury touched his sleeping wife lightly on the shoulder and said, "Suzanne, I have to go into town for a few hours. Should be back early afternoon. I'll pick up some souvenirs for my grandkids while I'm out."

Suzanne murmured something in reply and then settled back into her slumber. They had been married for five years, and it had not been easy. She was thirty-five, twenty years his junior, a former lawyer, and she had a wandering eye. Still, she served her purpose. Once made up, she could have passed for Princess Diana and was always ready to play the role of a loving and caring wife. Whatever she did when Kingsbury wasn't around was of no interest to him as long as she was at his side when the lights went up and it was time for her performance.

Kingsbury stepped to the phone in the living room of the suite they occupied at the Montego Bay Ritz-Carlton and called Mario, one of his two driver-bodyguards, to tell him to bring his rented limousine to the front. Kingsbury rarely went anywhere without Mario and Ralph, who both looked like they had played on the defensive line for the Baltimore Ravens in prior lives. When Kingsbury exited the elevator on the first floor, he paused to visit with several of his managers, explaining that he couldn't make the morning session because of a prior commitment. He saw Roger Boatwright and his wife in the dining room and made it a point to stop at their table to confirm that everything about the meeting was to their satisfaction. He promised to visit with them more that evening at the cocktail party.

The limo was waiting for him when he left the hotel. Ralph had the back door open. "Good morning, Dr. Kingsbury. Your Starbucks is in the drink holder, and the *New York Times* is on the seat."

Kingsbury nodded to him and got in the car. He greeted Mario, the driver, as Ralph took the front passenger seat. As they drove along the main highway leading into Montego Bay, Kingsbury reflected on the past three days. It couldn't have gone better. Of course, he wanted his managers and spouses to enjoy themselves. More importantly, he had played golf with Boatwright all three days and continued to bring up Exxacia, taking every opportunity to convince him it was a miracle drug that was destined to revolutionize treatment of bacterial infections. He was satisfied that he had Boatwright in his back pocket and FDA approval was close to being a mission accomplished.

The limousine stopped in front of a three-story building with a sign that announced it was the St. James Parish National Bank. Kingsbury entered the lobby to be greeted by a distinguished, gray-haired Jamaican and a younger man, bald but handsome.

"Dr. Kingsbury, I'm Christopher Cornelius, president of the bank. This is Kevron Tillman, senior partner in our bank's law firm."

They shook hands, and Cornelius led them to his corner office on the first floor. After coffee was served and the president's secretary had shut the office door, Kingsbury took over the meeting. "Gentlemen, as you know, I'm CEO of the North American subsidiary of Ceventa, but I'm here on personal business, not company business. Mr. Tillman, I want to establish eight offshore corporations. You can decide whether they are all to be in Jamaica or if some should be domiciled on other islands."

"My firm can handle that, Dr. Kingsbury," Tillman interrupted. "We have offices in several other places in the Caribbean. I will need to have some idea of the purpose of the corporations."

Kingsbury studied the two men. "Both of you must understand that what I am about to tell you is highly confidential. If word leaks out, we will all be in trouble. On the other hand, there is the opportunity for significant profit."

Mr. Cornelius put down his coffee cup and responded, "You can be assured that we are in the business of maintaining our clients' confidences at all costs."

Kingsbury nodded and continued. "The corporations will be used to invest in Ceventa. I expect our stock to skyrocket over the next two years. I am in the process of liquidating nearly all of my assets and will be wiring one hundred million dollars to this bank. Once received, Mr. Cornelius, you will be directed to divide those funds and wire them to the eight corporations established by Mr. Tillman. Mr. Tillman will be directed to buy Ceventa stock at market in lots of a size that will not attract the attention of authorities. The stock is the lowest it's been in ten years. That's about to change."

Tillman rubbed his hands together, and greed appeared in his eyes. "That can be accomplished with no problem, Dr. Kingsbury. Might I inquire why you think your stock is going to perform so well?"

Kingsbury rose to leave. "One word, Mr. Tillman, Exxacia. It will make us all rich. If you choose to buy in, please be discreet. You will be receiving further direction next week. Good day, gentlemen."

Kingsbury returned to the limo, satisfied that his plan was being properly launched. As Mario opened his door, he said, "On the way back, we've got to find a store. My grandkids will be disappointed if their grandpa doesn't return with something from Jamaica."

"Boss, I saw a store selling seashells just up the way a few blocks."

"Perfect! Let's get some big ones for my grandson and look for some small, pretty ones for my granddaughters," Kingsbury replied.

8

Ryan Sinclair parked his red Corvette convertible in the garage behind the FDA's Center for Drug Evaluation and Research. He unfolded his six-foot frame from the car, brushed a mop of blond hair from his eyes, and put on wireless glasses that he wore to create the studious image he sought. While most of his co-workers dressed business casual, he always wore an expensive suit and tie to the office. He would hang the coat on a coat rack inside his office until he left at the end of the day. While it wasn't necessary, he thought it was the right way to dress. Probably it came from his physician father who never failed to wear a suit and tie. Or maybe it came from his grandfather who made his money on Wall Street and left all of his grandchildren multimillion-dollar trust funds they inherited when they turned twenty-five.

Entering the building, Ryan reminded himself that this was only a stepping-stone to his ultimate career. His goal was the Centers for Disease Control, where he hoped to assist in conquering some of the most virulent infectious diseases that plague the poor of the world. He'd chosen to start at the FDA to learn the regulatory side of drugs. Another two years and he would be ready to move on.

Once inside, he stopped to talk Ravens football with the burly guard at the security desk and then joined others crowding into an elevator. He exited on the fourth floor and was walking past the corner office occupied by Roger Boatwright when he heard Boatwright's voice. "Hey there, Dr. Sinclair, come in here a minute."

Ryan stepped into his boss's office. Boatwright was behind his desk, tie askew and white shirt already looking as if he had been wearing it all day. He let Sinclair stand in front of his desk for two full minutes while he read a three-page memorandum. The contrast between him and Sinclair could not have been more dramatic.

Finally, Boatwright glanced up. He didn't like Sinclair. The young doctor was born with a silver spoon in his mouth—Harvard, then Johns Hopkins Medical School and internal medicine residency, followed by an infectious disease fellowship. He'd heard about Sinclair's trust fund. Sinclair didn't even have to work, but he'd chosen the FDA and was clearly the best medical review officer CDER had on infectious diseases, as well as the youngest. Sinclair was independent by nature, and Boatwright would have preferred to put him on agency scutwork. Still, if he didn't put Sinclair on major projects, particularly involving infectious diseases, his boss would wonder why.

"Dr. Sinclair, I have a new assignment for you."

"You know I always like a challenge, Dr. Boatwright. What is it?"

"Ceventa's got a new antibiotic. It's called Exxacia. Supposed to be revolutionary. According to Alfred Kingsbury of Ceventa, it wipes out bacteria causing community acquired pneumonia, bronchitis, sinusitis and tonsillitis."

Sinclair nodded. "Sounds promising, if it works. And I know Dr.

Kingsbury slightly. My dad golfs with him frequently. I joined them a couple of times back in my college days."

Boatwright did a slow burn at the thought of his junior scientist golfing at Kingsbury's club while he was out on the public links. "I have no doubt that it will do just what Kingsbury says. And, by the way, Ceventa has paid us the million dollars to put it on the fast track. That means that you and your team have six months to evaluate and approve the drug. That clear?"

"I'll have my assistant print a copy of the new drug application this morning, and we'll start this afternoon," Sinclair answered. He walked to his office thinking that Boatwright was an ass, and only minimally competent to boot.

Sinclair's assistant pushed a cart loaded with two large banker boxes into his office. "Where do you want these, Ryan? It's that new Ceventa drug, Exxacia."

"Two boxes, we'll put them on the floor here by my desk. Here, let me help you." Ryan rose and started around his desk.

"Not so fast, Ryan. Two boxes here and fourteen more in the copy room. You want them all?"

Ryan pulled the lid off one and found six three-inch binders labeled EXXACIA NEW DRUG APPLICATION. "Looks like these are the NDA. This other box contains exhibits. Probably that's what's in the other fourteen. Leave the application box and put the other fifteen in our file room. I'll find them if and when I need them. Make three more copies of the application for the rest of the team. I'll tell them where to find the exhibits."

A new drug was routinely assigned to a medical review officer in CDER, Sinclair or one of his colleagues, who would call on a team of researchers and statisticians as needed. Exxacia was now Ryan's drug, and he expected to spend the next several months learning everything he possibly could about it. He needed to understand its formulation and evaluate its efficacy and its safety. Did it really work in the ways that Ceventa's scientists said? Were there any significant risks to patients? He took his job very seriously. Some of his peers were prone to rubber-stamping NDAs. They figured that the pharmaceutical companies knew what they were doing and wouldn't submit an application until they were certain that it was a good and safe drug. Not Sinclair.

When it was all said and done, Ryan Sinclair was known to defer to no one. He could recommend approval of Exxacia and it would sail smoothly to market. On the other hand, if he found problems, he would certainly recommend that the application be rejected. He could be overruled by Boatwright or even someone higher up the food chain. So far, that hadn't happened.

After his assistant had taken one of the boxes away, Ryan put the remaining one on his desk and pulled the first binder from it. He read through the executive summary, finding that Ceventa wanted to market the drug for various respiratory problems and tonsillitis initially, and then come back for approval for other bacteria-caused illnesses at a later date. That immediately struck him as a little strange. Most antibiotics that worked in the respiratory tract were not usually effective elsewhere. He immediately questioned its value in fighting tonsillitis. Next he noted that Exxacia was already being marketed overseas and took that as a positive since most countries in Europe and South America had drug regulations somewhat similar to those in the United States.

Four hours later his assistant stopped at his door to say that she was leaving and asked if he needed anything else. "Nothing more than another set of eyes and a couple dozen aspirin," he replied. "Only kidding. I'm going to be here a while. Have a good evening."

9

Luke and Samantha left Houston just ahead of the moving van. As was usual when they rode together now, nothing was said, and the silence hung in the air even after they pulled into the driveway in San Marcos.

Luke was proud of the work that he and the contractor had done on the house. The last of the painters had finished only the day before. The exterior was a dark green that matched the leaves on the two giant front-yard oaks. Two rockers were already in place on the porch to the right of the door.

"Not bad," Samantha finally said.

"Come on." Luke grinned. "I'll show you around. You're gonna like it."

Luke bounded up the steps and threw open the heavy wooden door. He gestured for Samantha to go ahead of him. The floors were a freshly varnished oak. The ceilings were twelve feet tall, and wood paneling covered the first four feet of the walls.

"This is my office. My desk will go here by the front window. The fireplace was already here. I just modernized it. There's another one in the upstairs living room. This is my conference room. Used to be the dining room. The room across the hall at the front is for my assistant, which I don't have at the moment. And there's one more room over there, suitable for another lawyer, not that I expect to have an associate. You can have it for your office if you like."

Samantha let her guard down just a little. "Very nice, Father. You did a good job."

"Come on upstairs. It gets even better."

The stairway led to the residence. The living room was twenty by twenty and carpeted in a plush brown. The kitchen was at the back, separated from the living area by a breakfast bar. Luke had added an alcove to the side of the house, above the porte cochere. Suitable for a small dining table, it had floor-to-ceiling glass on three sides. The feeling was that of a tree house on a summer day. Samantha walked to the alcove and glanced out at the trees, saying, "That's cool, Father."

Luke smiled as he realized that she was thawing just a little. Good—particularly since he was about to surprise her. "The front bedroom is yours. Go ahead. Open the door."

Samantha opened the door to a room painted eggshell blue, only she wasn't looking at the walls. In the center of the room was a dog kennel. In the kennel was a ten-week-old golden retriever who barked a greeting as Samantha neared her.

"Go ahead. You can let her out. Her name's Cocoa. She's yours. Well, she's mine, too. I figured we could share her."

Samantha sat in front of the kennel, unlatched the door, and was met by a five-pound bundle of fur.

10

Samantha awakened early on the following Sunday morning, the day she would leave for Camp Longhorn, where she would be a junior counselor. She looked at the clock every fifteen minutes until it was eleven o'clock. Then she practically dragged her father down the stairs and out to the car, begging him to hurry.

Luke dropped Samantha at camp and turned the Sequoia back to

San Marcos. He breathed a sigh of relief that Samantha would be happy for twelve weeks anyway. Luke had already planned how he would use those twelve weeks.

The next morning he printed the names and addresses of all the lawyers in Hays County. He studied the locations over coffee and decided to start at the courthouse. He put Cocoa in her kennel, grabbed his briefcase, and walked up the street. When he entered the courthouse he visited every desk, introducing himself, passing out his business cards, and leaving résumés. A couple of the clerks remembered him from high school. He made his way to the second floor to a door that announced CHESTER A. NIMITZ, DISTRICT JUDGE. He opened the door to the outer office and found a plump middle-aged woman with a radiant smile.

"Good morning"—Luke looked at the nameplate on her desk—"Ms. Higginbotham. I'm Lucas Vaughan. Would Judge Nimitz have a few minutes this morning?"

"Well, you just call me Susie. Everyone else does," she said, smiling. "Besides, I don't like my last name. Too long. Should have changed it when I divorced the man that stuck me with it. What do you want to see the judge about?"

"Nothing important. I don't even have a case in his court. I'm new to town. Well, actually that's not right. I grew up here and practiced for nearly twenty years in Houston. Got fed up with the rat race and moved back."

"Oh, you bought the old Cramer place, didn't you? Nice job. Hold on. I'll tell Judge Nimitz you're here."

Five minutes later the door to his chambers opened, and a short, muscular man with gray hair, blue eyes, and a ruddy complexion stepped out. "Mr. Vaughan, come in. I'm Chuck Nimitz. Susie, bring coffee. How do you take yours?"

"Black, sir, if you please."

The walls and shelves in Judge Nimitz's chambers were overflowing with photos, plaques, and memorabilia. "Let me give you a quick tour. Everyone is always interested in this stuff I've been collecting for forty-odd years. Start with this photo. That's me graduating from the Naval Academy. I'm named after my uncle Chester, the World War II admiral who grew up over in Fredericksburg. Wasn't very hard to get in the academy after he put in a word. That's me and one of my classmates, John McCain, a real hell-raiser. Our careers kind of paralleled each other for a lot of years. We even flew from the same carrier for a while during the Vietnam War. I got shot down once, too, but was able to get my fighter over water and was rescued by our guys. Broke my hip. Still bothers me when the weather changes."

Luke saw an honorable discharge certificate that appeared to be from when Judge Nimitz was in his early forties. "Why did you get out of the navy, Judge?"

"After Vietnam there wasn't any prospect of another real fight. They eventually made me a squadron commander, mainly a desk job. After twenty I'd had enough. This wall here is my UT wall. Went to law school there after the navy. Best law school in the country as far as I'm concerned."

"You won't hear me disagree with that. Judging from your diploma, I was just a few years behind you. Of course, I hadn't put in twenty years serving my country."

"Have a seat, Luke. Tell me about yourself."

Luke spent the next fifteen minutes outlining his career, some of his verdicts, his ulcer, and his decision to move back to San Marcos. After giving the judge his résumé and business card, Luke thanked him for his time and left the courthouse.

Over the next several days Luke introduced himself to most of the lawyers in the area. Next, he went to San Marcos High School and found his old English teacher. She kept up with most of the graduates and was eager to give him information about the members of his class and their whereabouts. Armed with a new list of potential clients, Luke started the same drill.

One day he was leaving the Comal Cleaners, which was owned

by a classmate, when he heard a voice. "Luke, Luke Vaughan, is that you?"

He turned to see an attractive brunette, probably in her late thirties, smiling at him. Luke noted that her gray business suit hid what appeared to be an athletic body. Her blue dress shirt was unbuttoned at the neck, revealing just a hint of cleavage. With her high heels, she was almost as tall as Luke. She removed her sunglasses, revealing sparkling green eyes as she continued. "It is you, Luke. You don't remember me, do you?"

A little chagrined that he didn't remember such a good-looking woman, he could only say, "I'm sorry, I don't. Maybe you can jog my memory." He smiled.

"I'm Sue Ellen Taggert. I was in the ninth grade when you were a senior. I was always trying to get your attention then, but you were more interested in the cheerleaders. I heard you were a big-time trial lawyer in Houston. What're you doing coming out of Jim's cleaners?"

"I don't know about being a big-time lawyer there. Anyway, I'm just reacquainting myself with everyone. I live over on Live Oak Street. Bought the old Cramer place. My daughter and I live upstairs, and my office is on the first floor. What about you?"

"I'm a lawyer, too. Graduated from St. Mary's in San Antonio and took a job with the Hays County district attorney. I'm the chief felony prosecutor. I live in one of those old houses not far from you, and my only roommate is my ten-year-old son," she said with just the hint of a twinkle in her eye. "So we need to get together. Got to run. Judge Nimitz is calling his criminal docket at one. Oh, here's my card. I'll write my home number on the back."

11

———◆———

Ryan Sinclair had a house that very few employees of CDER could afford, in an upscale neighborhood fifteen minutes from their office. He invited the other members of his team there for a Saturday night barbecue. While they were expected to relax and unwind, the real reason for the get-together was to have a place and time where they could discuss their opinions about Exxacia without interference.

Mary Hawkins, Henry Schmidt, and Robert Walls, along with their spouses, arrived around seven. Mary was an infectious disease specialist, Henry was a pharmacologist, and Robert was a statistician. It was late fall, but Ryan cut the chill on the patio with a couple of heat lamps. His wife, Sara, had set appetizers on the patio table. Ryan escorted each couple on arrival through the house to the kitchen, where he offered drinks. The choices were Bud Light or red wine.

Football dominated the men's conversation. All of them had become Baltimore fans, and after a dismal start the Ravens were now making a playoff run; their young quarterback was the talk of the league. Then there was college ball. Texas, Florida, LSU, and USC were all in the hunt for the national championship. Ryan kidded that his alma mater, Harvard, should be in the BCS title game. After all, they, too, were undefeated. Finally Sara invited all of the women inside, where they made dinner preparations and found something more interesting than football to talk about. After two rounds of drinks, Ryan fired up the grill and took steak orders. In thirty minutes they were seated inside, where the guests congratulated Ryan and Sara on a fantastic barbecue dinner. After dinner, Sara cleared the table and served coffee. Ryan took over the discussion.

"If you spouses don't mind, we need to talk a little business."

"Thanks a lot, Ryan," Henry said, grinning. "You fill us full of barbecue and beer and expect us to sound coherent. Just kidding. We knew this was coming."

"Ryan's been talking about this Exxacia for months," Sara responded. "I feel like I'm a part of the team."

"You are, dear," Ryan said. "Only you don't get a vote. Mary, you go first."

"Tonsillitis is out as far as I'm concerned, but I may get overruled. And I'm old-fashioned enough that if it was my call, I'd eliminate sinusitis, too. Ninety percent of sinus problems will resolve themselves without medication. For the other ten percent we've got a bunch of antibiotics out there that have fifteen or twenty years of history. There aren't any more surprises with those drugs."

"Still, you know the problem, Mary," Henry replied. "We can't block a new drug application just because there are other drugs that do the same thing. I agree with you on the tonsillitis, though."

"Robert?" Ryan asked. "Your turn."

"I've still got safety issues. On the basis of less than a thousand patients in the Phase I, II, and III trials, I wouldn't feel comfortable putting this drug out there. Why take a drug for a sinus problem if you may lose your liver or have a heart attack? Sure, the chance may be only one in fifty thousand or a hundred thousand. Personally, I'd rather just run through a couple of boxes of Kleenex."

"I couldn't agree more," Ryan added. "My friend in London sent me the European after-market data. Besides liver and cardiac problems, some vision problems are on the radar screen, along with vasculitis. That last one doesn't make much sense and may be a coincidence, but it's out there. Let's take a vote. Thumbs up or thumbs down."

They all looked at Mary, who slowly turned her thumb down. She was followed by Henry and Robert, who looked at each other for confirmation they were doing the right thing and also turned thumbs down. Then all three turned to Ryan, who smiled and turned his thumb down as well.

"When are you going to tell Boatwright?" Emma asked.

"Monday morning. No use waiting. The advisory committee meeting is in four weeks, and we might as well start getting ready for it."

"Boatwright's going to be pissed, Ryan," Henry cautioned. "For some reason he's personally interested in this one."

"Yeah, I know. He can override me if he wants, but I don't think he has the stones to do it."

"What if he recommends a big clinical trial to the advisory committee? You go along with that?"

"Nope, not on this drug. As far as I'm concerned, the more patients taking Exxacia, the more adverse events. Only problem is that it may not be my call."

12

Ryan stopped by Dr. Boatwright's assistant's desk on the way to his office on Monday. "Lucille, can I see Dr. Boatwright sometime today for, say, fifteen minutes?"

Lucille looked up from her computer. "Dr. Sinclair, you know how busy Dr. Boatwright is, don't you? It's probably out of the question. I'll do my best to get you in to see him sometime this week."

"Whatever you say, Lucille. I would think that Roger would like to see me sooner rather than later."

Exasperation filled Lucille's face. "Dr. Sinclair, you know that Dr. Boatwright does not permit first names. I'll try to tell him you dropped by. Have a good day."

Lucille turned to read something important on her computer. Ryan saluted her and walked to his office. At four o'clock that afternoon Lucille called. "Dr. Boatwright will see you at four forty-five. You will have fifteen minutes. Be prompt."

"Yes, ma'am," Ryan said as this time he saluted the phone.

Ryan appeared at Lucille's desk at four fifty. It was intentional. Lucille looked at him in disgust. "You're late."

"Right you are, Lucille. I'll talk fast."

Lucille escorted Ryan into the office and retreated, closing the door behind her. Boatwright was again poring over some document. This time Ryan took one of the two chairs across from his desk, crossed one leg over the other, and waited for him to look up. Finally he did. "Dr. Sinclair, punctuality is a virtue. You're late."

"I agree, Dr. Boatwright, but I knew you would be reading that document and figured I could use an extra five minutes."

"What? How did you know what I was reading? Oh, never mind. What is it?"

"I thought you might like to know the final verdict on Exxacia, Dr. Boatwright."

"Of course, of course. I'm sure that you found it to be both efficacious and safe for all concerned, right, Dr. Sinclair?"

Ryan unfolded his legs and leaned forward as he spoke in almost a whisper. "Afraid not, Dr. Boatwright. My team has voted unanimously to send a nonapproval letter to Ceventa."

"You must be kidding," Boatwright erupted. "It's a joke, right? Your little joke. Dr. Kingsbury has assured me that the drug is a miracle in the making."

"Sorry, but my team disagrees. You'll be getting my formal report and recommendation tomorrow. There are too many red flags popping up for us to approve it, liver toxicity, vision, one heart attack, all from a small population."

"But, but, but, the advisory committee hasn't even met. They won't for four weeks."

"Look, Dr. Boatwright, I only do my job. So do my team members. What you do, or what our distinguished advisory committee members do, both are out of my control."

Boatwright rose and paced behind his desk for at least a minute, head down, deep in thought. "That'll be all, Dr. Sinclair."

As soon as Ryan left, Boatwright locked the door behind him and placed a call to a private cell number. "Dr. Kingsbury, Roger Boatwright here."

"Roger, my friend, delighted to hear from you. Did you forget that we're on a first-name basis? How's my NDA coming? About time for approval, isn't it?"

"That's what I'm calling about, Dr. . . . I mean Alfred. Ryan Sinclair was just in here. He's not approving the drug."

"Nonsense. You told him that you wanted it approved, didn't you? I thought that after we left Jamaica it was a done deal."

"Yes, sir, I did tell him. He thinks there are some safety issues with Exxacia, particularly dealing with hepatitis."

Boatwright, of course, couldn't see Kingsbury's face as it turned red and he fought to control his temper.

"Look, Roger, you're the guy in charge at CDER. Young Sinclair is becoming a real pain in the ass. You can overrule a narrow-minded pencil pusher like him, can't you now?"

Boatwright fumbled for an answer. "I have the authority, but I'm sorry to say that Sinclair is quite well thought of in the agency. If I overrule him, it's almost certain to get back to the commissioner. He's likely to send someone down from his staff to nose around and find out the reason for the disagreement. It would be a lot worse for you if I give you an approval letter and then have to withdraw it." Boatwright's voice dropped almost to a whisper as he finished.

"Dr. Boatwright, it's highly important to me, personally, to have Exxacia marketed in the United States." Dr. Kingsbury's voice rose as he continued. "We'll make sure it's a huge success, but I can't give it to my marketing boys until you give us the green light. It still has to go to the advisory committee, doesn't it?"

"Right, Dr. Kingsbury. That's in four weeks."

There was silence on the other end as Kingsbury puffed a cigarette and thought. Boatwright was about to ask if there was anything else when Kingsbury said, "This advisory committee has eleven members, correct? I suggest that you plan to attend their meeting and persuade them that my drug is safe and efficacious."

13

One Sunday afternoon Luke and Cocoa were out in the neighborhood when they passed Spring Park, which was on one of their regular routes. Only five acres, it usually held a few children playing soccer or football and some mothers watching toddlers roaming at one end. On this afternoon there were probably a dozen dogs and owners, too. Seated in a ragged circle, the owners chatted with each other. Some of the dogs were content to lie beside them. Other dogs were engaged in friendly contests. An older man had a Frisbee and tossed it as far as he could. His black Labrador took off, barking happily, as he followed the Frisbee. When it was four feet from the ground, the Lab leaped to catch it, did a small parade lap, and returned to his owner where he dropped the Frisbee and awaited the next toss. Luke smiled at the gathering. Cocoa was excited and strained at her leash to join the others. Then Luke spotted Sue Ellen Taggert.

Luke and Cocoa walked to the group. "Hey, Sue Ellen, can we join you?"

Sue Ellen broke off a conversation with another woman and pushed to her feet. She was wearing shorts and a Texas Longhorns T-shirt. *Wow,* Luke thought, *I'm sorry I didn't pay attention to her in high school.*

"Welcome, Luke. Everybody, this is our new neighbor, Luke Vaughan. He grew up here and disappeared into the vast wasteland of Houston before coming to his senses. He bought the old Cramer place. And this is his dog . . . ?"

"Cocoa. Cocoa's about four months. I'm teaching her to be a fierce attack dog." Luke grinned.

Sue Ellen introduced all of her friends and their dogs. "And this is my son, Josh, and Jackie, my border collie."

When the rest of the group returned to their conversations, Sue Ellen explained that the ad hoc club assembled most Sunday afternoons. Sometimes there were twenty people in attendance, sometimes only half a dozen. Dogs were their common interest. The only rule was that any dog that couldn't get along with the other dogs would not be permitted to return.

Sue Ellen motioned for Luke to sit beside her as Josh wandered off to toss a football with some friends. Luke looked around at the group. All of them seemed happy, contented, and relaxed. *Why didn't I opt for this lifestyle twenty years ago?* he thought.

The sun began to cast shadows on the park as people and dogs started to drift away. Luke was content to stay there until midnight. Stress was a distant memory, and Sue Ellen was a delightful conversationalist. Luke particularly enjoyed it when she would punctuate her comments by touching his arm and occasionally his knee.

"Probably time to go," Sue Ellen finally said. "Luke, why don't you and Cocoa walk with us back to my house? It's only a couple of blocks out of the way. I've got beer in the fridge."

"I'm for it. Lead the way," Luke replied as he got to his feet and extended a hand for Sue Ellen. Sue Ellen hollered at Josh, who caught one more pass from his friend and joined them.

Josh was a cute ten-year-old, well-mannered and big for his age. Luke took an instant liking to him. "Josh, you play any sports?"

"Yes, sir. Most all of them, depending on the season. Football, baseball, basketball, soccer. I like football the best."

"Who knows, maybe I'm raising a Longhorn quarterback," Sue Ellen said, the smile of a proud parent on her face.

They turned the corner, and Sue Ellen motioned to the second house on the left. "That's ours."

It was a smaller version of Luke's house, well maintained, painted light blue with dark blue trim.

"Have a seat on the porch. I'll bring those beers. Josh, you can join us or go watch television." Josh opted for the TV.

Luke took a seat and Cocoa was content to lie beside him and quickly dozed off into doggie slumber. Sue Ellen returned with two beers, then went back in the house and reappeared carrying a tray of assorted cheeses and crackers. They rocked, sipped their beers, and continued their small talk about old mutual acquaintances and caught up on life events.

Sue Ellen had graduated from Texas and then tended bar on Sixth Street in Austin for two years until she decided what next to do with her life. She settled on law school, but her grades were not quite good enough for UT Law. St. Mary's was a good second choice, and she moved to San Antonio. In her third year she dated a fellow student she expected to marry, but he was shocked when she announced she was pregnant and thereafter would have nothing more to do with her. She found herself in early labor during the bar exam and assumed that she had probably failed. Two days later Josh was born, and three months later she learned she was a lawyer. She admitted to no serious romantic involvement since that time.

After a second beer the sun was almost gone, and Luke said that he would be getting on back to his house. There was an awkward moment between the two friends as she extended her hand. Rather than taking it, Luke pulled her toward him and gave her a gentle good-night kiss. He promised to call her soon and waved as he got to the end of her sidewalk. In hindsight, Luke should have savored that moment, for stress would reenter his life by the end of the summer.

14

It was Friday night in San Marcos. Luke had reluctantly agreed with Samantha that since she was now in high school, she could go to the movies and to the mall with her friends on weekend nights, provided a parent drove and she was home by ten thirty. He was finishing up a real estate deal for a Hill Country developer when he heard a timid knock on the door. Before he could get up, Samantha hollered down the stairs, "I'll get it, Father."

Samantha bounded down from the second floor and ran for the door.

"Samantha, stop! Don't open that door yet."

Luke walked to the hallway and stared at the apparition that his daughter had become. "My God, Sam, what have you done to yourself? Halloween is over."

"You like it, Father? It's the new Samantha."

Luke could hardly speak. Samantha was wearing black jeans, black boots, and a T-shirt with Marilyn Manson on the front. In addition to a pentagram necklace, she wore a giant bracelet on each wrist and a chain around her waist. That was bad enough, but the worst was that she had dyed her beautiful red hair black.

"Sam, what did you do to your hair?" Luke stuttered as he tried to control his voice. "You can't go out like that."

"Father, calm down. All my friends dress like this. Let me show you."

She threw open the door to reveal a skinny kid, probably fifteen, with a pasty-white complexion. He was shorter than Samantha by two inches. His outfit was almost identical to Samantha's. His hair was black and sprayed into a spike, and he had a stud lebret hanging from his bottom lip.

"Father, this is Jimmy. He's been showing me how to be goth."

Luke looked with astonishment from his daughter to Jimmy and back to Samantha. Then he walked to the edge of the porch, where he saw Jimmy's mother sitting in the driver's seat of a ten-year-old Chevrolet, window down, puffing on a cigarette as she waited. Marilyn Manson reverberated from the open window.

"Samantha, go back in the house. You're not going anywhere like that."

"Father," Samantha yelled, "you promised. You didn't tell me there was a dress code."

Luke sized up the situation and debated what to do. Finally he said, "All right, Samantha. Take off that chain. You don't need it to hold up those jeans anyway. Leave the bracelets here, and you can go. Don't you dare be home one minute past ten thirty. Do I make myself clear?"

"Yes, Father," Samantha fumed as she removed the chain and bracelets. She tried to toss them on a chair in the foyer and missed. "Sorry, Father. You can pick them up. We're late. Let's go, Jimmy."

They ran down the stairs and jumped into the car. As he watched them drive away, he pulled his cell phone from his pocket.

"Sue Ellen, Luke here. Sorry to call you on short notice. I should be taking you out to dinner or something, only I need some advice. Can I come over? I'll even bring a bottle of Scotch."

Sue Ellen could hear concern in Luke's voice. "Come on, Luke. Forget the Scotch. I've got plenty."

Luke and Sue Ellen had been seeing each other on a semiregular basis for the past year. The potential for a romantic relationship, perhaps more, was there, but neither pushed it. They enjoyed each other's company and commiserated about raising kids as single parents.

Luke climbed the steps to Sue Ellen's house, but before he could knock, she opened the door, a Scotch and water in her hand. "About time you got here. Start with this one. Let's sit in the living room. Josh is upstairs playing some video game."

Luke sat in an easy chair across from the sofa, where Sue Ellen folded her legs under her and waited. He sipped his Scotch for a couple of minutes. "You know anything about goths?"

"I presume you don't mean the old European Goths, but the modern ones. Yeah, I do. I've run across a bunch of teenagers who are into the movement in criminal court."

"Oh, that's just great," Luke replied as he took another sip of his Scotch.

"It's usually nothing serious. Some drinking, a little marijuana, loud music disturbing neighbors, occasionally a DUI. Actually, they get into trouble about the same way that other teenagers do. Samantha into it?"

Luke described what had happened that night. "I'm at a loss. What's possessed Samantha? What happens from here?"

"Luke, Samantha's fourteen and she's rebelling, probably rebelling against you and certainly against society. Kids want to be part of a group. The outfit is part of how they identify who they are and what group they belong to. Sports teams have their uniforms. Gangs have their colors. Kickers identify each other by their boots and belt buckles. Goths are just a little more extreme."

"Wait a minute. Why would Samantha rebel against me? I've done the best I can as her father."

"I'm sure you have. At least from your perspective you have. May just be that Samantha sees the relationship differently."

Luke rose and turned to stare out the picture window into the darkness. "I'm sorry to say you're probably right. Okay, you seem to understand this goth stuff better than I do. What do you suggest?"

Sue Ellen rose, stood beside Luke, and circled his waist with her arm. "Do nothing, Luke. The more you protest, the worse it will be. Let her be a rebellious teenager for a while."

"Then what?"

"She'll outgrow it. Probably when she goes to college she'll mature out of the phase."

"You're telling me that I have to put up with this another three years," Luke said as he turned to face Sue Ellen.

"That's right, Luke. In the meantime, just love her," Sue Ellen said as she put her arms around Luke's neck and held him. Then she lifted her head and kissed him lightly. Luke responded by pulling her toward him and returning the kiss with one that was much more passionate and lingering.

Sue Ellen stepped back and looked into Luke's eyes. "So, Mr. Vaughan, exactly where is this going?"

"I think we both know where we're going. The only question is, when do we get there?" Luke smiled.

15

In the middle of Samantha's junior year, Luke gave up trying to be a good father. In fact, he really gave up on being a father at all. It was not intentional, but he realized he had tried everything and was out of options.

It was a chilly Saturday night in February. Samantha was out with her friends. Luke was relaxed in his big easy chair in the upstairs living area with a John Grisham novel. Cocoa was curled up at his feet, snoring quietly in front of a roaring fire. His solitude was broken by the roar of heavy metal music coming from a car in the street. Cocoa barked and ran down the stairs. *Sam's home,* he thought and then turned a page. Luke was resigned to Samantha's goth friends. He didn't like Sam's outfits or the latest pink streak in her black hair. He only hoped that Sue Ellen's advice that she would mature out of it proved to be correct.

Luke heard Samantha stumble over the front door threshold and trip as she made her way up the stairs. "Good evening, Father," she slurred as she got to the second floor. "I'm going to my room. Come on, Cocoa."

"No, you're not, young lady. You'll come right here," Luke replied as he put his book on the ottoman. "How much have you had to drink?"

"Nothing, Father."

"Sam, don't lie to me. How much?"

"All right. We split a six-pack of beer in the parking lot at the mall."

"Samantha, you are not to drink as long as you live under this roof."

"Come on, Father, all my friends drink. Besides, what gives you the right to be so high and mighty? You drink every night. I never see you after five o'clock without a Scotch close by. Good night, Father."

Samantha turned, motioned to Cocoa, and slammed the door to her room behind them.

Luke picked up his Scotch and started to drink it. Instead, he walked to the kitchen and poured the Scotch down the sink.

The next morning at nine, Luke pounded on Samantha's door. "Sam, time to get up!"

"Father, it's the middle of the night, for God's sake."

Luke opened the door and motioned to Cocoa, who was also just awakening. "Come on, Cocoa. Let's go for a run. Sam, I expect you to be up when we get back."

After the run he and Cocoa climbed the stairs and went into the kitchen, where he expected to find Samantha sitting at the breakfast table, probably reading the paper. He was wrong. There was no sound.

He walked to her door, threw it open, and commanded, "Samantha, get out of that bed right now. We need to talk."

Samantha stirred and rolled over on her stomach, pulling her pillow over her head as she did so. Luke threw back the covers and tossed the pillow on the floor. "I mean now!"

"Okay, okay, Father, if it's that important. Let me go to the bathroom first."

Luke stomped out of the room, poured himself coffee, and sat at the kitchen table. Finally Samantha came from her room, wearing a robe and slippers. She slumped in a chair across from her father.

"You want something to eat?"

"No thanks. My stomach is feeling a little queasy. Look, I know this is about last night. I'm sorry, Father. It won't happen again."

Luke tried to modulate his voice. "Damn right it won't. Until further notice you're grounded."

"Grounded! Father, what does that mean? I'm nearly seventeen."

"That means that you're not going out with your goth buddies anymore until I say so. You want to have your friends over here, that's fine, even those weirdos. Tell you what I'll do. I'll even provide a couple of six-packs of beer, provided it's drunk here and I can monitor the consumption of your friends. I'll probably even have a couple myself. How's that?"

"Oh, great. So I tell my friends to come over and drink with my old man. That'll go over like a pregnant elephant. No thanks. I'll serve my penance by myself. If you want to have me do a few Hail Marys, just say the word. Now can I be excused?"

Samantha knocked over the chair as she rose, didn't bother to pick it up, and stormed to her room.

16

Ryan found himself, once again, standing in front of Boatwright's desk as the director pretended he wasn't there. Boatwright finished proofing a letter and finally looked up. "Dr. Sinclair, the Infectious Disease Advisory Committee convenes in three days. There are a few minor matters, mainly follow-ups from previous meetings, but the bulk of the meeting will be a discussion of Exxacia."

Ryan nodded. "I've been working with my team, Dr. Boatwright. I'll be prepared to present our recommendation."

"That's what I want to discuss. Why don't you shut the door and have a seat?"

Ryan did as he was told. Boatwright leaned over his desk. "Dr. Sinclair, you and I disagree about this drug. I expect you to lay out your team's findings in full. However, I would ask that you not recommend a complete rejection of the drug. These committee members use antibiotics every day in their practice. They can hear what you say and draw their own conclusions. If they choose to reject the drug, so be it."

Anger welled up in Ryan. He took off his glasses, wiped them with his tie, satisfied himself that they were clean, and replaced them, all the while composing himself. "You want me to defer to the committee?"

"Precisely, Dr. Sinclair."

"Why would I do that? I'm a medical reviewer. My job is to evaluate drugs and make recommendations, not to pass the buck, Dr. Boatwright."

Boatwright rose from his chair and shook his finger at Ryan. "Your job is to do what I say. Otherwise, I'll accept your resignation right now, Dr. Sinclair."

Ryan wasn't ready to resign. He believed in his work. Someone in the FDA had to be accountable to the public. There were too many Boatwrights in the agency. If he stayed longer, maybe he could lead a quiet revolution and change the system. Besides, he wasn't quite ready to move to the CDC. He got out of his chair and replied, "I'll think about it, Dr. Boatwright. No promises, you understand."

The eleven members of the Infectious Disease Advisory Committee assembled from around the nation. Rarely could all attend; today nine were expected. Eight were medical doctors, and one was a scientist with a special interest in antibiotics. They had read a briefing paper prepared by Ryan's team and expected to question the staff, but first there was lunch. They assembled in a conference room on the second floor of CDER; place cards identified their seats. Dr. Ramon Salazar from San Antonio was at the head of the table. Dr. Boatwright sat to his left. The lunch conversation was about families, changes in faculty appointments at medical schools around the country, and NFL football teams. After the table was cleared, Dr. Salazar called the meeting to order.

"We're here today to discuss a new Ceventa antibiotic, Exxacia. I'm sure you've all had the opportunity to study the briefing paper. Dr. Boatwright, I understand Dr. Sinclair is available to discuss the drug with us."

Ryan had been sitting in the hallway outside the door, arms folded, doing a slow burn since he knew that Boatwright had intentionally denied him a place at the luncheon table. Boatwright went to the door and summoned him to a small podium at the front of the room. Ryan placed a briefing book on the podium, opened it, and looked around.

"Dr. Sinclair, am I correct that you have headed up the team that has been evaluating Exxacia?"

"Yes, Dr. Salazar. My team has been focused on it for over six months. I'm comfortable that I can answer any questions your committee may have."

"Very well, please proceed with your introductory remarks. We'll chime in from time to time."

Ryan paused for a sip of water. "We should start with the results of the drug in Europe and South America. Ceventa has marketed it overseas for nearly three years. As of the last available data several million prescriptions have been written, mainly for sinusitis, but also for bronchitis and pneumonia, with some doctors also using it for tonsillitis. Based on physician and patient surveys by Ceventa, the response has been very favorable."

"If I may interrupt, Dr. Sinclair," Dr. Anita Sebastian, an infectious disease specialist from Chicago, said, "one of your footnotes alludes to some problems with liver failure, both in after-market reports overseas and in Phase III clinical trials here."

Boatwright's glare at Sinclair conveyed a demand: *Don't overdo this, Sinclair.* Ryan caught the look. "That's true, Dr. Sebastian. There can be instances of toxicity to the liver." Ryan glanced at Boatwright as he continued. "We all know that is a trade-off that must be made with any antibiotic."

"If I may be heard." Dr. Holloway, a physician affiliated with Emory University, interrupted. "I don't see anything here that alarms me."

"Just a minute, young man," Dr. Rogers from Palo Alto said. "It looks to me like the reports of adverse events are much more frequent than with some of our more common antibiotics. We rarely see liver problems with ampicillin, for example, and it works quite well for bacterial sinus infections and even pneumonia. Plus, it's now been around long enough that it's a generic and a whole lot cheaper than whatever Ceventa will charge for this new one."

Dr. Craig from Miami popped up. "And what about those reports of cardiac irregularities? I don't like those one bit."

"Dr. Sinclair, you and your team have been living with this drug, as you say, for six months now. What's your recommendation?" Dr. Salazar asked.

Not liking the way the wind was blowing, Boatwright rose to his feet and interrupted before Ryan could answer. "Members of the committee, may I make a suggestion? From what I can determine, Exxacia has marvelous potential, particularly since our population is aging and, frankly, older antibiotics are just not as effective. Why don't we mandate that Ceventa conduct a large, randomized prospective clinical trial with patients throughout the country? I would suggest that we require an approval letter be subject to Exxacia passing such a trial with flying colors. If they don't want to spend the money for it, or if the trial doesn't produce satisfactory results, then we can reject Exxacia. And there's another benefit. By the time the trial is complete, we'll have much more data from other countries."

"I don't have any problem with that," Dr. Salazar said. "Certainly, more data can only help our decision. Everyone in agreement?"

Heads nodded around the table. Ryan had backed away from the podium and leaned against the wall, his arms folded. He didn't see the benefit of a trial. He was satisfied that Exxacia had far too many problems. Still, he was literally boxed into a corner. *At least,* he thought, *it'll take a year or more to do a study,* and he could always hope that more problems would surface.

17

Alfred Kingsbury directed his driver to park in a handicap space at the front entrance of the CDER complex. He pushed out the back door before Mario could get to it and burst through the front door to the security desk. "I'm here to see Dr. Roger Boatwright, young man," he bellowed.

"Is he expecting you, sir?"

"No, he's not, but he ought to be. You call up there and tell him Dr. Kingsbury is here to see him—immediately, you understand?"

"Yes, Dr. Kingsbury. Give me a moment." The guard dialed a number, and after a brief conversation, he handed a visitor badge to Kingsbury. "Please sign here. Someone will greet you on the fourth floor."

Kingsbury scribbled his name and marched to the elevator, where he punched the button three times before one arrived. On the second floor two young women entered, chatting about their children, and punched the third-floor button. Kingsbury continued to fume as they exited and he repeatedly pushed the button to close the door without success. Finally it slid shut, then opened on the fourth floor, where Roger Boatwright, thankful he'd had time to put on his coat and tie, awaited him.

"Afternoon, Alfred."

"Today it's Dr. Kingsbury to you. Where's your office?"

"Right this way, Dr. Kingsbury. Can I get you coffee?"

"No, Dr. Boatwright. This is not a social visit."

Boatwright told his assistant that he was not to be disturbed. He closed his door and was about to take his seat when he realized that Kingsbury remained standing.

"Look, Dr. Kingsbury, I know why you're here. You got the letter this morning."

"You're damn right that's why I'm here." Kingsbury stuck his finger in Boatwright's face. "I depended on you to get my drug through. My company and I have a lot invested in Exxacia. Aren't you the man in charge?"

Boatwright retreated behind his desk. "I am the director of CDER, but if I overrule one of my medical review officers, it raises red flags all the way to the top. Believe me, I want Exxacia approved, and I wish it could be today. The way things were going in that committee room, if I hadn't suggested the clinical trial, there was a likelihood they were going to vote down the drug."

"Damn it, Boatwright, that will cost my company a year and

hundreds of millions in profit," Kingsbury fumed. "And think what it will do to our stock. Once the word gets out, our stock will drop twenty or thirty percent when it should have doubled just with an approval letter."

"Calm down, Dr. Kingsbury. Think long term. Another year or so and then you'll be producing that hundreds of millions of profits every year."

Kingsbury finally took a seat. "All right, Roger. Sorry I got so pissed off. What do you want in that study?"

"Your call, Alfred. I suggest that you design a trial that will put Exxacia in the best possible light. I'll approve whatever you submit."

"I've got it, Boatwright," Kingsbury said with a smile. "We'll design a trial that will have twenty-five thousand patients, maybe one of the largest you've ever seen by a pharmaceutical company. We'll put it on a fast track, maybe less than a year, and then dump that data on Dr. Sinclair and his team. I'll depend on you to push them to make a quick decision. No way they'll be able to do a critical analysis of our data in a few weeks, right, Boatwright?"

Boatwright nodded his head in agreement. "You get us the data, and I'll set the time limit to either accept or reject the drug. You can count on me."

Kingsbury moved into action. First he assembled his marketing team and ordered them to run small classified ads in every medical trade journal in the country. He knew it wouldn't take much to attract physicians to apply to be clinical investigators. After all, the family practitioners and internists were among the lowest-paid physicians in the country. To participate in a clinical study was not only good money, it was easy. Really all the physician had to do was follow the protocol, monitor the patients, and report the results. On top of that, these were not really sick patients, particularly the ones with sinus infections and bronchitis. It wasn't like they were testing a new drug to treat heart failure or cancer. So the ad ran:

NEW DRUG APPLICATION

Major international pharmaceutical company seeks qualified physicians to investigate a revolutionary new antibiotic for treatment of sinusitis and similar respiratory infections. Contact us at Exxacia.com for further details.

As soon as the ads hit physician offices in November, the Exxacia team was overrun with e-mails. After minor screenings they selected nearly all of the family physicians, a few internists, and none of the infectious disease specialists. The team recognized that too much knowledge could be dangerous to the approval of their drug.

18

Luke heard the sound of a motorcycle on the street in front of the house. It stopped, and someone turned off the engine. He rose and looked out the window to see a Harley-Davidson in mint condition at the curb. Chrome reflected the afternoon sun; the saddlebags were a deep maroon; the body was a luxurious red. *My God,* Luke thought, *it's Morgan Freeman coming to my office.* Then he looked more carefully and realized that the rider merely looked like the actor. The slender, middle-aged man strapped his helmet to the handlebars, glanced at the house, and started up the sidewalk. Curious, Luke opened the door and met him on the porch.

"Afternoon, sir." The visitor spoke as he extended his hand. "Name's Wilson Moore. I'm a history professor over at Texas State. You got a few minutes?"

Luke took an instant liking to him. "Sure, you want to come in or sit out here on the porch?"

"Out here's fine with me. Too nice a day to be inside."

"Have a seat. Let me holler at my assistant to get us some iced tea."

While Luke went inside, Cocoa nosed her way through the screen door and sidled up to the stranger on her porch. Finding him to her liking, she permitted him to scratch her back until Luke returned with a tray complete with two tall glasses of tea and various sweeteners. "Now, what can I do for you, Professor Moore? You need a good lawyer?"

Professor Moore added Splenda to his tea, stirred it, and spoke. "First, just call me Whizmo."

"Kinda strange name. Where'd that come from?"

"High school buddies. Somehow they shortened Wilson Moore to Whizmo, and I've been stuck with it ever since. Even my students call me Whizmo—Professor Whizmo when the dean's around. Don't need a lawyer. I'm looking for a place to live, and I've been noticing that you have an apartment over your garage. Is it for rent?"

"Well, it's empty and has been since we remodeled this place. I've thought from time to time about renting it out. Just never got around to advertising it. I've got a daughter to put through college before long and could use the extra money. Don't you have a place to live?"

A frown crossed Whizmo's face as he fumbled for words. "Luke, I've been a history professor here for twenty years. I've even got a distinguished chair that pays me an extra forty thousand a year. I also teach a graduate seminar in computer science. There wasn't a degree in it when I was in school, so I'm self-taught but pretty damn good, if I say so myself. I've got a big old house on the west side of town. My wife and I raised two kids there. They're both out on their own now. One lives in Houston and the other in San Antonio." Whizmo paused and summoned the strength to go on. "I lost my wife to cancer last year."

"I'm sorry, Whizmo," Luke said, finding it easier to say the strange name.

"No need, Luke, only I've been rattling around in that house with memories everywhere I turn. I finally decided I needed to put it on the market and move somewhere else. I'm not sure where I'll end up, but your garage apartment looks like a good interim stop. It's close to campus. I can walk some days and other days ride my Harley."

"Don't you own a car?" Luke asked with some amazement.

"Got an old pickup out at the place. Don't use it except to haul wood and stuff. I've been riding Harleys since I was a kid. Second nature to me."

"How long do you want to rent the place?"

"I'll sign for a year and then evaluate my situation. Mind if I have a look?"

Luke rose and beckoned Whizmo to follow him around to the back. "I've got to warn you that it may be a little dusty. I'll get a maid to clean up if you decide you want it."

Luke opened the door and let Whizmo step in. The transformation from three years before was remarkable. Recessed lighting cast a pleasant glow throughout the living area and kitchen. Stainless steel appliances glistened from behind the kitchen bar. A fireplace occupied one wall. Two bedrooms shared an adjoining bathroom. The old windows had been replaced by modern picture windows with miniblinds to provide privacy.

Whizmo let out a low whistle. "Wow, this is more than I imagined. Frankly, I figured it would be your average run-down garage apartment. What do you want for this?"

Luke scratched his head. "You know, Whizmo, I don't have a clue. You tell me?"

"How about fifteen hundred a month? And if you'll let me have one of the garages I'll throw in another hundred."

"Done." Luke smiled. "Why a whole garage?"

"Oh, I've got another Harley. It was my wife's. It's the one thing that I just can't get rid of. Not yet, anyway. We had too many great rides and great memories to part with that, at least for now. Then, I'm into woodworking and I've got a few power tools. You need any furniture, I'm your man."

"Deal, Whizmo. No lease necessary. If I've got to have someone sign a lease for my garage apartment, I don't want that person living behind me. Now, let's go back to the porch and seal this with a beer."

Over the next several weeks Whizmo hauled furniture, all handmade, to the apartment. Luke volunteered to help with the heavy stuff. Then came the woodworking tools, along with a lathe, table saw, drill press, jointer, hand planes, and a large table, old and scarred. There was just enough room left for two motorcycles.

One Saturday Luke heard a low rumble and glanced out to see Whizmo turning into the driveway on a different Harley. He parked it in the backyard and proceeded to wipe it down with loving care. Luke wandered out to admire it with Samantha not far behind.

"She's a beaut, Whizmo," Luke said. "That one your wife's?"

"Yep, she put sixty thousand miles on it before she died. We knew every road in the Hill Country. Hell, we even made Sturgis a couple of times when we were younger. This your daughter?"

"Samantha, this is Professor Moore. He teaches history and computers over at the university. Samantha's a junior. She'll be heading to college in another year."

"My pleasure, Samantha. Just call me Whizmo like everyone else does. You ever been on a motorcycle?"

"No, sir, I mean Whizmo. I'm scared of those things. A friend of mine has a Kawasaki and shattered his leg. I'll stick to cars. I'll be getting my license soon, right, Father?"

"Probably about the time you go to college will be soon enough."

Samantha glared at him and, without another word, walked back to the house.

Whizmo stood and wiped off his hands. "Strikes me that you and Samantha have a few issues."

"More than just a few, Whizmo."

19

———◆———

Samantha and Jackie Sutherland, a classmate, stumbled out of the fraternity house a little after midnight. Two members of the fraternity chased them down the sidewalk.

"Samantha, you and Jackie can't leave. We're tapping another keg and have five more bottles of tequila. Besides, the band's going to play until two."

"Sorry, guys," Samantha slurred, "I'm already in too much trouble. I'm an hour past curfew as it is."

"Yeah," Jackie giggled, "and if I drink any more, I'll be barfing all over the lawn. Thanks for a good time."

When they got to Jackie's Chevrolet Malibu, Jackie handed the keys to Samantha. "Here, Sam. You drive. I'm too drunk."

Samantha hesitated. "My dad made me wait until I was seventeen to get my license. I don't want to risk getting it suspended."

"Dammit, it's only a few blocks to our neighborhood. You can do it. I'll watch out for cops."

The two girls got in the Malibu with Samantha in the driver's seat. "Jackie, I can't even get the key in the ignition."

Jackie grabbed the keys and pushed one into the ignition and turned it. The engine coughed once and then started. Samantha checked all her mirrors and pulled slowly out into the street. As they cut across campus, she made sure she drove five miles under the posted speed limit. She knew that she shouldn't be driving but was pleased that she seemed to be sober enough to obey the traffic signs and keep on the right side of the street. When they approached the edge of the campus, Jackie suddenly leaned forward and threw up a full night's worth of beer, tequila, Doritos, and cheese dip. Samantha looked over to try to help. "Hold on, Jackie, I'll pull over. Then we'll find a filling station to clean out the car before we get home."

Distracted by Jackie, Samantha never saw that the light at the intersection was red as she went through it, not until she got to the other side and saw a state trooper stopped at the light.

"Oh God, Jackie, I just ran a red light and a trooper saw us."

"Make a run for it, Samantha. He'll have to turn around, and we can cut down a side street."

Samantha looked in her rearview mirror and saw the trooper's lights come on at the same time she heard his siren. "Not gonna do it, Jackie. Maybe I can sweet-talk him out of a ticket."

Samantha pulled over to the curb, and the trooper stopped behind her. He got out of his car, carrying a large flashlight, and approached the Malibu. Samantha rolled down her window. "Evening, Officer." She gulped. "Did I do something wrong?"

"Yes, ma'am. That light was red." The trooper sniffed the inside of the car. "Whew, that's a powerful smell. Why don't both of you young ladies step out." He stepped back to confirm that no traffic was coming as Samantha exited the car. "Oh, and bring your purse so I can have a look at your driver's license."

The phone rang only once before Luke picked it up. "Sam, where the hell are you? Are you all right? Your cell phone's not working."

"I'm okay, Father. They took my cell phone away from me."

"Who's they?"

"I'm in jail," Samantha mumbled.

"For God's sake, for what? It's a mistake, right?"

"Er, I was driving Jackie's car and ran a red light."

"And they took you to jail for that?"

"There's more. They also charged me with DUI."

"DUI! You were drinking again and driving," Luke sputtered.

"I'll try to explain. Can you come down here and bail me out? I think it's something like a thousand dollars," Samantha pleaded.

Luke didn't reply. Instead, he slammed the phone down and walked to the bar, where he poured himself a double Scotch. *Now what do I do? This has got to be the last straw. I've done the best I can to be a good father. And I've failed.* "I know," he said to Cocoa, who could see he was upset, "I'll let her stay in jail a few days. Maybe that'll shape her up. What do you think, Cocoa?"

Cocoa whined and went up the stairs to Samantha's room, where she took her place on her side of the bed and waited for her roommate.

Samantha again burst into tears as she was led back to the cell. Then the tears turned to anger at a father who would do this to his daughter.

20

It was five o'clock before Luke managed to fall into a restless sleep. A ringing woke him at eight. He grabbed for the phone. "Hello."

"Luke, Sue Ellen here. I've got the weekend duty. Samantha's in jail."

"I know, Sue Ellen. She called me a few hours ago."

"Why aren't you on your way down here to bail her out? It's usually only a thousand dollars. In fact, I can probably get her released to your custody with no bail."

"Thanks, Sue Ellen. I've been wrestling with this all night. I've done all I can. Let the system deal with her."

"Luke, you can't abandon your daughter," Sue Ellen pleaded. "It's not like she robbed a bank or assaulted someone. Kids her age end up here every weekend. That doesn't make them bad kids."

"Thanks for your advice, Sue Ellen, but I've made up my mind." Luke returned the phone to its cradle.

Sue Ellen stared at her phone, not believing what she had just heard. Then she dialed the jail. "Omar, have you got an empty cell?"

"Yes, ma'am."

"Then would you get Samantha Vaughan out of the drunk tank and into that cell? She's a personal friend of mine."

"Will do, Sue Ellen."

On Sunday morning there was a rap on Luke's door. He went down the stairs in his bathrobe to find Sue Ellen and Whizmo standing on his porch.

"Can we come in, Luke?" Whizmo asked.

"Sure. Coffee's made. Come on upstairs. I'll grab some jeans and a T-shirt."

Luke poured his third cup of the morning and joined his friends in the breakfast alcove. "I know what this is about. I'm not changing my mind."

"Luke, I've got it all arranged. All you have to do is go with me to the police station and sign some papers saying that you'll guarantee she'll make her court appearance. Please, please, don't do this to yourself and to her, please."

Luke remained silent as he sipped his coffee and finally spoke. "All right. I give up. She's had two nights in jail. Maybe that's enough. Let me grab my keys."

Three weeks later Luke and a frightened Samantha sat on the front row in Judge Nimitz's court.

"The State of Texas v. Samantha Vaughan," the clerk called.

Luke rose with Samantha, who instinctively grabbed his hand as they approached the bench.

"Good morning, Mr. Vaughan. I presume this is Samantha."

"Morning, Judge. I'm here as Samantha's father and her lawyer."

Judge Nimitz leaned over his bench and peered into Samantha's eyes. "Young lady, do you realize that you could have killed someone that night?"

"Not at the time, no, sir. I guess I wasn't thinking."

"Well, you're damn lucky someone wasn't walking across that street, aren't you?"

"Yes, sir."

"I could lock you up for a year for what you did."

"No, sir. Please," she begged. "I want to go to college this fall."

"I understand. I've checked with your school and find you're a very good student. Here's what I'm going to do. Your fine for running the light is one hundred and fifteen dollars, which I presume your father will loan you. As to the DUI, I'm putting you on probation for one year. If you get in any kind of trouble with the law during that year, you will be locked up. Do you understand that?"

"Yes, sir. I understand."

"Mr. Vaughan, I presume that you will accept custody of her during the year of her probation."

"Of course, Your Honor."

"Very well, then. And one more thing, Samantha. I don't like these goths. They're troublemakers, if you ask me. As a part of your probation, you are not to mingle with any of them and you are to burn all of your goth outfits. Understood?"

"Yes, Your Honor."

"I understand you have beautiful red hair. The next time I run across you in town, I want to see your red hair, not that awful black with the pink streak."

Luke listened to the additional terms of probation and thought that maybe something good would come out of this after all.

21

―――――――

Even though it was spring and flowers were blooming in San Marcos, there was still a chill in the air at the Vaughan house. That chasm that Whizmo had discussed when Samantha was in jail was even wider now. Luke and Samantha rarely talked. It was as if they were two roommates who shared the same house but nothing else.

Since Samantha could no longer associate with her goth friends, she spent more and more time with Whizmo, who always seemed to be working in the garage when he was home. Samantha had been rocking on the front porch when she heard Whizmo's Harley rounding the corner. When he turned into the driveway, he waved at her. As soon as he cut the engine in front of his apartment, Samantha motioned to Cocoa, who bounded down the steps and around the corner. By the time Samantha caught up, Whizmo was sitting on his steps, scratching Cocoa.

"Hey, Sam. How you doing, girl?"

Samantha sat on a step below Whizmo and replied, "Not so good, Whiz. I'm counting the days until I get to spend my last summer at Camp Longhorn and then head away to college. I'm ready to get out of this house."

"Yeah, I've been hearing from your dad that things are pretty frosty in there. Still, I don't know why the two of you can't talk. From where I stand, there's plenty of blame to be shared."

"Come on, Whiz." Samantha's eyes flashed. "All I did was have one problem with driving."

"Sorry, Sam, but I gotta disagree. That one problem was a DUI, and you've been close to stepping out of bounds ever since I've known you. By the way, I like the color of your hair. That's one thing that Judge Nimitz got right."

Both remained silent as they listened to two mockingbirds chirping to each other. Then Whizmo spoke. "Speaking of college, you still making good grades?"

"I haven't made a B in all of high school." Samantha smiled.

"So, where are you going, Texas or A&M? Both first-class schools. Personally, I'd like to get you to Texas State, but I know you're ready to get out of San Marcos."

"Whiz, there's no way I'd go to Texas. That would mean I would be following in my father's footsteps, and that's not going to happen. I'm going to be an Aggie, hullabaloo, caneck, caneck and all that stuff."

"You told your dad?"

"Yeah, we had that discussion a couple of months ago, after I did my weekend in jail. He'd rather have me going to Texas, but he's okay with A&M."

"You thought of a major?"

"Nope. I figure there's time for that. One thing for sure is that it won't be prelaw."

22

School ended, and Samantha graduated second in her class of two hundred. Luke attended the graduation, and in spite of his problems with Samantha, he teared up when she crossed the stage. Then it was off to Camp Longhorn for one last time.

When he got back to the house after dropping Samantha at camp, he went to the kitchen for a Bud Light. Beer in hand, he and Cocoa went outside, where he sat in a rocker on the porch while Cocoa chased squirrels in the yard. As he sipped his beer, he sized up his life. Not exactly what he had anticipated when he graduated from law school. He'd made a decent living in Houston but never got rich. In hindsight, his ulcer was probably a good thing since it slowed him down and likely added twenty years to his life. He loved San Marcos. Looking back, he couldn't fathom why he ever left in the first place. His law practice was okay, and it didn't require him to work nights and weekends as a trial lawyer regularly did. Sue Ellen was now more than just a friend. He conceded he was in love and relished the emotion. Since Samantha was going to be off on her own, he vowed to focus on his relationship with Sue Ellen. They were on the road to a lasting relationship, yet for some reason he had avoided talking marriage. Sue Ellen didn't seem to mind, but he knew that once Sam was in college it would be time for a commitment. Then there was Whizmo. What a character, and what a delightful person to sit around and swap stories with.

Luke's face grew somber as he thought about the major failure in his life, his daughter. How could that have happened? He loved her. He always wanted to do what was best for her. He wanted nothing but happiness for her. In spite of all that, he recognized that he had failed her. Maybe it was best that she move away. Maybe the distance would mend the gap between them. He could only hope.

As he finished his beer and watched Cocoa trying to coax a squirrel out of a tree, he heard a familiar rumble, and Whizmo turned into the drive. He stopped beside the porch and took off his helmet. "You got another one of those I could buy off you?"

"Come on up, Whizmo. I'll go retrieve a couple more."

He went inside as Whizmo climbed the steps and settled into the second rocker. Cocoa abandoned her squirrel hunt to beg Whizmo for some scratching behind her ears. Luke kicked open the door and came out with a small cooler, containing six beers.

"I got nothing better to do, so I figure you and I can sit out here and get a little mellow."

"You missing Samantha already? I saw you loading her up for camp this morning."

"I couldn't admit it to her, but the answer is yes."

"Well, counselor, just why can't you admit it to her?"

"Good question, Whiz. When I come up with an answer, you'll be the first to know. I've been sitting here, contemplating my life. My law practice is pretty good, but I'm bored. I guess I need a hobby. Maybe I should take up woodworking."

"If you want to learn, I'm your man. Spending a few hours in a woodshop is guaranteed to clear the mind."

Cocoa had retrieved a stick from the yard and dropped it at Luke's feet. He picked it up and pitched it almost to the street. Cocoa bounded down the steps, retrieved it, and was back in fifteen seconds. Luke threw it again. "Now look what I've started. She wears me out every time. You know, Whiz, what I really think I'd like to do this summer?"

"Not a mind reader, Luke. Tell me."

"I think I'm old enough to ride a Harley. If I buy one, will you teach me?"

Whizmo gulped down the last of his beer and popped open another. "I'll go you one better. I'll tune up that blue Harley and you can learn on it."

Luke shook his head. "I can't do that, Whiz. That was your wife's. What would you do if I wrecked it?"

"Don't worry, Luke. Cheryl's gone and I've accepted her death. That bike's just sitting there. She'd probably like it if someone would ride it on occasion. We'll start in the school parking lot, and when you're ready, we'll get you a license. We can explore the Hill Country."

Starting with the parking lot behind the history building, in three weeks Whizmo had Luke riding the streets. Once he got his motorcycle license, Whizmo started leading him on weekend rides into the Hill Country, where Luke discovered that once he spent an hour maneuvering the hills, valleys, curves, and low water crossings he forgot everything but the pleasure of the ride. *I should have done this years ago,* he thought.

23

Ryan Sinclair watched as his dad sank a fifteen-foot putt. Ryan tapped his in from four feet away, and they walked to their cart.

"I've got a problem, Dad."

Maxwell Sinclair looked at his son with concern. "At home or work?"

"Not at home. Couldn't be going better with me and Sara. It's work. Your friend Alfred Kingsbury and his company have submitted a new antibiotic that I think is a bad drug."

Maxwell Sinclair got in the passenger seat, and Ryan drove to the next tee. "I thought you would be in a position to stop something like that."

"So did I, only Boatwright has taken a personal interest. I intended to block it at the advisory committee, but Boatwright wouldn't let me give them my recommendation. He pushed for a clinical trial instead. So now Ceventa has come up with a protocol that wouldn't get third place in a high school science fair. On top of that, I've been looking at the list of clinical investigators. I wouldn't let most of them touch my dog."

Ryan approached the tee, placed his ball, sized up the fairway, and let loose a drive that came close to three hundred yards.

"Well," Maxwell said, "I'm certainly glad those golf lessons I paid for when you were ten turned out to be worth the money."

"It's all your fault, Dad. If you had only started me when I was six, I'd be on the pro tour instead of having to deal with the FDA and drug companies who don't give a damn about anything but their bottom line. I feel like I wimped out at the advisory committee. I had been asked my opinion about the damn drug, but before I could say anything, Boatwright jumped in the middle of it. I deferred to him since he's head of the whole damn division. Bottom line is I didn't do my job."

"This is that new antibiotic, isn't it? What's the name again?"

"Exxacia."

"Yeah, I remember now. Kingsbury told me about it, bragged about how much money it was going to make for Ceventa. Told me if I bought their stock now, I'd triple my money in two years."

"Not if I have anything to do with it, and I will. Fortunately the clinical trial stands between Ceventa and approval. I'll have another chance to kill it, and I won't be so timid next time."

"It really is that bad, is it?"

"Damn right. The number of cases of liver failure and death is ten times higher in Europe than with any other antibiotic."

Maxwell lined up his tee shot, took a couple of practice swings, and hit one right down the middle, where it stopped at the 250 yard marker. After his shot, Maxwell walked up to his son and tapped the handle of his driver into Ryan's chest as he spoke. "Son, you watch your backside on this one. Something tells me the stakes are high."

24

Crowley, Louisiana, is in the heart of Cajun Creole country. There are still families there that speak only a French dialect, and gumbo is considered a staple. In fact, folks there take such pride in their family gumbo recipes that they are handed down from generation to generation and only by word of mouth. To put such a treasure in writing could mean it might be stolen and turn up on a neighbor's table. One of the best of the gumbo chefs was John Paul Batiste, DO, an osteopathic physician who officed in a small house on the highway leading to Baton Rouge.

Under six feet tall, he weighed three hundred pounds. In spite of his weight, he had a sign in front of his office that touted his specialty in weight-loss medicine. His size didn't bother his patients, mostly women. When they entered his office, the smell of gumbo drifted from the kitchen in back to fill the entire office. After he examined his patients, he took them to the kitchen, where he dished them up a bowl, whispering to them that while the pills he gave them would take off some weight, the secret ingredients in his gumbo would do more to help them shed pounds than any pill.

It was three o'clock one afternoon, and, as was his custom, Dr. Batiste took a bottle of vodka from the credenza behind his desk. He went to the kitchen and returned with a tea glass full of ice and poured the vodka up to the rim. He then leaned back with the glass in one hand and a magazine called *Louisiana Medicine* in the other. He flipped through the magazine until he ran across an ad from Ceventa, seeking clinical investigators for a new antibiotic. A smile crossed his face. He had been such an investigator too many times to count, enough times that he had learned how to manipulate the system to minimize his efforts and still fatten his pocketbook. He kicked his feet off his desk and turned to his computer to log on to the Ceventa Web site. In ten minutes he completed the application, and the message said to expect a packet of materials and drugs by FedEx within two days. Now he just had to start lining up subjects for the study, who were supposed to have one of the bacterial infections that the drug was developed to combat. Then he smiled as he thought that all of his plump patients almost certainly had the sniffles that could be caused by sinusitis. Certainly that would be his diagnosis.

25

Rudy Kowalski, Ceventa's officer in charge of the Exxacia clinical trial, was the first to notice. Ceventa had enrolled several hundred doctors, and they were approaching twenty thousand subjects. Kowalski was pleased at how smoothly the trial was progressing. He thought they should easily meet their deadlines as mandated by Dr. Kingsbury. He printed off an Excel spreadsheet to get an idea of the sites and physicians involved. As he studied the list, he was sipping a cup of coffee. Then he spotted a problem, not just one problem, but a lot of them. He put his cup down so hard that some of the coffee spilled onto the desk. He grabbed some Kleenex and wiped off the spreadsheet and then studied it some more.

The protocol called for no more than fifty subjects to be evaluated by any one investigator. He started talking to himself as he evaluated the information. "Here's one with seventy. More than approved, but not too bad. Here's one with a hundred and twenty-five. And, crap, here's some doctor named Batiste in Louisiana who's got four hundred and forty-three." He started writing down the names of the investigators who had more than fifty subjects and the numbers of patients. Finally he turned to the phone.

"Dr. Kingsbury, please. Rudy Kowalski calling. I only need about a minute of his time."

"What's up, Kowalksi? Make it fast," Kingsbury said.

"Sir, I'm a little alarmed by our study. We've got eighty-three doctors who have anywhere from seventy to over four hundred subjects enrolled in the Exxacia trial."

"How the hell did that happen, Kowalski? That's eighty-three red flags for the FDA. Why didn't you have someone monitoring this kind of thing?"

"I did, sir. She'll be looking for another job this afternoon."

Kingsbury thought for a few seconds. "Well, hopefully there's no problem we can't handle. We damn sure aren't going to start this study over. Get someone to do a site inspection on that doctor with four hundred patients. We'll start there and do random checks of others, depending on what you find."

26

The car was loaded. Samantha hugged Cocoa good-bye and climbed into the passenger seat. She was ready for college. She was also ready to get out from under Luke's thumb. After all, she was now a woman.

Luke got into the driver's seat, and after he buckled his seat belt, he handed Samantha a piece of paper with numbered paragraphs. "Here, Sam. I've drafted ten rules for succeeding at A&M. Take a look at them and we can talk as we drive to College Station." Samantha took the list and skimmed down the page before wadding it up and sticking it in her purse. Instead of having a discussion, they again drove in silence.

Once they arrived, they joined other parents and students who were unloading vehicles and carting the contents to dorm rooms. After the Sequoia was unloaded, Luke and Samantha stood awkwardly at the door to the dorm. Neither knew what to say. Then, much to Luke's surprise, Samantha stepped forward and gave him a hug. In return he kissed her on the cheek.

"Do good, Samantha."

"I will, Father."

Luke smiled and turned to walk to the car.

When he returned to San Marcos, Luke checked his e-mail and phone messages. Finding nothing that wouldn't wait until the next day, he went upstairs to change clothes, then came down again. Whistling as he went out the back door, he got what he now called his Harley and rode to pick up Sue Ellen. She was waiting on the porch.

"Hi, handsome. I haven't been on one of those since college. You sure you know how to ride it?"

"Had the best teacher in town, Whizmo's Riding Academy. Put this helmet on, and I'll take you out in the hills to a biker bar Whizmo showed me. Best cheeseburgers in the Hill Country."

It was Luke's first time to have a passenger, so he took it easy. *Keep it under the speed limit,* he thought, *and watch for gravel on the curves.* They got to the edge of town, went down a hill, crossed a low water crossing, and were on their way. The sun was slowly disappearing, mixing shadows with beams of light as they climbed a hill and cruised down the other side. The road followed the curve of a river as it wound through the hills, and finally they came to a bridge over the river with a ramshackle house and a parking lot full of motorcycles on the far side.

As they went around the house to the back porch, Luke said, "Just so you'll know. There are a few of the old bikers that hang out here, but most of the customers are modern-day professionals just trying to relive their youth."

When they stepped onto the porch, the bartender hollered, "Hey, Luke, who's your old lady and where's Whizmo?"

"Whiz is in San Antonio seeing his grandkids. This is Sue Ellen. Give us a couple of cheeseburger baskets and Bud Lights."

Luke and Sue Ellen settled into chairs at a table overlooking the river and watched the sun disappear behind the hills as Christmas lights that were strung from tree to tree were flicked on by the bartender.

"So, Luke, how's it feel—I mean, to be an empty-nester?"

The bartender brought their beers.

"Little too early to tell. I'm just glad I got her out of high school and into college. Hopefully she does well, and hopefully not living under the same roof will make it better for both of us." Luke reached across the table and took Sue Ellen's hands in his as he gazed into her eyes. "And it means I'll have more time for the second love of my life. Well, maybe the third if we count Cocoa."

The comment drew a poke in the arm from Sue Ellen. "I'll be willing to fight Cocoa for that number two spot. May the best girl win," she teased. "Actually, I'll be facing the same thing you are in a couple of years. Josh is determined to go to Texas and start at quarterback. I've told him that the Longhorns get their pick of the best prospects in the country. He just says, 'Bring 'em on.' He's a good kid. Maybe not as smart as Sam, but he makes up for it by busting his butt in everything he does."

A waitress dropped off two cheeseburger baskets.

"You eating onions?" Sue Ellen asked.

"You bet. You better, too, for self-defense if nothing else."

Sue Ellen nodded and loaded her cheeseburger, topping it off with mustard and ketchup. When she took a bite, she chewed with a smile on her face. "You're right. Best damn cheeseburger around. Promise to bring me back?"

"Not before tomorrow night, anyway."

Sue Ellen nodded her agreement. When they finished the burgers, they grabbed two more beers and walked along the river as the moon peeked over the hills to the east. Pausing on a boulder that jutted out into the river, they turned and wrapped their arms around each other. The kiss was long and passionate. When they broke away, Luke said, "See, we couldn't even taste the onions."

27

Sally Witherspoon marched into Rudy Kowalski's office, pitched her report onto his desk, and eased down into a chair. "We've got a mess on our hands down in Louisiana."

Kowalski leaned forward. "I'll read your report this afternoon, but give me the executive summary."

"This Dr. Batiste knows how to play the system. It's not bad enough that he has nearly nine times the maximum approved number of subjects enrolled. That alone will throw up a big red flag to CDER. He enrolled his entire family in the study, including cousins. Claims they're all subject to sinus problems. His main practice is pushing a bunch of pills to fat women for weight loss. From what I saw, he should have had them out walking around the parking lot instead. There's one batch with all the same blood work. Then there's another group that have the exact same vital signs on every visit. How likely is it that two women are each going to have identical blood pressure of 139 over 83 on repeated visits? How about twenty with that same pressure? Also, if the charts are to be believed, he signed up forty-three subjects all between seven and eight one evening. You think he had a Tupperware party or something?"

Kowalski buried his face in his hands. "Anything else?"

"Probably half of the consent forms are forged. The initials on each page look like they were made by the same person with the same pen. There's plenty more. It's all in that report."

"So what you're saying," Rudy sighed, "is that we paid the good Dr. Batiste a couple of hundred thousand dollars for crap."

"If that's a scientific term, Rudy, the answer is yes," Witherspoon said, nodding. "Oh, and I might add that there was not one adverse reaction to the drug out of all of his patients. You and I both know that's impossible. Surely some had liver enzymes climb enough to be reported."

"Okay, Sally. For now let's keep this just between us. I've got to figure out what to do before I break the news to Kingsbury."

28

Luke stopped a security guard on the A&M campus and asked for directions to Milner Hall, where he hoped to find Samantha in class. He parked in a visitor lot across the street, locked the door, and walked toward the building. At the entrance he paused, pulled a piece of paper from his pocket, and double-checked the room number. The class had been in progress for twenty minutes. Luke looked through the window on the door and saw a young professor who was lecturing about the American Revolution. When he opened the door, several students looked back momentarily and then returned their attention to the front.

There were two hundred students in the room, some taking notes on paper, some on computers, and some following the professor's lecture in a textbook. A few were text messaging, and some just stared off into space. Luke studied the students and spotted Samantha on the back row. Her arms were folded on the desk and she was resting her head on them. If she wasn't sleeping, she was putting on a good act.

He walked up behind her and shook her shoulder. Samantha raised her head, not sure where she was, and then realized it was her father. He motioned her to follow him out of the classroom. Samantha reached for her backpack and trailed behind Luke.

When they were in the hallway, she asked, "Father, what are you doing?"

"I just came from the admissions office. You're no longer a student here."

"What? You've got to be kidding."

"I'm dead serious. I got your midsemester grades. You were perfect. You have an F in every subject. Judging from how I just found you, I think I understand why. It's hard to stay up all night partying and expect to learn anything in class."

"Wait, it's only midsemester. I can pull them all up to C's. Give me a chance."

As they walked across the street to the car, Luke replied, "I told you that you only got one chance. You've had it. You're going back to San Marcos with me."

"But what about my room, my clothes?"

"I've got a mover with a security guard overseeing him right now. Your stuff will be back in our house by tonight."

Samantha turned to walk away. "I'm not going. I'll get a job here in College Station and take out some student loans. I don't want you in my life ever again!"

Luke grabbed her arm and whirled her around. "I'm not giving you an option. Get in the car. Now!"

Samantha did as she was told. She folded her arms and stared out her window for the next three hours. When they got home she greeted Cocoa and slammed the door to her room. For the next week she came out only long enough to get peanut butter, Cokes, and crackers from the kitchen. Luke tried to get her to go out to dinner with him. She refused. He tried to get her to take Cocoa for a walk. She refused. Weeks went by and nothing changed.

One evening Luke and Sue Ellen were talking quietly on the front porch. As usual Samantha was in her room.

"I'm out of ideas, Sue Ellen. I can't even get her out of the bedroom."

They had rocked quietly for several minutes when Sue Ellen said, "You know, Josh always knows I've got his back. Whatever happens, whatever he does, he knows he can tell me. We can talk through any problem. We even yell at each other a little, but then one of us apologizes and life goes on. When's the last time you showed Sam that you had her back, that you had confidence she would do the right thing, no matter what?"

Luke thought about his answer. "Probably before we moved to San Marcos, maybe when she was about eleven."

Sue Ellen reached over and took Luke's hand. "Then maybe it's about time to change that. She's an adult now. Give her a roof over her head, but let her be that adult. Show her you respect her decisions as a woman. If she screws up, let her deal with the consequences. Maybe even apologize for your behavior when you've been a jerk. Wouldn't hurt to try."

Luke nodded his head but said nothing.

The next Saturday morning he knocked on Samantha's door.

"What is it?"

"Can I come in?"

"I suppose. Just don't complain about how my room looks."

Luke opened the door and stepped over clothes, Coke cans, and cracker boxes. When he got to the bed he sat on the edge and took his daughter's hand. "Look, I'm sorry. I did my best, but I've been a lousy father. If you'll give me another chance, I promise to do better. And I want you to know that I now respect you as an adult. It's your life. Live it as you choose." Samantha stared at her father, not sure she could believe what she was hearing. Then Luke slipped a key into her hand. "Now look out the window. It's yours."

Samantha climbed from her bed and walked to the window. Shining in the driveway was a blue Camaro with T-tops. "Father, why? Why now?"

"It's three years old, but all I could afford. Consider it a symbol of our starting over. I trust you to drive it safely. I want you to know I have confidence in you, and I know my confidence won't be misplaced. You're welcome to stay here. In fact, I want you to stay here. But if you want to go back to A&M and get a job, it's up to you. I don't need to be making decisions for you anymore." Luke surveyed the room. "Now, this is only a suggestion, but it wouldn't hurt if you cleaned up a little."

Samantha lay back down on her bed and buried her head in her pillow, not sure what to think or do. Luke quietly closed the door.

29

Over the next several weeks Samantha elected to test the waters. On the Friday night after the conversation with Luke, she stayed out until three in the morning. When she entered the front door, Luke was nowhere to be found. She climbed the stairs, and only Cocoa greeted her. The only sound she heard was Luke snoring behind his closed bedroom door.

One afternoon Luke came home from seeing a client to find Samantha drinking a beer on the front porch. He smiled, kissed her on the cheek, went into the house, and came back out, beer in hand, to join her.

One evening she had four friends over and played computer games, accompanied by rap music, until the wee hours of the morning. Cocoa even howled along with some of the singers. Luke just shut the door to his office and worked.

Samantha threatened to return to her goth look. Luke pointed out that her probationary period had expired and she was entitled to dress however she pleased. Samantha smiled and left her hair its natural red and stuck to jeans and T-shirts.

If she had been grading her father's papers, Luke would have gotten an A.

One afternoon Samantha overheard Ruth, Luke's part-time secretary, telling him that she needed to take an indefinite leave of absence. Her daughter in West Texas was having a difficult pregnancy and had been put on bed rest by her doctor. Luke nodded his understanding and said he would figure out a way to get by.

After Ruth had gone, Samantha walked down the stairs and knocked quietly at Luke's open door. Luke looked up from his computer, smiled, and said, "Hi, Sam. When did you ever find it necessary to knock to come into my office?"

"Just being polite, Father. Can I sit down?"

Luke wondered what was going on. He didn't recall ever seeing his daughter with this attitude. He gestured for her to take a seat. "What's going on, Sam? You decide to go back to College Station to look for a job?"

"No, sir. I heard Ruth talking to you. I'm not doing much these days. I thought that if you need me, I could help out around the office. I can answer the phone. I'm a good typist. I even know how to make coffee," she added. "And I've been thinking. I can't blame you for everything in my life, particularly for my bombing at A&M. I made those five F's, not you. I think I've learned I have to accept responsibility for my actions."

Luke put down his pen and took off his glasses. He reached for a Kleenex and idly wiped them as he looked at his daughter. *What's happening here?* he thought. Then he realized that he at least had to give Samantha a chance. "Okay, you're hired. Hours are ten to three. Pay is ten dollars an hour," he replied, "plus room and board, of course."

Samantha stood and reached her hand over his desk. Luke was uncertain what she was doing until it dawned on him that she was expecting to seal the deal with a handshake. He also got to his feet and took her hand. "I accept, Father. I'll start tomorrow if that's okay."

Samantha was in her office across from Luke's at nine the next morning. Cocoa wandered back and forth between the two rooms, not sure what was going on. Finally she decided that since it was daylight, her proper place was in Luke's office on the rug in front of the fireplace. Samantha wore a dress and had her hair back in a bun, doing her best to look professional. She busied herself with rearranging the office and even brought a few photos down from her room for the walls. Around ten thirty she saw an African American couple of indeterminate age climbing the steps with two grocery bags. They knocked on the front door and waited for someone to greet them.

Samantha jumped to the door. "Morning, miss. Is Ruth here?" the gentleman asked.

"Ruth's away for a while. I'm Samantha. Please come in."

"No need, Miss Samantha," the woman replied. "We've had a good fall crop and just wanted to bring Mr. Vaughan some vegetables. Would you see that he gets these? We know he's a busy man, and we'll be on our way."

Samantha thanked the visitors as they turned to go down the steps. She walked to her father's office, and he smiled when he saw the two grocery bags. "Looks like the Watsons dropped by. Just take those up to the kitchen."

"Father, why are they bringing you vegetables?"

"They drop by three, four times a year, sometimes more. Their son was in a little trouble a few years ago. I helped him out. They live on a disability check, and Mr. Watson grows some vegetables in the back-yard. They couldn't afford a lawyer, so I didn't charge them anything. Ever since, I get fresh vegetables. I try to tell them it's not necessary, but they won't hear of it."

As Samantha turned and climbed the stairs to the kitchen, she thought that maybe there was a side to her father she'd never seen before.

"Vaughan Law Office. This is Samantha. How can we help you?" Samantha discovered that she liked answering the phone. Luke's clients were varied: old, young, male, female, all races, most of apparently modest means. Some wanted wills. Some wanted Luke to review documents before they bought a house or a piece of land. A few wanted a divorce; Luke didn't like doing those, but they helped to pay the bills. A couple of times a month a businessman would show up to discuss a real estate project or the purchase of a strip center. Samantha learned that would mean a good payday.

When Samantha saw the mailman drive up, she leaped from her desk to meet him, trading a bottle of cold water for the day's mail and a smile of thanks.

That other side of Luke kept popping up, she found. An elderly couple entered the office one day while he was on the phone. Samantha got drinks and invited them to take a seat in the hallway, which had become the reception area. When Luke got off the phone, he greeted them and went to Samantha's office. "Sam, these folks are here to sign their wills. Run out back, please, and see if Whizmo's there. If he is, tell him we need five minutes for him to witness their wills. You'll be the other witness."

Within a couple of minutes Samantha and Whizmo came through the back door. Luke introduced Whizmo as Dr. Moore, the famous history professor at the university. Whizmo obviously had done this a number of times, so Samantha followed his lead as she signed her name on the documents.

"How much do we owe you, Mr. Vaughan?" the man asked.

"Not a thing, Mr. Sampson. Simple wills are easy and something that I believe a lawyer ought to do as a service to the community. You folks have a good day now."

Luke, Whizmo, and Samantha adjourned to the front porch, where there was now a third rocker. "Father, don't you think that you ought to be charging those folks something? They look like they could pay two, three hundred dollars."

"That's not the point, Sam. We're not rich by any means, but we're making a decent living. Besides, they'll pass on a good word about me to a neighbor or someone at church."

"Sam, you wouldn't have any idea how many times I've been called up here to witness wills. Your father is generous with his professional time," Whizmo added. "If he ever went back to trying lawsuits, half the people in this town would be looking for a way to find for his clients, just because they know Luke or have friends that do."

Samantha rocked silently as she contemplated this other side of her father once again.

30

It was a strange thing about runners. They eventually became addicted. It usually took about a year. Then, if they missed more than a day or two, it affected their body and spirit. Luke had arrived at that point back when they lived in Houston. In San Marcos, morning was his time for a five-mile run; it cleared his mind and got him ready for whatever the day had in store. One morning he came out of his bedroom, dressed in his orange shorts, a white singlet, and New Balance running shoes. He found Samantha sitting at the kitchen table, also dressed for a run but wearing a maroon Aggie T-shirt.

"Mind if I join you?"

"Of course not, only you'll have to change that T-shirt. Just kidding." He laughed.

Samantha rose from the table. "You'll probably have to go slow for me at first. I haven't been running since I went away to school."

"Are you serious? You're running with an old man. Go easy on me. Tell you what, we'll let Cocoa set the pace."

Seeing what was happening, Cocoa barked, bounded down the stairs, and waited eagerly at the front door.

Luke and Samantha stretched while Cocoa ran circles around the front yard, checking out early morning smells. As they started their run, they concentrated on their breathing and working kinks out of muscles. When they passed Sue Ellen's house, Samantha asked, "How serious are you about Sue Ellen? I think she's pretty cool."

Luke thought about his answer. "I haven't said this to anyone but her. Sam, we're in love. You'll always be my first love, of course."

Samantha smiled.

"I figure on popping the question when the time is right. Expect a wedding before the end of the year, maybe beside a stream out in the Hill Country at sunset."

They ran two blocks before Samantha finally spoke. "You kinda took your time on that decision, didn't you? I mean, you've known her this time around for about five years, and as far as I know, you haven't dated anyone else."

Luke smiled. "Yeah, you're right. I don't think either one of us was in a big hurry. Neither of us had had a serious relationship in more than ten years when we met this time. Maybe we just knew we had a good thing going and didn't want to mess it up. It's a little hard to explain . . ." Luke's voice trailed off.

"That's okay. I think that's fantastic. I couldn't be more happy for both of you, honest. By the way, too bad Josh is younger than me. He's turning into a hunk. I'll bet every girl in high school is trying to get her hands on him."

After a few blocks they settled into a nine-minute pace, a speed where both runners could talk comfortably. "Sam, I need to tell you something."

Samantha looked at Luke with apprehension in her eyes.

"Don't worry. It's good. Every day I have a client tell me what a great daughter I have and compliment me for being able to raise you so well."

"Thanks, Father."

"I don't tell them that we had a few rough spots along the road. By the way, I take a water break at the park up ahead. You can run around the park a couple of times while you wait on your old man if you like."

"No thanks," Samantha replied as they reached the water fountain. "I'm ready for a breather."

Seizing her opportunity, Cocoa ran to the little lake in the middle of the park and leaped in and swam around while she waited for her family. Luke and Samantha both got a drink of water and then sat on a park bench to catch their breath.

"Uh, Father, I'd like to make a request."

Luke looked over at Samantha.

"Would you let me start taking some courses at Texas State in the spring semester? It starts in a couple of weeks. I'll still live at home and work in the office."

Luke nodded his agreement. "I'll make you a deal, Sam. You make a 3.5 GPA and I'll let you move to an apartment on campus next fall."

Samantha jumped to her feet and pulled Luke up into a bear hug. "Thanks, Dad. I want to take a class from Whizmo."

"Whizmo's liable to be tough on you."

"Oh, Dad, you know he'll be a pushover. I'll bet you ten dollars I'll top his class."

Luke hollered at Cocoa, who climbed out of the lake and, in usual doggie fashion, ran up to them and shook herself, showering the two runners.

"Cocoa," Samantha said, "where is it in the doggie gene code that says you guys always have to run to the nearest human before you shake yourself dry?"

Cocoa answered by shaking herself one more time.

As they resumed their run, Luke turned to Samantha. "And just when did I regain the title of dad and not father?"

"I'm not sure. Just a combination of things. I suppose now it just feels right. Let's race back to the house. Loser has to do the breakfast dishes."

31

Kingsbury leaned back in his executive chair, his hands behind his head. Rudy Kowalski sat across from him. "I need a status report on our clinical trial, Rudy."

"Yes, sir," Kowalski replied as he handed his boss a one-page summary.

Kingsbury skimmed it and tossed it on his desk. "Any major problems?"

"A few issues," Kowalski replied as he tried to downplay his worries about the trial, "but nothing that I would call major. We've spot-checked some of the investigation sites. We've got some doctors who appear to have been cutting corners and others who have gone way beyond our limit of fifty patients. Seems like the money must be too good. We've got that one doc in Louisiana who is guilty of both, but he swears everything is on the up-and-up."

"What about adverse events? Hold on a minute. I've got to get my cell phone."

Kingsbury glanced at the caller ID and smiled. "Is this the president of the United States? No. Then it must be the king of England. No. Well, it's the quarterback of the New York Giants. Oh, it's Teddy." Kingsbury laughed. "What's my favorite grandson doing using his mother's cell phone? Yes, I remember that I'm meeting you guys for dinner tonight. I'll see you then. Love you."

He hung up the phone. "Grandkids, Rudy, I recommend you have several. Now, back to the adverse events."

"Same kind as we've had reported in Europe—liver problems, cardiac, some vision. Frankly, sir, quite a bit higher than I would like to see. If the FDA drills down past our summary when it's done and analyzes the individual patient charts, we can expect to face some hard questions."

Kingsbury rose from his chair, walked around the desk, and sat on the corner, facing Kowalski. "Dammit, that's just what I don't want. How many subjects do we have enrolled?"

"We're right at twenty thousand."

"I told Boatwright we would have twenty-five thousand. I want at least that many. The more we have, the less likely CDER will have the manpower to study every one of the patient charts. Go get me five thousand more, and be quick about it. I want this clinical trial done in another three months. Clear?"

"Yes, sir. Perfectly clear. We'll have personal letters going out to some family docs no later than next week."

32

Samantha scheduled her classes at eight and nine every morning and from four to six in the afternoon. She liked working with her dad and rejected his suggestions that she could cut back on her hours. One afternoon while she was in class, Luke heard the back door open.

"Bring me a beer, too," he hollered.

The refrigerator door opened and closed. There were footsteps in the hall, and Whizmo appeared in the office door.

"Come on in, Whiz."

Whizmo handed him a beer and settled into an easy chair by the front window.

"Beautiful day, huh, Whiz? Maybe we ought to be planning a long ride next summer, maybe to Tombstone. I hear a lot of bikers make that trek."

Whizmo nodded. "Good idea, but that's not why I came over. I really just want to brag on your daughter. She's one of the brightest students I've ever had the pleasure of teaching. Seems as if she's memorized my damn textbook. She sits right in the middle of the front row, and if I get a date or fact wrong, she raises her hand and says, 'Whizmo, you know that's not right.' She breaks up the whole class when she does it. I'm trying to talk her into majoring in history. Truth be told, though, she's going to top whatever major she chooses."

Luke beamed. "Whiz, you know a boy named Brad McCoy?"

"Bradford McCoy, sure do. He's one of my seniors and a teaching assistant. Smart youngster. Good kid besides. I talked him into a double major of history and computer science. Why?"

"Sam's been talking about him a lot. They meet every afternoon after her last class at that pub across the street from the campus."

Whizmo nodded. "Yeah, he's my assistant in Sam's class. Now that you mention it, I do see them hanging around after class. You'll like him when Sam's ready to bring him for an introduction. Now, I'm going to the kitchen to get us a second beer. Shut off that computer and let's sit out on the porch. Spring is here, and we need to enjoy it."

33

Luke heard the door close and footsteps in the downstairs hall.

"Dad, you there? I'm bringing someone up."

"Come on. Cocoa and I are reading one of Whizmo's history books."

Samantha and Brad got to the top of the stairs. "Dad, this is Brad. Brad, this is my dad, Luke, and our faithful companion, Cocoa."

Cocoa wagged her tail at her name, and Luke got to his feet. Brad was close to six feet tall with trim black hair and green eyes behind stylish glasses, dressed in a Texas State T-shirt, jeans, and boots. He stuck out his hand. "Pleased to meet you, Mr. Vaughan."

"My pleasure, Brad, and call me Luke. If you can call your professor Whizmo, Luke will do just fine. Have a seat." Luke took an instant liking to the young man.

"How about instead, Dad, we grab a bite to eat. I figure you can spring for a cheeseburger for two starving college students."

"You're on. Let me get my keys and wallet. Cocoa, you stay here. You'll get a cheeseburger when we get back."

"While you're doing that, Dad," Samantha said, "I'm going to snag a couple of Tylenol. I seem to be having more headaches lately. Maybe I'm not used to having to stay up late and study."

As they left the front door, Luke noted a Ford pickup with a lot of years on it but in immaculate condition. "That yours, Brad?"

"Yes, sir. I bought her with money from summer jobs in high school. She's got two hundred thousand miles so far."

Luke nodded his approval as they climbed into the Sequoia. "About the same as this one. I'm aiming for half a million."

Five minutes later they parked in front of Jackson's, a restaurant on the Comal River, which meandered through town, and found a table. Luke and Samantha ordered Bud Lights. Brad chose a Coke.

"Tell me about yourself, Brad. I've heard a little from Sam and Whizmo."

"I grew up in San Marcos. Went to San Marcos High School. I'm a senior this year. Whizmo probably told you I'm one of his teaching assistants. I'm really into computers, but Whizmo convinced me that I need to broaden my thinking and talked me into a double major. That'll add another year before I start on a master's."

A waitress brought their drinks. Luke sipped his. "Yeah, I can see why you got lured into history. I'm reading Whizmo's treatise about the years from 1900 to 1940. He makes history sound like a novel."

"Dad, you ought to go to one of his classes. He teaches the same way. History, as told by Professor Whizmo, is never boring. When we studied the Spanish-American War, he came into class dressed as Teddy Roosevelt in a Rough Rider uniform and asked for volunteers to join him in taking San Juan Hill. Everyone in class raised their hand."

"She's right, sir, I mean Luke. His classes have almost perfect attendance. Nobody wants to miss the stories he tells. I've already taken all of his courses, but I'll still find a seat and listen to his lectures just for fun."

Their cheeseburger baskets came, and there was silence as they chewed for a while. Then Luke spoke. "I hear you guys are a two-some. Any truth to that rumor?"

Samantha looked over at Brad and nodded as she squeezed Brad's hand. "Yes, sir. We've both agreed that we're not seeing anyone else. Who knows, Dad, this could last for a long time."

Luke ordered two more beers. "Brad, you want one?"

"No, thank you. I don't drink. Another Coke will be just fine."

Luke looked at his daughter and the new young man in her life and thought that it had taken quite a while, but now all the pieces of the puzzle were coming together. "Well, all I can say is it looks to me like you've both made good choices. Brad, you're welcome at our house anytime."

Samantha beamed as she realized her dad liked her new boyfriend. Deep down she breathed a sigh of relief.

34

The street on the south side of Texas State curved around the university to the west and up into the hills. A small strip center squatted on it across from the campus. A liquor store occupied one end of the center, a place where there was a constant battle between college students with fake identification and Alcoholic Beverage Commission officers determined to separate the students and demon rum, generally a thankless task. At the other end was a convenience store where students could stock up on ice, chips, and other essentials for a day or a weekend back in the Hill Country. Between the two was a small office with a sign on the door that read VIJAY CHALLA, M.D., FAMILY PRACTICE.

Dr. Challa had been born in India and immigrated to the United States after completing a combined six-year medical school program in Mumbai. He found his way to Central Texas because he had an uncle who owned a liquor store and the office adjoining it. It took him two tries to pass the test that permitted foreign medical graduates to practice in the United States. He had hopes of becoming a surgeon but was never accepted in any surgical residency, so he moved next door to his uncle, where the rent was free. When the practice was slow, he placed a sign on the door that read BACK IN FIFTEEN MINUTES, locked the office, and assisted with the sale of liquor. The doorbell at the front of his office rang in the liquor store. When it did, he hurried out the back of the liquor store and through the back door of his office, grabbed a white coat, checked himself in the mirror, and unlocked the front door to find a potential patient, all the while apologizing that he had to step out momentarily to pick up a shipment of medical instruments.

Dr. Challa was a slight man, only five feet six inches and weighing perhaps one hundred and twenty pounds. He spoke English well but with a decided Indian accent. The students who knocked on his door liked him, particularly since he not only took care of colds, flu, and other minor ailments, but also because he was willing to prescribe "uppers" to his regular patients for the all-nighters that came with final exams and term papers.

One morning he parked his Volkswagen in the back of the center and walked to the office, shivering as the last winter breeze of the season blew through Central Texas. By any standards the clinic was small and run-down. Beside the back door was a unisex restroom. Across the hall from it was his office, outfitted with a metal desk, a swivel chair, and two metal chairs. His medical school diploma hung on the cinder-block wall behind his desk. Toward the front were three small treatment rooms that were rarely fully occupied. The reception area was ten feet square, with more metal chairs and whatever old magazines he'd retrieved from the convenience store owner before they were tossed into the Dumpster.

When he entered the office, he went to the front door, unlocked it, and turned the sign over to announce that the clinic was open. Returning to his desk, he hoped to find that the phone had a blinking light, announcing a call from a patient. There were no calls, so he took the coffeepot and filled it in the bathroom and soon had a strong black brew in front of him as he flipped through the mail from the previous day.

There were the usual bills from vendors, free magazines with a couple of articles to justify selling ads from the drug companies, and various statements from insurance companies, explaining why his bill of, say, $125 was being reduced to $37. Then he got to a professionally done envelope, thicker than most of his mail, with Ceventa in Maryland as the return address. He tore it open and found an announcement of a new drug called Exxacia and an invitation to be a clinical investigator. Dr. Challa had never filled such a role in his career. Still, he had heard that the money was good. He took a sip of his coffee and began to study what Ceventa had to offer.

When he got to the section on payment and read that he could earn $500 with $350 for him and $150 to the patient, he'd read enough. Challa put down the announcement and logged on to the Ceventa Web site. As he completed the application, he got to the section on board certification and checked that he was certified as a family physician even though he knew it was false. For good measure, he checked that he had been in practice for twenty years when it was only ten. If Ceventa did a background check on him and asked for proof, he would withdraw his request. A few days later he received a packet of materials and bottles of pills from Ceventa with a letter congratulating him on his selection. The packet also included detailed instructions and forms to be completed with each patient—a maximum of fifty, the instructions said. Well, he mused, since they clearly didn't do a background on him, who's to say that they would count? He'd worry about that after he enrolled the first fifty patients. Now his job was to start recruiting subjects for the study, and what better place than the campus across the street?

35

Samantha did it. She made a 4.0 GPA. She found a two-bedroom apartment a couple of blocks from campus that she could share with three other girls. Wanting to make up for the disastrous semester at A&M, she enrolled in summer school. Luke told her that she could quit working at his office. Again she refused. She enjoyed spending a few hours with her dad every day and also enjoyed talking with his clients. She left her Camaro parked at the house and found a secondhand bicycle to get around campus and to go back and forth to work with Luke. Most weekends she went back home for at least one night. It gave her a chance to get in a good run with her dad. She invited Brad to join them, but he declined, understanding that she needed the time with Luke.

One Friday afternoon, they stopped at Jackson's for a hamburger. She was about to order a Bud Light when Brad stopped her.

"Waiter, can you come back in five minutes?"

"Sure, man. Give me the high sign when you're ready to order."

"Sam, we need to talk."

A puzzled look crossed her face. "Okay, about what?"

"Your drinking, Samantha. You drink way too much, way too often—practically every night, and I'm worried about you."

"Brad, what's the problem? I enjoy a few beers. You ought to try one once in a while."

"Look, Samantha. I don't think drinking is a sin or anything like that. I actually drank until my freshman year. Then one night I was on my way home after a party and almost didn't see an old man crossing the street. I swerved and missed him." Brad buried his head in his hands and looked up. "I could have killed him. I quit drinking that night. I want you to stop, too."

Samantha leaned over and looked into Brad's eyes. "And what if I don't?"

"Samantha, I like you a lot. I may even love you, and I'm not one to throw down ultimatums, but I can't change on this one. If you want to keep drinking, then we need to go our separate ways. I'm sorry. I truly am."

Samantha rose from the table. Brad thought she was walking out on him. Instead, she walked over to the rail, where she gazed down at the river as it boiled and churned over a small waterfall. Then she returned to the table, sat down, and took Brad's hand. "Why don't you order me a Coke?"

Tears filled Brad's eyes. He leaned over to kiss her and then motioned to the waiter.

36

As Samantha was leaving her English class, she paused at the bulletin board on the first floor where jobs were posted, bicycles were offered for sale, roommates were solicited, that kind of thing. She had seen most of the postings, but a new one caught her eye. It offered a hundred and fifty dollars to participate in a clinical trial for a new drug, promising a minimal time commitment and no risk of ill effects. Samantha noted the name of a Dr. Vijay Challa who officed just off campus. She could use the money to put toward a new leather motorcycle jacket she planned to buy her dad for his birthday, she thought.

Samantha retrieved her bike and rode to the edge of campus. She stopped at the light and looked across the street to a sleazy strip center with a sign that hung crooked from a post, advertising a liquor store, a convenience store, and Dr. Challa's office. As she sized up the center, she started to turn around. Then the light changed and she found herself crossing the street. She parked in front of the clinic, chained her bike to a rusty bike rack, and entered the doctor's office.

Nothing happened. She called out, then called out again. "Hello, is anyone here?"

She was about to leave when she heard a back door shut. A moment later a small, dark-skinned man came through a curtain. "My apologies, miss. I just got back from an errand to the post office. My receptionist is off for the afternoon," Dr. Challa lied. "How may I be of assistance?"

Samantha looked around the shabby office and again started to turn and leave, only she didn't. "I saw a notice on the bulletin board over at the English Building, something about a clinical trial. Are you still looking for people?"

"Yes, yes indeed." Dr. Challa smiled, white teeth showing under his black mustache. "Please, have a seat."

Samantha took a seat across from the doctor while he pulled some forms from a desk drawer. "Your name, please?"

"Samantha Vaughan."

"Ms. Vaughan, this is a trial for a new antibiotic. I presume that you occasionally have some sinus drainage."

"Not really, only during pollen season."

"Well, I'm sure that is enough. If you'll fill in your name, date of birth, address, and so forth, I'll complete the rest of the form." Dr. Challa handed the first page of the form to Samantha, and she wrote in the information and returned it. "Now, if you'll just initial each of these pages and sign the last one."

"Shouldn't I read this first?"

"Certainly you're welcome to do so, but this is a mere formality."

Samantha shrugged her shoulders and did as she was asked.

"Now, let me go to the back and get you the pills and a check for one hundred and fifty dollars."

When Dr. Challa returned, he said, "I almost forgot, but I do need to take your temperature and your blood pressure and draw a little blood."

Samantha grimaced at the thought and then agreed. Dr. Challa found a vein at her elbow and inserted a needle. "Now, I'll need you to come back once a week for me to draw more blood and check your vital signs. That'll be for six weeks. Then there'll be a last visit in ten weeks. If you miss a time or two, that won't be a problem. Please take these pills, one in the morning and one at night for the next five days. If you have any problem, just give me a call."

Samantha took the pills as directed and made it back to Dr. Challa's office three times over the next six weeks. When she didn't show up, he reviewed her chart and estimated what her vital signs would be and carefully whited out the date from her last blood work and inserted a new one. Once he ran it through the copy machine, no one could detect the change.

37

The data arrived in a minivan. The boxes were unloaded and piled around the walls of a storage area in the basement of the CDER building. A metal folding table and four chairs were in the center of the room. A smaller box, containing the same data on discs, was placed on the table.

Roger Boatwright called Ryan into his office. "The Exxacia clinical trial is complete," he said, beaming. "Here's a summary of the results prepared by Ceventa. I must say that the clinical trial proved what we all knew."

"That is?"

"Exxacia is highly effective and absolutely safe. I'm convening the advisory committee in three weeks with a recommendation that the committee approve Exxacia."

Ryan took the summary from Boatwright and skimmed through it. "Wait a minute, Dr. Boatwright. Sounds like you're trying to bypass me and my team. We did some random inspections at a number of the sites. There were major issues with nearly every one of them. I need to see the raw data, not just a summary. Didn't Ceventa deliver it?"

Boatwright threw him a disgusted look. "Are you suggesting a distinguished scientist like Alfred Kingsbury would twist the results?"

"Look, Dr. Boatwright, I'm not suggesting anything. You and Kingsbury already know what I think about Exxacia. You've seen my e-mails."

"All right, Dr. Sinclair. The files are in storage room three in the basement. Do whatever you think best. You'll find a box of computer discs that have the trial data there, too. The meeting will be in three weeks whether you're ready or not."

After Ryan was gone, Boatwright called Kingsbury. Fifteen minutes later he pulled into the visitor lot at Ceventa, checked his tie in the rearview mirror, spat on his hand and wiped down the few loose strands of hair on his head, and hurried toward the building. When he got to the penthouse, he introduced himself to the receptionist.

"Yes, Dr. Boatwright, Dr. Kingsbury is expecting you. Please go through his office to the spa. The door will be to your right when you enter."

Boatwright walked toward the double doors, and as he approached, a buzzer sounded to unlock them. He entered an office that dwarfed his. It had to be thirty feet wide and sixty feet long. The desk in front of the windows at the far end was almost as large as his entire office. A Persian carpet that probably cost more than Boatwright made in an entire year covered the floor in front of the desk. There was a sitting area with an antique sofa and Queen Anne chairs arranged to face a fireplace with a mantle that appeared to have come from an Austrian castle. On the wall to the right were photos of Kingsbury with presidents, heads of state, and a variety of movie stars. There was even one with the queen of England smiling at his side. A door was in the center of the wall.

Boatwright opened it. "Come in, Roger. I'll only be a few more minutes, but we can talk while I finish my workout."

Boatwright found Kingsbury on an elliptical exercise machine, dressed in shorts and a T-shirt with the Ceventa logo on it, a towel draped over his shoulder. A wide-screen television was tuned to a financial channel. As Boatwright entered, Kingsbury reached for the towel and wiped sweat from his face.

"Roger, old boy, you ought to put one of these in your office. Help you take off those extra pounds around your waistline. Now, what's this about? I'm sure you've read our summary by now. Splendid result, if I do say so myself."

Not knowing what else to do, Boatwright stood in front of Kingsbury. "Yes, sir. It's excellent. Only there's a problem."

Kingsbury stopped the machine and clicked off the television. He walked over to a refrigerator and extracted two bottles of cold water. "Here, have a drink."

He sat on a bench and motioned Boatwright to sit beside him. "Let me guess. It's probably that damned Sinclair again, isn't it?"

Boatwright sat on the end of the bench. "I'm afraid so, Alfred. He and his team won't accept your summary. They're going through the data."

"Hellfire, Roger. There are twenty-five thousand patient charts. No way they can get those done. All they'll find is a few adverse events and some problems with the sites."

"I know, Alfred. That's what I'm worried about. Sinclair has already requested a criminal investigation on several of the sites, just based on some of the preliminary data. He even e-mailed me a few weeks ago, demanding that I stop the clinical trial."

"Yes, I heard about the site investigations. Fortunately, you didn't stop the trial." Kingsbury finished his water, wiped his face, and abruptly stood, stretched, and walked to the window overlooking the park. He was silent long enough that Boatwright wondered if he should leave. "Roger, you and I have gotten to be friends. I know you've got three daughters who are approaching college age. The cost of a four-year degree these days is outrageous, not even to mention graduate school or medical school."

"Tell me about it. My oldest is applying to several Ivy League schools."

"I want to help. I'll wire five hundred thousand dollars to a Swiss bank account in your name today. Consider it a loan. You can pay it back whenever you can. That ought to be enough to get all three of the girls into the Ivy League."

Boatwright continued to sit on the bench, his arms on his knees, staring at the floor. He would never have been so brazen as to ask for a bribe. Finally he decided that if he was going to take one and risk his career, he might as well go for broke.

"What's the matter, Roger? I thought you'd be ecstatic. I mean, I just made your life a lot easier."

Boatwright looked at Kingsbury. "I do appreciate it, Alfred, only I've got bigger problems than putting kids through college." Boatwright paused, wiped one eye, and continued. "Joanne, my wife, has ALS."

"You mean Lou Gehrig's disease? Roger, I'm so sorry. When was it diagnosed?"

"Just last week, sir. The girls and I are devastated, and Joanne is giving up. I'm so depressed that I'm starting Prozac."

Kingsbury shook his head. "I don't know what to say. Ceventa is part of a consortium of drug companies that are studying ALS. Right now, no cure seems to be in sight. How long does she have?"

"The doctors don't have any idea yet. Maybe months, maybe a year or two. She's determined to see our youngest graduate from high school." Boatwright stared at the wall and thought. Then he rose to face Kingsbury. "Look, Alfred, with all I've got to deal with, five hundred thousand dollars isn't enough. Even with insurance, the cost to keep Joanne alive is going to bankrupt me. I need a million."

This time Kingsbury rose. "Roger, I said I'm sorry about your wife, but don't get greedy. It's five hundred thousand. You can spend it however you see fit."

Boatwright considered his options. There would be another day. "Okay, okay. I'll get your drug through the advisory committee," he said as he started to leave.

"Wait a minute, Roger. You have to put a muzzle on Ryan Sinclair. Lock him in the closet on the day of the meeting if you have to. I don't want his opinions polluting the committee."

"Understood, Alfred. One more thing. I haven't told anyone at the office about Joanne. I prefer to keep my personal problems to myself." Boatwright walked out the door with his head down and shoulders slumped.

38

It was Sunday afternoon. Ryan and his colleagues pictured themselves as being trapped in a dungeon. Knowing there would be no air-conditioning, they sat around the basement table dressed in T-shirts, shorts, and flip-flops. They had two more days before the advisory committee met, and they were down to the last thousand charts.

"You know, guys," Ryan said, "I think we've seen enough. There's nothing in those last few boxes that's going to change my mind."

"I agree," Robert replied as he wiped up a bead of sweat that had dripped onto the chart that was open in front of him.

"Same here" was the response from the other two.

"Let's shut it down," Ryan said.

"You don't have to say that twice." Henry rose and started replacing the boxes along the wall.

"You guys get out of here. I'm going up and send an e-mail to Boatwright. If you see smoke rising from the vicinity of his office when you get here in the morning, you'll know who sparked the fire."

Ryan rode the elevator to the fourth floor and walked through the deserted office. While he waited for his computer to wake up, he composed his e-mail to Boatwright.

To: Roger Boatwright   October 4, 2009, 5:30 P.M.
From: Ryan Sinclair
Subject: Exxacia

Our team has completed its analysis of the clinical trial charts. My report to the advisory committee will cover our findings and will also include concerns about numerous data integrity issues along with potential fraud that raises serious questions about the validity of the entire clinical trial. Further, as you already know, several of the sites are the subject of an agency criminal investigation. Additionally, we have uncovered a significant number of adverse events that are not mentioned in Ceventa's report. The impact of Exxacia on a patient's liver, heart, and vision continues to be a significant problem. Last, there are more reports from Europe of continuing adverse events, even deaths, that add more questions about the safety of the drug. We still refuse to recommend approval.

"Dr. Sinclair, please come to my office immediately!" Boatwright barked into the phone.

Ryan walked the few steps down the hall, thinking that he and the rest of his team were about to be fired. He closed Boatwright's door without being asked.

"Dr. Sinclair, I'm only going to say this once. The advisory committee is not to be told about any allegations of fraud. There is nothing about fraud in any of the materials going to the committee. Those allegations are the subject of an agency criminal investigation, and we cannot compromise it."

"That's absurd, Boatwright, and you know it. We can have a closed-door session. We can go off the record if we need to. You can't have the committee evaluate this drug on just the data Ceventa wants to show them! Are you going to put a pair of rose-colored glasses at each member's place around the table?" Ryan asked, sarcasm dripping from his words.

"That's enough, Sinclair! Further, I'm instructing you to soften your opinions about the safety issues so that I'll have some wiggle room if I have to explain our decision somewhere down the line."

"Wiggle room! So you've already made up your mind. We're just going through the motions, is that it?"

"Not at all, Dr. Sinclair," Boatwright said in a calmer voice. "In fact, I've instructed Ceventa to present postmarket data from other countries of their choosing. There'll be more than enough justification for approval of the drug."

Ryan stormed out of the office, slamming the door behind him. He went to the stairs and took them two and three at a time to the first floor. Once outside, he paced a walking path around the building four times while he thought about what had just occurred. Kingsbury and Boatwright were going to present clinical trial data that was carefully whitewashed, backed up with foreign postmarket data of Kingsbury's choosing. He returned to the building and stopped at Henry's office on the third floor.

Henry glanced up. "Is that smoke that I'm smelling from the floor above? I haven't heard any fire alarms."

Ryan stood in front of Henry's desk, hands shoved in his pockets.

A plaque on Henry's wall caught his attention. It was recognition of distinguished service to the FDA for ten years. "I'll never get one of those. I'm out of here."

"Hold on, Ryan. Take a deep breath. Tell me what went on up there."

Ryan outlined the discussion and concluded, "Now you can see why I'm so pissed."

"Look, Ryan, stick it out for a while longer. If all of us who are trying to do the right thing leave, we might as well just hand the keys to the pharmaceutical companies. There'll be no one looking out for the health and well-being of the good folks of this country."

Ryan collapsed in a chair and stared at the ten-year plaque. "Okay, okay. A few more months, but I won't promise anything beyond that."

39

Ryan and Sara were in their bedroom on the second floor of the house when it happened. An explosion rocked them from sleep. Ryan rushed to their window and found his Corvette in flames. He glanced to the street to see a large, dark vehicle pull away. The lights were out, but it looked like a Lincoln. Ryan called 911 and then ran downstairs, followed closely by Sara. He stepped out the front door, sized up the flames, and knew he could do nothing but wait for the fire department. Other neighbors started coming out of their houses, wondering what had happened. Ryan had no explanation. Then a neighbor pointed to his front window. The glass was broken. Ryan studied it and then went into the house, where he found a note tied to a rock. A crude way to send a message, he thought. The note read *Get with the Exxacia program or this will be just the beginning.*

After the firemen and police left, Ryan went to the phone and dialed Boatwright's home number. Boatwright glanced at the caller ID as he picked up his phone. "Sinclair, why are you calling me in the middle of the night?"

"Boatwright, you son of a bitch!" Ryan yelled into the phone. "My car was just bombed in my driveway, and the bastards left a note about Exxacia. Other than my team, you're the only one who knows my opinion. You've cut a deal with Kingsbury, haven't you?"

"I, I don't know what you're talking about," Boatwright stuttered. "Have you been drinking?"

"How much is Kingsbury paying you to get his drug approved?"

"You're mad, Sinclair, stark raving mad," Boatwright replied, finally mustering the strength to yell back at his accuser.

"Hear me out, Boatwright. I didn't tell the police my suspicions before, but I'll be on the phone with them first thing in the morning. It's got to be you or Kingsbury, probably Kingsbury since you wouldn't have the guts to do something like this, but that doesn't mean you didn't know it was coming."

Before Boatwright could reply, Ryan hung up.

Boatwright listened to the dial tone for a few seconds as he considered what to do. Then he retrieved his cell phone and stepped out into the backyard, where he called Kingsbury. After he relayed the conversation, he continued, "I didn't have anything to do with the bombing, and I don't even want to know if you did, but—"

"Boatwright, I can assure you I had nothing to do with it either," Kingsbury interrupted. "The cops can sniff around all they want and they'll never tie me to it. Trust me on that. Good night, Roger."

"Wait, wait, Alfred, one more thing. That wire transfer. Is it secure? I mean, can anyone ever find out about it?"

"Perfectly secure, Roger. You can relax. I'll see you at the committee hearing."

. . .

Sara poured Ryan coffee and sat beside him at the kitchen table. "Ryan, quit the FDA. We don't need this in our lives, and we don't need the money. Look at me. I'm pregnant with our first child. Little Max needs a father," she pleaded as her eyes filled with tears.

Ryan stirred his coffee as he thought. "I'm not a hero, Sara, but I'm not a quitter either. You know that. I still intend to derail this drug. It's going to kill people. I'm just not sure how or when. Meantime, I want you to move in with my dad and mom."

Sara took both of Ryan's hands in hers and looked into his eyes. "Let it go for now. Pick another day for your fight. Boatwright is going to push it through committee anyway. Maybe you ought to go to Senator Grassley. He's on the Senate drug oversight committee. Once you've gone public and have Grassley behind you, Kingsbury will back off."

"I'll think about it. There'll be a way," Ryan said. Then he kissed his wife and led her to bed.

40

In San Marcos, Luke's phone rang. "Mr. Vaughan? I mean Luke. This is Brad. Can I drop by for a few minutes this morning?"

"Sure, Brad. Come on over. I'll put on another pot of coffee."

Ten minutes later Luke saw Brad climb out of his pickup, dressed in a T-shirt, jeans, and boots, and stride up the sidewalk. Luke met him at the top of the steps.

"Morning, Brad. What brings you over? You get a speeding ticket?"

"No, sir. Got my last one four years ago. Can we go into your office?"

Luke nodded, noting Brad's solemn manner, and opened the door. When they were seated at the coffee table by the fireplace, Luke tried again. "Brad, I can tell you've got some problem. Spill it."

"Sir, it's not about me. It's Samantha. She's started going to bed around eight, and even after twelve hours' sleep, she's sleeping through her first class. I'm worried about her."

Luke squeezed his hands together as he thought. "Now that you mention it, lately, when she comes over here to work, she's not as efficient as she was. In fact, she's almost listless. She claims she's just been up studying."

"I'm sure that's true, sir, but I think there's something else going on. I've tried to get her to talk, and she just says she's got some bug and she'll get over it. Only it's been going on for three or four weeks."

Luke frowned. "Thanks, Brad. I'll talk to her this afternoon. I appreciate your concern."

41

Dr. Kingsbury and two of his associates were already in the conference room when Dr. Boatwright entered. "Good morning, Dr. Boatwright. Beautiful morning, isn't it? These are my colleagues Dr. Allen and Dr. Escamilla. They did some of the research on Exxacia."

"Good morning, Dr. Kingsbury," Boatwright said. "May I have a word in private?"

Kingsbury nodded and followed Boatwright into an adjoining

room. Boatwright shut the door. His hands were shaking. He had also developed a nervous twitch in his right eye. He didn't appear to have slept in days. "Alfred, judging from what happened at Sinclair's house, it appears the price of poker is going up."

A look of horror came across Kingsbury's face. "Surely you don't still think I had anything to do with that. I was at home with Suzanne. No one else thinks I'm a suspect. Why should you? Maybe you're the one who did it, Roger."

"Look, Alfred, I'm desperate. I'm on the Internet every night. I've called people all over the world, trying to find something to help Joanne. Finally I've located a scientist in Austria who has come up with an experimental treatment for ALS. It's a two-year program that is going to run well into seven figures." He paused, then blurted, "I need five million dollars. You get me the money. I'll get your drug approved. If not, it won't get past this committee today."

Kingsbury sized up the situation. He wasn't sure that Boatwright wasn't mentally unbalanced at this point. Still, the committee was assembling just outside the door. It was now or never. He would deal with Boatwright another day. "All right, Roger. We've got a deal. Payment to be made once the drug is approved and on the market."

When Kingsbury and Boatwright reentered the conference room, the committee members were starting to drift in from the hall. Kingsbury had studied them on the Internet and knew enough about their backgrounds to comment about each of them or their institution or compliment them on something about their work. Drs. Allen and Escamilla handed each member a packet of journal articles on Exxacia, now showing the lead author of each as a prominent member of the infectious disease community. Each article also had a label, indicating in what distinguished journal they might expect to see it published in the next few months. No one mentioned that the articles had been written by scientists on the Ceventa payroll.

When eight of the eleven members were present, Dr. Salazar, the chairman, asked them to take their seats. The last person to enter the room was Ryan Sinclair, who chose to sit by himself along the wall. As he looked around, he saw the empty chairs at the oval table and studied the members in attendance. He concluded that no one in the room was seriously opposed to approval. Whatever he said was going to fall on deaf ears, particularly since Boatwright would be advocating strongly for the drug—and somewhere in the back of his mind he saw his burning Corvette and the note. As much as he hated to do so, he decided this was not the day to draw a line in the sand.

"Ladies and gentlemen," Dr. Salazar began, "we last met on this drug a little over a year ago and took Dr. Boatwright's recommendation to request a large clinical trial. Ceventa agreed to it. You received the summary results last week, and Dr. Kingsbury has been kind enough to join us. Dr. Kingsbury?"

Kingsbury stood at his place. "Thank you, Dr. Salazar. I'm pleased to advise that the clinical trial, one of the largest ever conducted by a pharmaceutical company, has proved just what we anticipated. Exxacia has a remarkable impact on sinusitis, bronchitis, pneumonia, and tonsillitis. It holds distinct promise for a number of other bacterial infections, but we are not seeking approval for those at this time."

"If I may interrupt, Dr. Kingsbury," Dr. Rogers from Palo Alto said, "I've studied your data very carefully. I can go along with your recommendations on the three respiratory illnesses, but I'll have to see more trials before I can approve Exxacia for tonsillitis."

Several other committee members nodded in agreement.

"Dr. Kingsbury," Dr. Sebastian from Chicago asked, "what about the issues we raised at our last meeting about Exxacia causing problems with the liver and heart?"

Dr. Kingsbury smiled. "I'm glad you asked. There were a few isolated events, but nothing more than with any other antibiotic, right, Dr. Boatwright?"

Boatwright, now calm and professional after taking a Prozac, stood beside Kingsbury and chimed in. "He's correct, Dr. Sebastian. CDER is prepared to give Exxacia its highest recommendation, and if this committee agrees, an approval letter will go out immediately."

"I might also add," Dr. Kingsbury continued, "your notebooks contain postmarket results from a number of countries in Europe and South America." He neglected to mention that they had omitted such results from a number of other countries where the reports of adverse events were considerably higher.

"I see Dr. Sinclair sitting over there." Dr. Craig nodded in Ryan's direction. "I understand he was the review officer in charge of this drug. Do you have anything to add, Dr. Sinclair?"

Ryan remained seated and folded his arms. "No, sir. Dr. Boatwright is in charge of this meeting. I'm just here as an observer."

"Just a minute, Dr. Sinclair. You've lived with this drug for over a year and you're telling us you have nothing to say. I find that hard to accept."

"Sorry, Dr. Craig, but Dr. Boatwright is speaking for CDER and the agency."

Dr. Craig was puzzled about Ryan's refusal to comment but said nothing further.

"Well, then, Dr. Kingsbury," Dr. Salazar said, "if you and your assistants will leave the room along with Dr. Boatwright and Dr. Sinclair, the committee will go into executive session."

The next morning Roger Boatwright posted a letter on the FDA Web site approving Exxacia for sinusitis, bronchitis, and pneumonia. Then he e-mailed Kingsbury and told him he would continue to push for approval for tonsillitis, but that approval would have to wait for another day.

42

Samantha pedaled from her last class to the house. She had to stop three times to get her breath and was sweating when she got home. She entered the front door and heard Luke on the phone talking to a client, so she went into her office and started opening the mail. Luke ended his call, crossed the hall, and took a seat.

"How was school today, Sam?"

"About the same, Dad. I may make a B in French, though."

"Don't worry about it. I know you're pushing yourself. Brad dropped by this morning."

"Brad? Why?"

"He's worried about you, Sam. He says that you've been sleeping through classes."

"Brad ought to be minding his own business," Samantha said.

"Sam, he's concerned. He's just trying to do what's best for you. Is he right?"

Tears filled Samantha's eyes. "Yes, sir. Dad, I don't know what's going on. I'm sleeping all the time. I'm not eating much either because I'm too nauseated."

"Sam, I don't quite know how to ask this but directly. Are you pregnant?"

"Dad, of course not. Brad and I aren't even sexually active."

Luke nodded his head and looked at his daughter as he thought. "Your face is looking sweaty."

"Yeah, I just rode home, and it's pretty warm out there today."

Luke stepped around the desk and looked more carefully at his daughter. "Sam, I want you to come out in the front yard so I can get a better look at you."

"Why, Dad? What if the neighbors see us?"

"Just for a minute. Come on."

Reluctantly, Sam followed Luke down the steps and into the sunlight. Luke took her hands and turned them over so that the underside of her forearms caught the sun.

"Sam, your skin is yellow. Look up at me. I want to see your eyes." She did as he asked. "The whites are yellowish. How long has that been going on?"

"I don't know, Dad. A few days, I guess."

"Okay, come back in the house. I've got another question."

When they were seated in Luke's office, he asked, "Sam, I may be getting too personal. Forgive me. When you go to the bathroom, what color is your urine?"

"It's pretty dark." Sam sighed as she slumped in her chair again.

"I'm taking you to see Clyde Hartman in the morning. He's the best internist in town, maybe one of the best in this part of the country. And you're spending the night here, not back at your apartment."

"Dad, I've got homework to do and classes tomorrow."

"Sam, this is more important. Stay here a minute while I call Clyde. Then you can go up for a nap."

Cocoa had been listening intently to the conversation. While Luke turned to the phone, she went over to Samantha, whined quietly, and lay down at her feet.

"Yes, ma'am. This is Luke Vaughan. Is Dr. Hartman around?"

Clyde Hartman picked up the phone. "Afternoon, Luke. As far as I know, I'm not getting sued for malpractice. So what can I do for you?"

"Clyde, Sam's jaundiced. I don't know if it's her liver or something else. Can you see her tomorrow?"

"You bet. Don't worry about an appointment. Just come on over. I'll work her in."

Luke thanked the doctor and told Samantha to take a nap. Sam and Cocoa climbed the stairs. It was the next morning before she woke.

43

The campaign was launched within twenty-four hours. Drug representatives had already been supplied with free samples and started leaving them with physicians all over the country. In turn, the physicians gave them to patients in place of other antibiotics.

Network medical editors were provided with briefing books and summaries of the studies. Always looking for ways to get more face time in front of the cameras, they were eager to talk about the new wonder drug.

A reader couldn't open *Time, Newsweek, Sports Illustrated,* or a major newspaper without being confronted with a full-page, multicolor ad with bold print touting the benefits of Exxacia. Six-point type at the bottom of the page that would require a magnifying glass outlined warnings of potential adverse consequences.

Ceventa bought time on all the major networks and cable outlets to run a commercial that featured an actor who had played a successful doctor on a long-running hospital drama. He was shown standing by a patient's bed, stethoscope around his neck. As the camera zoomed in, he turned and said, "As you know, I'm not a real doctor. If I were, I know exactly the drug I would be recommending to my patients with certain bacterial infections. It's Exxacia. The next time you have a sinus problem, bronchitis, or even pneumonia, ask your doctor about Exxacia. You won't be disappointed." The camera then backed away as the actor turned to place his stethoscope on the chest of the make-believe patient.

At the end of the month Ceventa released data on the remarkable sales of Exxacia, which were far greater than predicted by analysts. Overnight Ceventa stock rose 10 percent.

Kingsbury leaned back in his office chair and thumbed through the *Wall Street Journal* until he found the article. He read with satisfaction the analyst's assessment of Ceventa and the impact Exxacia would have on its stock price over the next two years. Finally, he thought, after all of the obstacles he had to overcome, he was seeing the results of his plan. Not as soon as he had originally expected, but better late than never, he surmised.

His eye caught the date of the newspaper, and he realized he had a minor problem. He turned to his computer contact information and pulled up the florist he used for special events. When a female voice answered, he said, "Morning. This is Alfred Kingsbury. I have a personal account with you."

"Yes, of course, Dr. Kingsbury. How can we be of assistance?"

"I just realized that my granddaughter's school play is in three days. I want to order two dozen Sterling Silver roses, you know, the light purple ones, delivered to her house day after tomorrow."

"We can certainly do that, Dr. Kingsbury," the florist replied. "But, we don't keep those in stock. They'll probably have to be shipped from France. On short notice, that will be quite expensive. We've got some beautiful red roses in stock."

"Don't worry about the expense," Kingsbury said as he glanced at the headline in the paper. "I can afford them and the overnight charge. Put on the card, 'To Kelley. Break a leg. Love, Grandpa.'"

44

Luke opened Samantha's door to find her sleeping with all of her covers thrown off. Cocoa was beside her. He walked to her side and felt her forehead.

Samantha stirred. "What is it, Dad?"

"I think you're running a little fever. It's time to get up. I want to get you over to Dr. Hartman."

"Can't I just sleep a little more?"

"Sam, you've been asleep fifteen hours. You can go back to bed after you see the doctor."

Samantha slowly sat up, and Luke looked into her eyes. He didn't say anything, but he didn't like what he saw.

They got in the car to make the five-minute drive to Dr. Hartman's office. Samantha dozed off before they got there. Once inside, Luke told the receptionist that Dr. Hartman was expecting his daughter. In a few minutes the nurse led them back to a treatment room, where the doctor greeted them.

Dr. Hartman was a large man with a mane of white hair complemented by a bushy white mustache. He had graduated from Baylor College of Medicine in Houston and probably could have stayed as a faculty member. Instead, he moved to San Marcos. As he put it, he wanted to be in a town where he knew his patients and would see them at church or the grocery store, not just when they were sick.

"Good morning, Luke. Sam, I hear you're a little under the weather."

"I think I've just got the flu or something."

"Okay, let's see. Put this thermometer in your mouth." He took it out when it beeped and glanced at the reading. "You've got a little fever, about one hundred and one. Let me look in your eyes. Look at this light. Yep, your eyes are yellow." Next he wrapped a cuff on her right arm and pumped it up, listening with his stethoscope. "Blood pressure is good. Lie back, please." Dr. Hartman listened to Samantha's heart and lungs. Then he pressed on her abdomen. Samantha grimaced when he did so. "That hurt a little?"

"Yes, sir."

"Sam, I'm going to draw some blood from your arm. You'll feel a little prick, that's all. Then I want you to take this little cup and go to the restroom, where I want you to leave me a urine sample."

As Samantha left the room, Luke asked, "What's happening, Clyde?"

"Something's going on with her liver. She ever had a problem with gallstones?"

"Never."

"If she doesn't have a stone in her common duct, she's most likely got some form of hepatitis. I'll get the blood and urine off to the lab this afternoon. I'm not sending her to the hospital for an ultrasound until we see those results. Bring her back day after tomorrow. I could talk to you on the phone, but I'd like to have another look at her."

Luke nodded.

Two days later Luke and Samantha were seated across the desk from Dr. Hartman. "All the test results are back. As I suspected, the liver function tests are elevated. The tests for hepatitis A, B, and C are negative. That leaves us with a hepatitis that is probably drug induced."

Luke was upset but tried to hide his concern with a poker face. Samantha wasn't sure what Dr. Hartman was saying.

"Sam, your liver is not working right."

"You can fix it, right, Dr. Hartman?"

"Probably, Sam, but I need to ask you some questions. Have you used any street drugs?"

That got Samantha's attention, and she sat up in her chair. "Absolutely not."

"How about alcohol? Do you drink much?"

"I used to drink about as much as most college students, but I quit last summer. My boyfriend didn't like to see me drunk."

The doctor thought for a minute. "How about any prescription drugs?"

"No, sir. I haven't been sick in two years."

"Herbs? Sometimes college students experiment with exotic herbs."

"Not me. Can we go back to the prescription drugs? I forgot something. See, there was this ad on the bulletin board in the English Building. This doctor was looking for volunteers for some drug study. He paid me a hundred and fifty dollars, and I took some pills for a few days."

"You never told me about that," Luke interjected.

"Sorry, Dad. It didn't seem like a big deal. He said that it was perfectly safe."

"What's this doctor's name?" Luke asked, his voice becoming louder.

"I don't know, Dad. He was in that little strip center across from campus. He has an office between the liquor store and a stop-and-rob."

"I know him, Luke. His name is Challa. He's from India originally. He's not much of a doctor. Sam, did he tell you the name of the drug or what it was for?"

Samantha thought for a minute. "He wouldn't tell me the name of the drug. He did say it was an antibiotic. He asked me if I had a sinus infection. I told him no, but he gave me the pills anyway."

"When was that, Sam?" Dr. Hartman asked.

"I don't know. Probably four or five months ago."

That rang a bell with Dr. Hartman. "Ah, yes. I think I remember getting something from one of the drug companies, inviting me to participate in a clinical trial. I threw it in the trash. I refuse to take anything from them, not even prescription pads or pens. We need their products, but like most giant companies, they're really in it for the money."

He turned to Luke. "As I recall, Sam's right. That trial was about some new antibiotic. Luke, one of the very rare but known risks of antibiotics is that they can cause problems with the liver. My best guess is she's got a reaction to whatever Dr. Challa gave her."

Luke stood and looked at the books on the shelves behind Dr. Hartman as if he were expecting to find a cure. "What do we do now?"

"Luke, I wish there was a magic potion, but there's not. You need to keep her home on bed rest as much as possible. Keep plenty of fluids in her. No alcohol and no pain killer with acetaminophen—Tylenol, for example—understand? Both can cause problems with the liver."

"But what about school?" Samantha asked.

"Sorry, Sam. You're out of classes for a while, hopefully only a couple of weeks. Your dad can probably arrange with your professors to get your assignments, only right now rest is the most important thing. Luke, I want to see her again in two weeks, sooner if you think she's getting worse."

Luke helped Samantha up the stairs and into her bed. Then he went to the kitchen and got her two bottles of cold water and a bowl of cereal with milk.

"Sam, I know you're not hungry, but I want you to eat as much of this cereal as you can. You've got to get some nourishment. Then I want you to drink this water, again as much as you can."

"Can I call Brad?"

"Sure. He can even come over. You're not contagious. I don't want him staying long, though. I'm going out for a little while. I should be back in an hour. Call me on my cell if you need something."

"You going to see a client?"

"No, Sam. I'm going to pay a call on Dr. Challa. I'm going to find out what he gave you."

Luke turned into the strip center and parked in front of Dr. Challa's office. He sized up the surroundings and couldn't imagine anyone walking through that door hoping to be made well. He got out of the car and walked to the door only to find it locked. He knocked loudly and waited. When nothing happened, he knocked again, this time even louder. Still nothing. Then he shouted Dr. Challa's name. A sound came from within, like a door opening and shutting. Then a small, dark-skinned man in a white coat opened the front door.

"Dr. Challa!"

"I am Dr. Challa," the man spoke in a quiet voice. "Please come in. How can I help you?"

"Doctor, my name is Luke Vaughan. Were you involved in a clinical trial for a new drug a few months ago?"

"That is correct. It was all very legal."

Luke looked around the shabby reception room, which was deserted, as usual. "My daughter is Samantha Vaughan. She says she was one of the patients in your trial."

"I'm sorry, Mr. Vaughan, but I don't remember her. I didn't really know most of the participants in that trial. Most of them were not my regular patients. And would you mind keeping your voice down?"

"Yes, I damn sure do mind, Dr. Challa. Do you have a list of the people who were in the trial?"

"Of course, but I'm a confidential investigator. I'm not at liberty to disclose anything about the trial. I signed a contract with the drug company."

Luke backed Challa up against the wall and grabbed the lapels of his coat, lifting him off the ground. "Look, you little pill pusher, either you get that list or I'll go back to your office and find it myself."

"Mr. Vaughan, let me down or I'm calling the police."

Luke took a deep breath and backed away. His tone changed. "Dr. Challa, my daughter, Samantha, has hepatitis, which probably came from that drug. I need your help."

Dr. Challa stared at Luke. "I don't believe that any drug I prescribed would do that. Still, let me check."

Challa went to the back and returned with a list. "Yes, your daughter was one of the subjects."

"What's the name of the drug?"

"I'm sorry, Mr. Vaughan, I signed a confidentiality agreement. I refuse to tell you the name of the drug or the name of the pharmaceutical company. Besides, the drugs were not marked. So even if I told you the name of the drug being evaluated, we wouldn't know if she got it or the benchmark drug."

"Damn it, she's got drug-induced hepatitis. I need to know the name of the drug!"

"I've told you all that I can, sir. Now you must leave."

"I'll leave, but you damn well better hope that Samantha recovers. Otherwise, you'll wish you never met me!"

45

Luke heard the sound of the Harley before he saw it. Then Whizmo turned into the driveway and parked in front of his apartment. The back door opened and closed, and Whizmo appeared at the office with a backpack.

"I've got Sam's assignments for the next two weeks, and I went by her apartment to pick up her computer and textbooks. Her roommates are worried."

Luke looked up from his desk with dark circles under his eyes. "They're not alone."

"Yeah, I can tell you haven't been sleeping much. I thought people usually got over hepatitis."

"I would have thought so, too. I've been researching on the Internet. If this were type A, I'd feel a lot better, but she got this from some pill that damn doctor gave her. She spends most of her time in her room asleep. I go up there every couple of hours to check on her. If I find her water bottle full, I wake her and make her drink at least half of it. I'm trying to keep soups in her and even made spaghetti last night, probably her favorite food in the world. She picked at a few bites and said she wasn't hungry."

"Can I go up to say hello?"

"Of course. Try to get her to drink some water."

Whizmo climbed the stairs and knocked quietly before he entered. Cocoa barked a greeting. Samantha opened her eyes, expecting to see Luke. When she saw Whizmo, she pushed herself up to a sitting position. "Hi there, Professor Whizmo. Sorry I'm having to miss your class."

Whizmo walked over to the bed and sat on the side of it. "No problem, sweetie. Here, drink some of this water." He opened an untouched bottle on her nightstand and handed it to her.

"You must have been talking to my dad. Every time he comes in here he does the same thing."

"I confess," Whizmo said, smiling. "It's important that you drink lots of water, even if you don't want to."

Samantha nodded and took a few sips. "Hey, Whizmo, how much longer are you going to live behind us?"

"I don't know, kid. You trying to get rid of me?"

"You know better than that. I just figured you'd stay a year or so and then buy another house."

Whizmo stood to look out on the apartment. "I've thought about it, sweetie. Only, you know, I like it here. It's all the space I need. By now you and Luke have become like family. I'll probably just stick around until you throw me out."

Samantha managed a grin. "I'd like that." Then her eyes shut and she was asleep.

46

Two weeks later Luke and Samantha were back in Dr. Hartman's office. He checked her over and shook his head as he did so. "Samantha, we'll draw some more blood. Sorry I have to be a vampire. Then I'll call your dad in a couple of days."

"Next time I come back I'm going to bring you a set of those fake vampire teeth. If you're going to act like one, you might as well look like one," Samantha joked.

Two days later Luke was at his desk when he got the call from Dr. Hartman. "Luke, this a good time to talk?"

"Any time is a good time for you, Clyde."

"She's not any better, Luke. In fact, her liver function tests and enzymes are climbing. Sorry to tell you, Luke, but that's not what we were hoping for."

Luke rubbed his eyes as he replied. "Actually, Clyde, I knew you were going to say that. I've gotten to know my daughter pretty well and haven't seen any improvement. What do you suggest?"

Clyde ran his hand through his hair as he replied. "I've been thinking about that. One of my good friends from medical school is a hepatologist in San Antonio, a professor at the University of Texas Health Science Center there. I've got a call in to him. I should hear back this afternoon or in the morning. He'd normally want to see her himself, but he knows that he won't find anything more on a physical exam than I would, and I've already e-mailed him Samantha's lab work."

"Thanks, Clyde. I'll be here. Otherwise, you've got my cell."

Luke stared at the phone and then gazed out the window for five minutes before he got to his feet and walked toward the back. He stopped in the downstairs kitchen and took two beers from the refrigerator before going out back to find Whizmo in his shop. Whizmo was measuring a top for a coffee table when Luke handed him a bottle.

Whizmo nodded his thanks, wiped the sweat from his forehead, and gulped half the beer. "So, how's Sam?"

"Just talked to Clyde. Not any better. In fact, she's worse."

"What's he recommend?"

"He's calling a specialist in San Antonio and will get back to me tomorrow. Whiz, I'm thinking about suing that Indian doctor."

Whizmo walked out to sit on the steps. "Have a seat. I saved one step for you. Exactly what do you expect to accomplish by suing Dr. Challa? That's not going to make Sam well."

"You're right. It won't, but I need some answers. Maybe I'll only find out what drug she took. Maybe there's an antidote. It may all be a waste of time. Something tells me I've got to do something. If I fail, at least I tried."

"How's your stomach going to react to all of this?"

"That's the amazing thing. Ever since Sam and I quit having problems, I quit having the stomach cramps. As to this lawsuit, it shouldn't be very complicated. I handled a lot of medical cases back in Houston. I'm just suing one doctor, looking for information. I might get a little money out of him for Sam, depending on what I find. Judging from the looks of his office, he wouldn't be able to pay a big judgment. On the other hand, he may have a little malpractice insurance. I can probably get my hands on that. Still, if I get the name of the drug, we'll see where it goes from there."

Whizmo downed his beer and belched. "Sounds okay to me. Let me know how I can help. And you better talk to your client upstairs. Make sure she's okay with it."

Luke nodded and returned to his house. When he got upstairs he found Samantha sitting in the breakfast nook, watching two squirrels chasing each other in the oak trees.

"Hey, Sam. Glad to see you're up. You feeling any better?"

Samantha turned to look at her dad, who tried to hide his dismay at seeing the yellow in her eyes. "Maybe just a little. At least I'm trying to convince myself that I am. I'm pretending that I'm a squirrel, running along an oak limb and flying through the air to land on the limb of another tree. That must be a great feeling. Not exactly a bird, but kinda like it."

Luke sat beside her and joined her in watching the squirrels. "I've got something to talk about."

"I know. I heard you talking to Dr. Hartman. My blood work still sucks, doesn't it?"

Luke nodded his head. "That's as good a word as any. He's talking to a friend of his in San Antonio to see what we do next."

Samantha nodded and returned to watching the squirrels.

"Sam, I want to sue Dr. Challa. You have any problem with that?"

Never turning away from the squirrels, she shrugged her shoulders. "Okay with me. Why?"

"Shorthand summary, Sam, is I'm looking for answers. All I've got is questions right now. I may find some and I may not. Think of it as a baseball game. If I go to the plate and take a swing, I may hit a home run or I may strike out. If I don't at least step up to the plate, we'll never know what will happen. I've got to sue in your name, but otherwise you probably won't have to be involved. He's a local doctor. I'll file suit in our courthouse right up the street. Shouldn't interfere in anything that Clyde and his friend decide to do to get you well."

"Go for it, Dad." Samantha managed a wan smile. "Only if you're going back to being a trial lawyer, swing for the fences."

Luke leaned over and hugged his daughter. "Don't worry, Sam. I intend to hit it out of the park."

"Hey, are you guys talking baseball up there?" a voice called from downstairs.

"Brad, come on up," Luke hollered.

"Dad, I don't have any makeup on," Samantha objected.

"Too late now," Brad said as he rounded the top of the stairs. "Besides, I love you with or without makeup. Makeup hides those cute little freckles on your nose."

Brad bent over to give her a peck on the lips before he sat down. Luke got up to excuse himself. "Brad, you know there are Cokes in the fridge. I'm going downstairs to finish a project."

After Luke was gone Brad asked, "How're you doing, baby?"

Tears welled up in Samantha's eyes. Brad handed her a napkin from the table. As she wiped her eyes, she said, "I'm sorry, hon, only I'm scared."

Brad scooted his chair around beside Samantha, put his arm around her, and pulled her toward him. Samantha laid her head on his chest and started crying quietly.

Brad didn't know what to say. All he could think of was to give her encouragement. "Hey, look, I knew a guy that got hepatitis when I was in high school. He was out of classes for a few weeks and then was fine. That's probably what's going to happen with you."

Samantha pushed away and looked at him. "You think so?"

"I'm not the doctor, but I'll bet it is. Besides, I'm here for you whatever happens."

Samantha put her arms around Brad's neck and hugged him. "Thanks. Just having you here makes me feel better."

Luke was sitting at his desk when Brad stuck his head in the door. "I'm heading out, Luke. I'll be by a couple of times a day if that's okay."

"Sure," Luke said, nodding. "You'll need to be Sam's personal spirit coach."

After Brad had gone, the phone rang. "Luke, Clyde here. I've talked to my friend in San Antonio. He wants to put Sam on alpha interferon. It's a subcutaneous injection. It's usually used for hepatitis B, but he is willing to give it a try with Sam's drug-induced hepatitis. He wants to try her on it for twenty-four weeks with an injection once a week. I've arranged for a home health nurse to come by every week to give her the shot. Tell Sam I'm sorry to have to put her through this. Let's hope it works."

Luke thanked Clyde and turned to his computer to begin drafting a petition in the case of *Samantha Vaughan v. Vijay Challa, M.D.* It was something that he had done so many times in his prior life as a trial lawyer that he could do it from memory. As he was running a spell check before he printed the document, the doorbell rang.

A gray-haired, heavyset woman carrying a small black bag stood on the porch. "Mr. Vaughan, I'm Mary Sanchez. Dr. Hartman has arranged for me to come by here once a week to administer your daughter's medication. Is now okay?"

"Good for me. Come in. I'll check on Samantha. Have a seat here in the foyer and I'll be back down in a minute."

Luke woke Samantha and explained what was about to happen.

"Dad, you mean I have to be stuck in the butt every week for twenty-four weeks? No way. Tell her to come back next year, or maybe in two years."

"Sam, come on," Luke pleaded.

"All right," Samantha said as she resigned herself to her fate. "Let's get it over."

47

The deputy stopped in front of Dr. Challa's office and knocked on the door. When there was no answer, he walked over to the liquor store. Dr. Challa, minus white coat, was behind the counter. "Afternoon, Deputy."

"You're Dr. Challa, aren't you?"

He handed Dr. Challa an official-looking document and turned to leave the store.

"Wait, Deputy. Why are you giving me this? I haven't done anything wrong."

The deputy turned and looked over his shoulder. "Doctor, I just serve the papers. You can read on there what you have to do."

Dr. Challa sat on the stool behind the counter and read the petition. The instructions from the summons attached to it said he had twenty days to file an answer. He knew that doctors got sued. He was told when he came to the United States that it was just a part of the practice of medicine. Still, it was his first time, and he was alarmed to see a claim of damages over a million dollars. He considered just packing his things and moving back to India. Instead, he locked the liquor store and went next door to his office, where he rummaged through cabinets until he found his file on Ceventa. When he got to an instruction sheet, he dialed the number of Rudy Kowalski.

"Mr. Kowalski, this is Dr. Challa. I'm calling from San Marcos, Texas. I was one of your clinical investigators in the Exxacia study."

"What can I do for you, Doctor? Wait, first of all, let me tell you we appreciate your help. Thanks to good physicians like you, Exxacia is now on the market and saving lives." He omitted that Ceventa was already making millions on sales of the antibiotic.

"Sir, it may be saving lives, but I've just been sued by one of my patients, a young woman named Samantha Vaughan who was in the study. She claims she's got hepatitis from the drug. Your company needs to represent me. She's claiming a million dollars in damages."

"Dr. Challa, maybe you didn't read the contract you signed. You agreed that Ceventa would have no liability to any of your patients. As a matter of fact, according to the contract, if we get sued, you can be asked to indemnify us."

Dr. Challa rarely raised his voice. This was an exception. "How can that be?" he shouted. "It's your drug! I just followed the instructions."

"Sorry, Doc. Not a thing we can do. Maybe next time you better read the fine print."

Rudy Kowalski knew what he was required to do. According to

the FDA, any adverse event was to be reported to the agency, where such events and their frequency could be monitored. Dr. Kingsbury had countermanded that mandate, issuing an edict that nothing would be reported to the FDA on Exxacia until he decided it would. Instead, Rudy went to his computer and clicked to a screen titled "Exxacia adverse events." He recorded the information reported by Dr. Challa. It was the forty-seventh report of a liver problem, and the drug had only been on the market a little over a month. If it was true that only about 10 percent of adverse events were ever reported to the drug company, they were about to have a gigantic problem on their hands. Kowalski knew that he could get in trouble if the FDA discovered he was holding back information, but he needed a job, and this happened to be the only one he had.

48

Dr. Challa slammed down the phone, cussing out Rudy Kowalski and Ceventa as he did. Next he chastised himself for deciding to make some easy money. Finally, he searched his desk until he found an insurance policy issued by Texas Preferred Doctors Insurance Company. He located the phone number to report a claim and did so. Next he faxed a copy of the petition to the claims person in Dallas, who called a lawyer in Austin that the company regularly used to represent its doctors.

Tom Lorance was a seasoned malpractice defense lawyer. He was short with a fringe of red hair and a matching complexion. His basic nature was to be polite to everyone, foe and friend alike. When the petition was faxed to him, he read through it and calendared the answer date. Then he went to the Texas Medical Board's Web site and checked out his new client. From what he saw of Vijay Challa's credentials, he was certainly not impressed. Last, he picked up the phone to call Dr. Challa.

"Dr. Challa, this is Tom Lorance. I'm an attorney in Austin. Preferred Doctors has asked that I represent you in this Vaughan case."

"Yes, sir, Mr. Lorance. Thank you for calling so quickly. I'm very worried about this matter. I only have a fifty-thousand-dollar policy."

"I've noted that, Doctor. You don't need to worry. I'll take care of you. Let me put out a couple of fires here, and I'll drive to San Marcos to meet with you later in the week."

"Yes, sir," Dr. Challa agreed. "However, Mr. Lorance, you should know that there's very little in the chart. I've got it here on the desk in front of me." Dr. Challa hesitated. "Right now I can't even find the consent form. I'm sure she signed it. It must be misfiled."

"Hmmm, that could be a major issue, Doctor," Lorance replied. "Please do your best to find it."

Tom Lorance's next call was to Luke Vaughan. "Luke, this is Tom Lorance from Austin. I'll be defending Dr. Challa. First I want to say that I'm sorry about your daughter."

Luke was a little surprised to get a call from a defense lawyer so soon, but also pleased. Considering Sam's deteriorating condition, the sooner the better. "What can I do for you, Tom?"

"Mainly I'm just touching base. I'll get an answer on file in a week or so. How's Samantha doing?"

"Not very good." Luke sighed. "We've got her on interferon, but I'm not seeing any improvement."

"Boy, that's too bad," Tom said. "I've got a teenage daughter. Sure would hate to have her in that condition. Can I ask you a personal question, Luke, and maybe give some advice?"

"Have at it," Luke said, somewhat puzzled at the offer.

"You sure you're doing the right thing? I mean, we all know that it's never a good idea to represent a family member. I could give you the names of a couple of good plaintiff lawyers who could handle

Samantha's case without letting personal involvement interfere with their decisions."

Luke hesitated, thinking about it. "I appreciate your suggestion, Tom. I really do. I did some soul-searching about taking this on, but I think that it's going to be pretty cut-and-dried. I'll make the right calls. By the way, how much coverage does Dr. Challa have?"

"Not much. Fifty thousand. Well, I just wanted to call so we can get this one off on the right foot."

"Appreciate it, Tom. By the way, I'm going to ask Judge Nimitz to put this on a fast track, and I'll be sending out a request for production of all of the clinical trial files in Challa's possession."

"I don't object to the fast track, Luke. If it were my daughter, I'd be doing the same. We may have a problem with the documents, though. I'll look for your request as soon as I file an answer."

49

Samantha and Cocoa appeared in Luke's door. "Dad, Cocoa and I want to go for a ride in the Camaro with the T-tops off. I want to feel the sun and the wind in my face."

Luke looked up from his computer, pleased that Samantha was up to an outing. "Your wish is my command. Let me shut down this computer and get the keys."

When they got to the car, he went to the driver's side.

"No, Dad. I want to drive. It's my car."

"Sam, are you sure you're up to this?"

"Come on, Dad. I'll take it slow, and you'll be riding shotgun."

Luke reluctantly agreed and went to the passenger side. Cocoa took her place in the backseat, close to the window so she could stick her head out.

Samantha backed slowly down the driveway and stopped at the corner. "Let's head into the hills, okay?"

"You're the driver. Your call. I'm just the copilot," Luke answered.

It was a beautiful day full of sunshine, with temperatures in the midseventies. It had rained enough the night before that when they got to the first low water crossing, they met six inches of water.

"Take it slow, Sam, but don't stop."

"Don't worry, Dad," Samantha assured him. "I've done this before."

Samantha got to the middle of the creek and then gunned the engine. As the car splashed to the other side, Cocoa barked when her snout was inundated with water.

After they climbed the hill on the other side, Luke glanced at his daughter. Her face was full of delight and excitement. *Thank God,* he thought, *we can still put a little happiness in her life.* Then he looked up into the azure sky. *Okay, God, I'm going to need a lot of help here. Please don't let us down.* For some unexplained reason, a sense of peace came over him.

After thirty minutes, Samantha pulled into a roadside park beside a quiet bend in the river. Cocoa bounded from the car, dove into the river, and swam across. When she got to the other side, Luke whistled, and she happily swam back. Luke and Samantha sat on the grass under the shade of a live oak and watched the river. He idly started picking up acorns and tossing them into the water.

"Dad, am I going to be all right?"

Luke had known this question was going to come, and he had been dreading it. "I hope so, Sam, but I can't promise. I can tell you that if there's any way on God's green earth to make you well, I'll find it. That's all I can do."

Samantha reached over to hug her dad, and when they pulled apart, both had tears in their eyes.

50

As soon as Tom Lorance filed an answer for Dr. Challa, Luke fired back a request for production. He asked for all of Dr. Challa's files on the clinical trial in which Samantha had been a patient. He didn't know the name of the trial, the drug, or the pharmaceutical company, so he simply referred to it as "the Clinical Trial." He didn't want only Samantha's chart but the charts on every one of Dr. Challa's patients in the Clinical Trial, as well as any instructions from the as yet unidentified drug company and communications to and from that company, whether by letter, e-mail, or fax. For good measure, he asked for records of any phone conversations in which the Clinical Trial was discussed. Luke knew that he couldn't possibly get everything he requested, but he could ask for all this information and take what the judge gave him.

Tom Lorance got the request and figured it was time to meet with his client. The next day he took the short drive to San Marcos. As he parked in the strip center lot, he tried to remember if he'd ever represented a client with such a run-down office. Before he entered, he stepped back to the street and used his cell phone to take several photos of the office and the center. He wanted to be able to show the insurance company what they were dealing with.

Lorance entered the office and waited. It wasn't long before a small, dark-skinned physician in a white coat came from the back and introduced himself as Dr. Challa. Lorance explained what to expect as the lawsuit progressed and then asked to see all of the files from the clinical trial.

"But, Mr. Lorance, aren't we violating federal privacy laws if I let you see any patient files other than those of Samantha Vaughan?" Dr. Challa cautioned.

Lorance pondered the question and then nodded his head in agreement. "I suppose you're right, Doctor. We'd probably better wait to see what Judge Nimitz does on the production request before I review the others. Just let me have a look at Samantha's and the communications between you and the drug company."

Dr. Challa did as requested and sat quietly at his desk while the attorney studied Samantha's patient chart. Lorance had been analyzing such charts as long as he had been practicing law. He looked through the vital signs on each visit and the lab results. "Dr. Challa, why is it that out of six visits, the lab results on three are identical?"

"That just happens sometimes, Mr. Lorance." Dr. Challa shrugged.

"No, it doesn't! Let's get one thing very straight. I'm your lawyer. I expect the truth from you. If there's a problem, I can figure out a way to deal with it. We have an attorney-client privilege, so let's try this again. Why are the lab results on three visits identical?"

This time the reply was different. "She didn't show up for those visits. The drug company insisted on lab work once a week. What could I do? I copied prior lab work and submitted the results."

"Well, for one thing, you could have just kicked her out of the trial," Lorance said with muted anger in his voice.

"But, Mr. Lorance, I'd already taken their money and already paid Ms. Vaughan."

"Okay. Sorry I raised my voice. You've told me the truth. I'll deal with it. Now, I see the drug is called Exxacia, manufactured by Ceventa. Haven't there been a bunch of ads running on television about this drug lately?"

Dr. Challa nodded. "You're correct, Mr. Lorance. It's been approved by the FDA, and doctors all over the country are prescribing it. I'm even recommending it myself."

Lorance continued to peruse Samantha's chart until he got to the back. "Dr. Challa, she had to sign a consent form to be a subject of a clinical trial. You still haven't found it?"

Dr. Challa grimaced. "First, I know that she signed one. All of the subjects signed one. I've searched all over this office. I've even looked in the charts of all of the other patients involved in the trial, thinking I must have misfiled it. It's gone, at least for now."

51

"Court, come to order. All rise!" the bailiff announced as the judge stepped through the door from his chambers.

"Good morning, ladies and gentlemen. This is our civil motion docket, and it looks like we have a big one. Who promises me that they can be through in less than five minutes?" A number of lawyers raised their hands and announced their cases. "All right, you'll be first. Fair warning, though, I'll cut you off at seven minutes and you go to the back of the line."

Knowing that they were going to take twenty or thirty minutes, Luke and Tom Lorance settled down to wait. *All part of being a trial lawyer,* Luke thought. *Hurry up to get here on time and then cool your heels.* Fortunately, he had some editing he needed to do on a real estate deal. He reached into his old briefcase and fetched a fat file and began to mark up various paragraphs with a red pen. After an hour and a half it was their turn.

"*Samantha Vaughan v. Vijay Challa, M.D.* Mr. Vaughan and Mr. Lorance."

"Morning, Judge," Luke said as he walked to the bench. "This is Tom Lorance from Austin. He says he's been in your court a time or two."

"Indeed he has." Judge Nimitz smiled. "Welcome back, Mr. Lorance. I see we've got a request for production. Mr. Lorance, it appears that you don't want to give Mr. Vaughan anything, not even his client's own chart."

"If I may explain, Judge?" Lorance asked. "To start with Samantha's chart, it would normally be discoverable. However, it's part of a clinical trial."

"I see that Mr. Vaughan has dubbed it the Clinical Trial."

"Yes, sir. The questionnaires, design of the trial, even the consent forms are proprietary, developed by Ceventa."

"Just a minute, Mr. Lorance," the judge interrupted. "Is there anyone in this courtroom representing Ceventa?"

Silence.

"Sorry, Mr. Lorance, but you don't have standing to make that argument. You will produce Samantha's chart, and I presume you would make the same argument about the communications between Dr. Challa and Ceventa. Am I correct?"

Tom Lorance saw he was fighting a losing battle. He had asked Ceventa to have a lawyer intervene, but he couldn't get their in-house lawyers to pay any attention to what they called a little pissant case in a small town in Texas. *Well,* he thought, *they made their bed.*

"Then, Mr. Lorance, I believe you know my ruling on those documents. That brings us to the other patient charts."

"Judge, I think I need to step in here," Luke said.

"Be my guest, Mr. Vaughan."

"No doubt those other patient charts have some information that would ordinarily be privileged. However, my client . . . my daughter . . . was part of a larger trial. These other patient charts may lead to relevant evidence and they may not. The only way to know is to see them."

"Seems reasonable to me. What say you, Mr. Lorance?"

"Judge, I haven't won a round in this fight yet. I honestly don't know what is in those charts. Personally, I was so concerned about privacy issues that I decided not to even look at them myself."

"Understood, Mr. Lorance. I think you probably made the right call at the time. Now I'm ordering you to turn over those charts along with the other documents to Mr. Vaughan. I'm sure Mr. Vaughan will sign a confidentiality agreement if you think it's necessary. Anything else, gentlemen?"

Both lawyers shook their heads and asked to be excused. When they got out into the hallway, Tom pulled Luke to the side. "Just so you'll know, I tried to get Ceventa to send a lawyer down here. They said they just didn't believe they needed any advice from me. Their mistake. We'll just see how it plays out."

Luke nodded but said nothing.

"One more thing, Luke. When you get Samantha's chart, you'll find that the consent form is missing. I'm just giving you a heads-up. We're not trying to hide anything. It's just that my client can't find it. If it turns up, we'll supplement."

Luke's eyes got wide at Lorance's confession. "Tom, if you don't find it, you need to be offering your policy limits. I'm not sure if I can even take your policy, but your client's got his ass in a crack."

52

Luke got the bad news on a Friday. On Monday he and Samantha drove to San Antonio to see Dr. Shepherd Stevens, the hepatologist who had been assisting Clyde Hartman in Samantha's care. They worked their way through the maze of buildings at the UT Health Science

Center to the hepatology department and signed in. When they were escorted to the treatment area, they were met by a distinguished looking physician with a calm, gentle demeanor. He invited them to take a seat.

"Samantha and Luke, I'm pleased that you could come on such short notice. Samantha, after looking at your last blood work, I thought it was time for a full work-up."

"I don't understand, sir," Samantha replied, her voice cracking with alarm.

"Samantha, your liver is still failing, even with the interferon. It's time to do more testing."

"Doctor, I'm only nineteen. Am I going to die before I'm twenty?" Samantha asked.

"Samantha, I have no intention of letting you die, okay?" Dr. Stevens replied as he handed her a Kleenex. "We may have to get you a new liver sometime soon. If we do, you'll live a pretty normal life. There are thousands of people in the country who have had liver transplants. The even better news is that with your youth and good health, your chances of a normal life are really quite good."

Samantha continued to sniffle. Luke had been quiet up to this time. "What's on tap today, Dr. Stevens?" he asked now.

"We're going to do a bunch of scans and imaging. CT, MRI, HIDA scan, ultrasound. They're all designed to focus specifically on the liver. Samantha, the only one that will hurt a bit is a liver biopsy. We're going to have to stick a needle in your abdomen and draw out a little piece of your liver. It'll be done under local anesthesia and will take about twenty minutes."

Samantha got through the day and was exhausted at the end of it. Dr. Stevens told Luke that he would call in no more than two days with the results. He lowered his eyes and refused to make eye contact with Luke as he spoke. Luke left, thinking he knew what the answer would be.

53

At ten the next morning there was a knock on the door. Luke opened it to find a FedEx delivery driver with a large box from Dr. Challa's office. Luke knew it contained Dr. Challa's charts. By midafternoon Luke, Whizmo, Sue Ellen, Brad, and Samantha were gathered around Luke's conference table. Luke had tried to talk Samantha into staying in bed since the day before had been traumatic. She refused, insisting it was her lawsuit and she would help. Sue Ellen had taken the afternoon off from prosecuting criminals. Whizmo had planned to do research for a paper he was writing on the effects of the Vietnam War on modern America. That could wait.

"Thanks for coming, everybody. Sam, if you start feeling bad, you need to go back to bed."

Samantha nodded her understanding, knowing she would stay until the last document was studied.

"I've already glanced through these. Ceventa is the manufacturer of the drug, named Exxacia."

"Hell, Luke," Whizmo interrupted. "I just saw some actor on television a couple of nights ago, telling people to ask their doctors about Exxacia. When it comes to drugs and advertising, we got one screwed-up system."

"I couldn't agree more, Whiz, only that system is for discussion on another day," Luke replied. "They've got a very detailed protocol, at least on paper, that outlines what Dr. Challa was to do. The subjects have to be between eighteen and sixty-five. They don't qualify if they don't have pneumonia, bronchitis, sinusitis, or tonsillitis. They've got to sign a detailed consent form and initial six other pages. The dates have to match. When they get the pills, they don't know whether they're getting the drug or the benchmark antibiotic. However, there's a numbering system so that, if Dr. Challa followed it, Ceventa knows which patients got the drug. We all know that Sam must have. Then the patients have to come back once a week for six weeks for a short physical—vital signs and more blood work—followed by a last visit at ten weeks. We need to check all of that on every one of these one hundred and five charts. Any questions?"

"Just one," Whizmo said. "At the end of the day, what are we going to do with our findings?"

"Let me save my answer until the day's over, Whiz, okay?"

Whizmo nodded, and they began to pore over the charts.

"By the way," Luke added. "If you run across Sam's chart, holler. Lorance has already told me the consent form is missing."

"But Dad, I didn't read anything. He just handed me a form and told me to sign the back page. Now I see that these forms had places to initial on each page. I don't remember doing that," Samantha protested. "I didn't have any sinus problem, either, not even a sniffle when I went into that office."

Luke walked around the conference table and patted his daughter on the back. "I understand, Sam. Believe me, I understand. One step at a time, though, okay?"

"Hey," Sue Ellen said to no one in particular as she thumbed through a chart. "Let me fire up my computer." Sue Ellen turned on her Dell, clicked through to the county clerk's Web site, and went to a section listing deaths in the county by year. "Aha! Just as I suspected. Here's a form completed by a dead guy, Francisco Saldana. I remember that name because I sent him to prison for cocaine possession a few years ago. I saw in the paper he died a while back. Must have been some powerful drugs he was doing. He came back from the dead, signed these forms, and even had a pulse and blood pressure."

"I'll be damned," Luke said. "Challa was reading the obituaries."

"I can get him for fraud, Luke," Sue Ellen replied.

"Not just yet. Let's see where this goes."

They spent the rest of the afternoon carefully analyzing the charts. When they finished, they'd found a handful that appeared to be valid in every respect. The rest had problems, including twelve charts completed by people who had died long before they supposedly volunteered for the trial.

54

The phone rang in Luke's office, and he picked it up. "Luke Vaughan."

"Mr. Vaughan, Dr. Stevens here. Is this a good time to talk?"

"Good as any, Dr. Stevens. What do you have to tell me?"

'I'm sorry, Mr. Vaughan. The results are about what we expected. Sam's liver is failing. The interferon we had her on hasn't worked as we had hoped. It's time to find her another liver."

Luke put the phone down, tried to regain his composure, wiped his eyes, and then retrieved the phone. In a halting voice he asked, "Doesn't that mean she's going to have to get on some damn waiting list? Aren't there a whole lot more people in this country that need livers than there are donors? Isn't a transplant expensive? Why can't I just give her my liver?"

"Mr. Vaughan, slow down a minute. Let me try to answer some of your questions." Dr. Stevens had been down this road numerous times and was prepared for the interrogation. "First, there is a waiting list. Based on her MELD score, a scoring system we use to evaluate potential liver transplant recipients, Sam will be in the top twenty-five percent on the list. That's good. As to cost, I'm afraid you're right.

The current cost is close to half a million dollars, and after the transplant the cost averages about twenty-five thousand a year."

"Is that for the rest of her life?"

"Afraid it is."

"How long will it take for her to get to the top of the list?"

"That, Mr. Vaughan, is the sixty-four-thousand-dollar question. Actually, the anomaly is that the more her liver deteriorates, the faster she moves up the list. Even when she gets close to the top, we still have to find a match to minimize rejection of the donor liver."

"What about my liver, Dr. Stevens?"

"I've already checked that. Living donors are becoming more common. We can take a piece of someone else's liver and it'll grow in the person who needs it. Then the donor's liver will grow back in a few months."

"Then let's do that."

"Mr. Vaughan, I took the liberty of checking your blood type with Dr. Hartman. The two of you aren't a match. Samantha has a rare blood type, and I need to tell you that that's going to make it even more difficult to find a suitable donor. What about her mother? I don't have any information about her. Is she still around?"

Luke searched his mind and came up blank. "I haven't heard anything about her in more than fifteen years. Last I heard she was in Tennessee. I'll see if I can find her."

Luke paused and stared out the window long enough that Dr. Stevens asked if he was still on the line.

"I'm still here, Doctor. How long does Sam have?"

"These situations can vary widely. My best judgment is at least several months. I've already taken the initial steps to get her on the national liver transplant list. Normally, she has to be interviewed by a number of people before she's approved, but I pulled a few strings. We're going to do our best, Mr. Vaughan. The good news is that people are living a lot longer with a transplanted liver than they did twenty years ago."

"Thanks, Doc. I'll be in touch." Luke replaced the phone and rubbed his eyes. Finally he rose and walked out of his office.

He found Samantha sitting at the bottom of the stairs, her face in her hands. "I heard all of that, Dad."

Luke sat beside his daughter and wrapped his arms around her. "It's going to be okay, Sam. I told you that. It's just that now we're going to have to get you a new liver."

Samantha jumped up from the steps and ran out the front door. Luke followed. She had curled up in one of the rockers. "I don't want to live like this, Dad. I don't even have a life. I want to die now, not when my liver finally fails."

"Sam, don't say that. Don't even think like that." He took her chin in one hand and gently raised her head until she was looking at him. "I promise, Sam. Trust me."

Samantha saw the horror on Luke's face. "I didn't mean it, Dad! It's just that I'm so tired. I'll stick it out." She sighed. "Now I'm going back up to bed."

Luke returned to his computer and started trying to locate his ex-wife on various Internet sites. After a half hour he paused and stared at the screen. Josie had died in a one-car accident ten years before, apparently drunk. He got up, paced the office, and then walked back out to the porch, where he sat in his rocker and contemplated his next step. He considered whether to tell Samantha about her mother and rejected the idea. Sam already had enough on her plate. Finally he returned to his office.

Luke spent the rest of the day trying to figure out where to raise half a million dollars. The equity in the house was thirty thousand. He had another forty thousand in his 401(k). He had a modest business line of credit, and his credit cards were all paid off. He figured that got him to roughly a hundred and thirty thousand if he maxed out his credit line and credit cards. Next he checked the Medicare/Medicaid site. Naturally, even as a small-town lawyer he made too much money to qualify for funds. He went to his personal insurance folder and read the medical insurance policy he had taken out for himself and Samantha when they moved to San Marcos. It was just as he remembered. He'd had an option to add a hundred thousand in coverage for any transplant and had decided to save a few hundred dollars a year in premiums. It had never occurred to him that either he or Sam would need such coverage. Now he mentally kicked himself in the butt. The Internet gave ideas for fund-raisers, but he had seen newspaper articles on such events, and apparently they rarely raised more than a few thousand dollars. Needing someone to talk to, he called Sue Ellen and arranged to meet her at the river for an early dinner.

55

Sue Ellen found Luke sitting at a table by the falls. Two empty beer bottles told her he had a head start. He rose and gave her a peck on the lips.

"Not good, huh, Luke?"

"It's worse than that, Sue Ellen," Luke said, his voice not much more than a whisper. "Sam's liver is barely functioning. She's got to have a transplant. She even briefly threatened suicide."

Sue Ellen's hand went to her mouth. "Oh my God, Luke. Was she serious?"

"I don't think so," Luke said. "I convinced her I'd get her a transplant, only there's one problem. It'll cost about half a million dollars, and I can't figure out a way to raise much more than a hundred and thirty thousand. On top of that, she's a rare blood type that's tough to match. I've made a promise to my daughter that right now I have no way of keeping."

"I've got twenty-five thousand in Josh's college fund. It's yours if you need it," Sue Ellen replied as she took Luke's hand.

"Thanks, Sue Ellen, but I'm not looking for charity. There's one more thing. I researched Sam's mother to see if she could be a donor. She died in a drunken car wreck ten years ago."

"Oh, Luke, I'm so sorry. Did you tell Sam?"

"Thought about it and decided not to tell her."

Sue Ellen shook her head. "That could be a mistake, Luke. She even talked to me once, wondering why her mother deserted her. On the one hand, it would be hard on her. On the other hand, it might ease her mind about being abandoned by her mother. I think she's entitled to know."

Luke stared down at the table as he spoke. "I value your opinions, Sue Ellen. You know I do. Only, I have to make the decision, and I just don't think this is the right time."

Luke and Sue Ellen sat in silence, both uncertain what to say next. Sue Ellen chose to change the subject. "What about your lawsuit against Dr. Challa?"

"He's only got fifty thousand in coverage. If Lorance offered it tomorrow, it wouldn't pay for a liver transplant.'

Luke ordered two more beers and invited Sue Ellen to order dinner, saying that he really wasn't hungry. Sue Ellen replied that she, too, had lost her appetite.

After the waiter brought their beers, Sue Ellen said, "Why don't you sue Ceventa? They're the ones that caused this problem, not Dr. Challa."

"I've actually thought about that, only I know how these drug companies handle litigation. They declare all-out war. They'll hire an army of lawyers and drag the trial out for two years. Then even if we were to win, they'll appeal for another three years. They have an unlimited budget in these things. I'm sorry to say that by the time we got through all of that, Sam would be dead." Luke shook his head. "It just won't work."

"Look, I don't think you've got any choice," Sue Ellen replied. "Your only hope is to put pressure on Ceventa. With Sam's life in the balance, Nimitz will give you a quick trial."

Luke sipped his beer slowly as he weighed his options. "I don't really know much about Nimitz as a judge. How sure are you that he'll put us on a fast track?"

Sue Ellen took both of Luke's hands in hers as she replied, "I'm as sure of it as I'm sure that Sam is going to die if you don't try it. I'll be beside you all the way."

Again there was silence as Luke contemplated what Sue Ellen was suggesting. Finally he nodded. "I'm for it, particularly if he will get us to trial in a few months. That may be all the time Sam has. I just have to clear it with her."

56

Samantha was sitting on the front porch with Cocoa at her feet when Luke returned to the house. She remained in her rocker as he bent over to give her a kiss and sat down beside her.

"Sam, Sue Ellen and I have been talking. I want to add Ceventa to our lawsuit."

"Dad, we already talked about that," Samantha replied with dejection. "You said that it might take two years to get to trial and more time on appeal. I know what the doctors have said. I don't have that much time."

"Hear me out. I'm going to ask Judge Nimitz for an expedited trial date, ninety days if he'll give it to us. Ceventa's lawyers will claim they can't get the case to trial that soon and will do everything they can to delay. Sue Ellen knows the judge well. She says he'll work with us. If we can push a trial date, we can be ready." He looked at his daughter. "It's our best shot."

Samantha was lost in thought. "What happens if we win in trial and they appeal?"

"Good question, Sam. No telling. Maybe they'll want to settle for a few hundred thousand if we get a multimillion-dollar verdict. We're not trying to get rich, just get you a liver." Luke stopped, not sure whether to broach this subject to Samantha. "And there's one more thing. I'll have to take out a second mortgage on the house to cover the expenses. I'll also have to turn down any other clients until the trial is over. If we lose, we may be on the street."

Samantha digested all the information. "Look, Dad, I know you want to do what's best for me. I agreed to sue Dr. Challa. Now you want to sue this giant corporation and risk everything we have. Plus, you're going to be consumed with the case." Samantha reached for her dad's hand. "If I don't have much time, I'd rather have you around than fighting with Ceventa. We can still sit out here and talk and sometimes go driving in the Hill Country. Does that make sense?"

Luke squeezed his daughter's hand. "Yeah, sweetie, it does. Forget I even suggested suing Ceventa."

A few hours later Samantha appeared at Luke's office door. He glanced up and smiled as she took a seat opposite him. "Okay, so I'm a woman, and a woman has a right to change her mind, right? Let's sue Ceventa."

Luke put down his pen and stared into his daughter's eyes. "What caused this change of heart?"

"Brad and I talked. We talked a long time. He said he doesn't want to lose me, and if there's even a slight chance that we can win and I can get a new liver, he says I should do it. Dad, Brad and I want to take that chance."

Luke continued to stare in silence at Samantha, then spoke. "Are you sure, very sure?"

"I am, Dad. Let's do it." Samantha paused as she faced up to reality. "There's one more thing. If I'm gone before the lawsuit's over, I don't want you to give up. If I die, at least I'll go knowing that I did what I could to stop Ceventa from killing others."

57

Luke was up early the next morning to draft the amended petition, adding Ceventa, along with the motion for an expedited trial. Without knowing for certain, he claimed Exxacia was defectively designed in that Ceventa knew that it could cause liver failure and death. Further, he alleged, the company failed to properly warn physicians and consumers of the risk. He also complained that Ceventa enticed innocent patients into volunteering as subjects in a clinical trial that turned them into guinea pigs. Next he beefed up the section on Samantha's condition, referring to a letter he had gotten from Dr. Hartman describing it in detail and confirming that her death was imminent if she did not get a liver transplant.

On his way to file the petition, Luke stopped by Sue Ellen's office. Law books were stacked all over her desk and overflowed onto the floor. She peeked from behind one of the stacks, saw Luke, and hurried around her desk to greet him.

"Sorry about the mess. I've got a brief due. One of these years the county is going to spring for Westlaw or Lexis. Until then I've got to do research the old-fashioned way."

Luke moved a few books from a chair and sat down. "I talked to Sam about suing Ceventa. At first she refused. Then Brad talked her into it. We're adding Ceventa today. Here's the petition."

Sue Ellen took the document and skimmed through it, pausing only to read the letter from Dr. Hartman. When she got to the motion for an expedited trial date, she said, "You know Ceventa won't be in the case by next week. Aren't you just buying yourself more work when they come in to try to continue it?"

Luke nodded his agreement. "Probably, only I'm planning to fight this battle in the court of public opinion, too. If I can get a couple of news reporters interested, maybe Ceventa will think twice about postponing a dying girl's trial. Or maybe Nimitz will feel a little pressure. I figure it's worth a try, anyway."

"Actually, I don't think Nimitz will need to feel any pressure. I told you that he'll give you a fast trial, and I meant it. I know him pretty damn well. One more thing, Luke, you know that you're declaring war on a multinational company. They'll hire one of the mega firms. You remember the wicked witch in *The Wizard of Oz*? She always had a bunch of flying monkeys doing whatever she asked. That's what you're in for. They'll be coming at you from every direction."

"Don't think I haven't thought about that. I figure on being outnumbered by about twenty to one. I keep reminding myself that David was a little overmatched when he fought Goliath, and it didn't keep him from winning."

"By the way, you'll be outnumbered twenty to two. I'll talk to the DA and arrange for a leave of absence when things start heating up. You're gonna need a second chair."

Luke put his hands in front of him as if to stop Sue Ellen. "You don't need to do that. I've always tried cases alone. Besides, I can't afford to pay you."

Sue Ellen rose and walked around her desk. "Did I say anything about getting paid? I'm doing this for Sam . . . and for you." She'd wrapped her arms around Luke's neck as she spoke and now pressed her lips to his. When she broke away she continued. "I won't take no for an answer. I expect to be at your side in this trial and, I might add, from this day forward."

Luke drew her to him and looked into her green eyes. "I want you by my side forever. You know that. Let's get through this trial and then we'll plan for the future. If you're right, that will be in only a few months."

Sue Ellen nodded her agreement with a smile as Luke picked up the petition and left her office. He walked the documents down the hall to the sheriff's office, where he paid the fee for FedEx to overnight the citation to the CT Corporation, Ceventa's registered agent for service in Dallas.

Luke's last stop was the *San Marcos Daily Record*. Like most small-town newspapers, the *Daily Record* was always looking for stories of local interest. Luke asked a young woman if he could talk to a reporter. He learned the paper only had two. One was sick, and the other was out covering a local volleyball tournament. Luke left the petition along with his card and asked for a reporter to call him.

When Luke entered the house, his office phone was ringing. The male voice on the other end said, "Mr. Vaughan, this is Allen Wentland. I'm the owner of the *Daily Record* and also the editor. Tell me about your daughter."

The front-page headline the following day read:

College Student Dying
Drug Company Sued!

Luke read the headline and story with much sadness mixed with a small dollop of hope.

58

Tom Lorance received his copy of the amended petition, read through it, and made two phone calls, one to Dr. Challa and one to Challa's insurance company. Then he e-mailed the papers to each. Within twenty-four hours he called Luke and arranged a meeting that afternoon in Dr. Challa's office. All he told Luke was that he had an offer.

Luke turned his Sequoia into the gravel lot and parked beside a Ford F150 pickup that he suspected was driven by Tom Lorance. As he approached the door, Lorance opened it and invited him in. Dr. Challa was sitting on one of the old reception chairs and rose to shake his hand.

"Thanks for coming, Luke," Tom Lorance said. "How's Samantha doing?"

"Her liver function tests are getting worse every week, but we're hoping for the best. Thanks for asking."

"Have a seat. Let me explain why I called this meeting. I read your amended petition, then talked to Dr. Challa and his insurer. Dr. Challa would like to settle his part of the case. I've prevailed on his carrier to toss in their policy. That'll give you a little war chest in your battle against Ceventa. Also, Dr. Challa would like to say something." Tom nodded at Dr. Challa, who couldn't bring himself to look Luke in the eye.

"Mr. Vaughan, I am personally devastated by your daughter's illness. If I had any warning that this might happen, I never would have signed on with Ceventa. I'd rather be selling liquor next door than be responsible for the potential death of one of my patients. Please forgive me, and ask Samantha to forgive me."

Luke walked over to the back wall and looked at a Texas medical license in a cheap frame, then turned. "Dr. Challa, I accept your apology. Tom, I'm sorry to say that I can't settle with Dr. Challa. If I settle with him, you know what Ceventa will do, don't you?"

Tom pursed his lips and nodded. "Yeah, Luke, I do. They'll try the empty chair. If he's not there at trial, they'll blame him for everything, particularly since the consent form is missing. I understand."

Luke looked at the two men for a moment. "Tell you what I'll do. If I get a verdict against Dr. Challa, I'll give you a handshake deal that I'll take only his insurance coverage, not his personal assets. In return, I want Dr. Challa's cooperation in my case against Ceventa."

Tom Lorance looked at Dr. Challa, who nodded. Tom walked over to Luke, hand extended. "Deal, Luke. Let's get those bastards and get Sam a new liver."

59

Judge Nimitz came from his chambers and motioned the roomful of lawyers to be seated. "Morning, ladies and gentlemen. Let's start with any unopposed motions." Luke and Tom stood. "We have a very short one, Your Honor."

"Step up, Mr. Vaughan and Mr. Lorance. I've read your amended petition and motion for expedited trial, Mr. Vaughan. Mr. Lorance, I'm surprised you're not opposed to the expedited trial."

"Judge, I've read the letter from Dr. Hartman. I certainly am not going to stand in the way of Samantha having her day in court. The sooner the better as far as I'm concerned." Tom avoided telling the judge that he and Luke had a deal to gang up on Ceventa and limit his client's risk.

"Mr. Vaughan, I'm willing to grant this, but what about Ceventa? You're naming them as a new defendant. I don't see anyone representing them. Have you talked to their counsel?"

"Judge, I know this is a little unusual," Luke said. "However, if I wait for them to answer, it could be another month. We can't afford to wait. I asked the sheriff to serve Ceventa's registered agent, the CT Corporation in Dallas, by FedEx. The return of service and notice of this hearing is in the court's file. As you can see from Dr. Hartman's letter, time is critical."

Judge Nimitz looked out in the audience as he spoke. "I don't want any of you other lawyers getting the idea that you can do this, too. I know Dr. Hartman. In fact, he's my personal physician. I want to put that on the record in open court in case he is called to testify." The judge paused to glance at his computer calendar. "I'm setting this case in ninety days. That work for the two of you?"

"We'll make it work, Your Honor. Thank you," Luke said.

The two lawyers were about to walk away from the bench when Susie approached the judge and whispered something to him.

"Hold up, gentlemen. There's a lawyer on the phone who says she represents Ceventa. Let's put her on the speakerphone and see what she has to say. Now, if I can just hit the right button without disconnecting her . . . Hello?"

"Judge Nimitz, this is Audrey Katherine Metcalf. I'm counsel for Ceventa, and I demand that you deny this motion for expedited trial. Ceventa hasn't even made an appearance yet."

A scowl came over the judge's face as he growled, "Ms. Metcalf, if you're going to be in this case, you'll learn right quick that you don't demand anything in this court. You must be from New York City."

"No, Judge. I'm from Dallas."

"Same thing," the judge said, getting nods and grins from the lawyers in the audience. "You Dallas lawyers always seem to think those of us in small towns got our law degrees from a Sears and Roebuck catalog. Just so you'll know, mine came from the University of Texas School of Law, one of the best around. Let's see, Mr. Vaughan and Mr. Lorance, aren't the two of you Longhorns, too?"

Both lawyers raised their hands in a "Hook 'em Horns" sign.

"You can't see that, Ms. Metcalf, but they're UT alums, too. You probably graduated from Harvard, right?"

Silence filled the phone, and then came the sound of Audrey Metcalf taking a deep breath. "No, sir. I went to Yale."

Judge Nimitz nodded. "Figured it had to be one of those Ivy League schools."

"Look, Judge Nimitz. I'm getting off on the wrong foot with you. I apologize for my demeanor. My client called this morning, yelling at me to get something done, and I obviously overreacted."

"Apology accepted, and I'm sure I'll hear no more demands from you, only requests. Now, to get you up to speed, I've just set this case for ninety days."

This time Audrey Metcalf spoke in a low, modulated voice. "Judge, could we make that six months? Ninety days makes it impossible to get a case like this ready for trial."

"No, Ms. Metcalf. We've got a young lady who may not live long. I suspect you're with one of those big firms. You just round up as many lawyers as you need. We've got a nice Holiday Inn out here on the highway. You may want to reserve a few rooms just for good measure. We look forward to meeting you."

Audrey Metcalf slammed the phone down and looked around her corner office on the fortieth floor of the Renaissance Tower in Dallas. The office overflowed with lawyers, paralegals, and secretaries, all listening in on the conversation. "That bastard has set this case for ninety days from now," she barked. "All of you shift whatever you're doing to others. You're now working exclusively on *Vaughan v. Ceventa* until further notice. Charlotte, start researching what motions we can file to delay the trial or get us an interlocutory appeal to put this son of a bitch off."

Charlotte Bronson, an appellate specialist, nodded her understanding.

"Samuel, get the Exxacia clinical trial data overnighted down here. I don't care if you've got to charter a plane. We need it in our office." Samuel Ashland, a seasoned paralegal, turned and left the room.

"Becky, the judge said something about a Holiday Inn on the highway. Call down there and book the top floor." Metcalf clapped her hands loudly. "Now get a move on. We've got a case to win!"

Audrey Metcalf watched as her team filed out of her office, putting quarters and dollar bills in a jar by her door on the way out. The young woman bringing up the rear suddenly turned around.

"Excuse me, Ms. Metcalf. I'm Mary Eames Livermore. I'm a new file clerk assigned to your team. Could I ask why there are jars of pink jelly beans around your office and people are dropping money in that jar by the door."

Audrey Metcalf relaxed as she eyed the nineteen-year-old, obviously on her first job out of high school. "Have a seat. Tell me your name again."

"Mary Eames, ma'am."

'What you see is evidence of my other passion, probably equal to my passion for the law. I had breast cancer six years ago."

"Oh, I'm sorry," Mary Eames said sympathetically.

"That's okay, sweetie. I've passed my five years. It made me stop and reexamine my life. Once I got over the fear of dying, I got involved in the movement to cure breast cancer. The Race for the Cure started right here in Dallas about thirty years ago. I put together a team for the event every year. A lot of the people that were just in this room are a part of it. I ask each of them to raise a thousand dollars. You want to be a part of the team?"

Mary Eames shifted uneasily. "Yes, ma'am, I sure would—but I don't know enough people with money to raise a thousand dollars."

"Tell you what," Metcalf said, "I'll help you this first year. I'll make a few calls and raise a chunk of it for you in your name."

"That'll be great," Mary Eames enthused. "Just one more question. Why all the jelly beans, and why are they pink?"

Metcalf pointed at the pink ribbon in the lapel of her jacket. "See that? It's pink, too. I always wear one. It's to remind people that we haven't cured breast cancer. Same with the jelly beans. When I was diagnosed, I had to quit smoking. A helluva struggle, by the way. Every time I had the urge for a cigarette, I grabbed for a jelly bean instead. Then I arranged for them to be shipped to me, all pink. I carry them everywhere and put them around the office. Anyone in my office can have a pink jelly bean for a quarter. The quarters go to fight for the cure. The money's not important, but it's a reminder that we're in a war with breast cancer, a war I want to win in my lifetime."

Mary Eames rose, thanked Audrey Metcalf for her time, and left the office, pausing to dip into her pocket, where she found a quarter to put in the jar.

60

When Mary Eames left her office, Audrey Metcalf's eyes focused on the wall opposite her. It told the story of her life. There was an undergraduate diploma, with high honors, from the University of Michigan, a law degree from Yale, a plaque recognizing her as editor of the *Yale Law Review,* another recognizing her two years as a briefing attorney for Justice Sandra Day O'Connor on the United States Supreme Court, and multiple photos of Metcalf standing beside Republican governors, senators, and presidents. In the center was a plaque she'd received for her efforts in fighting breast cancer. Missing were photos of any family members. Her parents had died in the crash of a private jet on their return from Italy when she was five, and she'd been raised by an elderly grandmother. She'd flirted briefly with the idea of marriage after law school and abandoned the idea, choosing not to carry the baggage of a family through her life. She was now forty-five. Her goal was to be on the Supreme Court in ten more years. That goal was within reach if the country would just elect a Republican president next time.

Her eyes drifted to a recent photo of her with the mayor of Dallas at a charity event. *I'm holding up pretty well,* she thought. *No sign of gray in my black hair; that surgery to straighten my nose along with a little nip and tuck on my eyes two years ago took off at least five years.* Surgery had also reconstructed the breast ravaged by cancer.

Her thoughts returned to the case at hand. She had a lawsuit to win. Metcalf picked up the petition and studied it again. Although it wasn't stated in the petition, she assumed that there was a connection between the plaintiff lawyer and the plaintiff. Was he her father? Surely not. It would be plain stupid for a father to represent his dying daughter. At some point his emotions were sure to get the best of him. If he was the plaintiff's father, she could only conclude that the case was weak. Otherwise, he could have found a good plaintiff lawyer to take it on a contingent fee. Metcalf turned to her computer and clicked on the Texas State Bar Web site and typed in "Lucas Vaughan." The basic information showed him to be a graduate of UT Law, board certified in personal injury trial law, and a sole practitioner in San Marcos with no disciplinary history.

Next she typed in variations of "lucasvaughan.com" until she found his Web site. Obviously done by an amateur from a template, it listed him as available to do wills, probate, deeds, and corporate documents. Strange, she thought, that he was board certified in a trial specialty but had an office practice. He probably wasn't much of a trial lawyer. *This case shouldn't be a challenge,* she mused. *Small-town lawyer, sole practitioner, in way over his head. Once we get up to speed, we'll drop one or two motions on him every week.* Sleep would soon become a distant memory to Mr. Vaughan. She twirled her red leather chair around to look at the Dallas skyline. Then her eyes were caught by two brass balls, sitting in a velvet-lined leather case on her credenza. She picked them up and clicked them in her hand as she thought of the day she made partner. The senior partner in the firm handed them to her, saying that they were to remind her that the balls that truly made a great trial lawyer were in the mind, not elsewhere on the anatomy—and that she clearly had the biggest balls of any lawyer in the firm.

61

Samantha appeared at her dad's office door, dressed in jeans, a long-sleeved shirt, and a leather jacket that she had hidden away rather than following Judge Nimitz's order to discard her goth clothing all those months ago.

Luke turned from his computer and said, "So, do I have to report you to the judge for disobeying his order?"

"You can't do that, Dad. You're my lawyer, remember? I want to go for a ride."

Luke knew that his daughter had very little happiness in her life these days, so he replied, "Sure, let me grab my keys. You want to go in the Camaro? I'm not sure you're up to driving."

"Nope." Samantha shook her head. "I want to ride with you on the Harley."

Luke raised his eyebrows. "Sam, this is a surprise. I thought you didn't like motorcycles."

"I didn't, Dad, but now things are different. You know that movie *The Bucket List*? Riding a Harley is now on mine. But I'm not into skydiving and some of that other stuff that Morgan Freeman and Jack Nicholson did."

"Sam, sit down for a minute. I promised you were going to be okay. You don't need a bucket list."

"Yeah, Dad, I know. You're doing everything you can, but some of it's out of your control." Samantha walked around Luke's desk, sat in his lap, and put her arms around his neck. "I've had a lot of time to think lately. Dad, we're all going to die. I've got a lot I want to do with my life, but when my time comes, I'm willing to accept it. Meantime I might as well live a little, don't you think?"

Luke fought back tears again as Samantha gave him a hug. "Now let's go to the garage," Samantha said. "I'm ready to be your old lady for the afternoon."

62

Sue Ellen walked up the steps and entered the house without knocking. "Anybody home? Bright, young, well, not too young, but good-looking lawyer, here to apply for a job."

Luke met her in the hallway and gave her a hug. "Welcome, beautiful associate. Sam's asleep upstairs. Come on into the conference room."

He sat at the end of the table, and Sue Ellen sat beside him to his left.

Luke had a laptop already plugged in and the basic structure of discovery loaded.

"How's Sam?" Sue Ellen asked.

Luke shrugged his shoulders. "About as well as could be expected. She sleeps a lot, and I keep forcing her to drink plenty of fluids. She's more inclined to eating various soups now. I'm okay with that as long as I can get a couple of bowls down her a day." Luke paused to control his emotions. "Clyde says she's going to need to go to the hospital soon for constant care. She's resisting. So am I, for that matter. I don't want to have to visit Sam in the hospital while I work on her case. I'm working on a compromise with Clyde."

"I'm sorry, Luke. I wish there was more I could do," Sue Ellen said as she squeezed Luke's hand. Luke nodded his appreciation, and she turned the talk to business. "Now, what are we doing?"

"Here's the plan, subject, of course, to modification if we both agree. I'm getting a notice out for the deposition of Dr. Alfred Kingsbury, CEO of Ceventa. I'll serve it as soon as they answer, which is in two weeks. I figure they'll stall until the last day."

"Wow! I like how you think. That ought to cause a few fireworks in Maryland. I seem to remember something about the rocket's red glare up in that part of the country a while back. Any chance you'll get to depose him?"

"Truthfully, I don't know," Luke replied. "Kinda depends on how it strikes Judge Nimitz. Win or lose on this one, they'll know we're serious."

Sue Ellen pondered as she gazed out the window. "Then why don't you let me argue this motion. I'll take my leave of absence before the hearing. I've already cleared it with the DA. I just have to give him a few days' notice. Chuck and I get along real well. He and the DA and I even go out to the Hofbrauhaus for a beer once in a while."

"Well, if you can call him Chuck outside of the courthouse, then this motion is yours. As to discovery, we'll draft some interrogatories and a request for production. Then a request for disclosure is standard. I want the names of the Ceventa employees who were in charge of the clinical trial, their job descriptions, etc. Let's see, the names of the people at the FDA who worked on the project, the results of the trial, medical files on all of the subjects who participated in the trial, summaries of the results, and all communications between Ceventa and the FDA. Figure on seeing a big FedEx truck pull up if the judge lets us have all we ask for."

"Maybe I can help there." They turned to see Whizmo standing at the door.

"Hey, Whiz, I didn't hear you come in," Luke said. "What can you help with?"

"Remember, I'm not just a history professor. I also teach computer science on occasion. You just get that study on a few discs. Then you tell me what you want to find, and I'll design a program to search all that data and spit out only what you want. Don't need any FedEx truck when you've got Whizmo around."

63

As two lawyers walked away from the bench, Judge Nimitz made some notes about his ruling on the case docket sheet and then called, *"Samantha Vaughan v. Vijay Challa, MD, and Ceventa Pharmaceutical."*

Metcalf and her two associates approached the bench, followed by Luke and Sue Ellen.

"Sue Ellen, are you lost? We don't have a criminal docket this morning."

Sue Ellen gave the judge her warmest smile and replied, "Judge, you know I don't ever get lost in this courthouse. I've taken a leave of absence from John's office for a couple of months. I'm associated with Mr. Vaughan on this case."

"Morning, Luke. Well, you must be Ms. Metcalf."

"Good morning, Judge. Audrey Katherine Metcalf, Michael Forsythe, and David St. James for Ceventa."

"Welcome, Ms. Metcalf. I hope we can get off to a better start than the last time we talked. By the way, you'll notice that Mr. Lorance is not here. He called Susie and said that since he didn't have a dog in this fight, he wouldn't make the drive from Austin. I've read the motions and your responses to discovery, Ms. Metcalf."

"If I may, Judge Nimitz," Metcalf interrupted, "I'd like to be heard."

Nimitz put up his hand like a cop stopping traffic. "Not yet, Ms. Metcalf. You and I need to get something straight. You objected to every single one of Mr. Vaughan's interrogatories and requests, and on top of that you waited the full thirty days to do so. I know what you're doing, Ms. Metcalf. I see it from you big-firm lawyers from all over the state. Your clients pay you to fight about everything, nitpick about every word, stall, delay, you name it. I've seen it all, and I don't like it one damn bit. You waited until the last day to file Ceventa's answer and waited the full thirty days to object to Mr. Vaughan's discovery. All of these damn objections were already in your computer. You could have just clicked a couple of times and sent them out."

"Judge—"

"I'm not finished, Ms. Metcalf. All of your objections are denied. There might even be a few in there that I might have granted if you had acted professionally, but you didn't. And we're not about to delay the trial. You've got five days to fully respond to this discovery. You can redact names and personal information about the patients, nothing more. Is that clear?"

Metcalf had to bite her tongue to control her temper at the judicial ass-chewing, but she did so. No one noticed when she slipped her hand into her jacket pocket and retrieved a pink jelly bean before she spoke. "Yes, Judge Nimitz, it's perfectly clear. We'll have complete answers by next Monday."

"No, Ms. Metcalf. That's seven days. I didn't say five business days. In fact, you have those answers in Mr. Vaughan's hands by this Friday. Now, about this deposition of Dr. Kingsbury. Mr. Vaughan, why do you need his deposition?"

"I'd like to answer that, Judge," Sue Ellen said. "He's the CEO of the defendant. He knows more about the company than anyone else. He's a scientist himself who undoubtedly had to give final approval to the submission of Exxacia to the FDA as a new drug. We can cover more bases with him in one day than we can in two weeks if we have to depose all of his managers. And remember, Judge Nimitz, Ceventa's already wasted about six weeks of our ninety days."

Judge Nimitz turned to Audrey Metcalf. "Now you may say something, Ms. Metcalf."

"Thank you, Judge. First, let me hand you a brief we've prepared on this issue." Forsythe passed a fifty-page brief up to the judge. "Judge, this is an attempt at an apex deposition. Over twenty years ago some enterprising plaintiff lawyer sued Walmart and wanted to depose Sam Walton. He even offered to go to Arkansas to do it. Walmart objected on the basis that Mr. Walton could hardly be expected to run his company if he had to sit for a deposition every time somebody slipped and fell in one of their stores. Our Supreme Court agreed and quashed the deposition. The situation is no different here. Dr. Kingsbury's knowledge about Exxacia and the clinical trial can only be secondhand. Certainly he didn't have any hands-on involvement in the drug. Let us respond to their discovery, and they can pick someone else to get the information from."

Judge Nimitz leaned back in his chair, put his hands behind his head, and gazed up at the ceiling, saying nothing. Finally he leaned forward and folded his hands on the bench. "Ms. Metcalf. I'm going to grant your motion to quash at this time. If some of the other documents or witnesses show that Dr. Kingsbury has more than passing knowledge about this Exxacia drug, I'll invite Mr. Vaughan to ask me to revisit the subject."

Audrey Metcalf twirled on her heel and started to walk away.

"Just a minute, Ms. Metcalf. You heard what I said about your stalling tactics. I'll consider sanctions if that happens again. Understood?"

"Yes, sir, it is. May we be excused?"

"You may. Luke, you and Sue Ellen have a good day. By the way, Luke, the district attorney will be mighty upset if you steal Sue Ellen on a permanent basis."

"I know, Judge," Luke replied. "I had to promise him it was only temporary."

64

Dr. Hartman came down the stairs from his twice-weekly visit with Samantha and found Luke in his office.

"How's she doing, Clyde?"

Dr. Hartman shook his head. "Not very good, Luke. The blood I had Mary draw yesterday shows her liver function still dropping. Now, we really need to put her in the hospital where she can be monitored twenty-four hours a day."

Luke slowly turned his head from side to side, not rejecting the idea but responding to the gravity of the situation. "Have you talked to Sam about this?"

"Not yet. I wanted to talk to you first."

Luke came from behind his desk. "Let's go talk to her."

They found Samantha asleep with Cocoa in her now almost constant position, lying beside Samantha, maintaining a vigil over her mistress.

"Sam," Luke said quietly.

Samantha opened her eyes. "Hi, Dad. What's Dr. Hartman doing back here? I thought he left."

Luke sat on the bed and stroked Sam's red hair. "Sam, Dr. Hartman thinks it would be better for you to go to the hospital now, where they have nurses who can check on you more often."

Samantha pushed herself up to a sitting position. "No, Dad. I won't go. I want to stay here with you. I'm helping with the lawsuit. That's what's keeping me going. I can't do that from the hospital." Samantha took a bottle of Gatorade from her nightstand and downed nearly half of it. "See, I'll do my part here." She paused and looked out the front window before turning to her dad and Dr. Hartman. "Besides, if I'm going to die, I want to be here with you and Cocoa."

Luke coughed to get his voice under control. "Clyde, what about this? We'll get Sam a hospital bed and set it up downstairs. I'll have Mary move in and live in Sam's room. She can take care of Sam when I'm not here."

Dr. Hartman thought about the option and then nodded his head. "I suppose we can give it a try. I'd rather have her in the hospital. Still, if Sam won't go, that'll have to do. I'll just plan to drop by here most evenings on the way home."

Sam nodded her agreement and lay back down with one arm draped over Cocoa.

65

"Okay, Sam, I'm going to get on one side of you with Whiz on the other. Hold on to our arms and we'll walk you slowly down the stairs."

When they got to the bottom, Luke explained what he and Whiz had done. "We cleaned out the reception room where you worked. That furniture is now stacked out in the garage. They just brought your bed and got it set up in here. I've arranged it so that you have a view out to the front street when the curtains are open. Your pictures are still on the wall."

Samantha sat on the edge of the bed and looked around. Her eyes drifted to a wheelchair in the corner. "I suppose I'm going to have to use that, huh?"

"Dr. Hartman said it would be better to save your strength," Luke replied.

"Dad, where am I on that liver transplant list? Do I have a chance?"

"Yeah, baby, you do. Right now the problem is that you have a rare blood type and it's harder to find a match." Luke avoided mentioning that there was a major problem with money.

Then there was a knock at the door. All three looked to the street and saw a FedEx truck.

Luke opened the door to be greeted by a friendly delivery man wearing a FedEx shirt and shorts. Luke knew him from other deliveries over the years. "Howdy, Luke. How's Sam doing?"

"As well as could be expected, Clarence. What do you have for me?"

"Package from Dallas. Looks like computer discs." Clarence handed Luke a clipboard, and Luke signed the receipt. "You tell Sam to take care of herself."

Luke returned to the house and retrieved a pocketknife from his desk to open the package. Inside he found eight discs. "What do you make of these, Whiz?"

Whiz looked at them. "Looks like a ton of data to me. Remember them saying it would take a truck to bring the study? Looks like they did decide to deliver by truck, only in a different form. Here, let me get on your computer."

"Dad," Samantha hollered from across the hall. "Come help me get in the wheelchair. I want to see, too."

Luke went across the hall, helped Samantha to the wheelchair, and returned with her to find Whiz rummaging through the first disc. "I found answers to your interrogatories. I'm printing them now. If we print the rest of this stuff, it'll fill your office and probably the hallway with paper."

Luke walked over to the printer to retrieve the interrogatory answers. "What do you suggest?"

"Here's what we're going to do. Let's burn another copy of these discs for me to take back to my apartment. Then you sit down and come up with some key words and phrases. I'll design a program to search the data. We may have to refine it as we go along, but I guarantee it'll be better than the old-fashioned way. I'll probably call Brad to come over to help."

Samantha's eyes lit up at the mention of Brad's name.

"How long, Whiz?"

"I may have to stay up all night, but I'll have it for you in the morning. Then we'll set up my computer along with Sam's, Brad's, and Sue Ellen's in the conference room, and we'll start downloading and printing."

Luke nodded his agreement with the plan and turned to call Sue Ellen to join them at eight in the morning.

"Whiz," Samantha said, "ask Brad to come by to say hello before you two settle down to work."

"You got it, sweetie. Now I'll bet it's about time for you to take a nap. I'm out of here, Luke."

By the time Luke had gotten Samantha into her bed, Sue Ellen was coming through the front door. "What have we got?"

Luke explained what they had received and what Whizmo intended to do. "I've printed off two sets of their answers to interrogatories. Let's go out on the porch and study what they've given us."

Luke went to the downstairs kitchen and returned with two glasses of iced tea and found Sue Ellen on the front porch already looking through the answers. He took another rocker and said, "By the way, I may have failed to mention it, but I just responded to their discovery. It was pretty standard stuff. Schools, doctors, hospital visits, etc. They'll learn about her DUI conviction and her flunking out of A&M."

"Not really a big deal in my opinion, when she's dying because of what they did to her. Looks like our friend from Dallas did what the judge told her. These answers look pretty complete to me."

Luke took a sip of his tea before he spoke. "Yeah, I think she knew she was on thin ice with Judge Nimitz. He would have sanctioned her if she pulled any more of that crap."

"So now what do we do with this information?"

"We don't have a lot of time. I'm still pissed that Nimitz wouldn't let us depose Kingsbury. He's out of subpoena range for trial, so I suppose we just have to scratch him as a possible witness. Let's try to pick out the one person who can provide the most information."

"Agreed. Then why don't we forget about Ceventa employees and look for someone from the FDA who was involved in the process? Maybe he or she'll be a little more honest about the trial."

"Excellent idea," Luke replied as he ran his finger down a list of names and titles. His finger went right by Ryan Sinclair, who would have been eager to come clean about what happened, and settled on Roger Boatwright. "Here's our guy. Roger Boatwright is the director of CDER, the division that oversaw the clinical trial. Let's go after him."

"Sounds good to me. He ought to know as much as anyone in the agency." Luke and Sue Ellen clicked their glasses in agreement, and the conversation turned to Samantha.

The notice to take the deposition of Roger Boatwright in Maryland went out on Friday.

66

Luke was up with the sun on Saturday. He wanted to go for a run, but had given it up because he thought it would not be fair to Samantha for him to run when she couldn't. He showered, shaved, and put on a pair of jeans and a blue golf shirt, then stepped out into the living area. He found Mary Sanchez seated in the dining area, reading the *Daily Record*.

"Morning, Mary. How's Sam?"

"About the same, Mr. Vaughan. I got her up to go to the bathroom. Then she insisted on putting on makeup because she thinks that Brad may be here today. That wore her out, and I put her back to bed. She was watching television when I came back up here."

Luke walked quietly down the stairs so as not to disturb Samantha if she was sleeping. He peeked around the corner to find her staring at him.

"Dad, you don't have to tiptoe. When I'm sleeping, I'm out of it. I doubt that a firecracker in the street would bother me."

Luke walked over and kissed her on the forehead. "You're looking good this morning. Already got your makeup on."

Samantha clicked off the television. "Well, I hear we're going to have a houseful of people. So I wanted to look my best. I've even changed into sweatpants and a T-shirt." She glanced out the window.

"Oh, there's Brad's pickup. You sure I'm looking all right? Help me get into my wheelchair."

Luke did as he was told, and Samantha was waiting beside her bed for Brad when he knocked on the front door. Luke let him in and led him into Sam's room.

"Hi, Sam. Looks to me like you're making some progress. Nice looking shirt."

Samantha managed a slight smile. "Shirt's okay. Can't say the same for this wheelchair."

Luke excused himself, saying that Brad could bring Sam up to date on what was happening on campus and with their friends. Within half an hour Whizmo and Sue Ellen arrived. Whizmo had a smile on his face. "We're good to go. Everyone fire up their computers. Sam, you can help Brad."

Samantha shook her head. "Nope, I'm still a part of this team. I'll work on my own computer until I need to take a break."

"Okay, then everyone to the conference table. I've got a program on a disc for each of you. Load it onto your computers. When you're ready, I'll give each of you a disc from Ceventa with some of their data."

Luke gave a list to each member of the team, outlining what they would be looking for. Sue Ellen passed out yellow legal pads and pens to make notes "the old-fashioned way," as she put it. Silence prevailed as they pulled data from the Ceventa discs and made notes. At one time Luke said, "I can't believe this crap."

Later Sue Ellen said, "Do they think they're dealing with fools?"

Whiz merely shook his head from time to time and let out a low whistle.

After two hours Sam retired to her room for a nap. Another hour went by, and Sue Ellen went upstairs to make sandwiches. When she announced that lunch was ready, Luke, Whizmo, and Brad joined her on the second floor. Between bites they discussed what they were finding.

"To start," Brad said, "I'm finding a bunch of sites that are completely missing, gone, vanished. Not hard to figure out. The sites are numbered and my disc starts with 102 and goes through 198. I'm missing six."

"I've got the same thing," Luke replied. "I must have the first disc since mine has sites from 001 to 101. Eight of my sites have disappeared."

"I'm missing twelve," Sue Ellen said as she sipped a Coke.

"Then I must win the prize," Whizmo said. "There are twenty-two missing from my group."

"Correct me if I'm wrong, Professor Whizmo," Luke said with astonishment showing in his face, "but that's forty-eight sites gone up in smoke."

"You'd make a good math teacher, Luke, and that doesn't count what Sam might have found. Here's another statistic that I did while I was working on this last night. There are twenty-one thousand four hundred and fifty-three subjects in the trial. Ceventa reported twenty-five thousand. I think we know what happened to those missing patients. We just don't know why."

"Next on the list is vital signs," Luke said. "What are we finding there?"

"I'll go first again," Brad replied. "I haven't counted them yet, but I'm finding some patients with the same vital signs on every visit at some sites, and at some of those sites several of the patients all have identical vital signs."

"Same here," Sue Ellen replied as Whizmo nodded with her.

"Dammit! It's impossible for one patient to show up two days in a row and have exactly the same temperature, blood pressure, pulse, and oxygen saturation. Hell, usually if a physician takes a patient's blood pressure twice in fifteen minutes it won't be the same."

"Luke, we're making progress here. We can spend the rest of the week pulling up these statistics. Trouble is I can't come up with a program that will identify forged signatures, initials, and so forth. So while you're in Maryland, we're going to have to take a look at every one of these charts and hunt for problems."

67

———————————

"Michael, find David, and both of you get in here in five minutes!" Audrey Metcalf demanded and then slammed the phone down.

"Morning, boss," the two younger lawyers said, almost in unison, when they appeared in answer to her summons. Michael took a handful of pink jelly beans from the jar on the front of the desk.

"Sit down," Metcalf ordered as she plopped down in her executive chair. "By the way; don't forget to pay for those on the way out. Now, we've got a problem to deal with in the Vaughan case."

Both men focused their attention on her, with pens poised to write on yellow legal pads.

"The plaintiffs have issued a notice to take the deposition of Roger Boatwright at the FDA next week, and they're subpoenaing the entire FDA file on the clinical trial."

"That's preposterous!" David St. James exclaimed.

"I'll get right to work on a motion to quash it," Michael Forsythe added. We can't let that file see the light of day."

"Forget it, guys. Nimitz isn't going to quash anything. I'll have Kingsbury deal with Boatwright and the FDA documents. I want you to get to Silver Spring and start preparing Boatwright. No, on second thought, I don't want him to have to testify that he met with us to prepare for his deposition. I want him to appear to be the objective government servant. Call the FDA in-house lawyers and work through them. I'll call Kingsbury to get their cooperation. Michael, you come up with questions that Luke Vaughan will ask and figure out the best possible answers. David, you're to work with the FDA lawyers. They can spoon-feed the questions and answers to Boatwright. No one will ever know that we were the ones that prepared him for deposition. Call me if you run into a problem."

In the Ceventa penthouse Kingsbury picked up a private line and called Boatwright's cell phone. "Roger, can you talk?"

"Just a minute. Let me shut the door." Kingsbury heard the sound of footsteps and the door closing. "Now it's okay."

"Roger, when Vaughan takes your deposition, he wants you to bring discs with the entire clinical trial on them. You and I both know that there are certain parts of that file that we can't let him have. It would be bad enough for the lawsuit, but if word leaked out on the Hill, you and I both would be subpoenaed to the Senate oversight committee. You know what to do, don't you?"

Boatwright hesitated and then said, "What's the status of my five million dollars? Joanne's deteriorating daily. Now you're asking me to lie under oath."

Kingsbury knew he had to keep Boatwright under control. "I'm sorry about Joanne. I really am. Understand me. It's not easy just to juggle the books and send five million overseas without it getting some attention. I've got a few hundred thousand being wired today. More shortly. It'll take a little while."

"We may not have a little while," Boatwright replied, his voice quivering.

68

Luke entered the CDER headquarters at nine forty-five for the ten o'clock deposition and announced himself to a guard behind the desk. He took a seat and stared at the clock above the elevator. At ten he watched the elevator bank, but no one exited to approach him. He picked up a copy of the *Washington Post* that a previous visitor had left behind and thumbed through the paper, his mind not really focused on what he was seeing. At ten fifteen he looked at his watch. At ten thirty he was ready to leave and fly back to San Marcos, where he would move for sanctions against Boatwright for failing to honor a subpoena. Then the elevator opened, and Michael Forsythe stepped out.

"Sorry to keep you waiting, Mr. Vaughan. Mr. Boatwright had some problem with his car this morning and just now got here. We met him for the first time five minutes ago." Forsythe smiled, trying to convey the message that they certainly had not worked with this witness to prepare him for his deposition.

The elevator stopped on the sixth floor, where Forsythe led Luke to a small, windowless conference room already filled to capacity with the court reporter, a videographer, Audrey Metcalf, David St. James, two legal assistants, and, of course, Roger Boatwright. Someone had turned the thermostat up to eighty-five. Luke sized up the situation and understood the game they were playing. Fine with him. He intended to be gone before he broke a sweat. Two chairs remained, one for Luke and one for Forsythe. The videographer was set up along the back wall with a camera pointed at Boatwright. Metcalf remained in her seat and said icily, "This is Dr. Boatwright. You may begin when you choose." Then she returned to doodling on her yellow pad.

Luke took his seat and nodded at the court reporter, who administered the oath. Metcalf noticed that Luke had nothing in front of him, no notes, no legal pad, not even a pen.

"You're Roger Boatwright."

"I am."

"You're the director of the Center for Drug Evaluation and Research."

"Yes, sir," Boatwright responded as beads of sweat broke out on his forehead even before there were any hard questions.

"Who have you talked to in preparation for this deposition?"

"Only the in-house lawyers for the FDA."

"You were served with a subpoena to produce the entire Exxacia clinical trial maintained by the FDA. Have you complied?"

Boatwright broke out in a fit of coughing, got control of his voice, and pushed a box of discs toward Luke. "Here's the complete clinical trial."

"And you swear under penalty of perjury that there is nothing more, that this is complete, and by that I mean every scrap of paper, e-mails, memos, and patient charts, kept here at the FDA on Exxacia?"

Boatwright squirmed in his seat and finally said, "Yes, sir. I swear."

"Madam Court Reporter, please mark these as Boatwright deposition exhibit one for the record," Luke said, then turned his attention back to Boatwright. "As head of the division that is responsible for clinical trials, do you permit your clinical investigators to forge the signatures of patients?"

"Of course not," Boatwright replied with poorly contrived astonishment.

"Do you allow your investigators to alter vital signs on patient charts?"

"Preposterous, Mr. Vaughan."

"Do you know what blood splitting is, Dr. Boatwright?"

Boatwright reached into his back pocket and pulled out a handkerchief, which he used to wipe the sweat from his forehead. "Perhaps you should explain, Mr. Vaughan."

"Blood splitting, Dr. Boatwright. Taking blood from one patient and using it to perform lab work for a number of other patients. Do you permit that in your clinical trials?"

"Absolutely not, Mr. Vaughan."

"How about editing of patient charts after the study is over?"

"Ridiculous, sir!"

Metcalf had quit her doodling and now was paying attention. A frown briefly crossed her face. *Is he just fishing?* she thought. *Or does he know more than we think?*

Luke stood at his place and placed his hands on the table, leaning into the witness. "You would agree, wouldn't you, Dr. Boatwright, that those kinds of practices would call into question the integrity of the whole clinical trial, right, Doctor?"

"Sir, we oversee our trials to ensure that those kinds of events never occur."

"Answer my question, Dr. Boatwright."

Boatwright looked at Metcalf, who had returned to her doodling, her poker face back in place.

"You're correct, Mr. Vaughan."

Luke switched gears. "Have you or any of your staff, to your knowledge, had any contact with Ceventa employees outside of work being done for the FDA?"

Boatwright tried to sidestep the question. "Well, I, I'm not sure what you mean."

"Not a very complicated question, Dr. Boatwright," Luke pressed. "You know, golf, dinner, travel, entertainment, off-the-record discussions about Exxacia behind closed doors, that kind of thing?"

Boatwright knew he had to lie again, but he figured a small-town lawyer like Vaughan would never catch him at it. Besides, he'd made a deal with the devil and could hardly back out. He straightened his posture, looked directly into the camera, and replied, "Of course not, Mr. Vaughan. I would never do such a thing and would fire any of my employees who did."

Luke hesitated as if he didn't know quite what to ask next. "By the way, how well do you know Dr. Alfred Kingsbury?"

"Certainly I've seen him, but always in a strictly professional capacity."

"You swear that there has been nothing improper about your contacts with Dr. Kingsbury, no lavish dinners, golf outings, corporate junkets, that kind of thing?"

"Absolutely, Mr. Vaughan, absolutely."

Luke put his hands in his pockets and stared at the ceiling. "One last question, Dr. Boatwright. You require drug sponsors like Ceventa to preserve all the data on every one of the clinical investigation sites, don't you?"

"Certainly, Mr. Vaughan."

"That's all, Dr. Boatwright. I'm out of here. I've got a plane to catch."

Luke turned and left a room full of surprised people who were expecting the questioning to go into the night.

The deposition of Roger Boatwright was supposed to be kept quiet, but such an event circulated on the CDER grapevine faster than an e-mail "reply to all." Nearly everyone in the building knew the date and even the time of the deposition. At the end of the day Ryan Sinclair stationed himself on the first floor and waited for Boatwright to step from an elevator, then followed him outside.

"Hey there, Dr. Boatwright, hold up for a minute," Ryan called as Boatwright circled the fountain between the building and the garage. Boatwright looked back, saw Sinclair, and quickened his pace.

Ryan caught up with Boatwright and grabbed his arm, forcing him to stop.

"Dr. Sinclair, please remove your hand from my arm. I'm late for an appointment."

"This won't take long. Just a question. I know you were required to bring all the Exxacia clinical trial data to your deposition today. I just want to know if you included the memos and e-mails from me and my team or not."

Boatwright started to walk away again.

"Simple question, Dr. Boatwright. Did you or didn't you?"

"That's none of your business, Dr. Sinclair," Boatwright said. "Now please get out of my way!"

"Look, Boatwright, I'm really pissed about how this whole Exxacia affair has come down. Let me make myself clear. I have a complete copy of the clinical trial on discs locked up at my house. If it comes out that you've provided something different, I'm going to be the first to accuse you of perjury, clear, Dr. Boatwright?"

Boatwright, trying to feign outrage to hide the fear that was inside, turned and marched to the garage. Once in his car, he called Kingsbury's cell phone and reported what had just occurred.

The Southwest Airlines plane carrying Luke landed at Austin's Bergstrom Airport at six in the evening. When he got in his Sequoia, he called home, and Mary answered, saying Samantha had already gone to bed. He was going to stop by Sue Ellen's house before he got home, he told Mary; he wanted to discuss the deposition with her and talk about where they should go from here with their lawsuit. As he made the forty-five-minute drive to San Marcos, he worried about his daughter. By now she was sleeping twelve to fourteen hours at night with a three-hour nap in the afternoon. Would she make it until the trial was over? Was all of this effort to bring down a giant pharmaceutical company going to accomplish anything? Was it merely a pipe dream that he might somehow get some money out of Ceventa in time to get Samantha a new liver? Then he thought that he had no other choice. The trial was now only a few weeks away. He prayed that Samantha would hang on and somehow a miracle would occur.

Sue Ellen met him at the door with a glass of wine. Josh was watching a baseball game on television in the living room, so they sat at the kitchen table, where Luke described the day's events.

"I'll bet they were surprised when you finished the deposition in twenty minutes," Sue Ellen said.

Luke shrugged his shoulders. "I got what I came for. Sometimes the best depositions are the shortest ones."

Sue Ellen nodded her agreement as she rummaged around the kitchen and retrieved a brick of cheddar cheese and some crackers. "Now, let me tell you what we found while you were gone. First, most of the investigators did their jobs. Still, even setting aside the sites we're missing, the only way to describe this study is shitty." She handed Luke a manila folder containing several pages of computer notes. "Here, Whizmo prepared this summary. It's all tied back into the database. Where do we go from here?"

Luke finished chewing his crackers and cheese and took a sip of wine before he spoke. "I was thinking about that on the way back from Maryland. Of course, we file a motion to compel the production of the charts and data from the fifty or so sites we're missing. Then we include a motion to sanction Ceventa for hiding the data. I doubt if the judge will fine them enough to make a big company wince."

"Yeah, Luke, you're right. Chuck's pretty conservative about things like that. Still, if we can catch them in more violations on down the line, the dollars will get bigger. I'll draft the motion and have it ready for you by tomorrow afternoon. We can probably get a hearing early next week."

69

The next day Ryan Sinclair got on the Internet and learned the name of the case and of the plaintiff lawyer. Armed with that information, he called the district clerk in San Marcos and was given Luke Vaughan's phone number. That night he dialed it.

The first time Luke's office number rang, at eight o'clock in the evening, he ignored it. Also the second time. When it rang again, he picked up the phone. "Vaughan here. Office is closed. Please call back during business hours."

"Wait, Mr. Vaughan. Don't hang up. This is Dr. Ryan Sinclair. You don't know me, but I work for the FDA and was involved in the Exxacia new drug application."

Luke settled into his office chair. "Sorry, Dr. Sinclair. Why are you calling me?"

"Please call me Ryan. I'm calling about the deposition you took of Roger Boatwright yesterday."

"Yes," Luke responded, reluctant to say more until he saw where this conversation was going.

"Luke, you need to know there's more than one version of the Exxacia clinical trial. I don't know what Boatwright gave you. When you have a chance to review it, please contact me at my home or on my cell. There's something strange going on at CDER about this drug. I don't know if there's a cover-up or not. If there is a cover-up, I don't know whether it's coming from Ceventa or if someone in my office is somehow involved, or both."

Luke processed what he heard and asked, "How do I know that I can trust you?"

Ryan paused, then responded, "Go to the Rockville newspaper and search for my name. You'll find a small story. Someone bombed my car while it was in my driveway. Trust me. I'm on your side."

Ryan had just placed the phone in its cradle when he heard the sound of breaking glass. *Jeez,* he thought, *another rock and a note.* He walked from the den into the living room to pick up the rock—and even though he had never seen a bomb other than in the movies, he knew he was in trouble. He turned and ran back to the den, diving through a window just as the bomb exploded. The concussion knocked him twenty feet. He was just returning to consciousness when the fire department arrived. As he staggered to his feet, an EMT grabbed him under the arms and pulled him away from the house.

"Anybody else in there?"

Ryan shook his head. "No, just me. My wife's safe."

The EMT examined Ryan and sat him against an oak tree, where he watched as the firefighters battled the blaze. The EMT tried repeatedly to get him to go to the hospital to be checked out. Ryan refused, saying he was a doctor and was doing just fine. Within a half hour the fire captain in charge hollered, "Forget the primary house. Protect the adjoining properties. This one's gone."

Ryan buried his face in his hands, thankful that Sara was safe. Then he thought, *Is she safe?* He borrowed a cell phone from one of the neighbors who had congregated on the street and called her. Relieved to hear her voice, he told her what had happened. Sara wanted to join him, and he insisted that she stay where she was. He would catch a ride over to his parents' house.

After a neighbor dropped him at the house his mother and father had occupied for twenty-five years, he made his way up the sidewalk. Before he could reach for the doorknob, the door opened and Sara pulled him into a hug. His dad stood beside her.

"Ryan, come into the living room. Let me look you over," Maxwell insisted.

"Dad, I'm fine. A little shaken up, but no broken bones and only a slight concussion."

While Ryan explained what had happened, his mother brought a tray with four steaming cups of coffee.

"Mother," his father said, "get that bottle of brandy and put a shot in Ryan's. One for me, too, for that matter. Ceventa behind this, Ryan?"

"Dad, I have no idea. First my car and now my house. I was talking to that lawyer that's suing Ceventa in Texas. Maybe my phone was tapped. No, that couldn't be it. The bomb came through the window within a minute after I ended that call. Wait, wait just a minute. I told Boatwright yesterday that I had a copy of the Exxacia trial at home. Boatwright must have told someone at Ceventa. I don't know, Dad. I'm exhausted. Let's go to bed, and I'll try to sort this out tomorrow."

"Not just yet, Ryan," Sara interrupted. "Look at me. I'm five months pregnant. Now I'm really worried that our son may never know his father. You need to quit the FDA tomorrow! Please!"

Ryan nodded his understanding. "Sara, believe me, I'm worried. That's why you've been staying over here. I can't forget what I know, only now the evidence to back up my word is destroyed. Whether I'm working for the FDA is immaterial at this point, but I'm not ready to leave the FDA to Boatwright." Then he paused as he thought through the idea that just hit him. "Dad, give me Kingsbury's home number."

While his family watched, Ryan punched in the digits.

"Maxwell, to what do I owe the honor of this call? You up for golf on Saturday?"

"Kingsbury, this is Ryan Sinclair. My house was just burned to the ground and, you lowlife bastard, I know you did it."

"Ryan, I'm so sorry. Are you and Sara all right?" Kingsbury replied in a calm and modulated voice.

"Cut the crap, Kingsbury. I'd like to see you behind bars. Instead, you've got what you want. I'm now officially out of the loop on Exxacia. You and I both know that your drug is killing people, but I'm not going to risk the lives of my family to prove it. I'll stay out of the way on Exxacia, and you leave my family alone. Deal?"

"Ryan, I don't know what you're talking about, but you can rest assured that I'll do nothing to harm you or your family. Good night, Ryan." As Kingsbury hung up, a smile was on his face.

70

Once again the courtroom was filled with lawyers, and this time there were several reporters from Austin and San Antonio newspapers and radio and television stations. Human interest attracted the media like flies to honey. Now everyone wanted to know about the dying girl fighting a pharmaceutical giant. Everyone rose as Judge Nimitz took the bench. He looked over the crowd in his courtroom and realized that the media was in attendance. "Before I call the rest of my docket, Mr. Vaughan and Ms. Metcalf, your case will be last. Judging from the other matters before you, it'll probably be about ten thirty before I'll hear your motion, Mr. Vaughan. You can be excused until then."

Luke and Audrey Metcalf rose and turned toward the door, but Judge Nimitz stopped them. "Ms. Metcalf, I notice you're always wearing a pink ribbon in your lapel. Is there something special about it?"

"Yes, Judge, there is." Audrey smiled, pleased to have something to discuss with the judge other than discovery motions. "I'm a breast cancer survivor and on the board of directors of the Susan G. Komen breast cancer foundation. That ribbon is my reminder that we haven't cured breast cancer yet. If I may, Mr. Vaughan, I'd like to give the judge and you a small bag of pink jelly beans, another reminder." Metcalf reached into her purse and handed one to Vaughan, then walked to the bench to hand one to the judge.

Judge Nimitz nodded his appreciation. "I'm sure that Luke won't report you for bribing a judge with jelly beans, and I admire your efforts. My wife is also a breast cancer survivor. I'll give these to her. Now you're excused."

At once the reporters rose and went into the hallway. They clamored for interviews with Luke as he and Sue Ellen walked by. Luke wasn't accustomed to trying his cases in the media and shook his head at each reporter. Once she and Luke were in her office, Sue Ellen shut the door behind them.

"That was some stunt that Metcalf pulled with those jelly beans," Luke fumed as he tossed his into the trash.

"Drop it, Luke," Sue Ellen cautioned. "Along with Judge Nimitz, every woman in the courtroom admires her efforts, and I know Chuck's wife. She had a tough time. I want to talk about something else. Ceventa is blasting us with commercials about the wonders of Exxacia. We need to put a face on this case that our potential jurors will remember when they're called in a few weeks. The judge hasn't entered a gag order. Let's go out on the courthouse steps and answer some questions."

Luke stared at Sue Ellen while he thought about her proposal. "I've never tried my cases to anyone but the judge and jury before." Then he smiled. "I guess there's always a first time. Let's go."

They stepped out the door to find the reporters still roaming the hall. Once the reporters saw Luke, they followed him out into the sunlight, where he stood on the steps with the courthouse behind him. The reporters stuck microphones and recorders into his face. Cameramen quickly adjusted their equipment. Sue Ellen stood off to the side.

"Ladies and gentlemen, I've decided to make a brief statement, and then I'll answer questions. Let me start by telling you there will be no interviews with Samantha. She's too sick. I took on this lawsuit for her, but there's also a higher purpose. I'm convinced that my daughter is dying because she took a drug manufactured and marketed by Ceventa. I expect to prove that and use this lawsuit to force Ceventa to take Exxacia off the market so this won't happen again. Today, we are here because Ceventa refused to honor Judge Nimitz's order to give us all of the documents related to the study that led to the FDA approving the drug. Once we get the rest of the study, we'll be ready to go to trial in a few weeks."

"Mr. Vaughan, Mr. Vaughan," a young woman asked, "can you tell us more about how Samantha is doing?"

Luke looked into the cameras. "She has good days and bad days, but no days like you and I have. On her good days she can get on her computer for a few hours or watch television. Sometimes I wheel her out on the porch, where she and Cocoa watch the birds and squirrels."

"Cocoa?"

"Oh, that's our dog. Cocoa stays with her constantly."

An older male reporter pushed his way to the front. "Will she testify at trial?"

"I really don't know. The way her health is deteriorating, I doubt it."

A reporter with a KLBJ logo on his shirt, obviously from the Austin radio station originally owned by former president Lyndon Johnson, raised his hand. "How can you be so sure that Samantha's liver damage was caused by Exxacia? Ceventa's answer to the lawsuit says it wasn't."

A frown crossed Luke's face. "That's the company line. I can tell you that I will produce evidence that will convince not only twelve jurors we're right, but even you cynical media types. Now, if you'll excuse me, I've got to get back to the courtroom."

Luke turned to walk back into the courthouse. Sue Ellen whispered that he had done just what they needed. When they got into Judge Nimitz's courtroom, there were two other lawyers arguing at the bench.

Audrey Metcalf, along with three associates and two paralegals, was at one counsel table. Luke and Sue Ellen took seats at the other. The reporters noisily followed behind them, talking among themselves as they found seats.

"Let's have order in this court," Simon Rothschild, the bailiff, commanded as he stared at the reporters until they all were quiet.

The other lawyers finished their hearing, and Judge Nimitz looked first at Luke and then at Audrey Metcalf. "You guys ready? If so, come on up. Ms. Metcalf, I only want you up here at the bench. The rest of your posse can keep their seats."

Judge Nimitz smiled at Luke, and his face turned somber as he looked at Audrey Metcalf. "Ms. Metcalf, I've read Mr. Vaughan's motion. He's attached an affidavit from Professor Wilson Moore over at the university. I know Professor Whizmo and have no doubt that if he swears to something, it's true. Are there some records that your client has been holding back?"

Metcalf spoke in a loud voice to emphasize her conviction. "Absolutely not, Judge Nimitz. We turned over all we could find. We even put them on discs to accommodate Mr. Vaughan."

As was his custom when he wanted to intimidate a lawyer or witness, Judge Nimitz leaned over his bench, getting his face as close to Metcalf's as possible. "Then, pray tell, what happened to the data from all these missing sites?"

"Judge, I can explain," Metcalf responded as a little nervousness appeared in her usually calm voice. "We're talking about tens of thousands of documents. After the motion was filed, we went back and did another search. There were some sites missing, and we're prepared to provide the information on them. In fact, I have another disc with me that I am handing to Mr. Vaughan. I apologize for creating the problem."

"Ms. Metcalf," Judge Nimitz said as his voice rose an octave, "do you understand that we're going to trial in four weeks and you are just now turning over critical information? I've read Dr. Boatwright's deposition, and he swears that Ceventa was required to preserve the entire study. Mr. Vaughan has also asked me to sanction your client for violating my orders. Here's what I'm going to do. I'm going to carry that motion along with the case. Tell your client that if I learn of any more conduct like this, I'll evaluate all of it at the conclusion of the case. That's all."

"Judge," Audrey Metcalf said, "there's one more thing."

"Ms. Metcalf, I don't have anything else on my docket on your case this morning."

"Judge, it just came up this morning. May I be heard?"

"Okay, make it brief. I have a tee time in an hour."

Metcalf turned to Luke. "Judge, this lawyer is attempting to try his case in the media. Just this morning he had a press conference out on the courthouse steps. I move that the court enter an order forbidding any lawyer or party from talking about this case to any member of the media."

"That true, Luke?"

"Yes, sir. It certainly is. I figured it's a free country and the media needs to know what's going on."

Judge Nimitz looked from lawyer to lawyer and then out to the reporters in the audience. "Motion denied."

A commotion broke out among the reporters, and the bailiff rose to bring order.

"That's okay, Simon. I can handle this. Ms. Metcalf, I've never looked up the net worth of your client on the Internet, but, like everyone else around here, I can't turn on my television without seeing a commercial for Exxacia. I think Mr. Vaughan is entitled to level the playing field. So, unless your client is willing to drop all of its ads, here and nationally, about Exxacia until our trial is over, Mr. Vaughan can talk to the media anytime, anyplace." Judge Nimitz then turned his attention to the audience. "As to you folks, you've heard my order. You're welcome in my courtroom, but my rules apply to you, too. If you disrupt my proceedings, you can forget about freedom of the press. You'll be out on the street. Is that understood?"

The reporters nodded in unison as the KLBJ reporter got to his feet. "Judge Nimitz, on behalf of my colleagues, we sincerely apologize. It won't happen again."

Judge Nimitz nodded his understanding as he spoke. "Don't any of you guys report that I'm sneaking out for a round of golf, either. Too nice a day to spend indoors. In fact, if any of you have your clubs with you, I'll get you on my course as my guest."

71

Whizmo came through the back door, computer in hand, and found the others in the conference room. "Okay, what have we got?"

Luke looked up from his computer. "Mainly more damn good stuff for us."

"All of these sites that they held back have more problems with fraud and forgery than any of the sites they first gave us," Sue Ellen added.

"Yeah, it's clear why they tried to deep-six this information. We've now accounted for right at twenty-five thousand patient-subjects," Luke said. "There's one major problem, though."

"What's that?" Whizmo asked as he plugged in his computer.

"They now have turned over Ceverta's copy of the consent form that Sam signed."

"It's my signature," Samantha said quietly. "Even the initials at the bottom of each page look like mine, but I don't remember initialing them. I didn't read any of the stuff. Dr. Challa said I didn't need to, that it was just a formality. He kept telling me that the drug was safe."

"Can't we keep that out of evidence?" Sue Ellen asked. "It was misrepresented by Dr. Challa."

Luke shook his head. "We'll give it a try, but it's a long shot. Buried on page four of six, in the fine print, is some language that describes the risk of liver failure as a side effect of the drug. They don't say there's a chance of death, but they'll argue that any adult would know that if your liver fails, you can die. Bottom line is that it will probably come into evidence and we'll just have to deal with it."

72

Metcalf tapped her pen on the conference table as her team gathered coffee and found seats. They had moved to the San Marcos Holiday Inn. Jeans, Nikes, and T-shirts met the dress code for this endeavor. "Let me remind you of the words of the late Vince Lombardi. If you're early, you're on time. If you're on time, you're late. If you're late, don't bother to show up. Just pack your bags. When I walk into this conference room, I expect to be the last to arrive. Clear?"

Heads nodded around the table, although Michael Forsythe had to hide his anger at being treated like a file clerk. After all, he was a junior partner.

"Okay, let's get started. We lost some ground at that last hearing."

"Yeah," Forsythe replied. "It never occurred to me that a small-town lawyer would have the time or resources to go through all those documents and figure out what we held back."

"There may be a message in there," St. James interjected. "This guy may be a little sharper than we figured. By the way, who's this Professor Whizmo?"

"I've had him checked out," Metcalf said. "He's a history professor over at TSU, something of a legend around the university. He also does double duty as a graduate-level computer prof. Seems to be a little odd; lives in a garage apartment behind Vaughan and rides a Harley around town. Still, the word is that no one outdoes him either in history or on computers. Now, what do we do to neutralize all the crap that is in this clinical trial?"

"I have an idea, Audrey," a soft voice said from the other end of the table. It was Charlotte Bronson. The appellate lawyer was the brains of the outfit. Short and plump, with mousy brown hair and horn-rim glasses, she wouldn't stand out in a crowd. She spoke quietly, but when she did, everyone listened.

"Go ahead, Char," Metcalf said. "What's your idea?"

"I think we can keep the study out of evidence."

That got the attention of everyone around the table.

"The clinical trial was to get approval of the drug for marketing. Samantha Vaughan was a part of the trial. Her doctor didn't prescribe Exxacia to her based on the results of the trial, FDA approval, what was on the label, or even advertising. What's relevant here is that she signed a consent form, which I understand we just produced. That's where we should draw the battle lines and argue that the rest of the clinical trial is not relevant to her case."

Audrey Metcalf again tapped her pen on the table as she thought through the argument. Everyone else waited for her to say something. They dared not speak until she expressed her thoughts about the plan. Once they perceived which way the train was going, they would vocally climb on board.

"I like it," Metcalf finally said. "Anyone disagree?"

Murmurs of assent came from around the table.

"Charlotte, you've got a week to get that motion and brief drafted. We'll file it as soon as I've given it the okay. Now, we have our mock

jury in Austin tomorrow at the Four Seasons on the Lake. I want everyone except the file clerks there at eight in the morning. Back to work,
everybody! By the way, if anyone wants to join me, I'll be doing a
five-mile run at six this evening."

73

Bruce Outland, a tall African American in his midthirties, still had an
athletic build. He'd played wide receiver for the Longhorns and tried
out for a couple of NFL teams. When he couldn't make the cut, he
returned to The University of Texas and got a doctorate in psychology.
After working for a jury consulting firm in Dallas for several years,
he returned to Austin to start Capital Consultants. Now he had a staff
of ten and went to cities and towns across Texas and several neigh-
boring states to consult with lawyers.

On the day that Metcalf's team drove to Austin, Outland was
going to do a mock trial to determine what prospective jurors would
be good for Ceventa and which ones might be more favorable to Samantha Vaughan. He and his team had already spent weeks evaluating the demographics of Hays County. They knew the percentage of
males and females, the numbers of young people versus older citizens, and, most importantly, the county's racial and ethnic makeup—
a hodgepodge of Anglos, Latinos, Germans, Poles, Czechs, African
Americans, and a scattering of Asians. Once Outland knew what he
wanted, he put his staff to work. They ran ads in the *Austin American-
Statesman* and on the Internet, offering one hundred and fifty dollars for
a day's work. In tough economic times, it was relatively easy to have
hundreds of takers. Next they pored through the application forms

until they came up with sixty people who would match a prospective jury in Hays County. The mock jurors were asked to arrive at the hotel at eight and were directed to a large conference room, arranged like a classroom. Five other smaller conference rooms were arranged for jury deliberations, each with a large conference table and twelve chairs.

Once assembled, they were told that they were to be a part of the judicial system: Rather than go to the time and expense of a trial, the parties to this litigation had decided to put on a summary of their case to those assembled in the room. They never knew that the entire production was funded by Ceventa. As they heard from each lawyer, the jurors each held a device with a keypad and buttons from one to ten. They were to hit ten when they were impressed with something a lawyer said and go as low as one if they had strong negative feelings about a statement. Or, of course, they could hit any number in between.

After the opening statements, they would be divided into five juries of twelve to deliberate on the questions in the case. In the spirit of full disclosure, they were advised that they would be videoed at all times, but only the lawyers would watch the videos. As consent forms were passed around, no one refused the opportunity to make an easy buck and a half.

74

Bruce Outland met Audrey Metcalf and her team in the lobby of the hotel.

"Audrey, nice to see you again. "What is this, the sixth time we've worked together?" Bruce asked.

"I think it's seven, but who's counting as long as you keep helping me win," Metcalf replied.

Outland shook hands with the rest of the team and led them to yet another conference room. This one was outfitted with half a dozen television monitors. Five showed the empty jury rooms. The sixth showed the large room where the jurors were milling around, drinking coffee, and reading the paper; in the center of the serving table was a large jar filled with pink jelly beans, and several people were eating them and reading pamphlets about the Race for the Cure.

Metcalf was surprised to find Alfred Kingsbury standing at the coffee table, talking on his cell phone. As they entered, he ended his call.

"Alfred, I didn't expect to see you here." Metcalf smiled as she hugged her client.

Kingsbury poured coffee for Metcalf and a cup for himself. He let the others fend for themselves. "Audrey, I pay a ton of money for these around the country every year. This one is setting us back a hundred and fifty thousand. I've never seen one before. I just figured it was about time. Besides, Exxacia is critical to Ceventa and, I might add, to me. The board wants a firsthand account of this case every step of the way." A twinkle appeared in his eyes as he continued. "Also, I thought that when we got through today, you and I might have drinks and dinner like we did when you handled that case for us in San Francisco. You know the old saying, 'all work and no play . . .'"

"I think we might be able to work something out." Audrey smiled again. "How's Suzanne?"

"Uh, she's just fine. Taking an extended vacation in South America."

"How about the grandkids?"

"Couldn't be better. Here, let me show you my granddaughter in her latest play."

Kingsbury reached for his wallet, and Metcalf dutifully admired the photos. Before she could say anything more, they were interrupted.

"Dr. Kingsbury, we're about ready to start. You can see my associate asking our jurors to take their seats," Outland said. "He'll explain what we're doing, and we'll get started. Mr. Forsythe is going to play the role of Lucas Vaughan. He'll have an hour to summarize the plaintiff's case. Audrey will play herself. We'll watch each of them on this large monitor. The jurors do not know that Mr. Forsythe is really a member of your team. His job is to lay out the plaintiff's case as forcefully and dramatically as he can." Outland turned to Michael Forsythe. "Mr. Forsythe, I think they're ready for you."

"Bruce, nice touch with the jelly beans and pamphlets," Metcalf said. "I appreciate it."

"It's not just for this one, Audrey. You got me started, but now I do it at every mock trial. I've even got those pink jelly beans in my reception area downtown."

Michael left the room, and they soon saw him on the television screen, approaching a podium in front of the audience. "Good morning, ladies and gentlemen. My client, Samantha Vaughan, is dying because she took a drug manufactured by Ceventa Pharmaceutical, the defendant in this case."

In the adjoining room, the Ceventa team watched a red line superimposed over Forsythe's image climb to ten on a graph and remain there. Kingsbury looked troubled.

"I've taught him well, Alfred," Metcalf said. "He knows how to grab the jury's attention with his first sentence."

Over the next hour, the red line never hit ten again but fluctuated between two and eight, more often in the range of five. When Forsythe finished, the jurors took a break, then reassembled as Metcalf entered the room.

"Ladies and gentlemen, right now, throughout the world, Exxacia has saved three hundred and seventy-five thousand lives."

The red line shot to ten.

When Metcalf finished, the jurors were invited to take sandwiches from a buffet table and go to their jury rooms to deliberate. They would have three hours. As they did so, the Ceventa team could watch each of the juries and turn up the volume to a room when they saw something interesting. At the conclusion of the deliberations, three juries found in favor of Ceventa and two were split in favor of Samantha. Once the jurors had filed out of their rooms and received their checks for jury service, Outland spoke to the Ceventa team.

"We've learned a lot today. We'll be giving you a detailed report along with videos of the proceedings. Preliminarily, it's clear that we want older men and as many people of Slavic descent as we can get on the jury. We want to avoid younger women, who will sympathize with Samantha, as well as Latinos, who are nearly always too compassionate."

"Audrey, what's your assessment?" Kingsbury asked.

Metcalf paused to collect her thoughts before she spoke. "We're going to be okay, provided we get the right jury. With the wrong jury we could have a problem. We damn sure want some of those Germans and Polacks, as many as we can get."

Outland nodded his agreement. As the Ceventa team left the hotel, Metcalf joined Kingsbury in his limousine.

75

Luke trudged up the steps to the porch, where he took off his coat and tie and tossed them onto a rocker. Then he walked around to the garage, opened the door, checked over his motorcycle, got on, turned the key, and pushed the ignition. When he roared down the driveway, Samantha watched him leave and wondered why her dad would be riding his Harley in the middle of the morning and with no helmet.

He hit the edge of town and started up the road to an area called the Devil's Backbone. Luke cussed to himself. *How the hell could this happen? How could Nimitz rule like he did?* Metcalf had filed a motion to quash the admissibility of the clinical trial. That trial was critical to their case. They had spent untold hours finding the fraud and forgery that ran rampant throughout the study. They would win if they could show the fraud and deceit perpetrated by Ceventa. Sue Ellen had written a brilliant response that he was convinced would carry the day, but now, on the eve of trial, they had lost. Not only did they lose the motion, but without the evidence of fraud, they almost surely would lose the trial. Sure, they might get a big verdict against Dr. Challa, but that would be a hollow victory. Ceventa would tout the verdict and claim that the American judicial system had found Exxacia to be safe and effective. And Samantha was going to die.

When he came over a hill and rode the crest of the Devil's Backbone, Luke let his anger spill out as he gunned the engine and pushed the Harley to a tooth-rattling hundred miles an hour. *The judge ruled against us. He bought into the argument that the clinical trial was not relevant to Samantha's case. How could he do that? Had Ceventa gotten to him? No, not Judge Nimitz. He's as straight an arrow as ever took the bench. He's just flat wrong, and there's nothing we can do about it until we appeal. Only for Samantha, that'll be too late.*

Luke slowed as he came to the stream where he and Samantha had sat and talked. He got off his motorcycle and walked to the riverbank. His mind lost in thought, he idly skipped rocks across the water. Sue Ellen had been in the courtroom. She knew what happened. He would have to tell Whiz, though. As for Sam, he'd just say they lost a motion, and that was just part of trying lawsuits.

When Luke climbed back on the Harley, he blew out a big breath and forced himself to relax as he left the stream. Returning to San Marcos along the Devil's Backbone, he mused that the ridge was appropriately named. The road twisted and turned for the whole distance, requiring a driver or rider to pay attention to avoid steep embankments and more than a few places where the side of the road dropped off a shear cliff.

From almost anyplace on the twenty-five-mile ridge, one could see the rolling hills for miles in either direction. On weekends the road was heavily traveled by sightseers. Not today. Luke rarely passed another car or motorcycle. As he rode, at least for the moment, he put his worries behind him and enjoyed the view and the wind in his face.

He was about ten miles from the edge of San Marcos when he glanced in his rearview mirror and saw a dark vehicle in the distance, closing rapidly. *Must be a crazy tourist,* he thought, one who didn't realize the danger of overdriving the curves on the backbone. He returned his gaze to the road ahead and slowed to make a sharp curve. When he looked back, the vehicle was almost on top of him. Now he saw it was a black Lincoln and could make out two men in the front seat. Assuming they were in a bigger hurry than he was, Luke moved over to the right.

The car accelerated, and as it came even with Luke, he saw it swerving toward him. Faced with a two-ton vehicle to his left and a small shoulder adjacent to a steep cliff to his right, Luke had only one option. He cut to the shoulder and laid his bike down on its left side. He skidded and bounced along the shoulder as the cliff loomed. At the last possible moment, he came to a stop two feet from the edge.

Luke lay there for nearly a minute before he managed to lift the Harley just enough to pull his left leg from under it. He staggered to his feet and surveyed his body. His left leg was scratched and bloody, but nothing seemed to be broken. Thank God, he thought, that he had slowed for the curve. Next he looked down the highway. The car was long gone. He checked the Harley; it appeared to be like his leg, scratched but not broken. Now, if he could just get it upright.

As he surveyed the bike, another rider stopped behind him. "Hey, man. You okay?"

"I think so," Luke replied.

"You hit gravel on that curve?"

Luke shook his head. "Some son of a bitch tried to force me off the road."

"Yeah, man," the other rider said. "I've had that happen. Some drivers just have it in for us. They're usually just trying to play games."

"This guy wasn't playing games. He wanted me at the bottom of that ravine. Can you help me get my bike up?"

Luke and the other rider uprighted the Harley. Luke checked it over, climbed aboard, started the engine, and rode it fifty yards before returning. "She's doing fine. Thanks, man," Luke said. The other rider gave him a salute, and Luke turned to ride back into San Marcos, watching for the black Lincoln at every curve and crossroad.

76

Luke turned into the driveway and drove around to the garage, where he found Whizmo puttering in his workshop.

Whizmo glanced up as he heard the Harley, then put down a screwdriver and walked over to Luke. "What happened, Luke?"

"Afraid I messed up your bike a little, Whiz."

"Not concerned about that. What about your leg? You need some stitches?"

"Naw, I think I'll be all right with a little iodine and a couple of bandages. I'm going in the house to call Sue Ellen and Brad. Join us in, say, thirty minutes."

Whizmo nodded as Luke limped into the house.

Sue Ellen dropped what she was doing when Luke called and told her what had happened. Fifteen minutes later she came through the front door, followed by John McClain, the district attorney. McClain was a big man with a bald head. He customarily dressed in a brown suit, checked brown and gold tie, and boots.

"When you told me what happened, I figured we better have John involved," Sue Ellen explained.

Whizmo came through the back door as Brad entered the front. Samantha was in her wheelchair, waiting for them in the conference room.

Luke described the events in detail.

"You sure it wasn't just an accident, Luke?" McClain asked.

"Positive, John. They swerved just as they got even with me. Someone wants me dead."

"Gotta be somebody at Ceventa," Whizmo said.

"Sue Ellen's been telling me about this case, and I've read about it in the paper. I don't know if Whiz is right or not, but I can't arrest anyone without evidence. Two guys in a black Lincoln don't get me there."

"You need a bodyguard, Luke," Brad said. "I have a license to carry. Let me do it."

Samantha had listened in silence. "Dad, no use in saving my life if you lose yours."

"Samantha, let me interrupt," McClain said. "Brad, thanks for your offer, but I think we need professionals. I'll get a deputy to escort your dad and Sue Ellen wherever they go until we get to the bottom of this. They'll each have one, twenty-four/seven. I'll also have a deputy parked in front of your house at all times, Luke."

"You think that's necessary, John?" Luke asked.

"If what you described is accurate, Luke, yeah, I do."

Luke considered all that had occurred before he agreed. "Okay, do it, but I want these guys to be discreet. They need to walk behind Sue Ellen and me, maybe half a block back. When they're staking out the houses, put them down the street a ways." He looked at the others around the table. "We've got to keep our focus on the trial. Do your best to pretend this is not happening. I trust John to do his job. Let's do ours."

77

Luke bought two new suits for the trial. He really had no choice: In his office practice, his business attire was a dress shirt and slacks; when he pulled his old trial suits out of the closet, he was dismayed to find that his waist had outgrown the pants. This was pretrial, so he picked the gray suit, saving the blue one with the thin pinstripe for jury selection tomorrow.

When he went downstairs, he found Whizmo in the conference room with two of his students. "I'll have the rest of my computer grad students here within an hour. As soon as you can get us those jury cards, we'll start digging for information."

Luke nodded in agreement. "This shouldn't take long. I ought to be back in a couple of hours." He turned to say good-bye to Samantha and found her door closed. He knocked quietly and then entered. Mary was taking up a pair of jeans to fit Sam's slighter figure while Sam was putting on makeup. "Morning, Dad."

"You're getting mighty dressed up, Sam. You feeling better?"

"Not really, but we're going to have a houseful of students today. I'm going to do my best to play hostess. I looked out the window and saw a sheriff's car down the street. I suppose that makes me feel safer," she said with a shrug.

Luke smiled, kissed his daughter, grabbed his briefcase, and left the house.

He walked up the street to the sheriff's car and was greeted by one of the deputies, who exited from the passenger side and introduced himself as Brian Wallis, his escort for the day.

"Brian, I want you to stay back half a block or so. Just keep your eyes open. I don't expect any problem."

Deputy Wallis nodded his agreement. His partner remained in the car.

While Luke walked the short distance to the courthouse, he considered the twists and turns in his life and what was about to happen. He intended to be a famous trial lawyer in Houston and failed. He married because he had to, not because he wanted to. He and his former wife had Sam, and then she deserted him. Well, that was one positive. He tried to raise Sam while they were in Houston and managed to alienate her. He made the decision to move to San Marcos to simplify his life, and it got more complicated when Sam separated herself from him, at least emotionally. He made too many bad decisions to count in her teen years and topped them all off by jerking her out of A&M. Then the miracle occurred and they managed to reconcile. They had one fantastic father-daughter year before Ceventa tore their lives asunder. Now Sam lay on the brink of death and he was walking to the Hays County courthouse, trailed by a deputy sheriff, in a desperate effort to salvage her life against odds so high that no one in Las Vegas would place a wager on his chances. "Help me, God," he said quietly but out loud. Then he turned the corner and discovered a three-ring circus camped on the lawn of the courthouse.

Remote vans with antennas filled the streets. Reporters were smiling into cameras as they discussed what was about to take place in this small Central Texas town. Other reporters and technicians tested microphones.

Luke paused, took a deep breath, and continued toward the courthouse. When one reporter spotted him, others followed to surround the small-town lawyer out to save his daughter's life. On this day, he elected to tell them he was late and had no comment, maybe tomorrow. Luke hurried up the steps and into the courthouse corridor, where he was greeted with smiles by everyone he saw. When he entered the courtroom he found Sue Ellen already at the table nearest the jury box, talking to Simon Rothschild and Tom Lorance. Lorance had been conspicuous by his absence once he had offered Dr. Challa's insurance coverage. Now, of course, he had to be here.

"Morning, Sue Ellen. Morning, Tom. Morning, Simon. How's your grandchild doing?"

"She's doing well, Luke. Thanks for asking. The wife ought to be able to come home in a couple of weeks."

"Sue Ellen, let's talk over by the window a minute."

The two stepped away and talked softly. "Any problems this morning?"

"None. My deputy's kinda cute." She smiled. "Don't worry. He looks just a little older than Josh."

The doors opened, and Audrey Metcalf swept in with her usual entourage. She was followed by reporters who filled up the seats and stood around the walls.

"Should we say anything to her about yesterday?" Sue Ellen asked.

Luke shook his head. "If it was Ceventa, I don't think she would have been involved. She's a tough bitch, but she wants to destroy us in the courtroom, not on the highway. Still, if we say anything, she'll just try to figure out some way to turn it to her advantage."

Simon motioned to the reporters. "Judge Nimitz doesn't permit any cameras or recording devices in the courtroom. If you have them this morning, please turn them off and put them away. Tomorrow we'll be checking each of you before you're permitted in the courthouse. You best not even have a computer, just a pad and pen to take notes."

The reporters grumbled among themselves about being transported back to the nineteenth century when they entered Hays County. Then Judge Nimitz stepped from his chambers. "Be seated, everyone. Good morning. In the case of *Samantha Vaughan v. Ceventa and Dr. Vijay Challa,* I'm calling for announcements."

"Plaintiff is ready, Your Honor," Luke said as he rose.

"Ceventa is also ready, Judge Nimitz," Audrey said.

"So is Dr. Challa, Judge," Tom Lorance joined in.

Judge Nimitz looked at Lorance. "Tom, I almost forgot about you. We haven't seen much of you lately. You still got a dog in this fight?"

"Yes, sir, but only a little one. I intend to take only a modest role in this proceeding."

"Very well, then, having received announcements of ready from all parties, we'll proceed with pretrial and pick a jury tomorrow. Luke, you're first. You have any motion in limine matters that I need to hear?"

"No, Judge," Luke replied. "Mine are the usual. I submitted them to Mr. Forsythe and he agreed."

Forsythe rose and acknowledged their agreement.

"Tom, I presume you've got nothing," Judge Nimitz asked as he looked in Lorance's direction. Lorance motioned with his hand to indicate the judge was correct.

"That leaves you, Ms. Metcalf. What are you looking to keep out of evidence?"

Metcalf stood at her table and folded her arms. "Judge, you've already ruled on the clinical trial data. I can assure you and counsel that we will not be opening that door. Not only would it be prejudicial, but it would also probably lengthen our trial by about a month."

Judge Nimitz nodded his head. "We certainly don't want a six-week trial. Mr. Vaughan, you are again instructed not to go into that clinical trial data unless you approach the bench and get my prior approval."

Luke didn't like the ruling but knew he was out of options, at least for now. "Understood, Your Honor."

"Now, let's talk about tomorrow. I can squeeze eighty prospective jurors in this courtroom if Simon brings in extra chairs. So that's the number you'll be working with. Simon, please give the lawyers the jury cards."

Simon took three jury lists from his desk and placed one in front of each lead lawyer. Each photocopied card on the list provided information about the prospect: age, sex, race, religion, address, occupation, marital status, number of children, prior jury service, and involvement as a party in other lawsuits. This basic information was frequently all the lawyers had about prospective jurors until they started asking questions. In this case, Luke knew that Whizmo's team would ferret out more details. Likewise, Luke knew that some of Audrey's flying monkeys back at the Holiday Inn were prepared to do the same thing.

78

When Luke and Sue Ellen got back to his house, they found the conference room filled with young men and women, all with laptops in front of them. Some were checking e-mails, some playing games, and a couple actually doing homework assignments. Samantha was sitting at the end of the table, also with her laptop open, and talking to Brad. Whizmo was walking around the room, visiting with each of his students.

"Brad," Luke said, "take these jury lists and make one set for everyone at the table. Whiz, please introduce us to your students."

Whizmo went around the room, naming the students and telling Luke and Sue Ellen a little about each of them.

"Now," Luke said, "I'm sure that Whiz has told you a little about what we'll be doing today. Let me cover it one more time to make sure we're all on the same page. The jury information cards that Brad is copying have some basic information on eighty people. We'll divide them among you. We've got access to LexisNexis here, PublicData, county property registration, vehicle registrations, criminal records, you name it. If there's a database out there, you'll have access to it. I want to know if these people live in a house or an apartment, whether they're paying their mortgage on time, what kind of cars they drive, credit status, credit card debt, political parties, marriages, divorces, other lawsuits. Don't consider anything so unimportant that you don't include it. Let us be the judge of what you find. Sam and I appreciate your help. By the way, we'll order pizza about noon."

By late afternoon Whizmo's team had completed the job. Samantha had long before excused herself for a nap. Luke thanked them all for their help and promised to keep Whizmo updated as the trial progressed so he could pass the information on to them.

When the students were gone, Whizmo took himself off to his woodworking shop. Mary cleared away the pizza boxes, Cokes, and Dr Peppers. Luke and Sue Ellen settled down to analyze the data. Using yellow highlighters, they marked any detail that would be a positive or a negative for them. Likewise, they highlighted any information that needed follow-up questions. As the sun was fading in the west, they called it quits and adjourned to the porch with wine in hand. Tomorrow it began for real.

79

It was a little after ten and Luke was in his office, preparing for voir dire, when his phone rang.

Looking at the caller ID, he answered, "Sue Ellen, what's up?"

"Luke, Josh is not home. He was studying over at a friend's but was supposed to be home by nine. I talked to his friend's mother, and she said he left about eight thirty. It's only a ten-minute walk from there to here. He doesn't answer his cell, and I've called all of his friends. Luke, I'm scared."

"I'll be right over. Call John and get him out of the sack."

Samantha was already asleep. He went upstairs and knocked on what was now Mary's bedroom. Mary opened the door a crack and peeked through. "I'm going over to Sue Ellen's. Should be back in an hour. Just wanted to let you know."

As he went down the steps the lone night deputy met him. "Any problem, Luke?"

"I've got to go over to Sue Ellen's for a little while."

"You want me to go with you?"

"No, it's only three blocks. I'll be okay. You stay here. Call me if you see anything suspicious."

Sue Ellen met Luke on her front porch. She was crying. "Luke, I just got a call. The man said that if I want Josh back, we have to drop this lawsuit. You've got to dismiss the case."

Before Luke could answer, John McClain drove up and jumped from the car. Sal Jenkins, the sheriff of Hays County, got out of the passenger door. "Sue Ellen, have you heard from him?"

Sue Ellen repeated the phone conversation as they climbed the steps and walked into the house.

"Dammit! Dammit to hell! I thought we had our bases covered. It never occurred to me that Josh would be in danger. I'm sorry, Sue Ellen. I'm so sorry."

"John, I'm not angry with you. I just want answers and I want Josh safe. Now what?"

McClain scratched his bald head before he replied. "As to the threat about the lawsuit, that's between you and Luke here. Besides, there are no guarantees that even if you dismissed the case tomorrow, Josh would be safe. Sal, notify the state troopers and put out an APB. Sue Ellen, we need a current photo of Josh. And, Sal, since we've got a kidnapping that makes it a potential federal offense, call the FBI.

You get your guys to canvas the neighborhood tonight. I don't care if you wake people up. We need to know if any of the neighbors saw anything strange."

"I'm on it, John," Sheriff Jenkins said. "Don't worry, Sue Ellen. We'll find him. Now, if you'll get me that photo."

After the DA and the sheriff left, Luke and Sue Ellen sat on the couch and hugged each other. Finally Luke broke away and wiped the tears from Sue Ellen's eyes. "Sue Ellen, I don't know what to do. How can this happen to two small-town lawyers? We started off trying to save Samantha's life. Now both of our kids are in danger. I'll drop the case if necessary, but if I do . . ."

Sue Ellen suppressed her crying and finished Luke's sentence. ". . . then Samantha's going to die."

"And if I don't, then Josh could die."

There was silence in the room for minutes while the two parents considered their dilemma and options. Luke broke it. "There's no right answer. We're dealing with some people who tried to kill me and now have kidnapped Josh. Even if we dismiss the case, like John said, there's no guarantee we'll find Josh alive. We think someone at Ceventa is behind this, but we don't know for sure." Luke paused as if to be certain what he was about to say was the right decision. "If we drop the case, Sam's gonna die, and even if Josh is released, we'll probably never know who's behind all of this. I'm afraid that we have no choice but to go forward with the trial and hope that all the law enforcement agencies can find Josh. There's one other thing, and don't think I'm saying this to try to convince you one way or the other. If they kill Josh, they've lost their leverage with us. That alone should encourage the kidnappers to keep him alive."

Sue Ellen rose, turned to look at Luke, shook her head, and without a word walked up the stairs. Luke watched her disappear and then walked out the front door into the night.

80

Luke showered and dressed the next morning, then went downstairs and knocked on Samantha's door. Samantha was just waking up when he entered. He sat on the side of her bed as he spoke. "Sam, something happened last night."

Samantha stared at him sleepily.

"Josh is gone. We think he's been kidnapped."

Samantha was suddenly awake and pushed herself up to a sitting position. "Who did it, Dad? Why?"

"We don't know, Sam. The district attorney, the sheriff, and the FBI are all looking for him."

Samantha looked out the window at the sheriff's car down the street. "It's about the trial, isn't it, Dad?"

Luke hesitated and then told her about Sue Ellen's phone call.

"Drop it, Dad."

"Do what?"

"Drop the lawsuit. Look, I'm probably going to die anyway. They tried to kill you, and now Josh may be next. It's not worth it. Josh didn't do anything to anybody."

Luke took his daughter by her narrow shoulders. "Listen to me, Sam. Sue Ellen and I talked this through last night. I'm going to keep going with the lawsuit. I don't have time to explain now, but I think it's the right decision. I promise you we'll take it day by day. I want you to trust me on this."

This time Samantha looked her dad in the eye. "Are you sure this is the right thing to do? Positive, I mean?"

Luke sighed. "Samantha, I can't be positive about anything anymore. I can tell you I believe this is the right decision. We can talk about it some more tonight."

Samantha nodded and lay down with her back to her dad as he left her room.

81

Luke and Sue Ellen walked to the courthouse, this time with deputies on either side of them. They ignored reporters who asked about their escorts. Two other deputies stood guard at the courtroom door, permitting only the lawyers to enter. When Audrey Metcalf arrived, John McClain met her and asked her to come talk with him in his office. After thirty minutes they returned to the courtroom. Metcalf was visibly shaken as she took her seat. Before she could tell her team what was going on, Judge Nimitz stepped from his chambers. When he took the bench, he motioned to his court reporter to record every word. His face was solemn as he spoke.

"Let the record reflect that the doors to the courtroom are locked. The only people present are counsel for the parties, District Attorney John McClain, Sheriff Sal Jenkins, my bailiff, and my court reporter. We have a very serious situation on our hands. Ms. Metcalf, I understand that Mr. McClain has briefed you."

"He has, Your Honor."

"So the record is clear, someone made an attempt on Mr. Vaughan's life just two days ago. Last night, Josh Taggert, Sue Ellen's son, was apparently kidnapped and has yet to be found. Understand, Ms. Metcalf, I'm not suggesting anything. The criminal investigation will be handled by Mr. McClain and Sheriff Jenkins. However"—the judge paused to choose his words carefully—"the only connection between the attempt on Mr. Vaughan's life and Josh's kidnapping appears to be this lawsuit."

"Your Honor!" Metcalf said.

"Please be seated, Ms. Metcalf. I'm not through yet. There are two parties who would like to see this lawsuit over before it even begins, Dr. Challa and Ceventa."

"Your Honor," Tom Lorance interrupted. "I'll be glad to bring Dr. Challa in from the hall and let you or Mr. McClain examine him right now."

"I appreciate that, Mr. Lorance. Now's not the time or place. However, I do want you defense lawyers to quiz your clients, particularly you, Ms. Metcalf. Although I doubt if Ceventa is involved, they're going to tell you."

Metcalf rose again. "Now may I be heard, Judge?"

Judge Nimitz nodded.

"Judge, you can rest assured that I'll get to the bottom of this with my client. I can further assure you that Ceventa tries cases all over the country. Ceventa is a good corporate citizen that believes in our judicial system. It's always been willing to present facts to a jury and abide by their decision."

"Understood, Ms. Metcalf. Now, what do we do about this trial? Luke, you and Sue Ellen can make the call. If you want it continued, we'll do so."

This time Sue Ellen rose. "Judge, under the circumstances, I will be the one to speak for our side. Luke and I talked far into the night about this. There's no clear-cut answer. Both of our kids are in danger. Samantha is near death. Any postponement could mean she will never have a trial or a chance at a new liver. I understand we've got multiple law enforcement agencies combing the area. For now I'm willing to defer to Mr. Vaughan's decision to go forward with our trial. If things change, we'll advise the court."

Judge Nimitz pondered the situation before speaking. "Sue Ellen, are you sure?"

"Yes, sir. I am."

"Very well, we'll start picking a jury in half an hour. No one is to breathe a word of this to anyone outside of this courtroom and your clients. If the media gets wind of it, I'll have to sequester the jury."

82

"Good morning, ladies and gentlemen. My name is Lucas Vaughan. I'm a lawyer here in San Marcos, and I'm sorry to say that I have to represent my daughter, Samantha, who is dying because of a drug manufactured by Ceventa Pharmaceutical, one of the defendants in this case."

"Objection! Objection, Your Honor," Metcalf yelled as she leaped to her feet. "He's already arguing his case. There's no evidence that Exxacia has caused any of Samantha Vaughan's health conditions."

"Ms. Metcalf, he's entitled to say what the case is about and what he's claiming," Judge Nimitz said sternly. "Objection overruled. And I'm not hard of hearing, Counsel, so please keep your voice down. Proceed, Mr. Vaughan."

Pleased to have won a small victory without having to say a word, Luke turned his attention to the jury. "How many of you have heard of this case in the media or elsewhere?"

Over half the audience raised the numbered cards that Simon had given to each of them. All the lawyers hurriedly wrote down their jury numbers. *Uh-oh,* Luke thought, *I've got to be careful or we'll bust this whole panel.* "Let me see if I can ask all of you who raised your jury cards this one question. Having read about this case in the newspaper or seen something about it on television, is there anyone among you who cannot set aside whatever you've learned before today and decide this case on the evidence that is presented in this courtroom?"

All the numbers went down except for two. Luke glanced at the information they had assembled on the jurors and determined both were students at Texas State. "Miss Frederick and Mr. Morales, you've still got your cards up."

Lacey Frederick stood. "Yes, sir. I had some classes with Samantha. I know she was a healthy straight-A student until she took some drug."

"Same with me, Mr. Vaughan," Franscisco Morales joined in.

Luke was disappointed that he had lost two good prospective jurors, but he liked what Lacey Frederick said in front of the entire panel.

Luke knew that there were at least twenty on the panel with Slavic ancestry. He wanted them gone. So he asked a series of questions about frivolous lawsuits, the rising costs of medical care caused by suits against doctors and drug companies, advocates of tort reform, and the need for tort reform in the state. It took an hour, but when he finished, eighteen of the twenty were gone.

Next he focused on damages. No one objected to awarding damages for medical costs, but ten other prospects were adamant that they could not justify damages for mental anguish or physical pain. Judge Nimitz agreed with all ten of Luke's challenges. As the lunch hour approached and Luke came to the end of his voir dire, he conferred with Sue Ellen, who sized up the remaining jurors and told him that by the time they used their peremptory strikes, she would be satisfied with the remainder.

It was twelve thirty when Luke finished. The judge asked the panel to be back at two o'clock, allowing a little extra time for the locals to run home for lunch if they saw fit.

83

Audrey Metcalf knew what she had to do. The sympathy factor in the case would be overwhelming. She attacked it from the start. "Ladies and gentlemen, the judge will instruct you that you should not let sympathy play any part in your deliberations. I'm sorry to say that Samantha Vaughan is dying, not because of a Ceventa drug but for other reasons that you'll hear as the trial progresses."

Luke gave Sue Ellen a quizzical look when Metcalf made that statement.

"I have sympathy for a young lady like Samantha, but to do my job, I've got to set aside my human feelings for her."

"The hell she does," Sue Ellen whispered to Luke. "The bitch and her client don't care who lives or dies as long as they win."

"Who believes that you just could not set aside your natural sympathy and judge the evidence objectively?"

Metcalf got what she wanted. It took her nearly two hours of poking and prodding, but she eventually disqualified sixteen jurors, mostly women and college students. Three more disqualified themselves because Luke had been their lawyer for one thing or another. Two were disqualified because a family member had been sent to the pen in Huntsville by Sue Ellen. The clock was approaching four when Metcalf conferred with her team and reported they had completed their voir dire. Judge Nimitz was about to announce that voir dire examination was complete when Tom Lorance stood.

"Judge, I think you forgot about me."

The judge shook his head at his own error. "Sorry, Mr. Lorance. Please proceed."

"Ladies and gentlemen, all I want to do is introduce myself. I'm Tom Lorance. I'm pleased to represent Dr. Challa." Dr. Challa got to his feet at Tom's urging and managed a nod to the jury. "You'll be hearing from him later in the trial. That's all, Judge."

"All right, you jurors are excused to stretch your legs. Don't anybody go home. You lawyers can make your strikes. Luke, I suppose you and Sue Ellen can use her old office. I think it's still vacant, awaiting her return. The Ceventa lawyers can use the jury room. Plaintiff gets six strikes. Ceventa gets four strikes, and Tom, you get two."

"Judge!" Metcalf yelped. "That's outrageous! Mr. Lorance's client is barely in this case. We should get six strikes."

"Ms. Metcalf, I suggest you find your indoor voice. Dr. Challa was the original defendant in this case. Unless your client is willing to indemnify him, he's still a defendant, and I'm giving the defense a total of six strikes. If you raise your voice again, I'll split them three and three."

Luke smiled, knowing that he and Tom had already agreed that while they could not work together to strike, Luke would strike potential defense jurors starting with the first juror, and Tom would do the same but starting with the last juror. Was it unethical? Probably. In his mind there was no doubt that the gloves had come off. He'd do whatever it took to win.

After the lawyers made their strikes, the judge called the names of thirteen members of the panel, twelve primary jurors and one alternate in the event illness or family emergency pulled one of the original twelve away. As they took their seats in the jury box, Luke sized them up: six women and six men. Three of the women were Anglo, two Hispanic, and one African American; among the men, four were Anglo, one Hispanic, and one African American. The alternate was a heavyset black man who said he was retired, but their research showed he was only forty-eight and had been on welfare for ten years. Luke liked the fact that he had two young people who would surely empathize with Samantha. It bothered him that two jurors were of German descent. Almost certainly they would be stingy with damages. On the other hand, they would probably insist on perfection or something close to it for Ceventa.

Now those thirteen strangers would take two or three weeks away from their jobs and families for the grand sum of forty dollars a day. They would have to listen to all of the evidence, some of it no doubt boring, and try to resolve the dispute between Samantha and Ceventa. All would go home that evening and grouse about having been chosen. Still, once it was all over, if they were like most jurors, they would find the experience challenging, fascinating, and fulfilling. For most of them, it would be their one chance to serve as an official in their judicial system. None of them would recall it, Luke thought, but our Pledge of Allegiance ended with four very important words: "and justice for all." He could only hope that justice for Samantha would be swift and would include some way for her to get a new liver—and that they would find Josh alive before the trial was over.

84

The next morning Luke opened the door of Sue Ellen's office and quickly shut it behind him to fend off questions from the reporters in the hallway. Sue Ellen looked up. Luke took one look at the dark circles under her eyes and knew that there was no good news about Josh. He walked around her desk and put his arms around her shoulders. "Nothing, huh?"

"John was just in here. Josh has disappeared from the face of the earth. Look at this."

Sue Ellen handed Luke a small box.

"You can open it. They've already dusted it for prints. It's potential evidence, but John's letting me keep it locked in my office."

Luke opened the box to find a Texas Longhorns baseball cap.

"It's Josh's. I found it on my front porch this morning. Somehow someone got past the deputy and left it."

"I'm sorry, Sue Ellen. I know they're doing everything they can."

"I . . . I don't know if I can take this much longer. I want Josh back." Sue Ellen grabbed a Kleenex from her desk and wiped her eyes. "I was up most of the night. Are we jousting at windmills with this trial? Without that clinical trial in evidence, our case is hanging by a thread. Every day we keep going, Josh's life is at risk. Is it going to be worth it?"

Luke walked back around Sue Ellen's desk and sat down. "Believe me, I didn't sleep much better. I think Dr. Stevens will get us past Ceventa's motion for a directed verdict, but it'll be close. Hopefully, your friend Chuck will let it go to the jury. If we can get it to the jury, we should get a favorable verdict. Then maybe we can convince Ceventa to settle."

Luke realized that he had just convinced his daughter to keep going forward the day before, and now he was having to convince Sue Ellen. Maybe it was wrong to jeopardize Josh, but he couldn't let his daughter die without giving it everything he had. "Stay beside me, Sue Ellen. It's going to be okay," Luke said with a modicum of conviction. As he rose to leave, he saw Sue Ellen bury her face in her hands.

The courtroom was packed when Luke entered. Sue Ellen trailed only a few minutes behind. It appeared that she had dried her eyes and reapplied her makeup. The audience was full of reporters. Luke spotted a group of Samantha's friends squeezed into the first row. He waved a greeting at them. Their shout of "Go, Sam!" brought a prompt rebuke from Simon.

When Simon was satisfied that everything was ready, he called for order and instructed everyone to rise as Judge Nimitz entered from his chambers. Everyone, Judge Nimitz included, then remained standing while Simon brought the jurors from the jury room. Once everyone was seated, Judge Nimitz looked at Luke. "Mr. Vaughan, call your first witness."

"Your Honor, plaintiff calls Dr. Vijay Challa."

Dr. Challa stood when his name was called. His eyes darted nervously from the audience to the judge, then to the jury and Audrey Metcalf before returning to the judge. As instructed by Simon, he stopped in front of the bench and raised his right hand.

"Do you swear to tell the truth, the whole truth, and nothing but the truth, so help you God?" Judge Nimitz demanded.

"Yes, yes sir, I do," the doctor replied in a voice that cracked with nervousness. Whatever Ceventa had paid him to be a clinical investigator, it was not enough to go through this.

Luke took a sip of water and began. "You're Vijay Challa, a medical doctor?"

Dr. Challa sat awkwardly in the witness chair. He couldn't figure out what to do with his hands. At first he let his arms drop to his sides; then he tried folding his arms in front of him. Finally he rested his hands on his knees. "Yes, sir."

"You went to medical school in India and then had to pass a test to be allowed to practice in the United States?"

"Correct, Mr. Vaughan."

"Tell the jury how long you've practiced in San Marcos and what kind of patients you see."

Dr. Challa turned to look at the jury. "I've been here for ten years. I'm a family doctor. I take care of patients from the cradle to old age. A lot of my patients are college students since my office is close to the campus."

"Were you one of the physician investigators in a clinical trial for a drug called Exxacia, manufactured by Ceventa Pharmaceutical?"

"I was."

"How did that come about, Doctor?"

"I got an invitation from Ceventa to assist them in confirming the safety and efficacy of what they considered a revolutionary new antibiotic. The study had been ongoing for several months, and they said they needed a few more physicians and, I think, a few thousand more subjects."

"Subjects, Dr. Challa!" Luke said, loudly enough that Simon started to rise to insist on order in the court. Judge Nimitz motioned him to sit down.

"Is that what Ceventa called your patients, subjects? Bunch of laboratory mice? Is that what they thought?"

Metcalf leaped to her feet. "Objection! That's argumentative and completely out of line."

"Sustained. Mr. Vaughan, please temper your questions."

Luke nodded and asked, "Ceventa did refer to your patients as subjects?"

Dr. Challa looked at the judge, who nodded he could answer. "Yes, Mr. Vaughan. All of the paperwork used that term."

"And one of those so-called subjects was my daughter, Samantha Vaughan, wasn't she?"

"I'm afraid so," the witness whispered. "I'm really sorry for what's happened to her."

"Approach the witness, Your Honor?"

"You may, Mr. Vaughan."

Luke handed a document to the witness while Sue Ellen displayed the first page on the overhead.

"Plaintiff's Exhibit One is a copy of the consent form used in the clinical trial, the one that was purportedly signed by Samantha Vaughan."

Dr. Challa glanced at the document, looked up, and nodded. "It is."

"Are you sure, Doctor? It's six pages long, all in fine print, isn't it?"

Dr. Challa stared at the form. "I, I presume it's the one signed by Samantha. I haven't looked at every page."

"Let's go page by page." Luke slowly turned the pages as Sue Ellen did the same. "There's a place to initial at the bottom of each page and a place to sign on the last page."

The witness nodded his agreement.

"Did you tell Samantha she needed to read all those pages before she initialed and signed the form?"

"No sir, I didn't. None of the subjects read the form. In fact, the regional supervisor from Ceventa said they were in a hurry to complete the clinical trial and for me just to get the form signed and give them the pills."

"Objection!" Metcalf was on her feet again. "Hearsay."

"Overruled, Ms. Metcalf."

Luke looked at the jury and shook his head in disgust. "How long was Samantha in your office, Doctor?"

Challa thought a minute. "Honestly, I couldn't say for sure about her. None of the subjects were there for longer than ten minutes."

Luke whirled and returned to his seat. "According to the protocol you were supposed to see Samantha once a week for six weeks and again one last time at ten weeks for blood work, vital signs, and so forth. Did you comply with the protocol with her?"

The witness stared at the clock in the back of the courtroom, refusing to make eye contact with anyone as he answered. "Very few of the subjects made all of their visits. So I would just make up vital signs and change the date on the blood work that I did have. I did that with most of my subjects."

Luke clenched his fists and tried to control his temper. "Well, let's talk about your other subjects."

"Objection, Your Honor," Metcalf said. "May we approach the bench?"

The judge motioned them forward.

"Judge, Mr. Vaughan is violating the court's direct ruling. He's injecting the clinical trial into evidence."

"Judge," Luke replied, "I'm only going to go into what Dr. Challa did. He's a defendant in this lawsuit."

"I agree with Mr. Vaughan, Ms. Metcalf. He can discuss Dr. Challa's conduct. Mr. Vaughan, please restrict your questions only to what Dr. Challa did. With that understanding, your objection is overruled."

Metcalf returned to her table and whispered to Charlotte Bronson. "There's one appeal point already. Start briefing it tonight."

Luke waited for Metcalf to take her seat and then picked up a stack of papers from the table. "Dr. Challa, these are the charts on your other subjects, as you call them. I want to make this brief. Out of all the subjects in your part of the clinical trial, most had falsified vital signs?"

"Yes, sir."

"Most had dates changed on lab work?"

"Yes, sir."

"Most failed to keep all of their appointments?"

"Yes, sir, particularly that last one at ten weeks."

"Once you had blood work from one patient that looked good, you used it on many other patients?"

Dr. Challa squirmed in his seat, stared out the window, and finally said, "I'm sorry to say I did."

"And even before Samantha ever set foot in your office you had ten subjects who had elevated liver function tests, some of them at toxic levels?"

"Yes, sir. I'm afraid I did."

"And did you report those findings to Ceventa?"

"Absolutely, sir. As we completed a patient, we sent the patient chart by e-mail to Ceventa's managers, and when all of the patient charts were complete, we did it again. Ceventa certainly knew about the liver problems. I assumed they would report the adverse events to the FDA."

Luke didn't try to hide the anger in his voice. "Your Honor, we offer Dr. Challa's patient charts—oh, I'm sorry, Dr. Challa, *subject* charts—as exhibits. Pass the witness, Your Honor."

85

Audrey Metcalf almost jumped from her chair and marched to the witness. Before she could get there, the judge interrupted. "Ms. Metcalf, you haven't tried a case in my court before, but I require that the first time a lawyer approaches any witness he or she seek my permission."

Metcalf stopped in her tracks. "Permission to approach the witness, Your Honor?"

"Granted, Ms. Metcalf." Judge Nimitz beamed. "Goes back to my navy days when anyone had to ask permission to come aboard a ship."

Several of the jurors smiled at the interchange, knowing the judge's background.

Metcalf dropped a thick notebook on the bench in front of Dr. Challa. "You've seen this, haven't you, Doctor? It's the detailed policy and procedure manual for the Exxacia trial. And if you'll go to the last page, you'll find what, Dr. Challa?"

"That's my signature, Ms. Metcalf."

"You acknowledged that you had read this and agreed to *strictly* adhere to those protocols, didn't you?"

Challa picked up the document and flipped through the pages.

"Didn't you, Dr. Challa?"

"Yes, ma'am. I suppose I did. I read the important parts, anyway."

Metcalf grabbed the document from the witness and turned to a page she had previously marked. Forsythe displayed it on the overhead. "Right here, Dr. Challa, it says that you are to report any irregularities to Ceventa's regional supervisor, doesn't it?"

Challa glanced at the document and then at Tom Lorance, seeking some help. Lorance ignored him. "Yes, Ms. Metcalf, it does say that. I might add that your supervisor told me to just get all of the charts completed. He told me not to worry about what was in the manual."

"Objection, Your Honor! Nonresponsive. Move to instruct the jury to disregard."

Luke smiled at the answer and the objection, knowing that telling the jury to disregard what they just heard from the witness stand was equivalent to telling a child to ignore a commercial for erectile dysfunction on television. Still, the judge sustained the objection and instructed the jury.

"And, Dr. Challa, you were also instructed that if any patient failed to show up for an appointment, that patient was to be dropped from the clinical trial and reported to Ceventa."

"Yes, that's true, but I'd already received the five hundred dollars for those subjects, and I didn't want to have to give the money back."

"That's the problem, isn't it, Dr. Challa," Metcalf sneered. "You didn't care about your patients. You were just in it for the money. You were paid over fifty thousand dollars, and you weren't about to give any of it back, were you?"

Dr. Challa tried to sit up straight as he answered. "Certainly I took the money. I thought I was a part of something important."

Metcalf returned to her seat and continued. "Right, Doctor. Let's tell the jury a little more about your background. First of all, you tried three times to pass the family practice boards and failed all three times, correct?"

Dr. Challa lowered his head and mumbled something.

"We can't hear you, Dr. Challa!" Metcalf challenged.

Challa raised his head and said a little more loudly, "That's true."

"Now, if we wanted to find your office we'd go to that little strip center across from the university. Your office is in the middle between a liquor store and a convenience store, isn't it?"

"Yes, ma'am. My uncle makes me a good deal on the rent there, and it's convenient to the students."

"Speaking of your uncle, you work in his liquor store about half the time because you don't have very many patients, correct, Dr. Challa?"

Challa squirmed in his seat. "I help him sometimes if I'm not busy and he has to run an errand."

"And, Dr. Challa, there's no hospital in this town that will give you privileges, is there?"

"I don't have hospital privileges anywhere," Challa said softly, his eyes flitting about the room as if looking for a way to escape.

"That's all for this witness, Your Honor. I've heard all I need to from him."

"Now, wait just a minute, Judge," Tom Lorance said. "I resent and object to the sidebar comment."

"Sustained, Mr. Lorance. Ms. Metcalf, you best keep those kinds of comments to yourself. Mr. Lorance, you have any questions of your client?"

"Just one, Judge. Dr. Challa, have you done your dead level best to tell the truth to this jury?"

"Absolutely, Mr. Lorance," Dr. Challa said as he turned and looked at the jury to reaffirm his answer.

"If Ceventa had bothered to ask you about your background, the kinds of questions Ms. Metcalf just asked you, would you have told the truth then, too?"

"Of course, Mr. Lorance."

On the morning break, Luke pulled Sue Ellen over to a corner of the courtroom. "What do you think?"

"Luke, you did the best you could, but he didn't help us much. The jury did get a little peek at a part of the clinical trial, but overall Metcalf proved him to be nothing more than a hack, looking to make a few easy bucks."

"You holding up okay?" Luke asked.

Sue Ellen looked down and slowly shook her head as she turned to go back to the defense table.

Luke watched her walk away and wondered if he was doing the

right thing. Then his thoughts returned to the trial and he gazed out the window, his mind searching for a way to get all of the clinical trial data in evidence or somehow pull a rabbit out of a hat. Unfortunately, he had neither a rabbit nor a hat.

86

Luke walked Clyde Hartman through his background—college degree, medical school, residency in internal medicine—and his decision to choose to practice in a small town rather than accept an academic appointment. Certainly he was a far different physician from Dr. Challa. When Dr. Hartman glanced at the jury, he nodded at three who were his patients. If they trusted the care of their families to Dr. Hartman, they would believe what he had to say.

"Dr. Hartman, what's Samantha's current condition?"

Dr. Hartman faced the jury. "Her liver is failing. She spends most of her time in a hospital bed at home. She needs to be in the hospital, but she doesn't want to leave her dad. Instead, Mr. Vaughan arranged for a home health nurse to move in with them. She can get out of bed for a couple of hours at a time, only she's too weak to walk. She has to use a wheelchair. I stopped by to see her this morning. Now her abdomen is distended, full of fluid. It's called ascites. The ascites is a sign that her liver failure is reaching end stage. I'm going to have to stick a needle in her abdomen this evening to drain that fluid."

A number of the jurors grimaced at the description of the procedure. Luke was caught off guard as shock replaced the poker face he normally maintained as a trial lawyer.

"I'm sorry, Luke. I didn't have a chance to tell you before I took the stand. You and I can handle it this evening."

Luke took a moment to regain his composure and continued. "Doctor, I'm putting a photo of Samantha on the overhead. What can you tell the jury about it?"

The photo had been taken before Samantha got sick. It showed a beautiful redhead with a couple of freckles on the end of her nose, wearing a Texas State University T-shirt, jeans, and a smile that would have warmed the heart of any young man. Cocoa was at her feet, her face turned up to her mistress.

"That's Sam before she took Exxacia. She was a vibrant, beautiful young lady who was making straight A's at Texas State. I'm—"

Metcalf got to her feet. "Objection, Judge. He's trying to tie her illness to Exxacia, and he hasn't been shown to have the qualifications to express that opinion."

Judge Nimitz thought for a minute and even stared up to the ceiling as if looking for divine guidance. "Sustained, Mr. Vaughan, unless you can establish his credentials as a liver specialist."

Luke nodded his understanding. "No problem, Your Honor. Our hepatologist is the next witness. Dr. Hartman, is that how Sam looked before she came to you with hepatitis?"

"Yes. She was a beautiful girl."

Sue Ellen removed the photo and replaced it with a recent one, showing Sam in a wheelchair, much thinner, with washed-out hair and an obvious yellow tinge to her complexion.

"That's Sam as she looks now. She's lost about thirty pounds. Her skin is yellow; it's a little hard to see in this photo, but the whites of her eyes are also yellow."

Luke took a deep breath before he asked the next question. "How much longer does she have to live?"

Silence filled the courtroom. The jurors and everyone in the audience awaited Dr. Hartman's answer.

Clyde shook his head. "I wish I could be more optimistic, but at the very best a matter of months without a liver transplant, maybe only weeks. Dr. Stevens can be more precise."

Luke took a Kleenex from the box on the table and wiped his eyes as he said softly, "No more questions, Your Honor."

Audrey Metcalf knew she had to go easy on a local doctor. "Doctor, you're not qualified to say what caused the hepatitis, are you?"

"No, Ms. Metcalf, I'm not. However, I can say that it's a drug-induced hepatitis, and the only drug she had taken in at least two years before she got sick was Exxacia."

Metcalf started to object and then thought better of it. No reason to emphasize the point. She shifted to a different subject. "Doctor, you know that Samantha was a heavy drinker, don't you?"

"I know that as a teenager she did like a lot of teenagers. I suspect she had a little too much to drink a few times, but I understand she quit drinking when she returned from a semester at A&M."

"Now, Doctor," Metcalf said as she placed a document on the overhead, "you know that she was—"

Luke jumped to his feet, jerking the document from the overhead as he did. "Your Honor, we need to approach the bench."

Nimitz had a chance to glance at the document before it was pulled from the overhead and was already prepared to jump down Metcalf's throat.

"Judge," Luke whispered at the bench, "she just put up a copy of Sam's DUI conviction. She knew not to put it on her exhibit list because she knew you wouldn't allow it in evidence. You're the one who accepted her guilty plea and put her on probation. It's about to be expunged from her record. That conviction isn't admissible for any purpose. I demand sanctions!"

Nimitz tried to control his anger. "You lawyers come over to the side of the bench away from the jury." Judge Nimitz turned his chair away from the jury and waited for them to reach him. "Ms. Metcalf, I'm appalled at your conduct. If it wouldn't delay this trial, I'd hold you in contempt and have my bailiff throw you under the jail."

Metcalf tried to put a spin on her conduct. "Judge, it was just to emphasize her drinking problem, and we all know that heavy drinking can cause cirrhosis of the liver and many of the same symptoms Samantha has. I fully intended to advise the jury that it was a probated sentence that was removed from her record."

Judge Nimitz drummed his fingers on his bench as he thought. "Okay, here's what I'm going to do. At the next break, we're going to mark that conviction for the record, not to go to the jury, but for an appellate court to know what you've done. And, Ms. Metcalf, that's twice you and your client have conducted yourselves in a way that should be sanctioned. Two black marks and we're just barely into the trial. Don't you believe for a minute that I'm not keeping a running tally. This will be dealt with at the conclusion of the trial. Are you through with this witness?"

"No, Judge," Metcalf replied, not the least bit chagrined. "I have a couple more questions."

The lawyers returned to their seats as Judge Nimitz spoke to the jury. "Ladies and gentlemen, Ms. Metcalf put a document on the overhead that was not admitted into evidence. She and her client directly violated our rules of evidence. It was only up there briefly, but if any of you had a chance to see it, I command you to disregard it."

The jurors nodded their heads. Two studied Metcalf with looks of disdain.

"Dr. Hartman," Metcalf asked, "isn't it true that you ordered Tylenol for Samantha's headaches?"

Luke and Sue Ellen looked at each other, wondering what the relevance of the question was.

"Ms. Metcalf, I don't know if I ordered Tylenol, but I did note in my chart that she periodically had to take Tylenol for headaches. Tylenol seemed to give her the most relief."

"Thank you, Doctor." Metcalf smiled. "No more questions."

The last witness for the day was Shepherd Stevens, MD, the San Antonio hepatologist. His testimony was blunt. Samantha had only two or three months to live. It was imperative that she get a liver transplant, but that would cost half a million dollars. Her problem was further compounded by her rare blood type, severely limiting prospective donors. Over Audrey Metcalf's strenuous objections, Judge Nimitz permitted his opinion that the hepatitis and liver failure were directly caused by Exxacia.

87

Luke told Sue Ellen he would call her later in the evening, pushed past the reporters, telling them that he had to get ready for the next day, and hurried the three blocks to his house, pulling a large briefcase and dreading every step of the way. He wrestled with how to tell Sam that Clyde was going to have to put a needle in her abdomen and finally settled on a straightforward description of what was to be done and why. As he turned the corner, he saw Clyde's Chevrolet pickup parked in front of his house. Clyde rose from a rocker on the porch and met him at the steps with a look of concern on his face and a black bag in his left hand.

"How bad is it, Clyde?" Luke asked.

"She's got quite a bit of fluid in her abdomen. I've been monitoring it and trying to control it with a low-salt diet and diuretics. In addition to not eating, she's having some difficulty breathing. Draining the fluid will give her a lot of relief."

Luke knocked quietly on Samantha's door and then entered. Sam was curled into a ball under a single sheet, her breathing noticeably labored. Luke mentally kicked himself for not noticing the problem before, but he had been too wrapped up in trial preparation. Cocoa got up from her place at the foot of the narrow bed, stretched, and walked over to be petted. Luke hated to wake Samantha but knew he had no choice.

"Sam, Sam," he said quietly as he placed his hand on her shoulder. "Wake up, Sam."

Samantha stirred and then opened her eyes. The yellow in them seemed even more prominent. "Oh, hi, Dad. You already through for the day? Dr. Hartman, why are you here again?"

Luke sucked in a breath and sat on the edge of the bed. "Sam, Dr. Hartman says that the reason you're not eating is because there's fluid in your abdomen. He's going to get it out. Then you'll feel better and will be able to eat."

The pupils in Sam's eyes grew big. "How's he going to do that?" she asked, knowing that she wouldn't like what she was about to hear.

"Sam," Dr. Hartman said, "I'm going to put a needle into your abdomen. The only time you'll feel any pain is when I inject some local anesthetic."

"Dad, I don't want to do this. I hate needles," Samantha said as tears streamed down her cheeks.

Luke stroked Samantha's hand as he took a Kleenex and wiped her eyes, then his own. "I know, baby. We have to do it."

Samantha squeezed her eyes shut and said, "Okay. Get it over with. I don't want to look."

Clyde opened his bag and pulled out a bottle of Betadine, a small needle and syringe, a larger needle and syringe, some tubing, and a sterile quart-sized container. He raised Samantha's pajama top to expose her abdomen. "Okay, Sam, I'm going to clean the area. You'll just feel a cool liquid." Clyde gently rubbed the abdomen with Betadine and then picked up the smaller syringe and inserted the needle into a small bottle. "Sam, this is that little prick I told you about. It'll sting for just a few seconds, and then the area will be numb." As

Clyde injected the anesthetic, Samantha winced in pain and squeezed her dad's hand harder, then relaxed as the sensation dissipated.

"Okay, Sam, we're going to wait about a minute to make sure the anesthetic is effective. Then I'm going to put in a bigger needle and get rid of that fluid." Clyde picked up a large-bore needle and inserted it. Once he was satisfied it was in place, he removed the syringe and replaced it with a tube that was connected to the bottle he had placed on the floor. Dark yellow fluid filled the tube.

When the bottle was almost full, the flow from the tube went from a stream to a drip. It seemed like an eternity to Luke. Dr. Hartman gently removed the needle. "Okay, Sam, that's it. I'm going to wipe the area with a topical antibiotic and put a big Band-Aid on it. You can open your eyes. You're going to feel a lot better now."

Samantha blinked open her eyes as Luke again wiped tears away. He felt tension he had not even noticed drift from his body. "Sam, I'm going to get Mary to make you a chocolate milkshake. Thanks, Clyde."

Clyde nodded, told Samantha he would check on her the next day, and made his way to the front door.

"Sam, I'm going to be in my office. Call me if you need anything." Luke turned to go across the hall.

"Wait, Dad," Samantha said as she pushed the control button to raise her bed to a sitting position. "How's the trial going?"

"We're off to a good start." Luke smiled.

"What about Josh?"

"No word on him yet. I suspect he'll turn up in the next couple of days."

"Dad, are you still sure we're doing the right thing?"

"Yeah, baby, I am," Luke lied.

88

Ryan Sinclair walked to the end of his parents' driveway and picked up copies of the *Washington Post* and the *Montgomery County Sentinel*. He waved at a neighbor who was already heading into Washington to work and walked back into the house, where everyone else still slept.

Ryan poured a mug of coffee and buttered two English muffins when they popped out of the toaster. Then he sat at the kitchen table to catch up on the overnight news. As was his habit, he picked up the *Post* first. A two-inch filler caught his eye on the back of the national section. It was about the case involving Samantha Vaughan and Ceventa. All it said was that a young woman was dying and had sued Ceventa, alleging the company caused her condition.

He put his coffee down and picked up the *Sentinel,* which he knew had a beat writer who covered the pharmaceutical industry that was such a large part of the local economy. He flipped through the pages until he found a full story about Samantha Vaughan's case against Ceventa. Two doctors, one a liver specialist, had testified the day before that Samantha was dying and Exxacia was the cause. Alfred Kingsbury was quoted as saying that he felt sorry for the young lady, but he was certain the court and jury would find that her liver failure was not caused by Exxacia. In fact, he said, they had extremely strong scientific evidence to show no possible connection between her liver failure and Exxacia.

"Horseshit!" Ryan yelled out loud and then hoped that he had not awakened Sara and his parents. He picked up his coffee and walked out to the backyard, where he paced the deck and thought about what to do. He knew that Exxacia must have caused the girl's liver failure. He'd had the data to prove it until his house was fire bombed. After his Corvette was destroyed and then his house, he had promised Sara that he would not get involved. That was until he read what Kingsbury had to say. Maybe it was the last straw. Maybe it was the straw that broke the camel's back. Whatever it was, he realized he could not sit idly by on the sidelines while Kingsbury defended Exxacia. If Kingsbury won this case, doctors all over the country would continue to prescribe Exxacia. The result would be patients experiencing more liver problems and death, all because of a drug no better than ampicillin. It had suddenly hit him that he couldn't go through the rest of his life watching the adverse event reports appear on the FDA's Web site and counting the deaths he could have prevented. Twice he'd had the chance to stand up and state his opinions about this drug, and twice he had bowed to pressure from Boatwright. If he'd done his job, Exxacia would never have seen the light of day. Maybe he couldn't save Samantha's life, but he had one more chance to voice his opinions, this time in a public forum, and he was going to do it. If he was going to be convincing, he needed something to corroborate what he would say, only his evidence was gone. Then it hit him. Within twenty minutes he had showered and kissed Sara good-bye and was on the freeway to the office.

The guard on the first floor tried to talk sports. Ryan told him it would have to wait until later as he punched the elevator button, then punched it a second time when one didn't appear immediately. Finally the door opened. A few seconds later he was exiting on the fourth floor. He rushed by Lucille's desk. She looked up and tried to stop him.

"Dr. Sinclair. You're not on Dr. Boatwright's appointment calendar this morning, and he's on a very important phone call."

"He's about to get off that call, Lucille," Ryan said as he burst through Boatwright's door and locked it behind him.

Boatwright was indeed on the phone and stared at Ryan with

incredulity that Sinclair would dare enter his office unannounced. Ryan walked to his desk, reached over, and pushed the disconnect button on the phone.

"Dr. Sinclair, have you gone mad? This will certainly go in your personnel file. Now, turn around and march back where you came. I don't have time to talk to you."

"The hell you don't. I'll stay here until I get what I want. Give me the complete version of the Exxacia clinical trial, including all of my recommendations from beginning to end."

Boatwright nervously adjusted his tie and then stood to confront Sinclair. "Well, Dr. Sinclair, you really are mad. That version and your recommendations no longer exist. My policy is to destroy everything done on a preliminary basis once the study is submitted to the advisory committee."

Ryan moved deliberately around the desk and seized Boatwright's tie, shoving him against the wall. "You're lying, Boatwright! I know you always keep a personal copy of the complete clinical trial data on every drug that goes through this department. You either give it to me right now or I'm going straight to Capitol Hill to the Senate oversight committee. You and Kingsbury can explain to the committee about the clinical trial and how you destroyed the backup data."

Boatwright's voice trembled as he said, "All right. Let me go. I'll give it to you on one condition."

"And that is?" Ryan asked as he released his hold.

"You won't give it to Congress or to the media."

"Deal. Turn it over."

Boatwright walked to a locked file cabinet and punched in the combination to one of the drawers. When it opened, he handed Ryan a box of computer discs. Ryan seized them from Boatwright and turned to leave.

"Hey, why do you want it?" Boatwright asked.

"None of your damn business," Ryan replied as he slammed the door behind him.

When he got to his office, he did a quick search of each disc to confirm that the clinical trial data appeared complete. Next he confirmed that all of his recommendations were still there. Last, he typed in "Samantha Vaughan," and her file appeared on the screen. He recognized Dr. Challa's name as one of the clinical investigators who had multiple problems and had been part of an ongoing investigation. He was about to leave the site when he noticed the date that Samantha Vaughan became a subject. "Double horseshit!" he said. "She was one of the last few subjects. Why didn't Boatwright and Kingsbury listen to me?"

Ryan knew that Lucas Vaughan would be in court and he couldn't track him down until that evening. He counted the hours until he could place a call.

89

As soon as Boatwright could compose himself, he shut the door to his office and called Kingsbury's cell. It rang four times, and Boatwright assumed he would have to leave a message, but then he heard, "Kingsbury here."

"Alfred, it's Roger Boatwright."

"Roger," Kingsbury boomed, "how are you? How's Joanne? Sorry if I sound out of breath. I'm on the golf course and was leaving the fourteenth tee when I heard the phone ring. What can I do for you?"

"Alfred, Ryan Sinclair stormed into my office just now and demanded the complete version of the Exxacia clinical trial, the one I had locked up."

Kingsbury walked away from the golf carts as the other members of the foursome were returning. He lowered his voice. "You didn't give it to Sinclair, did you?"

"I didn't have any choice. He threatened to go to Congress if I didn't. I did get him to agree that he wouldn't turn it over to Congress or the media. That's the best deal I could make."

"Dammit, Boatwright, I told you to destroy that data."

"Alfred, what kind of a fool do you take me for? Those discs were my insurance policy to make sure you kept your part of our bargain." Boatwright hesitated. "And I'm losing patience pretty damn quick. I need the rest of that five million in my account."

"All right, Boatwright, simmer down. I'm working on it. If Sinclair does what I think, this whole thing could unravel. I can't let that happen. Give me a week and I'll make it right with you."

Kingsbury clicked off his phone and told the other three golfers that he had a business emergency. His cart mate volunteered to drive him back to the clubhouse; on the way he commiserated with Kingsbury for having to leave such a fine round before the end.

Kingsbury stepped from the elevator at the penthouse and told his assistant that he was not to be disturbed. He locked the door behind him and went to a secure phone. His two primary bodyguards were in Texas, but he had backups who were capable of doing the job. He placed a call, advised the recipient of his mission, and negotiated the financial arrangements. When he hung up the phone, he thought about all he had done to ensure the success of Exxacia. All of the problems seem to have stemmed from that damned case in Texas. Clearly it was time for him to do a firsthand assessment.

90

There was another delivery to Sue Ellen overnight. This time it was one of Josh's Nike running shoes. Sue Ellen called Luke at six in the morning.

"Luke, one of Josh's shoes was on my front porch," Sue Ellen cried into the phone. "I don't think I can go on."

Luke hesitated, unsure what to say or do. "Sue Ellen, stick it out one more day. The combined task force is now over a hundred officers. They're bound to find Josh soon." Luke paused and continued. "I need your help. So does Sam."

Luke heard a quiet click on the line, and Sue Ellen was gone. When he got to the courthouse, though, he found her sitting at their counsel table, head down and hands folded in front of her. He touched her shoulder and said, "Thanks."

At the end of the previous day, Luke had evaluated their case after the testimony of Dr. Stevens. The ruling that kept out the clinical trial data left them with their epidemiologist, several of Samantha's friends to testify about her life before and after developing hepatitis, and Samantha herself. Over Metcalf's strenuous objection, Nimitz had granted Luke's request that Samantha testify by video feed from home.

Ruth Ann Crawford, MD, PhD, the epidemiologist, was short and a little stocky, with her gray hair in a bun. Her expertise was statistics, particularly in the field of medical trials and drug efficacy. She had been prepared to launch a scientific attack on the entire Exxacia trial, but the judge's ruling cut her testimony by eighty percent. Still, Luke thought he could get some value from her.

"Dr. Crawford, tell the jury a little about your background and education," Luke said after she had been sworn in and given her name for the record.

An experienced witness, she turned to the jury and tried to look each one of them in the eye as she spoke. "I have a medical degree from Baylor College of Medicine in Houston, and my PhD is from the University of Texas. I'm what's called an epidemiologist. That's a medical numbers person. We usually study diseases and their prevalence in certain populations. We also get involved in clinical trials to evaluate the risks of new drugs that are being studied."

Luke watched the jury and saw that they were quite interested in what was ordinarily a very dry subject. *Too bad,* he thought, *we couldn't lay out all the problems with the complete clinical trial.* "Dr. Crawford, I want you to focus only on the Exxacia clinical trial data that was prepared by Dr. Challa. Is that clear?"

Judge Nimitz nodded toward Luke, pleased that he was not going to intentionally violate his rulings.

"I understand, Mr. Vaughan. I know that Judge Nimitz has ruled that the rest of the data won't come into evidence."

Oops, Luke thought as he looked at Judge Nimitz to see if he was going to get a reprimand because his witness injected the judge's ruling into the case. Judge Nimitz maintained a poker face. Audrey Metcalf started to object, thought better of it, and returned to her seat.

Luke handed Dr. Challa's patient charts to the witness. "Doctor, based on your experience and training, how do you evaluate this portion of the clinical trial?"

Again Dr. Crawford turned to the jury. "Frankly, this is about as sloppy a piece of work as I've ever seen. Not only should it not be relied on by anybody evaluating Exxacia, but further, the incidence of liver problems is higher than with any antibiotic I've ever seen."

Luke looked at Sue Ellen, who nodded. "Thank you, Dr. Crawford. That's all I have."

Audrey Metcalf tapped her pen on her table long enough that she was about to be chastised by Judge Nimitz when she finally spoke.

"Of course, Dr. Crawford, you would agree that no one should rely on so little evidence to determine the efficacy and safety of any drug."

"I agree, Ms. Metcalf," Dr. Crawford said, nodding. "If you like, I'll be happy to discuss the remainder of the clinical trial."

Luke jumped to his feet. "Your Honor, we certainly have no objection if Ms. Metcalf wants to get into it."

Metcalf figured she'd better give up on Dr. Crawford. Questioning some witnesses was like Br'er Rabbit and the tar baby. Obviously, Dr. Crawford was one of those witnesses.

Metcalf rose. "Your Honor, I appreciate Mr. Vaughan's offer, but I decline. No more questions."

Two jurors on the back row looked at one another. One whispered that he didn't understand why they couldn't learn more about the drug.

Samantha's friends took up the next several hours. Luke timed it so that the last hour would be for Samantha. Each of them described her as the all-American girl who was capable of doing anything in life she chose, that is, of course, until she got sick. Brad was the last friend to testify. He tried to be strong and stoic but finally broke down and testified between loud sobs. Two women on the front row grabbed for Kleenex.

It was four o'clock, and Luke announced, "Judge, we are calling my daughter, Samantha Vaughan."

The jurors looked toward the door, expecting to see Samantha wheeled in, until the judge said, "Ladies and gentlemen, we're doing something a little different here. I've ruled that Samantha can testify by video from her home. Bailiff, would you roll the television to the usual place where all the jurors can see it."

As he did so, a technician paid by Luke clicked it on and called his counterpart at the Vaughan house. Momentarily, Samantha appeared on the screen, seated in her wheelchair beside her bed. Sue Ellen had left the courtroom and was standing behind her. Judge Nimitz administered the oath.

"Sam, can you hear me?" Luke asked.

"Fine, Dad."

"Sam, you can't see us, but thirteen jurors and the judge are watching you, also Audrey Metcalf and her team for Ceventa. How are you feeling today, Sam?"

Sam smiled at the camera and replied, "About the same as most days."

"Most days you're sleeping twelve to fourteen hours at night and then take a long afternoon nap?"

"Yes, sir. Mary just got me up thirty minutes ago and helped me put on a little makeup. I'm sorry, ladies and gentlemen, for how I look."

All of the women on the jury smiled in understanding.

"When did this start, Sam?"

"Dad, you know that you and Brad are the ones that first noticed it. I thought that I was just studying too hard and staying up too late. It was a few months after I quit seeing Dr. Challa, I think."

"Sam, I don't want you to get too tired. So that's all I'm going to ask. I'll see you when I get home."

Judge Nimitz had walked over to stand by the jury to watch Samantha. From there he asked, "Ms. Metcalf, do you have any questions?"

"Just one, Judge. Ms. Vaughan, even before you took Exxacia, you took Tylenol regularly, didn't you?"

Samantha frowned as she thought. "Well, ma'am, when I would get a headache I would take a few Tylenol until it went away, just like anyone else would."

"That's all, Your Honor."

"Sam, we're going to turn off the television now," Luke said.

Luke checked his notes and then spoke to the judge. "Your Honor, plaintiff rests."

The judge turned to face the jury. "Ladies and gentlemen, here's the good news. You're getting out early today. The better news is that tomorrow is Friday and we won't have court. Now, don't you go telling your neighbors that Judge Nimitz takes Fridays off and goes fishing. I've got a full docket of motions in the morning, and in the afternoon I've got to hear criminal pleas. I'll see you Monday morning at nine o'clock."

91

Luke looked in on Samantha and found her asleep, so he went upstairs and changed into shorts, a blue golf shirt, and sandals. After checking messages, he went out the back door to find Whizmo in his wood shop, sander in hand and safety goggles covering his eyes. It took a moment for Whizmo to realize Luke was there, but then he shut down the sander and removed the goggles.

"How goes it, bro?" he asked.

Luke extended his right hand and made a wavering motion. "Comme ci, comme ça," he said. "Actually, Whiz, not even that good. We've got a boatload of sympathy on our side. We had jurors crying today, but our liability case is weak without the entire clinical trial in evidence."

Whiz wiped the sweat from his face and hands. "Luke, you know I'm not very religious, but I always liked that saying that when God closes a door, somewhere he opens a window. You've just got to find that window."

"Easier said than done." Luke grimaced. "This trial is gonna be over by the middle of next week. If God's going to open a window, he better do it fast."

When he got back in the house, he saw Sue Ellen coming through the front door, still dressed in her courtroom suit and with a determined but somehow frightened look on her face. Her eyes were red.

Luke met her at the door and tried to kiss her. She dodged his effort. "They dropped the other shoe," she said.

"They what?" Luke asked.

"Josh's other Nike was on my front porch when I got home. Luke, I'm not sure how much more of this I can take."

"I'm sorry, Sue Ellen. I still think we're doing the right thing."

"You may think so," Sue Ellen erupted. "It's not your child whose life is in danger!"

"Yes, it is," Luke replied quietly.

Sue Ellen stared at Luke in dismay. "You just don't get it, do you?" Then she turned and stormed from the house.

Stunned by Sue Ellen's comment and her demeanor, Luke returned to his desk, where he reevaluated what he was doing and the impact on all of their lives. Now he realized he was also risking losing Sue Ellen. Still, when he weighed all of the potential outcomes, he knew that he would risk the loss of Sue Ellen and Josh if it meant that somehow he could save his daughter. He had been dealt a hand that he was not sure would be a winner for anyone. Still he was convinced that he had no choice but to play it until all the cards were on the table.

Then the phone rang. The voice on the other end said, "Luke, this is Ryan Sinclair. I think I can help you now."

92

Luke spent a fitful night, trying to sleep. It was almost like he was a kid on Christmas Eve. He awoke to check the alarm clock every thirty minutes. When the first light of dawn crept over the horizon, he was up and showering. As directed, he wore an orange golf shirt and black pants. Having remembered to make the coffee and set the timer the night before, he filled a large go-cup. He found a Texas Longhorns baseball cap in the downstairs closet, the last part of his outfit intended for identification. He tried to tiptoe past Samantha's room and was almost out the front door when he heard her voice.

"Dad, I'm awake."

Luke opened her door to find her bed in the upright position.

"I couldn't sleep. I kept thinking all night that Dr. Sinclair is going to help us win our case. Will he?"

Luke sat on the edge of her bed as the sun began to stream through a crack in her curtains. "I don't know, kiddo. He says what he has is going to blow Ceventa out of the water. Don't get your hopes up. It may turn out to be nothing. Still, his plane lands in two hours. We should be back here before noon. Cross your fingers."

Samantha crossed fingers on both hands. "I think I'll say a few prayers, too."

"That might just work," Luke said as he leaned over to kiss Samantha good-bye.

When Luke went down the front steps, the deputy saw him and walked over from his car. "Mr. Vaughan, we didn't expect you to be leaving this early. I'm the only one here. Let me call for another deputy to escort you to wherever you're going."

"Thanks, Brian. That won't be necessary. I'm going to Bergstrom to pick up a witness. I'll watch my backside. You stay here and take care of Samantha."

"Okay, sir." Brian frowned. "Only I'd feel better if I was going along with you."

Luke drove slowly through an awakening San Marcos to I-35, where he turned north for the short drive to Austin's Bergstrom Airport.

As he drove, his spirits were lifting. Finally they were getting a break. Maybe Whizmo was right about God opening that window. Sinclair hadn't told him much, only that he had located a version of the clinical trial data that he was certain Ceventa had not produced, the complete study, he called it. Sinclair said he was sick of the FDA doing the bidding of the big drug companies, but he had been scared off by the threats to his family. Now he had changed his mind and realized that he had to do the right thing. He was willing to testify. Luke could only hope that his resolve would remain strong. He would find out in a few hours.

Luke parked his car in the visitor lot and flipped the lock as he shut the door. A glance at his watch told him he was an hour early. Time enough for an Egg McMuffin and another cup of coffee. He stopped at the Hudson News stand for an *Austin American-Statesman* and then found McDonald's. Choosing a table away from other travelers, he flipped to the local section of the paper. There it was on the first page, a story about Samantha and the trial. The reporter, who had been in the courtroom when all of Samantha's friends testified and Samantha appeared on video, had taken a human interest angle and had even gone to the campus to interview some of Samantha's other friends. All in all, it was a well-written story. Luke could only hope that one or two of the jurors subscribed to the Austin paper.

Luke finished his Egg McMuffin and carried his coffee with him to the security checkpoint at the Southwest Airlines concourse. Sinclair had described himself and said he would be wearing a yellow golf shirt, tan pants, and Nike running shoes. Half an hour to go. Luke sipped his coffee and scrutinized each man who came through the checkpoint. As the time approached, he walked the few steps to the monitors displaying arrivals and departures. The flight from Baltimore was on time. Five minutes after the plane arrived at the gate, people were coming through the checkpoint, some hurrying to baggage claim, some being greeted by family and friends. Luke knew he was in the right place when a woman asked her husband how the flight from Baltimore was. He waited. After twenty minutes no one looking anything like Ryan Sinclair had approached. Luke looked at his watch and began to worry.

Where was he? Did he miss his flight? Maybe he was on the next one.

Luke walked back to the displays to find that another flight by way of Dallas was to land in an hour and a half. Sinclair must be on that one. Luke took one last look down the concourse and cussed himself for not asking Sinclair for his cell phone number. No choice but to wait. The hour and a half crept by. Luke wandered through the airport shops, pausing at least every five minutes to check his watch. Again he returned to the Southwest concourse and checked the monitors. The plane was en route from Dallas, expected to arrive on time. Then he turned his attention to the disembarking passengers. When the plane landed, he edged closer to the checkpoint. No one fitting Sinclair's description walked past. When he realized that Sinclair was missing in action, he found a relatively quiet place on the concourse and pulled out his cell phone. Maybe Sinclair had had a change of plans, maybe a family emergency. There was probably a message on his machine back home.

He dialed information for the FDA in Silver Spring and was directed to another number for the Center for Drug Evaluation and Research. Finally a female voice answered, "Dr. Sinclair's office."

Not wanting to give his name to a stranger in CDER, Luke just said, "Dr. Sinclair, please."

The voice on the other end replied cautiously, "May I ask what this is about?"

"Yes, ma'am. I was supposed to meet with Dr. Sinclair this morning, and he didn't keep the appointment."

"Sir, I have access to his appointment calendar, and it shows only that he was taking a personal business day today."

Luke was getting exasperated. "Look, that personal business was with me. Can you please give me his cell phone number?"

There was silence on the other end of the phone. Luke wondered if his cell phone had disconnected. "Ma'am, are you still there?"

"Sir, Dr. Sinclair died last night."

Stunned, Luke almost dropped his phone. "What happened? A car accident?"

"Sir, I'm not at liberty to discuss his death. I suggest you call the Rockville police. Good day, sir."

93

Luke slowly closed his phone and stood quietly, oblivious to the crowds around him. Now what? Nothing came to mind. Then he paced the corridors, trying to sort out all that had happened.

What the hell is going on? Luke thought. *Sinclair calls me yesterday. Says he can blow Ceventa out of the water. Now he's dead and the police are involved.* He knew nothing about Sinclair. Car wreck? Suicide? Murder? That was a distinct possibility. Who would want to murder a young doctor? There was only one logical suspect. After what had happened to him and Josh, it had to be Ceventa. But why? Why would Ceventa engage in murder and kidnapping because of a new drug? Just how big were the stakes in this game he was playing? Only one way to find out more about Sinclair's death. He checked the departure monitors. A flight to Baltimore left in twenty minutes. He made his way to the Southwest counter. "You have a seat on the next flight to Baltimore?"

"Let me check, sir," the agent said. After studying her computer, she continued, "Two seats left. It makes one stop in Nashville. Shall I book one? You'll have to hurry. The flight leaves in fifteen minutes."

"Please. Here's my driver's license and American Express card."

"Checking baggage?"

"No, ma'am," Luke said, "just carry-on." Luke had nothing with him but didn't want to take a chance that a passenger with no bags would trigger some kind of security alert.

The agent checked his license, glanced at his face for comparison, and returned it and his credit card. "Here's your ticket. Have a good flight."

Luke trotted back to the security checkpoint and paused to get his breath before handing his ticket and license to the first agent. Fortunately, the line was short. He emptied his pockets, took off his belt and shoes, and walked through the metal detector. As he hurried down the concourse he called home. Mary Sanchez picked up. "Mary, I'm in Austin. Is Sam awake?"

"No, Luke. She went back to sleep after you left."

"Don't bother her. Just tell her I'm flying to Baltimore. I should be back tomorrow night. I'll explain later."

Luke clicked off the phone and punched in Whizmo's number. Whiz picked up on the first ring. "You got him?"

"Sinclair's dead, Whiz."

"What? When? You just talked to him last night."

"All I know is he's dead and his secretary told me to talk to the police if I wanted more information. I'm catching a flight to Baltimore in ten minutes. Get on the Internet and find the address of Maxwell Sinclair. That's Ryan's dad. Sinclair and his wife have been staying with Ryan's parents since their house was bombed. I hate to bother his wife or family, but I don't have any choice. If I can catch her today, I'll be out of here first thing in the morning."

"You got it, Luke," Whiz replied. "Call me when you land. And I think I'll do a little more Internet research this weekend. Good luck."

94

Luke's plane landed in Baltimore at five thirty, an hour late after a delay in Nashville. He checked his watch as the plane taxied to the gate. When the plane stopped, even before the attendant announced they could disembark, Luke was out of his seat and bolting down the aisle.

"Sir, you'll need to return to your seat. The captain hasn't given the signal," the voice on the speaker commanded. Luke ignored her. What could she do? Kick him off the plane? The tone sounded and passengers started scrambling from their seats. Luke was first to the front, where the attendant met him.

"Sir, I'll need to get your name. You put our passengers in danger."

Just then, another attendant opened the door. Luke pushed past both of them and was on the gangway. He sprinted to the Hertz counter, wishing that he had called ahead to use his Gold Card so that a car would be waiting.

"I need a car," Luke said to the agent. "Here's my driver's license and my American Express. I'm a Gold member."

The young woman behind the counter popped her gum as she pulled up his information. *Come on, come on,* Luke thought.

"You have a preference?"

"I'll take any car you've got as long as it's quick. I'm late for a meeting. Oh, and I need one with a GPS."

"You're in luck, Mr. Vaughan," she said as she handed his license and credit card back. "I don't need your credit card. We have it on file. A Malibu just came from the wash. Catch the bus across the street and look for your name on the display when you get to the lot. The keys will be in the car."

Luke thanked her and ran for the door just as a Hertz bus pulled away. *Dammit,* he thought. *Now I just lost five minutes I can't afford.* He reached into his pocket, yanked out his cell, and called Whizmo.

"I thought I'd hear from you sooner. You have a problem?" Whiz asked when he picked up his phone.

"Yeah, thunderstorms in Nashville, and I couldn't even get cell service. I'm trying to get to the Sinclair house before dark. You get the information?"

Luke dug through his pockets until he found a scrap of paper and took down the address and phone number. There was still no Hertz bus in sight. Realizing he had a couple of minutes, he rushed back into the terminal and found a newsstand, where he bought the *Montgomery County Sentinel* and the *Washington Post.*

When he left the terminal for the second time, he saw the bus stopped and its doors starting to shut. He yelled at the driver, who nodded at him and opened the doors.

"Thank you, sir," Luke said as he climbed aboard.

"Hertz is here to please," the driver said, smiling. "Find a seat, and it'll be a five-minute ride to the Hertz Center."

Luke took a seat and started reading the headlines in the *Sentinel.* The story was on the third page.

A doctor with the FDA was found dead in Rock Creek Park this morning. An early morning jogger found the body near the trail that winds through the park. The doctor was Ryan Sinclair, an infectious disease specialist with the Center for Drug Evaluation and Research. Dr. Sinclair was found, dressed in a suit and tie, one hundred yards from the east parking lot, where he apparently left his car. There was a gun in his hand and one bullet wound in his head. A police spokesman stated that it appeared to be a suicide, but the investigation is ongoing.

Luke skimmed the rest of the article and was interrupted by the driver's announcement. "Gold Club members, please exit here. Please look for your name on the display and you'll find the number of the space where your car is located. Have a great stay in Baltimore or wherever you may be going."

Luke got off the bus and found his name. His car was in space 341. While the other customers were retrieving their baggage, Luke jogged to his rental car. He started it and input the Sinclair address into the GPS. The estimated driving time was over an hour. Too late. By then it would be dark. He decided a visit to Sara Sinclair would have to wait until morning.

95

Luke put Rock Creek Park into his GPS and discovered it was about thirty minutes away. *I'm not a detective,* he thought, *but I'm too close not to check out the scene.* Luke parked at the east lot, where Sinclair's car was found. Several other cars were in the lot. Probably joggers. There was only one path leading from it, following the creek that meandered through the park. Estimating he had about fifteen minutes of daylight, he started down the path at a brisk walk, passing occasional joggers heading in the other direction. Quite a bit of activity for this time of the evening. Suicide or even murder, it must have occurred later, when the trail was probably deserted. Luke rounded a curve and found crime scene tape blocking the trail. Chalk outlined the position of the body. As he studied the scene, more joggers passed. One stopped.

"Hey, man, you a detective?"

"No." Luke shook his head. "I'm just a friend of the victim. Wanted to have a look at the scene."

"Tough, man. I heard he was a doctor. Don't know why he was out here in the dark, dressed in a suit and tie. See you."

Luke nodded as the jogger ran away. He realized he was out of his element but agreed with the jogger that something wasn't right. Luke turned and walked slowly back to his car, started the engine, and returned to the freeway, where he started looking for a Target or a Walmart, somewhere to buy a clean dress shirt and toiletries, maybe even a sport coat for his meeting with Sara Sinclair the next day. When he spotted a Target, there was a La Quinta next door. *Perfect,* he thought.

Fifteen minutes later Luke left the Target with a blue dress shirt and a blue checked sport coat that was a little too big but okay, along with a razor, shaving cream, a toothbrush, and toothpaste.

He checked in, requesting a room in the back away from the freeway noise, and pulled around the motel. He entered his room, dropped his purchases on the bed, and flipped on CNN as he called home. To his surprise, Samantha answered.

"Dad, what are you doing in Baltimore? Are you all right?"

"I'm fine, sweetie. Let me tell you about my day."

Luke described the events that led him to a motel in Baltimore.

When he finished, Samantha exclaimed, "My God, what's going on, Dad? Why would this Dr. Sinclair commit suicide, and where is the stuff that he was going to bring us?"

"I wish I could answer your questions, Sam, only I can't. I'm going to Sinclair's house tomorrow. Hopefully I'll find the discs Sinclair was talking about. You doing okay?"

"I'm doing as good as I can, Dad," Samantha said softly. "I was really excited about what Dr. Sinclair was bringing. Now I think I'll just curl up under the covers and pretend this day didn't happen."

"I'm sorry, Sam," Luke replied. "Don't give up hope yet."

96

Luke showered, shaved, and dressed, then checked himself in the mirror. He hadn't bothered to buy a tie but concluded that he looked reasonably professional. After a quick breakfast at the motel buffet, he was in the car and headed to Maxwell Sinclair's house.

Once he was in the neighborhood, the voice from the GPS directed him through several turns until he found the house. One car, an Infiniti, was in the driveway. Luke left his car and walked up the sidewalk. *Jeez, I hate to do this,* he thought. Then he thought about Samantha and rang the doorbell. An older man, dressed in gray slacks, a white shirt, and loafers, opened the door.

"Dr. Sinclair?" Luke asked.

"Yes."

Luke fumbled for words. "Look, I'm sorry to bother you, but could I talk to Sara for a few minutes?"

"Absolutely not," the man replied sternly. "I don't recognize you and Sara's too upset to see anyone."

The man started to shut the door, and Luke put his hand up to stop it. "Dr. Sinclair, my name's Lucas Vaughan. I was supposed to meet Ryan in Austin yesterday."

"Let him in, Max," a woman's voice from inside the house said.

Ryan's father reluctantly opened the door. "You'll need to make it very brief, Mr. Vaughan."

Luke entered to find Sara Sinclair, obviously pregnant, sitting on the sofa with a television playing in the background. She appeared to be paying no attention to the program.

"Ms. Sinclair, I'm terribly sorry about your loss."

"Thank you, Mr. Vaughan," Sara replied as she wiped her eyes. "Please have a seat. What do you need?"

Luke chose a side chair close to the sofa. "Mrs. Sinclair . . ."

"Call me Sara."

"Sara, I was supposed to meet Ryan in Austin yesterday. When he didn't arrive, I started checking and found out what had happened. Again, I'm sorry about his suicide."

Sara leaned forward. "Luke, Ryan didn't kill himself. I'm his wife. He and I were ecstatic about a son coming into our lives. It was murder."

"But he was found with a gun in his hand."

"We don't even own a gun."

Luke hesitated and then asked, "This is not why I'm here, but would you tell me what happened?"

Sara rearranged herself and tucked her feet beside her on the couch. "Ryan came home, well, to this house, which is our temporary home, and told me he had confronted Boatwright, demanding some other version of the Exxacia clinical trial. Then he went into our bedroom, where he has a desk—"

Luke motioned for her to stop. "I'm sorry to interrupt, Sara, but are you saying he got that version from Boatwright?"

"Exactly. He went into our room, and I heard him talking on the phone. He said your name. When he came out, he told me he had purchased a ticket to Austin, leaving yesterday morning, and would be back in a few days. Then his cell phone rang. Ryan looked at the caller ID and returned to our room and shut the door." Sara paused. "That was strange. He never before had shut that door. We didn't have any secrets.

"When he came out, he had his coat on and was carrying his briefcase. He told me he had to leave for a few minutes. That's the last time I saw him alive," Sara said as great rivers of tears rolled down her cheeks.

Ryan's dad had chosen to leave Luke and Sara alone. Now he

stepped into the living room and interrupted. "Mr. Vaughan, it's time for you to leave."

Sara stopped him. "No, Max, it's all right. His daughter's dying. I want to help if I can."

Max shook his head and returned to his office.

"Who called, Sara?"

"Ryan didn't say. He took his briefcase with him, so I figured it was Boatwright or someone else from the office."

Luke sat silently as he allowed all of the information to sink in, then asked, "What was in the briefcase?"

Sara shook her head. "It was never found. The police searched his car and the park. There was no sign of it. That's another reason I know it wasn't suicide. Someone had to have stolen it."

Luke rose. "Sara, you know I hate to be bothering you now, but I need those discs. Do you think he had them with him? Do you think they're around the house anywhere?"

Sara stretched her hands out in front of her. "I'm sorry, Luke. Strange as this may sound, I knew those discs were important to Ryan and to you. I woke up last night and couldn't force myself to fall asleep. So I searched this house high and low. I even searched Ryan's new laptop, the one he got after our house was bombed. I'm pretty good on computers. If there was something there, I could have found it. That data is not in this house or on his computer."

Luke blew his breath out of pursed lips. "Then the discs had to have been in that briefcase. I agree with you, Sara. Ryan didn't commit suicide. I'll be leaving now. If you find anything useful, here's my card. Call me anytime, day or night. Again, I'm sorry about your loss."

"I will, Luke. I hope your daughter gets through this."

97

As Luke pulled into the driveway at dusk, he saw Samantha, Whizmo, and Brad all gathered to greet him. Sue Ellen was conspicuously absent. He forced himself out of the mood that had settled on him and hugged Samantha and tried to give a cheery greeting to Whizmo and Brad. Then he sat in one of the rockers and told them about his day.

"Bottom line is that I came up short. The version that Ryan Sinclair told us about is nowhere to be found."

"That sucks, Dad," Samantha said. "What do we do now?"

"Here's what we do, Sam," Luke responded. "We finish this trial. The jury can still go our way."

Whizmo had remained silent, quietly sipping on his beer. "Well, Brad and I have some good news. Brad, tell Luke what you found."

Brad had been sitting on the steps. He got up to face Luke. "I searched PubMed and all of the medical databases I could find. There are some European journal articles that have been coming out recently that are pretty critical of Exxacia. There's one very positive American article that praises Exxacia, only I did some digging about the authors. Every one of them has taken money, so-called honorariums, from Ceventa. In fact, one of the authors is a full-time employee of Ceventa. I'll bet he wrote the whole damn thing. Paper copies of the articles are on your desk."

Luke nodded his appreciation. "Thanks, Brad. Now I've just got to figure out how and when to use them. We'll see who Metcalf calls on Monday and make the decision on the fly. Now, Whiz, what have you been up to?"

"First of all, Luke, you know I teach computer science. What you may not know is that I'm one of the world's great hackers. Given enough time, there's no server in the world that I can't get into." Whiz smiled.

"Go on, Whiz, get to the point," Luke insisted.

"I got into Ceventa's server, and here's what I found."

Whizmo bent over and picked a manila folder up from the floor. He extracted computer printouts of Ceventa documents and handed them to Luke, who flipped through them before he let out a low whistle. "Wow! Now we've gotta hope that Metcalf calls someone I can use these with."

"Well," Whiz said, "I think it was some philosopher who said that it was always darkest before the dawn. I do believe that the sun is about to rise."

98

Luke got the call at seven o'clock on Sunday morning.

"Luke, you've got to come over here," Sue Ellen said.

"What's up? Did they find Josh?"

"No, just get over here now. We need to talk face-to-face."

Luke hung up the phone, not liking Sue Ellen's tone. He slipped on a pair of shorts, a T-shirt, and thongs and left the house. Brian again approached him, and again he told Brian that he was only going three blocks to Sue Ellen's. Brian returned to his patrol car and called his counterpart at Sue Ellen's to alert him that Luke was on his way.

Luke opened Sue Ellen's door to find her on the couch, a Kleenex box in her lap. Without a word she handed him a packing envelope.

When he extracted the contents he found a San Marcos High School T-shirt with blood splattered on the front, as if someone had landed a fist on Josh's face.

"That's Josh's shirt," Sue Ellen sobbed. "Luke, we can't go on with the lawsuit. Look at this note that was with the T-shirt."

Luke took the note from her. It read, *If this lawsuit continues, the next delivery will be a finger from Josh's throwing hand. So much for quarterbacking for the Longhorns.*

Luke chose to tread lightly as he sat beside Sue Ellen. "What do you want me to do?"

"Dismiss the lawsuit tomorrow morning, Luke! I can't take it anymore. I love Samantha, but I love Josh more."

Luke ran his fingers through his hair and rose to stand at the window. Then he turned. "Sue Ellen, we'll be through with this case in two days. It'll all come out all right," he pleaded.

Resolve appeared in Sue Ellen's face. "No, Luke. I've gone as far as I can go. If you won't dismiss the case, I won't be beside you tomorrow. Maybe whoever is doing this will notice that I'm off the case. I love you, Luke, but you're on your own. I'm sorry."

Sue Ellen bolted up the stairs to her bedroom. Luke contemplated following her but instead turned and left the house.

Desperate, Sue Ellen regained her composure and called Whizmo.

"Hey, Sue Ellen, any word on Josh yet?" Whizmo asked.

Sue Ellen explained what had happened that morning. "Whizmo, you've got to convince Luke to drop the case. He won't listen to me. Maybe he'll listen to you."

Whizmo thought about the request and responded, "Sue Ellen, I'm not willing to do that yet. I know what you're going through—"

"Dammit, don't say that! No one knows what I'm going through," Sue Ellen interrupted.

"You're right," Whizmo said softly. "I can't imagine what it must be like, but I'm not willing to interfere with Luke's decision. Still, I've got an idea. I know a few folks in the Hill Country, some of them that wouldn't cooperate with the law if a trooper handed them a thousand dollars in advance. I may have better luck. Let me wind up a little project for Luke and I'll hit the road this afternoon. Don't give up hope."

99

Whizmo, of course, was talking about his biker friends, not the lawyers and doctors and stockbrokers, but the ones who worked as mechanics and laborers to maintain their biker lifestyle. A number of them also supplemented their income dealing dope and wanted nothing to do with anyone remotely connected with law enforcement. Whizmo knew most of these bikers in Central Texas. What they did for a living was not his concern. They had the common bond of the Harley, and he treated them as equals. His search for Josh would be with them. While it was possible that one of them could be involved, Whizmo really doubted it. All he was looking for was a lead. Besides, like Luke and Sue Ellen, he was convinced that Ceventa was somehow behind the kidnapping.

After Whizmo got off the phone with Sue Ellen, he surveyed the trial projects Luke had given him and figured he could take the rest of the day off. He went to his desk and picked up a photo of Josh, a copy of the one that the law enforcement officers had plastered around San Marcos. He looked at Josh's handsome face and thought, *Hang in there, young man. I'm coming for you.*

Whizmo headed west. He didn't need a map. He knew the roads and knew the hangouts where he was seeking a lead. The first one was barely outside the San Marcos city limits. The patrons there were a mixture of the old hog riders and some of the young professionals. There were maybe a dozen Harleys along with a handful of pickups in the gravel parking lot.

Whizmo walked through the front door and was greeted by the bartender and got hand waves from some of the customers. "Whiz, where you been?" the bartender asked as he handed Whizmo a Bud Light.

"Gotta pass on the beer, Howie," Whiz replied. "I'm going to be doing a lot of riding today." Whiz pulled Josh's photo from his pocket. "I'm looking for this kid, name's Josh Taggert, big kid, six feet, two hundred pounds, sixteen. He's been missing for nearly a week. You seen him or maybe something out of the usual around here lately?"

Howie studied the photo and shook his head. "Nope. Never saw him. Troopers have been by here, asking the same questions. As to anything unusual, the answer's no. We've had a couple of fights, but that's just par for the course."

Whizmo nodded his thanks and took the photo to each of the customers, asking the same questions and getting the same answers. Then, his shoulders a little slumped, he left, mounted his bike, and went to the next bar on his mental list.

By ten o'clock that night he was fifty miles from home and had struck out. At his last stop he threw five hundred dollars down on a table where three of his biker buddies sat and said, "Look, dudes, this kid didn't just disappear. I can't get back out here for another day, maybe two. Put the word out and see what you can stir up. Here's my cell number. Call with anything. I don't care how small or insignificant you may think it is. Understood?"

"We'll do what we can, Whiz," one replied. "Can't promise anything, though. It's a damn big country."

100

Judge Nimitz took the bench before the jury entered. As was his custom, he surveyed the status of his courtroom. "Counsel, is everyone ready? Mr. Vaughan, I notice Ms. Taggert is absent. I presume she's running late. Do you want to give her a few minutes?"

"No, sir. Ms. Taggert is ill. I'll be going it alone from here on out."

The judge guessed what the problem was but chose to keep his opinions to himself. "Ms. Metcalf, please call your next witness."

When the witness had been sworn, Metcalf asked him to introduce himself.

"My name is Horton Thornberry. I'm a hepatologist, ladies and gentlemen. That's a liver doctor."

Audrey Metcalf liked how Dr. Thornberry looked and handled himself. He was in his sixties, had a white mustache and a gleaming bald head. His manner was self-assured and his demeanor gracious. Clearly the jury was interested in hearing what he had to say.

"Tell the jury a little about your background, Doctor."

"I graduated from USC with a degree in microbiology and went to medical school at UCLA."

"Go on, Doctor," Metcalf urged.

The witness turned to the jury. "I did a three-year residency in internal medicine at USC and then a fellowship in hepatology at Stanford."

Metcalf sized up the jury and decided to get to the issues at hand. "Doctor, are you familiar with a drug called Exxacia?"

"Certainly, Ms. Metcalf. There's an article in the *Annals of Hepatology* that recently came out. I was one of the coauthors. The purpose of the article was to evaluate Exxacia and any risk of liver damage with it. That's something important to do with any new antibiotic."

"Doctor, I'm putting a copy of that journal article on the overhead. Is this the one you're talking about?"

"Correct, Ms. Metcalf. May I suggest you turn to the conclusions on the last page."

Metcalf had those conclusions highlighted. "Doctor, can you summarize what you and your colleagues found?"

"Certainly. I'm sure the jury can read what's highlighted, but the bottom line is that Exxacia has approximately the same toxicity to the liver as do most other antibiotics. The risk is small but always there."

Two male jurors on the back row nodded in agreement as they listened.

Now Metcalf was ready to drop a bomb. As near as she could tell, Luke never saw it coming and was not prepared to counter it. "Dr. Thornberry, one more thing. Do you have an opinion as to the cause of Samantha Vaughan's liver failure?"

The witness took off his glasses and turned to Luke. "First, Mr. Vaughan, I want you to know that I'm extremely sorry for what has happened to your daughter. However, in reasonable probability, the Exxacia she took did not cause her liver failure. We know that she had a history of heavy drinking for several years. That undoubtedly left her with some cirrhosis, or scarring on the liver. Then she appears to have taken Tylenol on a frequent basis for headaches. Tylenol is a wonderful drug, but the medical literature is full of articles warning about the risk of liver toxicity in certain people who take acetaminophen, the primary ingredient in Tylenol and a number of other headache remedies. In fact, the FDA just decided to reduce the recommended maximum dose of Tylenol because of its impact on the liver. My opinion is it is far more likely that Samantha's liver failure came from the combination of cirrhosis and acetaminophen."

"Just how certain are you of that opinion, Doctor?" Metcalf asked.

"Oh, I'm quite positive. I was on a team that studied the effect of acetaminophen on the liver as far back as twenty-five years ago. Since that time there have been dozens of other studies all over the world." He turned to the jury. "Please understand, ladies and gentlemen, I'm not suggesting that you should not take Tylenol. For the vast majority of people, it's a superb painkiller." Dr. Thornberry paused, searching for an example. "Think of it like peanuts. Personally, I like peanuts. I'm sure most of you do. However, there are some people who are so allergic to peanuts that the smallest amount of peanut oil in food can send them to the hospital, even cause their deaths. Samantha developed a reaction to acetaminophen. It's not really the acetaminophen, but a rare individual reaction to it, that causes the liver failure. I'm not even sure that any doctor understands why, but there are too many reports in the literature to conclude it was anything else. Does that clarify my opinion for you?"

Several jurors nodded their understanding.

Audrey Metcalf smiled, stood, and said, "Pass the witness, Your Honor."

"Very well, let's take our morning break."

As the jury filed out, Luke went to a back corner of the courtroom and reached for his cell phone. *Dammit,* he thought, *I didn't see this coming. I've got some ammunition for Dr. Thornberry, but the Tylenol issue is a problem. I was too focused on Exxacia.* When Brad picked up, he told him to research Tylenol and its effects on the liver. Could Samantha have taken Tylenol for years and suddenly have this kind of reaction?

Following the recess, Luke began his cross-examination. "Doctor, let's talk about that journal article you're so proud of. Fact of the matter is, you and the other authors were paid to write that article by Ceventa, true?"

"Absolutely not, Mr. Vaughan," the witness replied, indignation in his voice.

"Wait a minute, didn't you receive twenty-five thousand dollars from Ceventa?"

"Mr. Vaughan, that money went to my research foundation."

Luke thought about the answer and threw out a question he didn't know the answer to, violating one of the cardinal rules of cross-examination. "Well, then, Dr. Thornberry, isn't it true that you're paid a monthly salary by that foundation?"

"That's true. I spend a lot of time in research, and it's only fair that I be paid."

Luke went to an easel and wrote "$25,000" with an arrow pointing to the words "Thornberry Foundation" and another arrow going to "Dr. Thornberry."

"Some people might call that money laundering, right, Doctor?"

Thornberry's face turned red, and he stood in the witness stand. "Mr. Vaughan, I resent that."

"Dr. Thornberry, you'll need to take your seat," Judge Nimitz commanded.

Thornberry looked at the judge. "Sorry, Your Honor. I was upset."

"And you know that all of the other authors were paid by Ceventa, don't you?"

"Mr. Vaughan, I can't say for certain, but I presume they or their foundations received a similar stipend."

"Stipend means money, dollars, doesn't it, sir?"

Dr. Thornberry had begun to nervously bounce his right leg up and down, up and down. Some of the jurors took note and began to see the witness in a slightly different light.

Luke knew he had Thornberry on the run. "Isn't it also true that the article was actually authored by Dr. Andrew Grizilli, a full-time employee of Ceventa? You and the others just looked it over and signed off."

"Mr. Vaughan, Dr. Grizilli is a distinguished scientist. I read every word of the article and saw no reason not to approve it."

"Just didn't bother you a bit that Ceventa wrote an article, whitewashing their drug, as long as you got your twenty-five thousand dollars!" Luke nearly yelled.

"Objection, Your Honor! Objection! Argumentative."

"Sustained. Mr. Vaughan, please keep your voice down."

Luke nodded to the judge. He was not concerned that the judge had sustained the objection. The point was made.

101

Luke turned his cell phone on over the lunch break. Since he no longer had the use of Sue Ellen's office, he walked back to his house to check on Samantha. As he mounted the steps, the phone rang.

"Luke, it's Sara Sinclair. I was hoping to catch you on your lunch break. Is this a good time to talk?"

"What's going on? You okay?"

"I'm doing as well as could be expected. Ryan's funeral is this afternoon, and we've got a house full of people. A FedEx truck just delivered a package addressed to Ryan. I opened it and found some computer discs marked *Ceventa Clinical Trial* and one thumb drive. He must have mailed the package to himself before he was killed. Maybe he did it when he got that phone call."

"Wow! Did you take a look at the data?"

"I excused myself from the family and locked myself in Ryan's office. The discs appear to contain the clinical trial. The thumb drive has summaries of various sites and other information along with Ryan's memos to Boatwright. Several of the memos show copies to Ceventa."

Luke paced back and forth as he listened. "Sara, I know this is a bad time, but I need that data ASAP."

"I know, Luke, that's why I called. What do you want me to do?"

Luke pondered the situation, knowing that Sara couldn't be late to her husband's funeral. "Is there someone who could load that thumb drive on Ryan's computer and e-mail it to me?"

Sara nodded even though Luke couldn't see her. "My cousin is going to house-sit while we go to the funeral. We've had an outbreak of robberies when a funeral announcement is placed in the paper. He can do it."

"Great! And I've got one more request. Can you ask him to make copies of the discs and the thumb drive and hide them somewhere in the house? Maybe you can take them to a safe deposit box tomorrow. Then, if you're okay with it, I'd like him to take the discs to a FedEx Office location and have them overnighted to my office for delivery first thing tomorrow. Can you do that?"

"I'll get it done. There's a FedEx location not ten minutes from here. I really want to help. Maybe at least this way Ryan's death won't be in vain. Luke, you need to win this case for Samantha and for Ryan."

"I will, Sara. I promise." Luke clicked off the phone and punched in Whizmo's cell phone. It rang four times. *Come on, Whiz, don't be in class,* Luke thought. *Please pick up.* Then he did.

"What's up, bro? I thought you were in trial."

Luke explained. "Whiz, can you go to my office and start reviewing the data on the thumb drive?"

"You got it. I'll get Brad to join me," Whiz replied. "By now we have a pretty good idea of what you're looking for. Remember what I said about that sunrise. It's getting brighter in the east, my friend."

"One more thing, Whiz. You do any good with Josh?"

"Struck out so far, but I haven't given up."

After lunch Metcalf called two Ceventa scientists to the witness stand. Both praised Ceventa as a company that was dedicated to saving lives through research and marketing of drugs. Each had been carefully selected for his complete lack of knowledge of Exxacia and the clinical trial. She had long ago decided to leave Rudy Kowalski in Baltimore. He knew too much. About all Luke could do with them was establish that they were paid by the defendant and would lose their jobs if they criticized the company. Of course, their stock reply was that there was no reason on earth to be critical of such a wonderful company.

102

Midafternoon brought another expert. Ramon Salazar, the chairman of the advisory committee that had approved Exxacia, was a distinguished professor in the department of infectious diseases at the University of Texas Health Science Center in San Antonio.

"Your Honor, for your planning and so the jury will know, Dr. Salazar will be Ceventa's last witness. We expect to rest our case after he testifies."

"Very well, Ms. Metcalf," Judge Nimitz replied. "I'm sure the jury is delighted to hear that. Please proceed."

Audrey Metcalf walked Dr. Salazar through his credentials and then asked, "Doctor, why do you take the time out of a busy schedule to advise the FDA?"

"Well, they pay me a small fee," Dr. Salazar said with a smile, "but that hardly covers the time it takes me to read about new drugs and attend several meetings a year. Some of us doctors believe we owe such service to our profession and to the public. I'm happy to do it."

Metcalf liked having a local touch to her experts, particularly a Latino physician who would appeal to the Latinos on the jury. "Doctor, were you on the advisory committee that approved Exxacia?"

"I was. We had meetings over about two years before we were satisfied that the drug was safe and effective."

"Doctor Salazar, based on all you read and particularly based on the extensive clinical trial done by Ceventa and supervised by the folks at CDER, did your committee vote to approve the drug?"

"We did. The jury should know that our committee first rejected Exxacia. We wanted more data. Ceventa launched the largest clinical trial I believe I've ever seen. Based on the results of that clinical trial, we certainly had no reason not to approve the drug for bronchitis, sinusitis, and pneumonia."

Satisfied that she still had the upper hand, Metcalf passed the witness.

Luke smiled to himself as she concluded. *We finally got a break.* In the heat of battle, she didn't realize that she had just opened that door that the judge had locked. She actually asked Dr. Salazar about the entire clinical trial. Now he was going to ask a few preliminary questions and charge through it.

He rose and stood at his table, a quizzical look on his face. He took another shot in the dark and prayed he would hit the target. "Doctor, since you're an infectious disease doc and since you headed the committee to approve Exxacia, I presume you regularly prescribe it to your patients."

Dr. Salazar shook his head. "Matter of fact, right now I'm not using Exxacia with my patients. I rarely use any new drug for two or three years after it's approved. I like to see how a new drug is received in the medical community and watch for postmarket reports of problems."

Bull's-eye! Audrey Metcalf was stunned. She hadn't anticipated this line of questions. Still, she couldn't think of an objection.

"However, Mr. Vaughan, it may be that I'll start using Exxacia in another year or so. I need to evaluate the postmarket data."

"Well, Doctor, since you raised postmarket data, actually Ceventa's scientists submitted some European postmarket data to your committee, didn't they?"

Dr. Salazar searched his memory for a few moments and replied,

"I believe you're correct, Mr. Vaughan. It must have been satisfactory. Otherwise, we wouldn't have approved the drug."

Luke rummaged through papers on his table until he found an article. "Doctor, first, you would agree that postmarket data may or may not be reliable, right? I mean, doctors or patients would have to report complications, and they may or may not do so. Then the drug companies have to report the complications to the FDA or similar agencies in other countries. Wouldn't you agree that postmarket data may underestimate complications by as much as ninety percent?"

The doctor rubbed his temples as he thought. "I agree in part. I'm not sure about your ninety percent, but there's no doubt that such data underestimates complications. Still, even with problems inherent with postmarket data, it can be useful."

Luke turned on the overhead projector. "Doctor, have you seen this European study, published in *Lancet,* about Exxacia?"

The witness looked at the overhead. "I don't recall it. May I see the entire article?"

"Certainly, sir," Luke replied as he took a copy to the witness. "I'm not surprised you haven't seen it, since it was published just two months ago."

Dr. Salazar skimmed through the article, pausing to carefully read the conclusion, and then looked up at Luke, waiting for the next question.

"Doctor, that article is reporting an extraordinarily high incidence of liver failure and deaths with Exxacia in Europe, isn't it?"

Dr. Salazar nodded. "Certainly higher than I have seen before. It may be that we will need several other studies before we can be more certain if Exxacia is causing liver failure or something else induced the reported liver toxicity. Just like one swallow does not a summer make, neither can one study confirm or reject the use of any drug."

Luke smiled. "Doctor, we've just heard Dr. Thornberry discuss an article where he was one of the authors. As you just stated, you wouldn't rely on any one article for decisions regarding your patients, would you?"

"Mr. Vaughan, I know Dr. Thornberry and know he is highly respected, but you're correct."

Luke put away the article and looked back at the witness, knowing his next question was going to cause an eruption of volcanic proportions from the other table. "Dr. Salazar, since you and Ms. Metcalf have been talking about the Exxacia clinical trial, let's turn our attention to it and some of its problems."

Audrey Metcalf leaped to her feet. "Objection, Your Honor. He's intentionally violating your pretrial ruling."

"Not so, Judge," Luke replied calmly. "She opened the door."

Judge Nimitz looked at the clock on the wall. "Ladies and gentlemen, I sense this may take a while. I'm going to release you for the day. See you back here promptly at nine unless the bailiff notifies you otherwise. Doctor, you're also excused until nine tomorrow. Have a good day."

Once the courtroom was cleared, the judge asked Audrey Metcalf, "Why have you now opened the door to the entire clinical trial? You intentionally asked questions that incorporated the whole damn thing and established that Dr. Salazar and his committee relied on all of the data."

Metcalf was clearly thrown off guard. Had she created a mess that she couldn't get out of? The last thing she wanted was to have the clinical trial and all of its problems be presented to the jury. She looked at Charlotte Bronson and turned to the judge. "Your Honor, obviously this is an important matter. Might I suggest that we postpone this discussion until in the morning? I'd like to have time to brief the subject and give you some case law to support our position."

Judge Nimitz looked at Luke. Luke was thinking that he had information coming from Rockville that could change the course of the case. He also needed to get to the bottom of the Tylenol question. A few more hours could work to his benefit. "I have no objection to what Ms. Metcalf requests. Just for good measure, I propose that we take this up at nine tomorrow and have the jury return at one." Luke didn't say it, but he knew that by then Whiz would have the computer discs in his hands and would have had time to give them a quick once-over.

"Agreed, Judge," Metcalf said.

"Well, I hate to delay the trial like this. A lot of these jurors need to be getting back to work. However, if the two of you are in agreement, that's what we'll do. See you tomorrow at nine."

103

Luke stuffed the materials from his table in a large briefcase. Then he was out the door and down the steps. Reporters hollered questions, and all he said was that the case was going well.

When he got home, he found Whizmo and Brad, along with Samantha, in the conference room. "Hi, Dad, I just got up from my usual three-hour, midday nap," Samantha said. "Where's Sue Ellen?"

Luke paused to think about how to answer the question. "Sue Ellen's not feeling well."

"She's worried about Josh, isn't she, Dad?"

"Yeah, she is, sweetie. We're going to have to do without her for a while."

"Boy, I really feel sorry for her. Why can't anyone find Josh?"

"They're doing all they can, Sam. We have to let the law enforcement guys handle that. We've got a lawsuit to deal with."

Brad handed Luke two journal articles, almost hot off the presses. One was American and had been published only the week before. The other came from a French journal but had been translated and published simultaneously in an American journal on infectious diseases. Luke flipped to the conclusions on both and smiled.

"Good work, Brad," Luke said. "Right now I'm really more concerned about Tylenol and its effect on the liver."

Brad shook his head. "Not good, Luke. Dr. Thornberry was right. All you have to do is Google 'acetaminophen' and 'liver toxicity' and you'll get dozens of hits. It can definitely cause liver problems. Usually, they go away when the patient stops taking the pills, but there are a few reported cases of severe liver failure and even death. For some strange reason, a few people have taken the drug for years and all of a sudden they have liver problems. Bottom line is it's a plausible theory. Because that drug has been around for so long, for every study we can find on Exxacia, they can find a dozen on acetaminophen."

"Dammit to hell!" Luke exploded. "Sorry, everyone. Brad, print off those acetaminophen articles. I'll stay up tonight reading them. Maybe I can find something to use with Salazar to neutralize the issue."

"Luke, I'm not a lawyer," Whizmo said, "and I'm only partway through that thumb drive, but I've got some really good stuff. It could turn the whole case. What's the big deal about acetaminophen?"

"Whiz," Luke replied, "that's all well and good, but right now the judge's ruling is still that the clinical trial doesn't come into evidence. Metcalf may have screwed up and opened the door this afternoon. We now have a good shot that Nimitz will change his ruling. We're arguing that at nine tomorrow. Still, if the judge continues to rule against us, Tylenol becomes a huge issue. Bottom line, our best shot is to make sure we get the real clinical trial, along with the forgeries and that other stuff, into evidence."

Whizmo rubbed his hands together. "Then call the FedEx office

and authorize me to pick up the package. I'll be there when they
open at eight. That'll get us two more hours. As to the thumb drive,
you'll have what you need from it in a few hours."

Luke went around the conference table to the wheelchair where
Samantha sat beside Brad. He tried to hide his concern for how thin
she was and how much more yellow her skin had turned. He gave her
a big hug and said, "Hang in there, Sam. Tomorrow could be our day."

"Is there going to be a bright glow in the eastern sky?" she asked.

"Prettiest sunrise you ever saw, and that's a promise," Luke replied.
"Now let's all say a prayer for Sue Ellen and Josh. Pray that Josh will
be with us tomorrow."

"Amen," Samantha said.

104

Luke looked at the old grandfather clock in his office, one he'd
bought at a yard sale in Kerrville a couple of years ago. It was eleven
o'clock. Anyone who thought the life of a trial lawyer was glamorous
and exciting had never spent the night reading medical articles written in language usually understood only by doctors. He put down an
article on liver toxicity and went to the back to pour his first and only
Scotch of the evening. As he returned to his desk, he heard the back
door open.

"That you, Whiz?"

"Damn sure better be. Who else you figure would be coming in
your back door at this hour of the night?" Whiz replied as he came
through the office door and plopped down in a chair. "Luke, we have
a visitor."

"Go on," Luke said, a questioning look on his face.

"One of my students works as a night desk clerk over at the Holiday Inn. He's been monitoring the comings and goings of the Ceventa team. Hasn't run across anything interesting until now. He just called. A black limo pulled up about thirty minutes ago. The driver got out and hurried around to the passenger door. A tall man, probably six and a half feet tall, got out. Gray hair and beard. Dallas Cowboys cap pulled low over his eyes, Dallas Cowboys T-shirt, jeans. As he entered the hotel, the elevator door opened, and Audrey Metcalf met him."

Luke flew to his feet. "Hell, it's Kingsbury!"

"You got it, Sherlock Holmes." Whiz grinned. "Now what are you going to do with him?"

"He can't be here to testify. Metcalf damn sure isn't going to call him as a witness, and she knows I'd subpoena his ass the minute he set foot in the courthouse. Whatever the reason he's here, he'll be gone in the morning. We need to get him served, but they won't let us get close to that floor of the hotel they rented. I hear they even have armed guards."

"I'll take care of it, Luke. You get over to that computer, print a subpoena, and sign it. I'll get him served."

105

"Alfred, what the hell are you doing here?" Metcalf asked as she poured them each a cup of coffee and they settled into easy chairs in her suite.

"I thought you knew me well. This case is the most important event in my life right now. My career, among other things, is riding on it."

A quizzical look crossed Metcalf's face. *Why is this case so important?* she thought.

Kingsbury continued, "I learned long ago that e-mail reports and telephone calls weren't good enough. They don't always convey the whole message. We're near the end of the trial, and I wanted to see you face-to-face to satisfy myself that this is going as expected."

Metcalf put down her coffee and walked to the balcony. She slid back the door and stepped out. Once she had surveyed the parking lot and the street in front of the Holiday Inn, satisfying herself that no one was around to see Kingsbury's arrival, she returned. "Look, I'll stay up all night to bring you up to speed if necessary, but you're taking a major chance. If Vaughan and his team knew you were in town, they'd get you served and you'd be on the witness stand."

"Believe me, Audrey, I thought this through carefully. I've been a risk taker my whole life. That's what got me where I am today. Once we're through talking, I'll be heading back to Austin. My jet will be refueled and I'll be gone. No one's going to know that I dropped by in the middle of the night."

"Okay, I'll try to make this as quick as I can, but it'll probably take a couple of hours. By the way, did you have to choose a Lincoln limo for a forty-five-minute ride? Most folks who visit Holiday Inns don't arrive in a long black car with a driver."

This time it was Kingsbury who walked to the balcony and looked down on the limo, now parked in the lot. He shrugged. "Well, I figured at this hour of the night, the usual rental places would probably be closed."

106

The limo driver was snoozing in the car when his cell rang. "Yes, sir. I'll be in front when you get there."

He started the engine and drove around to the front of the building. Then he got out of the Lincoln, looked at his watch, and figured that he had time for a couple of puffs on a cigarette before Kingsbury arrived. He pulled a Winston from its package and found his Zippo lighter. While he was lighting the cigarette, he walked to the back of the car and inhaled deeply. As he did he glanced up at a cloudless night with nothing but stars and a sliver of the moon off on the horizon. Then he heard a sound. He turned to see a black man wearing a hooded sweatshirt step from the shadow of the building. He was carrying a squeegee in one hand and a bucket in the other.

The man walked up to the limo, dipped the squeegee in the bucket, and began to wash the windshield.

The driver crushed his cigarette under his shoe and yelled, "Hey, man, get away from there."

"Service of the hotel, sir," Whizmo replied as he cleaned the driver's side of the windshield. "Of course, if you have any spare change, I'd accept a tip."

The driver started toward Whizmo, who moved around the front of the car and continued what he was doing on the passenger side.

Not sure what to do, the driver said, "Well, make it quick. My client is on his way down here right now."

"Figured as much," Whiz said. "Saw you leave the parking lot and drive around here to the front."

That caught the driver's attention. "Hey, just who the hell are you, anyway? On second thought, get the hell away from my car."

It was too late. The tall figure of Alfred Kingsbury pushed through the door and hurried to the limo. The driver opened the rear door, but Whizmo stepped between Kingsbury and the car.

"Alfred Kingsbury?" Whizmo asked.

"Yes, please get out of my way."

"I'm Professor Wilson Moore. Just wanted to confirm you're Dr. Kingsbury. This is for you." Whizmo handed him a subpoena. "See you in court in a few hours. Have a nice night."

Kingsbury stared at the paper in his hand and then looked up in time to see the hooded figure disappear around the corner of the building. For some reason he was singing.

Plenty of sunshine heading my way
Zip-a-dee-doo-dah, zip-a-dee-ay

107

At a quarter till nine Luke was standing at the top of the courthouse steps, talking to another lawyer, when Audrey Metcalf walked by.

"You son of a bitch," she hissed at Luke as she hurried past them. The other lawyer asked what that was all about, and Luke just smiled.

Luke barely got through the courtroom door before Judge Nimitz stepped from his chambers. With no jurors due until one o'clock, he was dressed in a white shirt and tie and matching suspenders. "Have a seat, everyone. I'll pull a chair up to one of the tables. Now, what's this about?"

"It's an outrage, Judge. That's what it's about," Audrey Metcalf erupted. "Mr. Vaughan had someone assault Dr. Alfred Kingsbury, CEO of Ceventa, in front of the Holiday Inn in the middle of the night."

The judge frowned at Luke. "Have criminal charges been filed, Ms. Metcalf?"

"Not yet, Your Honor. We wanted to bring this up with you first."

"This sounds very serious. Mr. Vaughan, what do you have to say for yourself?"

Luke met the judge's eyes with his own. "Judge, I'm afraid that Ms. Metcalf is, shall we say, overstating what occurred. I learned that Dr. Kingsbury snuck into town about eleven last night."

"Judge, he didn't sneak anywhere," Metcalf interrupted.

Now the judge was getting upset with Metcalf. "Ms. Metcalf, please let Mr. Vaughan speak. I'll tell you when it's your turn again. Go on, Luke."

"He arrived at about eleven last night in a chauffeured limo and was leaving at around two in the morning. When we heard he was in subpoena range, I asked Professor Moore to serve him with a subpoena. As you probably know, Whizmo has been helping us with some computer research."

Luke told the entire story of the service, including Whizmo's singing as he walked away.

"Was he really singing 'Zip-a-dee-doo-dah'? I haven't thought about that song in a hundred years." Judge Nimitz tried to suppress a grin.

"Yes, sir, he was. And you know Whizmo. All he did was hand Kingsbury a subpoena. No way did he assault the guy."

"Well, I'll deal with Whizmo if Kingsbury files charges. That's for another day. Now I understand why we're here. Ms. Metcalf, I presume you're trying to quash the subpoena he served on your Dr. Kingsbury last night."

Metcalf stood and walked around her chair and put her hands on the chair back. "Yes, sir. And I apologize for my outburst earlier. You've already quashed one attempt to have him testify. We argued the law on an apex subpoena, and you sustained our motion at that time. This is the same thing."

Luke started to say something, but Judge Nimitz raised his hand to stop Luke.

"Not quite the same thing, Ms. Metcalf. He voluntarily came to San Marcos. Mr. Vaughan is well within his rights to subpoena anyone who comes within a hundred and fifty miles of this courthouse. I haven't measured it, but I believe the Holiday Inn is only about three miles from here."

"But, Your Honor, Dr. Kingsbury has a very important board meeting on the East Coast this afternoon."

"Sorry, Ms. Metcalf. He should have thought about that before he set foot in Hays County."

Metcalf tried one last time. "Judge, if you're going to make him testify, I could call him myself, but I'll lose credibility with our jury. I told them I'd be resting after we're through with Dr. Salazar."

"Ms. Metcalf," the judge continued, "again, I didn't create your problem. You figure out what you're going to do, but I expect you to have Dr. Kingsbury out in the hall at one o'clock when we start up. Now, let's talk about whether you've opened the door to that clinical trial data when you were questioning Dr. Salazar yesterday."

"Judge," Luke said, "there's been another development. We were advised that there's yet another version of the study that was never produced to us, along with some memos from Dr. Ryan Sinclair, an FDA infectious disease expert who oversaw the clinical trial for Exxacia. He was killed under very mysterious circumstances."

Luke had the judge's attention.

"I have many of the clinical trial documents that were e-mailed to me yesterday. Whizmo picked up a package containing the remainder of the study at the FedEx office about an hour ago. I think that I can establish the predicate to admit the entire study on the fly like we used to do in the old days. Ms. Metcalf can make her objections, and we'll deal with them one at a time."

Metcalf tried to control the anger that was boiling inside her. "No, Judge, that won't work. He's springing some documents on us that we've never seen."

Judge Nimitz rose to his feet and placed his hands on the table and glared at Metcalf. "If what Mr. Vaughan says is true, your client has had this version all along! Now it may be that your client has been holding back relevant evidence that I ordered produced. If so, that may be another reason for sanctions. We're going to do it Mr. Vaughan's way. I'll see you all at one o'clock."

The judge pushed his chair back so hard that it tipped over and clattered to the floor. Then he stormed to the door of his chambers and slammed it so that it rattled the windows in the old court-room.

108

Whizmo was tired after his nighttime escapade, but what else was new? Like most trial teams, by this time they were all living on nervous energy spiked with large doses of very strong coffee. Whiz smiled as Luke walked into the conference room.

"Got it. I showed up at seven this morning, an hour before they opened. One of my former students works there, and he let me in. Gave me another hour to work through this stuff."

"Whiz," Luke asked, "is there any place in town where you don't have a student or former student somewhere on the premises?"

Whizmo smiled again. "Now, have a seat beside me. That program

I designed has helped me pull up the documents you want. I've moved them to a separate file."

"There's one thing I want to see first, Whiz," Luke said. "To get past a hearsay objection, show me something that authenticates this as an official government document."

Whizmo clicked to an index he had created, then punched in two numbers, and there it was, an official-looking document with the seal of the FDA and an affidavit signed by Roger Boatwright, PhD, director of the Center for Drug Evaluation and Research, certifying the Exxacia clinical trial as complete and accurate.

"That'll do it," Luke said. "Now show me what else you've pulled."

Whizmo spent the next two hours displaying documents as Luke noted the contents and index numbers on a yellow pad.

Finally Luke said, "I know you've got more, but that's enough to destroy Kingsbury, and Exxacia along with him."

"What's your move now, Luke? Don't you still have Dr. Salazar on the stand?"

Luke gazed out the window while he thought. "I think we have no more questions for him right now. I suspect that Metcalf will rest, and then we can call Dr. Kingsbury."

"What happens if she calls Kingsbury first?"

"I don't think she will. She knows she loses credibility with the jury if she calls her CEO now. He's always been available, just a private jet away. The jury would figure that she thought her case was crumbling and she needed him to fly in like Mighty Mouse to save the day. We'll take our chances. Now, let's roll."

109

When the jury and Dr. Salazar had settled into their seats and Judge Nimitz nodded at Luke, he stood and said, "Pass the witness, Your Honor."

Metcalf was caught off guard. She turned to look at Luke and conferred with Forsythe. "No more questions, Your Honor. May this witness be excused?"

Judge Nimitz looked at Luke for his agreement.

"Judge, we may find it necessary to call Dr. Salazar as a rebuttal witness," Luke said. "So we request that he remain in the hall until further notice."

Dr. Salazar turned to the judge. "Your Honor, I do have patients in San Antonio who need my attention. This is a serious imposition on my time."

Judge Nimitz nodded his understanding. "I fully appreciate what you're saying, Doctor. However, this is a very serious case. I suspect you have some other good doctors on your staff who can see your patients for the afternoon. If you like, you can wait in my office. I've got some fine history books about World War II and an excellent anthology of Longhorn football. You're excused, sir. Ms. Metcalf?"

Audrey Metcalf surprised Luke. "Your Honor, Ceventa calls Dr. Alfred Kingsbury."

Surprised, Luke turned to watch Kingsbury stride into the courtroom. There was one good men's store in town, and it appeared that Ceventa must have commandeered it for the morning. While his suit wasn't from Fifth Avenue, it was the best one could find in the small town. Dark blue with a thin pinstripe, it appeared to have been tailored for his lanky frame. The coat hung perfectly; the sleeves stopped just above the wrist, and the pants barely touched gleaming new black shoes. Quite a change from the man Whizmo briefly encountered early in the morning.

Kingsbury acted as if he were stepping into his own boardroom where he expected to be in complete command. He nodded at Luke as if to say, *I've gone up against the best lawyers in the world in courtrooms and Congress; you won't lay a glove on me.* Next he smiled at the jury and walked to the front of the bench.

As he raised his right hand, he said, "Good morning, Judge Nimitz. I'm pleased to be in your court."

When Judge Nimitz gave him the oath, he turned to the jury and responded, "So help me God."

Quite a performance, Luke thought. *Let's see how he does when an old country lawyer cross-examines him.*

Audrey Metcalf had also undergone a transformation with her client on the stand. Gone was the strident, demanding personality. In its place was a warm, soft-spoken one that she hoped would help to sell Kingsbury as a gentleman and a caring professional.

"Please introduce yourself to the jury, Dr. Kingsbury."

Kingsbury turned slightly to look at the jurors. "I'm Alfred Kingsbury. I'm originally from England, but I came to the United States thirty years ago. As they say, I got here as soon as I could. Ten years after my arrival, one of my proudest moments occurred when I became a United States citizen."

Several of the jurors were themselves only second- or third-generation Americans, and they nodded in agreement with Kingsbury's comment.

"Dr. Kingsbury, tell the jury about your education and what you've done with your life."

"I was born in the Cotswolds region of England. My parents were both schoolteachers, and I grew up in a small town. I played goalkeeper on our football team . . . well, we call it football there. I now know it as soccer. I really wanted to play forward and score goals, but I was always the tallest player on the team, and my coaches always said they needed me as goal. I was fortunate to get a partial scholarship to Oxford. From there I got a PhD in pharmacology, followed by medical school. After medical school, I was torn between returning to my hometown to be a family doctor and going into research. I finally chose Ceventa, where I just had my thirty-second anniversary as an employee."

"Was there one particular thing that turned you toward Ceventa, Dr. Kingsbury?" Audrey asked, knowing, of course, the answer they had rehearsed as Kingsbury was being fitted for his clothes.

Kingsbury hesitated as if he hated to bring up the memory. "Yes, yes there was. My best friend when I was a lad and just starting to play soccer, a teammate, was struck down with polio and to this day has to walk with crutches and braces on his legs. That devastated our team, and me in particular. It wasn't long after that Dr. Jonas Salk developed the polio vaccine. I always regretted that he hadn't gotten it done a few years earlier. Anyway, when I was making my decision, I kept thinking back to my friend and finally decided that I could do more good in the world with Ceventa than in my hometown."

Metcalf let silence fill the courtroom to allow the story to sink in. Luke stared at Kingsbury, recognizing that he might have a slightly more difficult job than he anticipated.

Continuing in a quiet voice, Metcalf asked, "How long were you a research scientist?"

Kingsbury stared at the ceiling as he thought. "Nearly ten years, and then I was asked to go into management."

"That was probably an easy decision, wasn't it?"

Kingsbury folded his hands on the bench in front of him. "Actually, it was another difficult one. I enjoyed research and was part of a team that produced a couple of drugs that helped in the continuing battle against influenza. Again, I had to weigh where I could do the most good and decided that if I could help Ceventa grow, we could spend more on research. And that's what we've done over the past twenty or so years. Our research budget goes up every year."

"Now, you're CEO of the company?"

"No, no. My boss would be upset if he heard me say that. I'm CEO of the North American subsidiary. The CEO is in our home office in Copenhagen. Still, I might add that my subsidiary is sixty-five percent of the company."

Metcalf wanted to show the jury something besides the professional side of her suddenly key witness. "Are you married, Dr. Kingsbury?"

"Happily so." Kingsbury smiled at the jury. "I have one daughter and three delightful grandchildren. They're really quite charming. I could show the jury photos of my grandchildren if you like."

"That won't be necessary, Dr. Kingsbury. I'm sure the jury will take your word for it."

Figuring she had put the right spin on Ceventa and Kingsbury, she asked, "Your company developed a drug now called Exxacia?"

"We certainly did," Kingsbury said. "It took us ten years and nearly a billion dollars, but we produced a new kind of antibiotic that is revolutionizing how we treat respiratory illnesses."

Luke decided he needed to break the flow of the examination. He stood and said, "Objection, Your Honor, nonresponsive. Request that the witness be instructed to answer the questions and not make speeches."

"Sustained, Mr. Vaughan. Dr. Kingsbury, please merely answer the question. Your lawyer is quite capable of getting the information from you that she wants to present to the jury. Proceed, Ms. Metcalf."

"Dr. Kingsbury, did you immediately introduce Exxacia into the United States?"

The witness shook his head. "No, ma'am. We started in South America, and after two years we introduced it to countries in Europe. So there will be no misunderstanding, we weren't using those countries and their citizens as guinea pigs. Their equivalent of the FDA had restrictions on new drugs at least as tough as this country."

"Tell the jury what results you had with Exxacia overseas."

Before Kingsbury could answer, Luke rose from his chair and wandered over to the window, where he stood, back to the courtroom, and gazed out on the town square. Another ploy to distract the jury. It worked. As Kingsbury was answering the question, every juror was watching Luke and wondering what he was doing. Luke also hoped to convey the message that what Kingsbury was saying now was really not important.

At last Metcalf rose. "Your Honor, would you kindly instruct Mr. Vaughan to take his seat at counsel table?"

Luke turned with a questioning look. "Sorry, Your Honor. I had a cramp in my leg and was just stretching."

"Dr. Kingsbury, when you introduce a drug into the United States, I'm sure that it has to have FDA approval. What's your relationship with the Food and Drug Administration?"

"Very cordial, of course. After all, they make the final decision. Also quite professional, but they keep us at a distance. They have excellent scientists who study any new drug most carefully. They are charged with protecting the health of our citizens and making sure that drugs are both safe and effective. I believe it says something like that in their mission statement."

Metcalf had conceded to herself that she had accidentally opened the door to the clinical trial with Salazar and decided she had no choice but to go into it. "Did they do that with Exxacia?"

"Certainly they did. We submitted data that would fill half this courtroom. Of course, it was on computer discs. Along with our research we had after-market data from half a dozen countries, but they still weren't satisfied. Their Infectious Disease Advisory Committee wanted more. So we commissioned one of the largest clinical trials ever for a new drug, twenty-five thousand patients. The success rate was remarkable. We submitted the results of the study to the FDA, and within a matter of weeks the advisory committee approved it. The rest is history."

"Can you elaborate, Dr. Kingsbury?"

Kingsbury took off his glasses and turned to the jury. "Exxacia has been on the market in the United States for less than a year, and by our estimates, just in this last flu season we probably saved at least a hundred thousand lives."

Luke watched the jury and concluded from their expressions and body language that they were impressed with Kingsbury and what he had to say. *He's quite a salesman,* Luke thought.

Metcalf could have done more, but she had also sized up the jury's reaction and elected to ask Kingsbury no more questions. Their case was strong. "Pass the witness, Your Honor."

"Thank you, Ms. Metcalf. We have to quit a little early today. I have a meeting with the other judges. We've made good progress." He turned to the jury. "I think I can assure you that we'll give the case to you by tomorrow afternoon."

110

When the Ceventa team got back to the Holiday Inn, Metcalf asked Kingsbury to change out of his suit so that they could get it pressed for the next day, then to join her in the conference room by the elevators in thirty minutes.

Kingsbury opened the door to his suite and was met with a shock. Roger Boatwright was sitting in the living room next to the window.

"Boatwright! What are you doing here? How did you get past the guards?"

Boatwright kept his seat, but his hands were trembling. "One question at a time. How did I get past the guards? Not very difficult. When I got to this floor, one of Metcalf's young lawyers that was at my deposition was talking to the guard. I explained that you had asked me to meet you in your suite. He got a guard to let me in."

"This is outrageous!" Kingsbury thundered. "I'm going to have you thrown out."

Boatwright's right eye ticked furiously. "Maybe you better hear me out before you throw me out, Alfred."

Kingsbury finally took a seat and waited for Boatwright to continue.

"You and I made a deal when I got Exxacia approved. It was five million dollars. Since that time I've called repeatedly, and you've ignored me. You said to wait a week. Well, I'm damn tired of waiting. Now Joanne is on a ventilator and I'm so depressed I can't take enough sedatives to get any sleep at night. I want the rest of that money wired to my Swiss account by eight o'clock tomorrow morning. Otherwise, I'm going to Luke Vaughan."

"You can't do that. You'll destroy your career!" Kingsbury sputtered.

"Alfred, at this point, I don't really care. My life is in shambles anyway. Look, I know you had Sinclair killed. You think anyone will believe it's a coincidence that he got those discs from me and died that same night? I figure that when you weigh that five million against what you've got to lose, you'll make the right decision. If that money is not transferred, I'll destroy you and your company. I'm staying in this hotel, down three floors. Let me know when the money's transferred."

When Boatwright was gone, Kingsbury walked over to the window and angrily punched in a number on his cell phone. When the other person answered, he said, "I've got another job for you."

111

Sue Ellen spent every waking minute at the command center established by the FBI in the basement of the courthouse. Every lead they developed had fizzled out. She had felt her life being destroyed each time she got a delivery from the kidnappers. Now the deliveries had stopped, and her panic escalated. The FBI agents and Sheriff Jenkins assured her that they were doing everything they possibly could and would continue to do so. Their assurances no longer meant anything to her. When she got back to her house that afternoon, out of desperation she called Whizmo. Thirty minutes later Whizmo climbed her steps and was met at the door.

Whizmo didn't like what he saw. Sue Ellen had black bags under her eyes. She had noticeably lost weight in only a couple of days. She had a tall glass of Scotch in her hand. "Thanks for coming, Whiz," she said as she hugged him.

"Glad to do so. You're not looking so good. You getting any sleep?"

"I can't, Whiz. I lie awake, staring at the ceiling and waiting for the phone to ring. The task force has come up with nothing. I guess the only good thing is that they haven't found a body." Sue Ellen burst into sobs. After she wiped her eyes and regained her composure, she asked, "Have you got any leads?"

Whizmo shook his head. "I've got my posse out there. They've struck out, too. I'm sorry."

Sue Ellen collapsed into a chair. "I don't know what to do. Help me, Whiz. Please do something," she pleaded.

Whizmo realized he had to make one last effort, not just for Sue

Ellen, but also for his own peace of mind. "Tell you what, all I've got left to do is run the computer for Luke tomorrow. Brad can do that. I'm not promising anything, but I'll hit the road again first thing in the morning. That's all I can do."

112

Audrey Metcalf was seated at the defense table, looking over her notes, and Kingsbury was in the first row of the audience as they waited to start the day. A legal assistant came through the hallway door, approached Metcalf, and whispered something. Astonishment overcame her, and she turned and stared at Kingsbury. Then she motioned him to follow her out into the hallway and down to an empty room one floor below. When she shut the door, she exploded. "What the hell are you doing?"

"I don't understand," Kingsbury replied.

"Roger Boatwright was found hanging from the showerhead in his room three floors below us. Someone used his tie to hang him, probably to make it look like suicide. The tie gave a little, and one toe was touching the tub. He's not dead yet, but the doctor says he may not survive. Alfred, I didn't even know he was here."

"Why are you yelling at me? I didn't either."

"That's a goddamn lie, Alfred! I also learned he was in your room yesterday!"

"All right, all right, I did talk to him. He was depressed. Said his wife had Lou Gehrig's disease. He tried to blackmail me. I told him to go screw himself. He left my room, and I never saw him again. I presumed that he left town. It probably was a suicide attempt."

Metcalf lowered her voice. "So that's it. Ryan Sinclair commits suicide in Maryland. Boatwright attempts suicide in San Marcos. You know, Alfred, I don't believe a word you're saying. I'll do anything to win a case, even bend the rules when necessary, but murder is not in my playbook. I'd withdraw as your counsel right now, but Judge Nimitz would never let me do it at this late stage. I'll do my job and do my best to win for Ceventa. After that, I never want to see or hear from you again."

113

Luke was getting nervous. They were about ready to start the day's evidence, and Whizmo wasn't there to handle the computer and exhibits. Then Brad walked into the courtroom, carrying his computer. "Where's Whiz, Brad?"

Brad shrugged his shoulders. "Don't know, Luke. He called early this morning and said he had something else to do. I'm handling the computer today."

Luke nodded as the bailiff called for order.

Luke rose and, remembering the judge's rule, asked to approach the witness. As he walked toward Dr. Kingsbury, Luke displayed a small pill bottle to the jury. He set it down in front of the witness. "Can you identify that bottle, sir?"

Kingsbury picked it up, examined it, shook it slightly, and said, "It's a bottle of our antibiotic, Exxacia. I presume the pills inside are our antibiotic. As I've already said, it's the most effective antibiotic to come along in the last twenty years."

Luke took the bottle from Kingsbury and walked to the jury box, where he set it on the rail. Turning to Kingsbury, he said, "It's also one of the most deadly, isn't it?"

"Absolutely not, Mr. Vaughan! It's been approved by agencies in over twenty countries. They certainly wouldn't approve a drug that wasn't safe."

"You know, don't you, Dr. Kingsbury, that my daughter is dying of liver failure because she was a *subject* of your clinical trial?"

Kingsbury replied very quietly, "I'm very sorry about your daughter, but I understand her liver problem is not related to Exxacia. We had very few problems with our clinical trial."

"Well, let's just see about that, Doctor. We've been able to get the real version of the Exxacia trial. Brad, would you put that authentication page on the screen?"

Brad hit two keys on the computer, and the document appeared.

"You see, Doctor, it has the FDA logo at the top and a verification that this is the final version of the Exxacia clinical trial, and it's signed and sworn to by a Roger Boatwright, PhD. Please note the date. Now, Brad, please put up the other one."

Brad replaced it with an identical document but with a later date.

"Your Honor, Your Honor." It was Metcalf, on her feet. "May we approach the bench?"

Judge Nimitz motioned for the lawyers to come forward. "Your Honor, this was not listed as an exhibit. We object. Besides, it's hearsay."

"Judge, I just took care of the hearsay objection. It's an official government document. And they can hardly be surprised, since I'll prove that they had this version all along."

"But, Your Honor—"

"Enough, Ms. Metcalf. Your hearsay objection is overruled. I'll carry your other objection along for a while until I see where Mr. Vaughan is going. Proceed."

"Both of these came from the FDA, only you convinced Roger Boatwright to submit the second one to the advisory committee because it had been whitewashed of problems and any staff memos critical of the drug, right, Dr. Kingsbury?"

Kingsbury stood at the witness stand and pointed a finger at Luke. "Absolutely not. We would never do such a thing. I don't know what you're talking about."

"Dr. Kingsbury, you need to take your seat," Judge Nimitz said sternly.

"Thank you, Your Honor," Luke said. "Here's an e-mail memo from Ryan Sinclair, MD, addressed to Roger Boatwright. You knew Dr. Sinclair, didn't you?'

"I did, sir. Fine young doctor. Committed suicide only last week."

"Actually, he was killed, wasn't he, Dr. Kingsbury?"

"Not according to what I read in the papers."

"This memo describes all of the problems with the Exxacia clinical trial. You and the FDA knew that this trial was full of forged patient signatures, false documentation, manufactured vital signs, protocol violations at nearly every site. I could go on and on."

"Of course not, Mr. Vaughan," the witness replied, his voice a little more subdued this time.

"Did you know that one of your investigators in Louisiana is serving a five-year federal prison sentence because he falsified nearly every one of more than four hundred patient charts?"

"Yes, sir." Kingsbury nodded. "I did hear about that after the drug was approved."

"But look here, Doctor, Brad has just put up another memo, this one from your very own staff long before the drug was submitted to the advisory committee, detailing all of the problems with that doctor in Louisiana. Ceventa ignored it and submitted all those results as part of your data, correct, Doctor? You even talked with Dr. Boatwright about this investigator and convinced him to leave his results in the version that went to the advisory committee without mentioning anything about his fraud, didn't you?"

Clearly, Kingsbury was no longer in command. It had never occurred to him that he would meet his match in a small town in Texas. All he could say was "I had numerous conversations with Dr. Boatwright. I can't remember them all."

"Can't remember, Dr. Kingsbury, or just choose not to do so?"

Kingsbury said nothing. Instead, he reached for a cup of water. The jury watched his hand tremble as he brought the water to his lips. Luke knew he didn't need to push for a verbal answer and moved on.

"Now, going back to Dr. Sinclair's memo, do you see where he said that Exxacia is far more dangerous than any other antibiotic currently on the market? The incidence of liver failure and death is at least ten times more than with other antibiotics. And at the bottom, it shows an e-mail copy going to you, right, Dr. Kingsbury?"

Kingsbury managed to regain his composure. "It does, sir, but I don't read all of my e-mails."

Luke shook his head as he walked to the jury box and placed his arm on the rail, exuding the confidence that he was beginning to feel. "Doctor, you know that Dr. Sinclair wanted to submit the real, complete version of the clinical trial and you convinced Boatwright to block it."

"Sir, I know no such thing."

"Well, then, look at this memo from Boatwright to Sinclair. He's replying to a memo from Dr. Sinclair, who wanted CDER to make full disclosure to the advisory committee. Instead, Boatwright says the FDA is investigating the irregularities in the Exxacia clinical trial and it would interfere with the investigation to disclose all of the problems with the trial like Sinclair wanted. Instead, they got the version with the problems eliminated, didn't they? And it shows a blind copy of that e-mail going to you. I guess you didn't read that one either, huh, Doctor?"

Kingsbury refused to make eye contact with the jury and instead gazed out the window as he mumbled, "Sorry, again I just don't remember."

Metcalf turned to her team and whispered to each of them, searching for some way to stop this bloodbath. No one had any suggestions. They just stared ahead with glum expressions on their faces.

114

Whizmo left at 8:00 A.M., knowing that he wouldn't find any bars open before ten, and headed farther west beyond Fredericksburg, where he knew of at least a couple of other bars. At the first one he found only the bartender cleaning up for the day. Whiz showed him the photo and asked his standard questions and once again struck out. He returned to his bike and rode another fifteen miles, then stopped in front of a deserted bar. Tables filled the front porch, and a sign announced it was open. Rob Scott, the owner, had heard the approaching Harley and was standing in the door.

"Morning, Whiz. What brings you out so early?" Rob asked.

Whizmo dismounted and left his helmet on the seat. "Morning, Rob. I'm on a mission, but everywhere I turn I hit a dead end." He handed Josh's photo to Rob. "You seen this kid?" The bartender shook his head.

"Haven't seen him around these parts. You want a beer?"

Whizmo hesitated. "A little early, but why not. I may be at the end of the road anyway. Give me a Shiner."

Rob returned with the beer and sat opposite Whizmo while he told him the story and slowly drank the beer.

"Anyway, it looks like I made a promise I can't keep. I've been in every bar between here and San Marcos. Nobody's seen Josh. I suppose I'll just have to head back and give his mother the bad news."

Rob scratched his head as he considered the situation. "You been out to Charley's?"

"Charley's? Oh, you mean that place out on the Llano River. Is it still open?"

"Last I heard it was. It's a pretty good piece out there, but there's nothing around for miles. Damn good place to hide out. Might be worth a try."

"Got nothing to lose, Rob. Thanks."

Whizmo climbed on his Harley, buckled his helmet, and was off to one last biker bar. He turned off the highway onto a dirt road that wound down to the water's edge, where there was a shack with a small deck facing the river. Five Harleys of various vintages were scattered around the parking lot. Whizmo stopped at the open front door and walked inside. The only light came from the door, a couple of windows, and the sliding doors to the deck. Even at ten in the morning, the bikers had beer in front of them.

All of the occupants glanced up from their beers and conversations as Whizmo stood at the door. Finally the bartender recognized him. "Whizmo, is that you? You're a long way from home."

"Morning, Charley. You're right. It's been a while."

Whizmo explained what he was doing as his eyes became accustomed to the semidarkness. When they did, he spotted two bikers he knew. Whizmo walked over and pulled a chair up to the table where a short redheaded biker and a tall one with tattoos down his arms were nursing their first beers of the morning. "Monkey, how are you and Buzz hanging?"

"Doing good, Whiz. How about you?" the short one called Monkey replied.

Whiz pitched Josh's photo onto the table. "I'm looking for this kid. You seen him?"

"Haven't seen the boy, but we've seen the picture. Some state troopers have been by here a couple of times. We didn't tell them anything. You know how it is, Whiz. We ain't gonna talk to Deputy Dawg. If we did, the next thing we know, they'll find some reason to look in our saddlebags and we'll be facing some charges for guns or marijuana or something."

"Understand, Monkey, but I'm not the man."

"Whiz, I haven't seen the boy, but I did see a big ol' black Lincoln turning down a dirt road a couple of miles back," Buzz said. "There's an old cabin about half a mile down there. Wondered why that car was out here."

Whizmo's eyes brightened. "Black Lincoln our here in pickup country. Worth checking out. Can you show me the road?"

"Damn right. Anybody else want to go?"

The other three men rose at once.

"Let me warn you guys, this could be dangerous."

"That's no problem." Monkey grinned. "We haven't had any fun in quite a while, right, guys?"

The others nodded their heads in agreement.

"Any of you have any weapons?"

"You're kidding, right, Whiz?"

115

The six riders stopped on the highway at the edge of the dirt road.

Whizmo sized up the situation. "We got to leave our bikes here. Who's got a gun for me?"

Five bikers unlocked saddlebags and each handed a gun to Whizmo. "Thanks, guys, but one's enough," Whizmo said as he selected a Glock. "You guys spread out in the woods. I'll be the decoy. I'll walk down the road and get their attention. They could recognize me, but I doubt it," he said as he pulled a baseball cap from his rear pocket and pulled it down low over his face.

Whizmo waited a few minutes to give the others a chance to get through the woods. Then he began to shuffle as he walked, appearing to be an old man who lost his way. He rounded a bend in the road and saw the cabin. The Lincoln was parked beside it. Two goons were sitting on a small front porch, smoking and talking.

One of them pointed at Whizmo. "Hey, look here. We got a visitor."

Whizmo's imitation of an old man was so convincing that neither of them rose as he approached.

"Hey, old man, you make a wrong turn?"

"Yes, suh. Looks like I surely did. I was looking for Ms. Appleton's place. May be I turned one road too soon. I surely do apologize if I disturbed you fine gentlemen."

Out of the corner of his eye, Whizmo saw Monkey coming around the corner of the house, gun in hand. One of the men saw his glance and turned to see Monkey at the edge of the porch. He went for his gun, but before he could get it from his shoulder holster, Monkey shot him in the leg. His partner saw what was happening and lunged at Whizmo just as Whizmo pulled the Glock from its place in the small of his back.

"You hold it right there!" Whizmo yelled. "Your buddy got it in the leg. I figure I can put a slug right between your eyes from this range."

The big man stopped at the edge of the porch when he saw the gun and then glanced around to see five other guns pointed at him. He slowly raised his hands over his head. "Okay, you got me." He nodded toward his friend, who was writhing in pain on the floor. "Can someone help him?"

"Not yet," Whizmo said. "Where's the boy?"

"Listen, we didn't hurt him. Weren't going to. Just trying to scare his old lady."

"You're working for Kingsbury, right?"

"Don't know no Kingsbury, man."

Whizmo walked to the edge of the porch and pointed his gun at the kidnapper's right eye. The big man flinched. "Now that I've got your attention, let me ask that question once more. You're working for Kingsbury, right?"

The man's eyes darted from gun to gun and back to Whizmo. "Yeah, it's Kingsbury."

"Now, you play ball with us and we'll try not to put a hole in you. The boy inside?"

The kidnapper nodded.

"Monkey, frisk them, and someone put a belt around that guy's leg above the wound. Looks like Monkey hit an artery. I'm going inside."

Whizmo stepped around the kidnappers and entered the cabin, where he found Josh tied to a chair with duct tape on his mouth. "Josh, this may hurt just a little," Whizmo said as he pulled the tape off.

"Whiz, how'd you ever find me?"

"Long story, son. Let's get these ropes off you. We'll use them to tie up those guys on the porch. I'll have my buddies hang around until the cops get here. We're going back to the highway and head home to San Marcos. There's a general store a few miles away. We'll buy you a shirt and some flip-flops. Your mama's been worried."

116

Luke returned to his seat. "Now, Doctor, we're going to a different subject."

Brad put up a document titled "Alfred Kingsbury Expense Account."

Kingsbury leaped from his chair. "Where did you get that? I demand you take it off the screen. It's private. If you hacked into our server I'll have the federal prosecutors on you."

Metcalf had given up objecting and said nothing. The judge said, "Order, order! Dr. Kingsbury, please take your seat."

Kingsbury sat down, his face red and looking like he could have a stroke at any minute.

Luke turned to Brad. "Mr. McCoy, please put up that clip from Dr. Boatwright's deposition." Momentarily, Boatwright appeared on the screen, swearing that his relationship with Dr. Kingsbury was strictly professional and he had never received anything of value from Ceventa, and further that it would be improper to do so. When the clip ended, Luke turned back to Kingsbury.

"You told the jury about how you have to keep your distance from the FDA, but here's an entry where you spent about twenty-five thousand dollars to take Dr. Boatwright and his wife on a junket to Jamaica."

"That was business, sir."

"A week at the Montego Bay Ritz-Carlton, nice business. And all of these lunches and after-work drinks with Dr. Boatwright, business, too? In fact, Dr. Kingsbury," Luke demanded, "you and Dr. Boatwright have both lied under oath, haven't you?"

Kingsbury, his confidence gone, could only nod.

Judge Nimitz interrupted. "Dr. Kingsbury, you must give a verbal answer."

Kingsbury turned to look at the judge. "Your Honor, I can't speak for Dr. Boatwright, but I'm trying to give truthful answers."

Several jurors shook their heads in disagreement.

Often in a trial there is a turning point when a seasoned trial lawyer knows that he has the case won. Luke looked at the jury and concluded he had reached that point with Ceventa and Kingsbury. Still, he continued. He wanted to destroy Kingsbury.

"And right here among all of these entries involving Dr. Boatwright is an entry that documents two wire transfers, one for five hundred thousand dollars and another more recent one for two hundred thousand, to a numbered Swiss bank account with the notation of

'Government Relations.' You have a lot of business in Switzerland, Dr. Kingsbury?"

"No, sir. We sell our drugs to pharmacies and hospitals there. That's all. It's a small country."

"So, Doctor, those transfers totaling seven hundred thousand dollars went to Roger Boatwright, the head of CDER, to buy his approval of Exxacia, didn't it?"

Kingsbury mumbled something.

"We can't hear you, Dr. Kingsbury. Why don't you look at the jury and tell them the truth for once?"

By now Kingsbury was leaning forward, his arms resting on his knees as he stared at his new black shoes. He looked up and replied, "Sir, I don't know anything about those transfers or how they got on my expense account."

Again Luke looked at the jury and found them to be staring at the witness with disbelief.

"And one more entry, another wire transfer to a bank account in Maryland for twenty-five thousand dollars. Is it a coincidence that transfer took place on the same day that Ryan Sinclair's body was found?"

Kingsbury looked at his lawyer, who was now staring out the window. Then he noticed the bailiff had left his desk close to the judge and had taken a position at the courtroom door, his right hand resting on his holstered weapon. Finally he responded in a barely audible voice, "Must be, Mr. Vaughan."

"Well, we'll see later. I'm sure the authorities can track down who that was wired to. Dr. Kingsbury, isn't it a fact that once Exxacia was promoted in other countries, the adverse event reports, particularly those involving liver failure and death, started to rise at an alarming level?"

Kingsbury straightened up in the witness chair. "I wouldn't call it an alarming level, but they have risen. We have a team investigating."

Luke nodded at what appeared to be a semitruthful answer and continued. "Doctor, I'm handing you the most recent adverse event data available from the FDA's Web site on Exxacia. I printed it this morning. In this country, in spite of your claimed success with millions of prescriptions, there are only five reports of adverse events. You know it's a violation of federal law, but you directed Rudy Kowalski to hold those reports back, didn't you?"

Kingsbury turned to the jury. "No, ladies and gentlemen, I did no such thing."

Knowing that he had Kingsbury on the run, Luke bluffed. "Brad, please put up that memo from Dr. Kingsbury to Dr. Kowalski."

Brad masked a smile as he reached for a blank sheet of paper and pretended to be adjusting the overhead before displaying the memo. Kingsbury interrupted. "Now that I think about it, I do believe I issued a memo early on in the production of the drug. It was probably interpreted that way."

The courtroom was silent when the back door opened. Luke looked around to see Whizmo escorting Josh and Sue Ellen in. Luke leaped to his feet and started toward them. Kingsbury wanted to run but knew he couldn't. The judge sized up the situation and ordered an immediate recess.

At the end of the recess Sue Ellen walked up to Luke's counsel table. "Luke, Josh is safe. Now finish kicking Kingsbury's butt."

Luke nodded. "We got one of our kids back. Now I aim to save the other one."

When the judge called the court back to order and the jury returned, Metcalf thought that Luke had to be finished. How much more damage could he do? She thought she had smooth sailing, and then her ship took a fatal blow to the bow just when the port was in sight. Luke had one more memo.

"Brad, if you please." As the memo appeared, all of the jurors as well as the judge studied it. "Another memo from Dr. Sinclair, correct, Dr. Kingsbury?"

"Appears to be, sir."

"It's an e-mail directed to Boatwright and copying you. It says,

'I demand that this clinical trial be stopped immediately. Otherwise more lives will be lost.'"

"I see that, sir. By then we had decided that Sinclair was a trouble-maker. That was confirmed by Dr. Boatwright."

"Troublemaker, Dr Kingsbury?" Luke asked, astonishment in his voice. "Not fifteen minutes ago, when we were talking about Dr. Sin-clair's death, you described him as a fine young doctor. Which is it? Or maybe the fact that he was a troublemaker had something to do with his death?"

Now most of the jurors nodded along with Luke.

Kingsbury searched for the right answer. "I misspoke when I said he was a troublemaker. We must have had some other reason for re-jecting his recommendation."

"In any case, Dr. Kingsbury, it was a lucky break for you and Cev-enta that Dr. Sinclair is no longer with us."

"Objection, Your Honor," Metcalf said. "Argumentative."

"Withdraw the question, Your Honor. And you see the date on this memo. It's six weeks before Samantha Vaughan became a subject in your trial. If you had followed Dr. Sinclair's recommendation, the trial would have been stopped and my daughter would never have received the drug."

"I suppose if your dates are correct, that would be true."

"And if you had heeded Dr. Sinclair's advice, Samantha wouldn't be dying of liver failure?"

Kingsbury slumped in his chair, ran his hand nervously through his hair, and replied, "I suppose that's possible."

Luke looked at the jury and concluded he had completed his mis-sion. "I'm finished with this witness," he said, disgust dripping from every word.

Metcalf stared at the clock on the wall and watched a minute tick off. Even as a seasoned trial lawyer she could think of no way she could rehabilitate her client. Finally she rose and said, "No questions, and Ceventa rests."

The judge looked at the jury, but before he could say anything, Luke rose. "Your Honor, at this time we are dismissing our case against Dr. Challa, and we have one very short witness in rebuttal. We recall Dr. Salazar."

When Dr. Salazar took the stand, Luke directed Brad to display the last memo from Ryan Sinclair. "Dr. Salazar, if you had seen this memo where Dr. Sinclair demands that the Exxacia clinical trial be stopped to save lives, would your committee have approved the drug for marketing in the United States?"

Dr. Salazar studied the memo and then said, "Absolutely not, Mr. Vaughan!"

Luke rose to his feet and buttoned his coat. "At this time plaintiff Samantha Vaughan closes."

117

The next morning the courtroom was overflowing with reporters, college students, and lawyers. The jury took their seats, followed by the judge. Sue Ellen had returned to her chair beside Luke. The courtroom was silent as they waited for the judge to call for closing arguments. Then there was a squeak of the hallway door as it opened. Every eye turned to watch as Samantha was wheeled into the courtroom by Brad. Whizmo followed behind. Luke held the swinging door behind the counsel tables open as Brad pushed Samantha to a place beside Luke's table.

"Judge, ladies and gentlemen, I'd like to introduce my daughter, Samantha."

Samantha had asked Mary to take in her favorite blue dress with yellow flowers so that it fit her much smaller frame. She had carefully applied her makeup and had her hair in a ponytail. Samantha smiled at the jury and got thirteen smiles in return. One man in the back row gave her a thumbs-up sign.

"Mr. Vaughan, you may begin," Judge Nimitz said.

Luke walked to the jury box. He had no notes. He didn't need them. He had been thinking about this moment from the day they sued Ceventa. "Ladies and gentlemen, I rise to speak for my daughter." He paused and looked at each of the jurors. "I also rise to speak for all of you, and for you, Judge, and even you, Ms. Metcalf. What you have seen over the past two weeks is the product of a carefully crafted system gone bad. The Food and Drug Administration was established to protect each of us from dangerous drugs. Instead, over the years, the drug companies developed an incestuous relationship with the FDA that was so strong that the upper management of the FDA forgot their mission and began to look at the giant pharmaceutical companies as their clients. The connection has become so strong that whatever the drug companies want, the FDA makes sure they get.

"We, you and I and Samantha, can sever that connection, and we can get Exxacia off the market. We've got enough antibiotics that don't kill people. Why do we need to risk death to clear up our sinuses?

"How do we do this? You have to return a verdict big enough to resonate throughout the country, all the way to Washington, Silver Spring, and, yes, even to Copenhagen. It's certain that Ceventa and the FDA knew Exxacia was dangerous, and what happened to Samantha could have been prevented. Ceventa is clearly responsible for Sam's condition, and you should so find. As to her actual damages, I'll leave it in your hands. Last, you've been asked to consider punitive damages against Ceventa for their conscious indifference to Samantha and to the citizens of this country. If you make the number big enough, they'll get the message. Thank you."

Luke looked each one of the jurors in the eye and turned to hug Samantha before he sat down.

Audrey Metcalf rose, thanked the jury for their service, and in a monotone went through all of the evidence that she had presented to show the good side of Ceventa and Exxacia. Clearly her spirit was shattered, and the jury could feel it.

118

It was five fifteen when Luke climbed the steps to his house. Samantha and Cocoa were waiting on the porch. "Did we get a verdict, Dad?"

"Not yet, kiddo."

"Does that mean we're losing?" Samantha asked, a frown on her face.

Luke sat down beside Samantha and scratched Cocoa's head. "Not at all, Sam. You never know what a jury is thinking. Best guess is we'll win. We turned the corner when we got that study from Ryan Sinclair's wife. Still, long ago I quit trying to second-guess juries."

Samantha reached for her dad's hand. "Thanks, Dad. I don't care what happens. You're the best dad in the world."

It took a few seconds for Luke to control his emotions before he could speak. "I love you, too, Sam."

The father and daughter gazed out into the evening, content to be alone with each other. Suddenly the office phone rang.

"Probably some damn reporter. I'll get rid of him." Luke walked into the house. Samantha could hear him talking but could make out only a few words.

Luke barged through the door. "Sam, that was Metcalf. She says her company will pay five million dollars to settle before the jury comes back. The only stipulation is that it has to be confidential, meaning we can't tell anyone the amount. That'll get you a new liver and lifetime follow-up care. I'm going to call her back and tell her it's a deal."

Samantha was silent as she thought about what her dad had said. Then she again grasped his hand. "No it's not, Dad."

Luke was stunned. What had gotten into his daughter? Maybe her illness was now affecting her brain. "Sam, what are you talking about?"

"Dad, I heard your argument. I believed what you said. Ryan Sinclair died because he wanted to get Exxacia off the market. I don't want to die, but I think the jury will do what you asked. If we get a big verdict, it'll do something that I would never be able to do again in my life. Tell them no. The jury will take care of me."

Luke held his daughter's hand and said nothing for several minutes as they rocked quietly. "You're an adult, and you get to make the call. Are you sure, Sam?"

A determined look came over Samantha's face as she nodded. "I'm sure, Dad."

119

The courtroom was again packed the next morning. Metcalf took Luke aside and tried to get him to persuade Samantha to take the money. Luke shook his head and returned to his table, where Sue Ellen and Samantha sat. After two hours the sound of two buzzes from the jury room announced the jury had a verdict.

Judge Nimitz came from his chambers, and the jury filed in. No one could read their faces. "Ladies and gentlemen, do you have a verdict?" the judge asked.

"We do, Your Honor," a middle-aged woman on the front row replied. She handed the verdict to the bailiff, who carried it to the judge. Judge Nimitz flipped through the pages and confirmed it was in order and unanimous.

"In answer to Question One, as to whether Ceventa is responsible for the injury to Samantha Vaughan, the jury answers yes. In answer to Question Two about actual damages, the jury finds one hundred million dollars."

The courtroom erupted. Several of Samantha's friends yelled. Simon Rothschild demanded order. Eventually, everyone sat down and watched the judge.

"In answer to the question about punitive damages, the jury finds one billion dollars."

"Your Honor," Audrey Metcalf said as she rose to her feet, "Ceventa gives notice of an immediate appeal!"

120

Sue Ellen and Josh walked up the steps to the Vaughan house. As they stepped inside, Sue Ellen called, "Bright, young, well, not so young, but good-looking lawyer requests permission to come aboard."

Luke rounded the corner from his office and put his arms around her. Then he turned to Josh and looked him up and down. "Well, son, you don't look any the worse for the experience."

"No, sir. Matter of fact I'm kinda a celebrity at school these days. Where's Samantha?"

"She and Brad are out in back, watching Whizmo make some toy for one of his grandkids. Come on out."

"Wait just a minute, Josh. I want to say something to Luke," Sue

Ellen said. "Luke, I'm sorry I created such chaos during trial. I'm just glad it didn't distract you. All I can say is that I'm a mother first."

Luke hugged her again. "I'm the one who ought to be apologizing. We both made decisions that we thought were best for our kids at the time. We were all caught up in a nightmare. Fortunately, we survived. Now, let's go outside."

They found Samantha in her wheelchair, talking to Brad and Whizmo, who were seated on the steps to the garage apartment. Whizmo got to his feet as they left the house.

"Well, well," Whizmo said. "Looks like the gang's all here."

"I've got some news," Sue Ellen said. "Kingsbury's being charged with Josh's kidnapping. Those two goons turned on him. Boatwright is still barely alive, and they won't admit to anything about him. The DA thinks he'll be able to nail Kingsbury on that, too. We just don't know if the charge will be murder or attempted murder. And the authorities in Maryland are close to indicting him for Ryan Sinclair's murder."

"Thank God," Samantha said.

"Sue Ellen, if you're through, we have some news, too," Luke said. "Samantha, you want to tell them?"

Samantha turned her wheelchair so that she could see everyone. "It's this way. This is all supposed to be confidential, but you're part of my team. Ceventa offered me five million dollars to settle before the jury came back. I turned them down because they wanted it to be kept quiet."

"Wow, sweetie, you've got some backbone," Whiz said.

"By then, Dad had already told me that we were probably going to win. I wanted to send that message that Dad talked about in closing argument."

"Go on, Sam," Brad said. "There must be more."

"Well." Samantha smiled. "Just this morning Ceventa raised the offer to twenty million, payable immediately. Dad and I talked, and I decided to take it if they would issue a press release saying that they were withdrawing Exxacia from the market."

"And they agreed!" Luke interrupted. "Papers are being drawn as we speak. Exxacia should be off the market by the end of the month. Thanks, everybody. We couldn't have done it without each of you."

It was the middle of the night when the phone rang. Luke shook the cobwebs from his head and answered.

"Luke, Clyde here. We've got a liver that matches. Dr. Stevens is waiting for you at his hospital in San Antonio. I'll be by to pick you and Sam up in fifteen minutes."

An hour later they were pushing Samantha through the emergency department door, where Shepherd Stevens met them with a smile on his face. "Samantha, there's been a tragedy, but out of it comes hope for you. A twenty-year-old college student was killed in a traffic accident. When her parents realized there was no chance she would survive, they signed an organ donor authorization. You and she have the same blood type. You ready to go?"

"I've been ready for a long time now, Dr. Stevens." Samantha smiled.

They wheeled Samantha to the operating room holding area where the transplant team had assembled. Luke kissed Samantha and said, "I'll see you when you wake up."

The surgery took four hours. Luke figured he must have walked ten miles up and down the corridor outside the operating room visitor area. Then the double doors opened and Dr. Stevens and Clyde stepped out. "Everything went fine," Dr. Stevens said. "She's going to do well. We've got her in the PACU, and she's starting to wake up. You can come in."

Luke followed the two doctors back into the recovery room. Samantha had already been extubated and was breathing easily. Luke sat beside her bed until she murmured, "Did it go okay?"

"Couldn't have gone better, kiddo. You'll be back to normal in no time."

Then Samantha drifted off.

The next morning she was moved to a room. Luke came in, bringing yellow roses. "I seem to remember you bringing me some of these back in another life."

Samantha smiled.

Luke sat beside her bed and took her hand. "I've been thinking, Sam. Next semester, if you want to return to A&M, I'm good for it."

Samantha looked at her dad and squeezed his hand. "No thanks, Dad. I'm going to live at home with you until I graduate. Then I'm going to law school at Texas. I expect to be a junior partner in the Vaughan law firm in a few years."